Dedalus European Classics
General Editor: Timothy La

An English Family
(Scenes from Oporto Life)

Júlio Dinis

An
English
Family

(Scenes from Oporto Life)

translated and with an introduction by
Margaret Jull Costa

Dedalus

Dedalus would like to thank the Direção-geral do Livro, dos Arquivos e das Bibliotecas, Portugal, and Arts Council England for their help in producing this translation.

Published in the UK by Dedalus Limited
24-26, St Judith's Lane, Sawtry, Cambs, PE28 5XE
email: info@dedalusbooks.com
www.dedalusbooks.com

ISBN printed book 978 1 910213 83 4
ISBN ebook 978 1 912868 46 9

Dedalus is distributed in the USA & Canada by SCB Distributors
15608 South New Century Drive, Gardena, CA 90248
email: info@scbdistributors.com   web: www.scbdistributors.com

Dedalus is distributed in Australia by Peribo Pty Ltd
58, Beaumont Road, Mount Kuring-gai, N.S.W. 2080
email: info@peribo.com.au

First published by Dedalus in 2020
An English Family copyright © Margaret Jull Costa 2020

Printed and bound in Great Britain by Clays Elcograf S.p.A
Typeset by Marie Lane

The Translator

Margaret Jull Costa has translated the works of many Spanish and Portuguese writers, among them novelists: Javier Marías, Benito Pérez Galdós, José Saramago, and Eça de Queiroz, and poets: Sophia de Mello Breyner Andresen, Mário de Sá-Carneiro and Ana Luísa Amaral. She won the Portuguese Translation Prize for *The Book of Disquiet* by Fernando Pessoa in 1992 and for *The Word Tree* by Teolinda Gersão in 2012. With Javier Marías, she won the 1997 International IMPAC Dublin Literary Award for *A Heart So White*, and, in 2000 and 2011, she won the Weidenfeld Translation Prize for, respectively, *All the Names* and *The Elephant's Journey*, both by José Saramago. In 2008, she won the Pen Book-of-the Month-Club Translation Prize and the Oxford Weidenfeld Translation Prize for *The Maias* by Eça de Queiroz. In 2015, she won the Marsh Children's Fiction in Translation Award for *The Adventures of Shola* by Bernardo Atxaga, and in 2017, with her co-translator Robin Patterson, she won the Best Translated Book Award for *Chronicle of the Murdered House* by Lúcio Cardoso. Most recently, she won the 2018 Premio Valle-Inclán for *On the Edge* by Rafael Chirbes.

In 2013, she was appointed a Fellow of the Royal Society of Literature; in 2014, she was awarded an OBE for services to literature; and in 2015, she was given an Honorary Doctorate by the University of Leeds. In 2018, she was awarded the Ordem Infante D. Henrique by the Portuguese government and a Lifetime Award for Excellence in Translation by the Queen Sofia Spanish Institute, New York.

Cover Image

It has not been possible to credit the copyright holder of the cover image as we have been unable to locate its origin, despite extensive searches. If the copyright holder could get in touch with us, we will rectify this omission.

Introduction

Júlio Dinis was the pen-name of Joaquim Guilherme Gomes Coelho and he was born in Oporto in 1839. His father was a surgeon, and his mother was of Anglo-Irish descent. She died of tuberculosis when Dinis was not quite six, but he was brought up very much in the traditions of Oporto's British community, which played a prominent role in the port wine trade. Dinis studied medicine, but having inherited the tuberculosis that carried off his mother, his maternal grandmother and, one by one, all eight of his siblings, he knew that his health would not be robust enough for him to undertake a career as a doctor. Instead, he took up a teaching post at the medical school from which he had graduated. Struggling with the physical symptoms of his illness, for which, at the time, there was no cure, his only escape, he wrote, was "to wander the worlds of his imagination". He retreated to the Portuguese countryside, as well as spending two long sojourns in Madeira, where the warmer climate was thought to be beneficial. During his final stay there, he apparently ate and drank furiously, in a last-ditch attempt to stem the implacable disease. When he saw there was no hope, he returned to Oporto in May 1871: "to find a hole to hide in and wait for whatever fate God has in store for me". He died in September of that year, just a few weeks before his thirty-second birthday.

7

As a boy of fifteen, he had already tried his hand at writing, producing sketches for the amateur theatre group to which he belonged. Although he didn't go on to write plays, that early experience definitely honed his skills as a writer of dialogue, which is such a prominent and pleasurable feature in all his novels. He also wrote poetry, and his poems often make an appearance in his books too.

Before his first escape to the countryside in search of health, Dinis had already written *An English Family,* which is set in Oporto itself. All his subsequent novels and short stories, however, are set in the provinces, and he often based his characters on people he had met there.

Dinis wrote *An English Family* in 1862, but, perhaps fearing that its gently satirical depiction of Oporto life might offend, he decided not to publish it immediately. However, after the success of *As Pupilas do Senhor Reitor* [*The Rector's Wards*] in 1866, he overcame any doubts he may have had, and *An English Family* appeared in 1867, initially in serial form in *O Jornal do Oporto*. As well as a collection of novellas and short stories, *Serões da Província* [*Provincial Evenings*] (1870), he published two other novels: *A Morgadinha dos Canaviais* [*The Heiress to the Canaviais Estate*] (1868), and *Os Fidalgos da Casa Mourisca* [*The Noble Family of Casa Mourisca*] which was published shortly after his death. His books were enormously popular in his day; since then, there have been many film and television versions in Portugal, and his books are still on the syllabus in Portuguese schools.

Dinis' contemporaries (with, perhaps, the exception of Eça de Queiroz) were more influenced by French literature than by English writers. Dinis, though, read George Eliot, Thackeray,

Introduction

Jane Austen and Dickens, indeed, Mr Richard Whitestone, the novel's pater familias, obsessively re-reads and quotes from Laurence Sterne's *Tristram Shandy* and Henry Fielding's *Tom Jones*.

Like so many other British families, Dinis' family on his mother's side had settled in Oporto for commercial reasons, and *An English Family* is in many ways an evocation of his own family history. It also evokes a particular class and a particular kind of Englishman, in the form of Mr Richard Whitestone. This is how Dinis presents him to us:

The familiar, almost brick-red complexion; the rather prominent blue eyes, bright as sapphires; the fair hair and sidewhiskers, which, it would not be going too far to describe as tongues of fire licking his plump cheeks; the regular teeth, like a string of pearls and white as mountain snow; the erect posture, the quick movements, and the permanent look of smug contentment.

And here is his typical diet:

His lunch was a veritable hecatomb of oysters. The market in Oporto could barely cope with the demands of the molluscivores in the English colony, among whom Mr Richard occupied an eminent position. Roast beef, ham, mustard, potatoes, crackers, beer, and Cheddar cheese were also present at these lunches, tailored to satisfy that robust Anglo-Saxon stomach, a descendant of stomachs, which, according to Alexandre Herculano in his book Jersey to Granville, *had still been cannibals in the fifth century.*

And in true English fashion he refuses to speak Portuguese correctly. His two English friends, Mr Morlays and Mr Brains are equally stereotypical, one the soul of gloom and doom,

9

the other bubbling with enthusiasm. All three are caricatures, and yet, while all are held up as figures of fun, Mr Richard is convincingly human in his devotion to his daughter Jenny and in his awkward relationship with his goodhearted, but feckless son Carlos. And that, I think, is the great strength of the novel. All the characters, however stereotyped, convince us as characters. Mr Richard's daughter Jenny and her friend, Cecília, are perhaps impossibly beautiful and good, but their devotion to their respective fathers and households is very real, as are their feelings for their absent mothers, for, like Dinis himself, both are orphans. Carlos or Charles (brought up in Portugal, but in an English-speaking household) is equally engaging as a charming and intelligent young man who lacks direction. And Manuel Quintino, Mr Richard's chief book-keeper, is both absurd in his love of rigid routine and inability to delegate, but also extraordinarily touching, particularly in the chapter where he is told, cruelly and erroneously, that his daughter Cecília is ill, and he barely survives the desperate, solitary rush home through the dark streets.

The novel's subtitle is *Scenes from Oporto Life*, and Dinis presents us with vivid and often very funny descriptions of the world of commerce, the tight-knit, dull and gossip-ridden world of the British community, and the bohemian world of young men, who frequent bars and Carnival balls and chase after women, although not, of course, women of their own class. For the plot of this novel very much turns on those social divisions. The Whitehouse family belong to the wealthy upper bourgeoisie, who employ the likes of Manuel Quintino whose family belongs to the respectable petit bourgeoisie, who, in turn, employ the working classes, the servant class. The latter are often described as *almost* members of the families they work for (for example, Kate the nanny now sinking into dementia and still cared for by the Whitehouse family, and Carlos' butler who has known him since he was a boy), but who definitely know their place, and, of course, do all the hard work. There is no intermarriage between classes, indeed, in order for the novel's two lovers to marry, Cecília's father has to be promoted up a class by being made a partner in the Whitehouse company.

Class and the dangers of crossing the class divide are a perennial topic in the nineteenth-century novel (think only of Jane Austen and Thomas Hardy). Another topic is the divide between the sexes. Middle-class young men are expected to sow a few wild oats, to sit in bars and josh with their friends, but ultimately, they are expected to work, marry and be the breadwinner. Middle-class young women are far more constrained. No wild oats for them. They must avoid all scandal, and – especially those who have lost their mothers – must run the household, organise the servants, and have no ambition beyond marriage, although, interestingly, at the end of this novel, we do not know what marital fate awaits our heroine, Jenny, who is repeatedly referred to as 'the angel of the house'.

Dinis has often been accused of sentimentality, and he himself said that he took pleasure in exploring characters whom he liked in all their flawed humanity, and had no interest in exploring evil or depraved creatures. There are no out-and-out scoundrels, only gossips, who have no real power and duly get their comeuppance. He consciously wrote for a female readership, for the kind of woman '…who will rejoice at the marriages at the end of the novel, sincerely mourn the death of the heroine, dream about the handsome hero and loathe the father, uncle or guardian who opposes the chaste desires of the two lovers...'

His novels celebrate ordinary, domestic lives. His depiction of a normal evening in the home of Manuel Quintino and his daughter is beautifully done and terribly touching – a word I keep returning to. Re-reading the novel for the nth time in order to write this introduction, I was again drawn into the plot, amused and (yes) touched by the characters. There is an element of caricature, there is, I suppose, sentimentality, but both these things spring from the author's genuine affection for his creations and, heartbreakingly, given his own tenuous hold on life, for the everyday pleasures of nature, food, family and friendship.

By way of a Prologue and in which the Reader is
introduced to one of the Main Characters

Among those of Queen Victoria's subjects resident in Oporto at
the beginning of the second half of the nineteenth century, none
was more beloved or more favoured, and few as phlegmatic
and thoroughly English, as Mr Richard Whitestone.

This was the name – known throughout the city – of a
wealthy businessman and brilliant entrepreneur with a highly
developed commercial sense, whose credit in the principal
markets of Europe and the Americas, especially in Britain's
vast emporiums, had been built on tried and tested foundations.

One would have found plenty of evidence to justify this
flourishing career in the archives of the Bank of England, as
well as those of certain joint stock banks and private banks in
the City or the West End.

Mr Richard Whitestone was not a man to follow the usual
beaten paths, nor to blanch at setting off along unknown tracks,
where he would find himself quite alone, accompanied only by
his own energy and tenacity.

He had sometimes risked his capital by setting up companies,
establishing new branches, helping nascent industries, and
thus providing profitable examples to be followed later on –
when profits were safely guaranteed – by his colleagues, who
were, in the main, more cautious and conservative and always

mistrustful of innovations.

Despite this, any crises – those devastating storms so frequent in the world of commerce – had always passed over the Whitestone establishment, leaving it unscathed. Mr Richard's honest firm had, with its customary splendour, shone through the black clouds that so often cast a shadow over the financial markets, while the fates had smiled less kindly on those firms who, for reasons of punctiliousness, caution and, yes, egotism, had shrunk from taking any risks at all. Yet another occasion to trot out that tired old cliché: *Audaces fortuna juvat*, fortune favours the bold.

This immunity, due in part to the brilliance and intelligence with which Mr Richard watched over his various enterprises – and due in part to the benign or perhaps happy spirit to which fortune often seems subordinate – afforded him the unbounded trust of everyone with whom he worked, a trust of which he never once proved himself unworthy, even in the most frivolous of circumstances.

His daily appearances in the Praça – the name we Oporto natives still give to Rua dos Ingleses, the city's main centre of commerce – were greeted with benevolent smiles, extravagant bows, ingratiating words and affectionate handshakes, depending on each individual's degree of friendship with Mr Richard.

Everyone felt obliged to show some such sign of respect whether because of the prestige of Mr Richard's large fortune and liberality or – as those who prefer to think well of men would say – because of his long, impeccable past record, his rectitude and gentlemanly behaviour, all of which were weighed in the balance each and every day.

Mr Whitehouse, however, did not allow himself to be swayed by the homage paid to him by his confrères, however deserved such homages might be.

Vanity was definitely not one of his defects. When he inhaled what one might call that moral incense, which can turn even the most ungiddy of heads, he felt no clouding of the crystalline quality of his reason, which was, besides, little given to swooning fits.

It would take more than that to melt the ice in a heart brought up and educated on the 51st parallel north.

Eulogies, encomiums (capable, even in prose, of intimidating less elusive modesties), or hyperbolic words of outright veneration, were all heard coolly and without so much as a hint of that pleasant, voluptuous titillation of the soul – if you'll permit such an expression – felt by almost all we children of that first victim of flattery, Eve, when exposed to panegyrics intoned by other people.

It was with the same indifference, the same if not absolute impassivity, then at least rational immutability, with which, one after the other, he downed glasses of beer, port and Madeira, rum, cognac, kümmel, ginger beer and even absinthe – libations that would have put anyone less Englishly restrained at risk of rampant alcoholism; and that same indifference and impassivity protected him from the no less inebriating effects of the flattering remarks constantly filling his ears.

He would often receive the courtly eloquence of his many admirers while distractedly and unaffectedly whistling 'God save the Queen', keeping time with his head or his walking stick.

He never bothered repaying one compliment with another. Those whose custom it is to sow compliments only in order to reap them met with barren ground in Mr Richard Whitestone; their compliments lay where they fell.

If by 'delicacy' you mean certain turns of phrase, certain subtle gallantries, certain conventional ways of walking and

15

looking and talking, which are fashionable in salons and vary from age to age, then you would hesitate to describe Mr Richard as 'delicate'.

That was definitely not his brand of delicacy, which lay instead in feelings and actions inspired by the eternal and unvarying rules of conscience and reason, and was, therefore, above the capricious fluctuations of fashion. His was a natural delicacy.

A true Englishman from old England, sincere, frank, and sometimes brusque, but never mean or base, he could be taken for the very personification of John Bull.

Indifferent to and little given to metaphysics, he was unmoved by the transcendent, philosophical matters that were the unhealthy preoccupations of the intelligentsia of the day; he remained entirely focused on the positive side of life, although without getting caught up, like certain excitable optimists, in pondering the future fate of humanity; he also avoided the talons of the demon Hypochondria, unlike many other men, whose prolonged meditations on the ills afflicting humankind end up poisoning their minds.

On the other hand, Mr Richard had that quality of mind – and in high degree too – so necessary if one is to do battle with life's occasional difficulties, a quality which, according to Sterne, is known by the name of *perseverance* in a good cause, and of *obstinacy* in a bad one.

Another of our man's important qualities was that he never wallowed in self-doubt or, rather, never gave any external sign of such a thing.

To judge by appearances, it would seem that his heart was encased in a thick layer of stoicism, which kept him safe from the malign influence of stimuli that tend to cause pain to that organ so vulnerable to numerous affections.

In this world, to which the Heraclituses of the Christian age gave the mournful, elegiac name of 'Vale of Tears', no event, no catastrophe, could, for very long, alter Mr Richard's accustomed expression, or even cause his rosy cheeks or – as the expression goes – his high colour to turn pale, and this gave him a slightly self-satisfied air, which, in turn, provoked the more than justified envy of his fellows.

This is a more common phenomenon than you might think in those Englishmen whom the ocean waves wash up on our shores on a daily basis.

Each of those Britons is like a silent, but eloquent rebuke to the old preconceptions of poets and writers from the South, who insist that the bright rays of our unclouded Sun or the clear face of our peninsular Moon – where they do not, as the poet says, have 'to break through the leaden skies' of London – are indispensable if our souls are to be filled with joy and our faces lit by their glow; they imagine our English allies to be fatally afflicted by *spleen*, eternally gloomy and glum, as if they had just emerged from the depths of a coal mine.

These people are entirely wrong, unless, of course, the English are highly skilled at deceiving us.

For this is an illusion – or deception – long belied by the indelibly beatific expression imprinted on the bright faces of those men from across the Channel, for they seem to walk among us surrounded by a dense atmosphere of perennial contentment, pleased with the world, pleased with other men and, more especially, pleased with themselves.

It is hardly surprising that the English writer, G.P.R. James, should dare to begin a poem of his with the following words: 'Ho, merry England, merry England, ho!'

And why shouldn't England be called 'merry'? How did the ill-founded belief that an Englishman must, by definition, be melancholic become so widespread?

It is one of those clichés, to give it no worse a name, that no one has ever bothered to counter with the necessary philosophical nous.

The impartial reader need look no further than the other members of the English colony, to see that the jolly chorus placed in the mouth of the aforementioned author's hero, the legendary Robin Hood, did not belong only to an age before civilisation and industry had devastated Britain's dense forests. No, the modern Englishman, faithful depository of that carefree national character, could still sing it now amid the smog and smoke from the factories.

I have long taken it as a point of faith that while melancholy may well be endemic in Great Britain, it is not as prevalent beneath the skies of London as many appear to think.

According to Dryden, English comedies are far superior to anyone else's. And do you know what reason some people give for this supposed superiority? Why, the climate, the very same climate that some accuse of fomenting hypochondria and suicide.

England's fickle climate, they say, favours the development of the strange, eccentric characters who are the backbone of Britain's comic spirit. Yes, jollity thrives in that mighty empire.

Tom Jones and Falstaff are perhaps more typically English than any of the sombre characters made fashionable by Byron.

And, despite his rather conventionally stern exterior, Mr Richard Whitestone, that worthy reader of *The Times* and sworn enemy of France, was, in fact, a pure, unadulterated Englishman.

In any awkward situations, when constrained by his respect for English pragmatism, his face betrayed the fact that such constraint was entirely artificial.

As for his physical appearance, Mr Whitestone was also characteristically English. Will these words serve in place of a more detailed description? Given the vast and varied assortment of masculine types, am I alone in hesitating to attribute only one type to old Albion, the daughter of mists, the queen of the seas, that land of meetings, puddings and so many other things?

Well, all those characteristics, all the distinguishing features of other perfect exemplars of his class, were brought together in the person of Mr Richard Whitestone, like a birth certificate without a hint of forgery.

The familiar, almost brick-red complexion; the rather prominent blue eyes, bright as sapphires; the fair hair and sidewhiskers, which, it would not be going too far to describe as tongues of fire licking his plump cheeks; the regular teeth, like a string of pearls and white as mountain snow; the erect posture, the quick movements, and the permanent look of smug contentment.

Almost the same could be said of his clothes. Even they did not betray him, for they, too, were authentically English.

A light tailcoat of blue cloth, made by the finest tailors of Yorkshire or the West of England; narrow trousers, in which his bony legs could play the part of pistons; long, slender boots that sacrificed elegance to sturdiness; the brilliantly white cravat and waistcoat, like those worn by a member of the House of Lords; and, in winter, an overcoat made of gutta-percha, a substance which, in these prosaic, utilitarian times, has come to replace the impenetrable armour of the Middle Ages – such were the main items of that worthy businessman's wardrobe. All this was crowned by a hat, invariable in shape, like a high fortress inaccessible to the destructive waves of fashion; an unshakeable bulwark against the contrary winds of human faddishness; a hat whose classic shape gives a certain group of Englishmen an appearance that is unique to them; the hat as symbolic expression of the industrial, manufacturing nature of that famous island, for it reminds one of the chimneys with which their most heavily industrial cities bristle.

Having breathed the scented air of our southern climes for more than twenty years, and having, during that time, drunk at source the beverage most favoured by British dining tables, namely, port wine – that nectar, whose aromas are more pleasing to the English nose than our sweet Portuguese air – Mr Richard Whitestone, despite those two influences and all the other charms of Portugal, had still failed to make two important changes: the adoption of the local way of life, against which he rebelled with every fibre of his British body, and due respect for Portuguese grammar, which he abused with an irreverence and downright impudence that would have provoked the most indulgent of schoolmasters.

Mr Whitestone merely confirmed what Alexandre Herculano once wrote, that whenever an Englishman is forced to speak a foreign language, he distorts, abuses and mistreats it with all the barbarism of a Cimbri warrior.

Indeed, the ashes of grammarians Lobato and Madureira must have been spinning in their graves whenever Mr Whitestone spoke Portuguese, because he trampled on the most trivial laws of gender and agreement with a coolness, indifference and ruthlessness comparable only to that of a member of the Jockey Club as he rides his horse over some inoffensive passer-by or over a fellow rider fallen on the track.

The Latinate prosody of this particular corner of the world fared no better.

Mr Whitestone's grammatical constructions in Portuguese bore a very British stamp. Had Venus heard Portuguese spoken like that, she would not perhaps have looked on Portugal quite as favourably as described in Camões' *Lusiads*.

His sentences seemed somehow shot through with the liberal confidence of a true citizen of London. The conciliatory, conservative spirit, the deep-seated constitionalism of that English mind, and his adherence to the interventionist principles adopted by his country, appeared to have been applied to the field of Portuguese syntax, causing Mr Whitestone, in his eagerness to impose harmony on all things, to try and make nouns and adjectives agree in a way that took no account of such troublesome matters as gender and number, and to tamper with the grammatical constitution of an ally, just as England likes to tamper with its own political constitution.

The cumulative effect of his pronunciation and his syntax sounded so comical to the not always respectful ears of his business colleagues that they would sometimes struggle to suppress a mischievous smile, which threatened, for a moment, to ruffle their customary professional gravitas.

Mr Whitestone would see their smiles and guess what might be the cause, but this was a matter of total indifference to him. If, on the other hand, anyone should ever contradict him over the pronunciation of an English word, however disputed, or if he saw someone smirking when he was speaking his native tongue, then, ah, then, he could come very close to threatening that imprudent individual with a demonstration of the noble, almost divine, art of boxing, which, ever since Jack Broughton's day, has been cultivated in London 'with fanaticism and taught with talent' – to quote a writer who was an expert on the subject.

And yet he responded to the smiles that greeted the atrocities he perpetrated on foreign grammar with rank indifference, or possibly even with a flicker of pride and pleasure.

II

Two more Introductions, and that concludes the Prologue

The honourable head of the Whitestone household had two children: a delightful, delicate young woman from the North transplanted to our southern climes when she was only two years old, and her younger brother, who had been born in Portugal.

Their names were Jenny and Carlos.

Jenny was one of those Englishwomen whose pleasingly perfect figure, delicate white skin and pure gold hair lends them such a subtle, airy, I would almost say, celestial look, that we expect at any moment to see them rise up from the earth and vanish like a luminous vision by which our eyes were briefly dazzled.

Delicate as ermine, which seems almost to withdraw at our touch, these poetic northerners seem so vague and ethereal that, in their presence, we gross, profane creatures are gripped by a kind of invincible constraint, as if we feared we might destroy them with a breath, scorch them with a glance, bruise them with a gesture.

Other people's desires do not trouble them, for they are surrounded by an atmosphere of virginal chastity, in which desires – those winged children of the imagination – slowly suffocate.

Beauties like her were doubtless the inspiration behind the

images of virgins in the poems of Ossian – or whoever the real author was – the virgins whom that bard compared to snow upon the heath and whose hair was like the mist of Cromla gilded by the rays of the setting sun.

Jenny's tender blue eyes did not burn with the fiery passions of an ardent heart, or reveal the telltale glitter of exalted fantasies, they glowed instead with a soft, mysterious light, as if reflecting the innermost depths of her soul; her thin, almost tight lips were never prey to tumultuous emotions, but were fixed in a smile of gentle affability, promising peaceful, enduring happiness; her breast, always modestly covered, did not heave in a voluptuous, seductive manner, but serenely rose and fell, a sure sign that this was a woman whom God has destined for family life; she was one of those sympathetic figures, whether mother, sister or wife, whom everyone has known or dreamed of at least once, planets immune to the violent storms that so often threaten the domestic horizon, conciliatory angels full of warmth and affection, consoling and rewarding everyone with tears and smiles; if thoughts of love surfaced when one looked at Jenny, it would always be the love of a chaste wife who, offering her innocent brow to her husband's affectionate kisses, still lowers her eyes as modestly as if this were the very first time they had met, and fixes them instead on the cradle of the sleeping child over whom she is watching.

The young Englishwoman's slender figure, the way she walked with none of the languid mannerisms of our own would-be elegant women, her pure, comely face crowned by a diadem of beautiful, unadorned blonde hair, her gaze half-affable, half-melancholy, her sweetly sonorous, cadenced voice, everything, in short, in some inexplicable way, like sundry phrases plucked from the mysterious language of beauty, spoke of charm and gentleness, of a person so immune to worldly wiles that one might describe her as angelic.

On seeing her, one felt that, for her, love would never be a mere pastime, a whim that begins with laughter and ends in tears. She might never be gripped by a violent passion, but, if she were, that passion would be like one of those plants, which, while it may not produce lush foliage and flowers, sends down deep, tenacious roots into the soil from which it sprang.

Such a troubling, passionate love would be unlikely to reveal itself in Jenny, unless someone found it out, and if that happened, then that love would have to be transposed into the love of a wife or mother, if not, it would slowly consume her, indeed, could prove fatal if, victim of a misunderstanding, her love failed to undergo that sacred evolution.

Such souls as hers are made for one of two things: either heavenly bliss or infinite torment, for I know of no greater torment than that of those who keep their suffering to themselves and repress all signs of grief, when, sometimes, to reveal it could bring relief. For the moment, though, Jenny's sky remained unclouded, and her life flowed sweetly along.

A rapid, near-imperceptible pursing of the lips, a faint frown and – although this might be pure imagination – a slight darkening of those lovely pure-blue eyes, were the only indication of the rare inner battles fought between her powerful, albeit female reason and some romantic impulse, a battle that reason always won.

Those clouds were rare, though, as rare as they were diaphanous, and as diaphanous as they were transitory.

Normally, her heart was as serene as the expression on her face.

But don't go thinking she was cold or insensitive. She was also full of the enlivening rays of all the essential emotions that bind us to the Earth, but rays that never give off any destructive flames when caught up in the flow of life.

Is the warmth of the sun any less welcome or any less energising because it does not set fire to forests and cities as do the fires started by mankind? For while one covers the fields with green and fills the branches with blossom and illumines the whole earth, the other scorches the plants it embraces and rapidly spreads its fatal light. Which, then, is the more powerful and effective?

In Jenny, any heartfelt affections were like the flames of those sacred lamps that light the temples built in God's honour and evoke only thoughts of heaven.

Such beings sanctify everything; passions which, in some, encourage vices, in them become spurs to sublime virtues.

The chalice which, in profane hands, presides over banquets and orgies, when consecrated on the altar, is transformed into a mysterious symbol of the most august religion.

God also enters many souls in order to create out of their original passions a bonfire worthy of Him.

Carlos was, in many respects, very different from his sister.

English by virtue of blood, Latin by virtue of the country where he had been born and spent his childhood and experienced his first adolescent stirrings of the heart, his character was evident in that almost-dual nationality.

From Portugal he took his enthusiasm, his lively imagination and his rarely repressed emotional impetuosity; from England he took a will power, persistence and stoicism that sometimes surprised those who thought they knew him; from England, too, he had inherited certain paternal traits, as if he had been inoculated with Englishness, something he could never have denied if, that is, he ever tried.

Carlos was something of a hothead, but he had a generous,

compassionate heart, a soul sensitive to other's misfortunes, and eyes that often filled with tears of pity.

If, by some lack of restaint on his part or some thoughtless word, he was ever himself the cause of tears, he would be the first to take the blame, to apologise and do all he could to dry them.

Since he was as capable of heroic acts of self-denial when helping others as he was of forgetting any favours granted, how could we criticise him when, accustomed to granting large favours himself, he never expected gratitude from those he helped, apparently unaware that such gratitude was his right?

Courageous to the point of recklessness, liberal to the point of prodigality, sincere to the point of rudeness, his greatest faults were really noble qualities taken to excess.

What he couldn't do was keep those qualities at the orderly, middle-of-the-road level so beloved of society.

His young blood led his head astray: his generous instincts were the torment of his heart, because if, in a moment of over-excitement, his head managed to ignore the generous scruples of his heart, his response was always the same, and would oblige him to repent, owning up to and even exaggerating the not always reversible consequences of his mad caprices. Carlos was one of those men who carry and cherish in their heart their own worst enemy.

Carlos and his father felt the purest affection for each other, although in both men this was concealed beneath a very British coolness and reserve. They rarely sought each other out, and whenever daily life brought them together, they barely exchanged a word. Mr Richard Whitestone was usually at his most loquacious after a family supper over a final glass of wine, but, even then, the conversation tended to be more of a long, rambling monologue on his part, which was interrupted by Carlos with just a few words of agreement, in which the word 'Yes' predominated, and accompanied by an indulgent smile, which was, however, no guarantee that he was actually listening.

Carlos respected his father and loved him almost too much, to the extent that he would have made enormous sacrifices for him, and yet he avoided him, as if he did not feel at ease in his company.

And he didn't.

Carlos could not bear any constraints, always feeling that they were something from which he must either break free or avoid.

He kept silent when he could not freely abandon himself to the vagaries of some trifling conversation; he became sad when unable to give vent to some spontaneous, irresistible outpouring of joy, which would, inevitably, strike others as merely puerile. Given the freedom to be foolhardy, he might have proved quite sensible, but when obliged to be sensible, he became sombre and irritable.

Mr Richard Whitestone's austere habits, his rigid idea of decorum and respect for the rules of English etiquette had just such a constraining effect on Carlos, and since he lacked the courage to rebel against that constraint, he preferred to avoid it altogether.

He tended to see his father as a stern, unbending judge, ready to pass judgement on him and possibly condemn him, and so, since he always felt some youthful misdemeanour pricking his conscience, and had little confidence in his ability to pretend otherwise, Carlos would, whenever possible, steer well clear of scrutiny by that paternal jury, even though such scrutiny was usually entirely in his imagination and could not have been further from Mr Richard Whitestone's actual intentions.

Mr Whitestone, for his part, was equally devoted to his son, and as indulgent of any youthful indiscretions as he himself had wanted and needed his own parents to be. He must have found it very hard indeed to maintain that sensible, conventional façade, so at odds with his naturally carefree, jovial self, a façade, however, that never managed to erase the smile that seemed as if imprinted on his lips.

He felt, though, that as father and natural mentor to a hothead son, who quite often merited far harsher punishments, it was his duty to preserve that air of manly brusqueness.

His English love of concision was averse to long moralising speeches or prolix sermons. In such matters, he was, by nature and by nationality, a man of few words, and when he felt he should call the straying lamb back to the fold, he never resorted to parables.

A single 'Oh!' spoken in the way that only a British larynx can produce, an aspirated, guttural, eloquent – in short – English 'Oh!', combined with a rapid, disapproving shake of the head and a few tut-tuttings, were the only signs of impatience and displeasure Mr Richard Whitestone ever showed, and Carlos feared those signs, as he would have any still more concise formula, because they revealed his father's disapproval.

On days when that fateful 'Oh!' had rung in his ears, he could no longer give himself over entirely to pleasure, instead, a cloud darkened the otherwise clear blue sky of youth.

He would promise then to mend his ways, a solemn promise made only to himself and quickly forgotten until it was renewed later on in similar circumstances.

Carlos' feelings for his sister were quite different.

Jenny was his good angel, as she was for the entire family,

the gentle, benign fairy whose gaze could calm storms and clear the clouds from the sky.

She could quell any torments of the heart with a smile. However weak and delicate her arm, Carlos had often found it had come between him and a precipice or was simply there as a support. Slender and diffident it might be, but it was always strong and firm when it came to saving her brother from some imminent fall or else helping to raise him up. Her voice might be soft and gentle, but it was the only voice he could hear above the roar of passion's tumult.

They had no secrets from each other. Even as a boy, Carlos would tell Jenny almost everything that happened to him, both good and bad.

He would openly tell her what he had been thinking, and, more than once, had held back when about to give in to the temptation to behave less than generously, simply so as not to have to tell his affectionate judge about it later on and receive a friendly, smiling reproof, or see a flicker of displeasure cross those lovely lips, something that always cut him to the quick.

He found remorse equally painful if he ever tried to avoid punishment and conceal his crime. Then his conscience would scold him for such lapses, on the rare occasions they occurred.

Jenny, who held sway over both brother and father, used that dual influence to bring harmony to the whole family whenever discord threatened.

She could extinguish, with a word, any irritation that Carlos' excesses might have provoked in their father, and with another could dispel her brother's slightest tendency to rebel – so natural, given his age and temperament – against any repressive measure taken by his father, always very rarely and always as a last resort.

Jenny's small purse had often opened to pay off debts

imprudently contracted by Carlos or to remedy the unfortunate consequences of some other folly of his. She was always ready to take his side and minimise his faults.

If she could not persuade Carlos to do something, then no one else could.

A silent plea from her became an entreaty, and the smallest request – however timidly expressed – an urgent order. And yet she never made this power of hers apparent; indeed, she did her best to disguise it.

She had learned the thousand and one mysteries and vagaries of the human heart more through thinking than through experience, and her admirable female gifts of diplomacy lay in knowing how to impose her wishes in as lighthearted a manner as possible, in accepting and being grateful for what her conscience told her were the results of her hints and entreaties, as if these had been granted to her spontaneously.

In almost every one of those conversations with her brother, Jenny managed to come up with a perfect and perfectly conceived strategy, a virtuous and kindly hypocrisy to which Jenny was obliged to stoop.

When the angels dissemble as we mere mortals do, they always preserve their innocence and remain angelic. Their wings may brush the mud of this world, but they emerge immaculate.

Jenny had spent her life almost entirely in the bosom of her own small family, so who could have taught her this science of the heart, which some say can only be acquired after many years of dealing with people and with the world? We have already mentioned that she thought deeply about things, and one learns far more from a profound reading of just one book than from leafing idly through a thousand volumes. The same applies to the study of character. There are some who, after years and years of dealing with people, die in utter ignorance of mankind's true nature, and there are others who, in the solitude of their study, see in their own hearts the secrets of the rest of humanity and decipher them, because once you have discovered the principal laws of human nature, it is easy then to divine the lesser rules, which is where the differences lie. It's always surprising when a man emerges from some obscure corner, a man unknown to everyone and yet who seems to know everyone. How and where did that man learn all those things? Through dispassionately observing himself or the people closest to him. It is thus that intelligence, invigorated by this process – and following seemingly insignificant paths – draws its most fertile conclusions.

Carlos could never resist his sister's reasoning for very long. Without even realising it, he would retreat step by step. He would edge towards the objective to which his skilled opponent wanted to lead him, and, when he reached it, would be surprised to have made so effortlessly what he had thought of as sacrifices, when, only moments before, the mere idea of doing so would have driven him to despair.

Mr Richard Whitestone's character – generally considered to be somewhat inflexible – was also putty in his daughter's hands.

So skilled was Jenny at concealing these small, but important victories, however, that it never even occurred to the good gentleman that, even as he was confidently boasting of his resolve and steadfastness, his very actions gave the lie to this.

These were the three main members of the Whitestone family who we will get to know more intimately in the next chapters of this very simple tale, in the course of which – for we would not wish to give any false hopes – the action will proceed unimpeded by any complicated adventures.

III

In the Golden Eagle

It was one of the last nights of Carnival in 1855.

There were more masks in the streets than there were stars in the sky. February – that month as fickle as a highly-strung woman – was in one of its bad moods, but playful Carnival laughed at such glumness and danced to the sound of the wind and the rain beneath the canopy of dark clouds approaching from the south. And thanks to unusually high waters in the Douro, the lower part of the city could easily have been a parody of the Venice Carnival.

Crowds gathered outside the theatres; the loud cries of ticket-sellers and the shrill falsettos of carnival-goers were positively deafening. The improvised wardrobes set up in shops located near the main dance halls were filled with costumes from every age and every nation, although it wasn't always easy to ascertain quite which age, nation or social class they belonged to.

Many people stopped to look at the displays of masks for sale and thus made the streets almost impassable to traffic. The fascination aroused by those rows of masks was similar to the effect that one of Hoffmann's tales has on excitable imaginations, for the comic diversity of expression resembled a swarm of Mephistophelian heads gathered together to mock human folly.

These window-shoppers would be rudely woken from their reveries by the vigorous curses of coach drivers ready to run them down, or by the none too harmonious shouts of the litter-bearers, who were obliged to lurch and dodge around them in the exercise of their worthy, beneficent work. Then, albeit reluctantly, the crowd would disperse, only to regroup a few steps further on.

If it is valid to compare great with small, one might see them as the inoffensive dreamers of this world, who are always cruelly roused from their dreams when they bump up against weary workers engaged in hard, useful labour.

The whole city was celebrating.

Everyone was eagerly bustling around… and pretending to be having fun, when they were, in fact, deeply bored.

Something was happening at the Golden Eagle too, the oldest of our inns, the veteran confidante of almost all the city's political, personal and artistic secrets, yes, something was happening in that modest yellow house in Largo da Batalha, something that attracted the gaze of passers-by.

Since three o'clock in the afternoon, the clink of glasses and china, the popping of corks, as well as loud guffaws, tumultuous shouts and deafening hurrahs, had been pouring forth in a torrent from the unassuming portal of that familiar building; and for a long time, just as happens with the waters of mighty rivers as they flow into the sea, that torrent was quite distinct from the great hubbub filling the streets.

The servants scuttled up and down the stairs, passed or collided with each other in the corridors, paused, perplexed, when given contradictory orders, chivvied their colleagues in the kitchen or palmed off impatient customers with promises.

Meanwhile, the one modest customer whose stomach had called him there to enjoy a humble cutlet – the inn's main

33

culinary trophy – was pretty much ignored, until, grown tired of waiting, he slipped sadly and silently away.

Beneath its modest appearance, the Golden Eagle seemed to glow with a majesty worthy of its emblem.

The dim light of a streetlamp shone on that bird of Jupiter sitting atop the inn sign, making it shine more brightly than usual, or so it seemed.

This was clearly a solemn night for the inn, which had been the subject of discussions among ministers and impresarios.

Down below, the waiters in the café were speaking softly, their eyes filled with a slightly anxious gleam, while their faces revealed a certain air of importance, as if something of real moment was happening upstairs.

At the time, the walls of the café were still decorated with paintings of the battles that had restored Greece's independence, and it was a décor that looked likely to last. The rather stuffy room was, though, entirely deserted, and the feeble light of the lamps failed to dissipate any shadows lurking in corners. Indeed, the scorer at the billiard table was almost falling asleep.

The masked balls had even lured away the men of politics. That night, any debates about the Crimean War – the main topic of conversation at the time – would be taking place to the sound of waltzes and mazurkas, and in the theatres.

It is not, therefore, this melancholy, almost lugubrious place where I intend to leave the reader.

Let us go upstairs and, pushing past any servants we may meet on the stairs or in the corridors, let us enter the room that is the source of all these festive noises.

The reader doubtless knows this room. Its architectural details hardly merit description.

What we have come to see is a young man's supper party.

We have, however, arrived late.

Cigar smoke fills the room and dims the lights, and although supper is almost over, the noise is at its height.

Glasses have already been broken, expensive wines spilled, the guests are either seated or standing around the table in every conceivable pose and position, some of which defy description.

The noise is deafening. One imagines that this is what Babel might have been like.

Everything is being talked about simultaneously; transitions between subjects take place with a rapidity that surprises and confuses even the interlocutors themselves; if you lose concentration for a second, you'll be lost for good, and will never pick up the thread of the conversation again; sometimes the talk grows more general; moments later, there are different groups discussing different topics; then the conversation again becomes more general; sometimes, everyone is talking at once and each individual is listening only to himself; at other times, a single orator manages briefly to be heard by everyone, until, that is, some comment or incident or gesture reestablishes the original Babelian disorder. There are genuine overlappings of conversations; someone at the far end of the table responds to something that was said at the head of the table, while those in between amuse themselves with other topics; it's a jumble of words, from which it would be very hard to extract any clear thought.

Over there the talk is of literature and, now and then, someone mentions the name of some well-known or fashionable novelist or poet; over here, they're discussing politics, and all the major figures of the day, financial, diplomatic and military, are dismissed in an instant; further along the table, two lads sitting opposite each other are discussing affairs of the heart, while two others, sitting diagonally across from them, are expounding on the latest styles in jackets; another group is getting all excited about the opera and debating whether to boo or cheer; alongside them, two fans of horse-racing are exchanging picaresque tales of horse-trading and the qualities, good or otherwise, of their equine purchases. Even German philosophy provides food for lively discussion, all interspersed with guffawings, songs, foul language and exclamations in various languages.

It would be equally difficult to say what common element unites the individuals gathered there.

They are a very mixed bag indeed: there's the young priest who has tested the skill and patience of barbers to the limit in his futile attempts to disguise his tonsure, and there's the highly civilised, mild-mannered army officer who finds even hunting a shocking, barbarous activity; there are men of all ages, from the boy fresh out of school, still beardless and intoxicated by the first stirrings of adolescent life, to the old man who, naively believing that time has neglected to keep count of the years, has abandoned his own generation and insists on living a young man's life in the company of young men; they come from very different financial circumstances too, from the capitalist who is happily spending his money, smug in the belief that the source of his wealth is inexhaustible, to the spongers and victims of fashion, the emptiness of whose pockets puts a daily strain on their imaginations as, regardless of the humiliations this might entail, they struggle to think of ways to remain in that fashionable atmosphere, which, to them, is the very breath of life; there are young men of all degrees of intellect too, from the celebrated author, who, with or without the aid of patronage, has made a reputation for himself in the world of letters, to the rank illiterate, whose idiot utterances are greeted with gales of laughter no one even bothers to suppress.

In short, this meeting of heterogeneous individuals represents a section of society that arrogantly dubs itself elegant, and for which it is hard to understand quite what the membership qualifications can be, since its members are not even particularly elegant, in the proper sense of the word.

The reason for the supper? Well, there is no reason, and that pretty much sums it up. A supper does not, of course, need to have a reason since one could, in philosophical terms, say that 'its existence was reason enough in itself'.

Among the company there is someone we've already met.

And since I have, so far, only introduced the reader to three people, it will require no great perspicacity on your part to guess which of the three it might be.

Yes, Carlos Whitestone is one of the guests, and not one of the most circumspect either.

He was sitting near the head of the table, and he was the one who most often succeeded in becoming the centre of attention, the one to whom Virgil's words, *conticuere omnes* – and all fell silent – could most easily be applied. Admittedly he did not command the total silence achieved by the hero of Troy, since he did not have the destruction of an Illium to describe nor a patient audience of Tyrians to listen to him.

Carlos Whitestone had a reputation for being very up to date on the kind of comical, scandalous gossip for which there is always an insatiable appetite.

That's why everyone was happy to listen to him.

Regrettably, we have arrived too late to hear the beginning of the story he is already halfway through telling. Lighting his cigar on that of his journalist neighbour, Carlos was saying: 'Despite the warning he'd been given, our man decided that in the best of good faiths…'

'Which must mean the good faith of husbands,' commented the priest *sotto voce.* He was somewhat behind in the gastronomic stakes, and was only now tucking in with gusto to a pigeon timbale, which, miraculously, was still intact. Then he added: 'I personally know of no better good faith.'

'Apart, that is, from the good faith of ingenuous lovers,' said Carlos.

'That has fewer consequences though…' retorted the priest.

'Silence, Father Manuel,' roared sundry voices. 'Go on, Carlos. So what happened next?'

'Then,' Carlos went on, 'having donned all his finery, perfumed himself, bejewelled himself, curled his hair…'

'And dyed it, don't forget that,' came a voice from the end of the table.

'Yes, and dyed it too,' said Carlos, 'having thus equipped himself, he set off for the rendezvous.'

'And how did he get to this rendezvous?' asked a soldier.

'In a most unusual manner,' said Carlos. 'Each night, having left hat, stick and gloves on the grass below, he would climb, squirrel-like, up the beech tree next to the balcony and…'

'You're joking!' cried some, laughing.

'It's true!'

'With a belly like his, that positively defies the laws of mechanics,' said an undergraduate.

'On the contrary,' said another, 'it's his belly that helps him to rise. Remember Archimedes' principle, think of balloons…'

'The councillor's fall would be a fine experiment for a course in physics…'

'And most amusing too,' said a voice.

'Yes, one exemplifying the laws of universal gravitation, because no one has more gravitas than him,' concluded the first voice.

These fellows liked to push puns to their limit.

'Let Carlos speak. What happened next?' said the more curious types.

Carlos went on: 'That night, however, the councillor was in for a nasty surprise, for as he climbed the tree, he spied another man.'

'Vítor?'

'Exactly, Vítor. You can imagine the ensuing conversation.'

'Oh, it would have been priceless. A duel between nightingales!'

'The councillor perhaps began by saying: *Tytire, tu patulae recubans sub tegmine fagi... Formosam resonare doces Amaryllida silvas.*'

'I object to that *recubans*, since Vítor was in a rather less comfortable position.'

'Well, *mutatis mutandis.*'

'Father Manuel, you're a Latinist, what verb would you use to describe Vítor's position.'

'Don't ask the father. Can't you see that he, like all the ancient Roman augurs, is busily consulting the entrails of a bird? A little respect for such a solemn act, please.'

'But tell us, Carlos, what were the consequences?'

'They were what you know them to be, the councillor...'

At this point, Carlos' story was interrupted by one of the waiters, who came over and handed him a letter.

'Excuse me a moment, gentlemen,' said Carlos preparing to open the letter.

'Bravo!' exclaimed the journalist. 'A letter from some impatient Echo!'

'*E un foglio a me lasció,*' warbled a music-lover, turning his chair round so that its back was facing the table.

'It's a note of surrender from a besieged Troy,' said the soldier.

'Sounds like a put-up job to me, some backstage shenanigans.'

'I foresee a lot of complimentary tickets being handed out, from which few of us will escape.'

Carlos smiled as he opened the letter.

'Careful, Carlos, sudden shocks are very bad for the digestion,' remarked the medical student.

'Don't worry, I'm used to such excitement,' retorted Carlos.

Suddenly, though, he looked very serious.

'Bad news!' said some.

'The plot thickens.'

'The lady's demands have reached new heights.'

'No, I reckon another councillor was climbing up another beech tree and is calling down revenge on his colleague, in this case, Carlos.'

Carlos was no longer listening. He stood up, went over to the sideboard and hurriedly scribbled a response on the back of the letter he'd been given.

While he was doing this, his fellow diners were pretending to dictate a response: 'My angel, if, up in the heavens...'

'...you are flying on the wings of love...'

'I, shipwrecked, like another Leander...'

'My dearest Heloise, if poor, unlucky Abelard...'

'Juliet, when the nightingale...'

Carlos returned to the table, having first sealed the letter and returned it to the waiter.

He was struggling to keep a smile on his lips, but this was clearly quite an effort, and this, of course, cancelled out the desired effect.

'What's up?' asked the soldier, who was sitting opposite

him. 'You look as if that letter smelled of the plague.'

'Will our Manrico have to rush off and save his Leonora from the arms of the dastardly Conte di Luna?' said the music-lover.

'Ulysses has returned to the domestic hearth, which is tantamount to an eviction order for the...'

'No, it's just some very solicitous shopkeeper insisting on prompt payment of a large bill for trinkets supplied.'

'Or a carnival-goer expressing his ingratitude...'

'That's enough hypothesising,' said Carlos, filling his glass with wine and trying to maintain the jolly tone of the evening. Then he added: 'It was just a note reminding me...'

'Oh, a reminder...
Tu souviens-tu, de même,
De nos transports brulants... '

'Reminding me that today is my birthday,' said Carlos, finishing his sentence.

'Really?'

'Yes, really.
Quand tu m'as dit "je t'aime"
J'avais alors vingt ans.'

'But why didn't you say it was your birthday?'

'I'd completely forgotten. If I'd remembered, I wouldn't be here with you lot.'

'You mean you'd have invited us all to your house?'

'No, not that either. I usually spend such days with my family.'

'Oh dear, bring on the violins.'

'How very British! Feet warming before the hearth, a jug of punch on the table, a copy of *The Times* in his hand. And the occasional monosyllabic grunt or some interjection that burns the throat like prussic acid. Delightful!'

'Heavenly!'

'An English heaven, slightly obscured by mist.'

'And smog.'

'Stir in a paraphrase of some Biblical text.'

'And a few variations on "God save the Queen".'

Carlos smiled and said: 'You may scoff, but the occasional day spent like that is not without its pleasures.'

I would like to believe that many of the men there, if not all of them, felt the truth of what Carlos had just said, and were equally capable of appreciating such family pleasures, but they would have been ashamed to say so out loud and in the middle of a Carnival supper. What do you expect? It's not fashionable to wear your heart on your sleeve. The custom now is to treat all expressions of emotion as ridiculous, as petty weaknesses which, like so many others, should only be confided to the four walls of our own room.

Carlos, however, was no good at pretending. He had spoken those words with real conviction and genuine feeling, and he was rewarded with a lot of epigrammatic allusions to what his fellows termed 'tendencies to bourgeois respectability'.

The letter that triggered this scene and which seemed to have genuinely upset Carlos, was from his sister and said only:

Charles,

Today is the 19th February. Your twentieth birthday. I didn't think it would be necessary to ask you to give us the pleasure of your company. Your father was expecting you.

Love, Jenny

To which Carlos responded:

Jenny,

You put too much faith in my memory, and I genuinely did

forget. I do hope you'll believe me when I say that I'm sure I would never forget either your or our father's birthday. I can't prove this now, alas. And now I have to stay with my fellow madmen, and when I do leave them, I'm not sure I'll be in a state to sit beside you without profaning the family supper table. As you see, there is little point in celebrating the birth of yet another numskull. Tomorrow, I'll come and beg your forgiveness. Whatever was I thinking being born on the first day of Carnival?!

Your wicked brother,
Charles

Finally, after a few more explanations, one of the guests stood up and, raising his glass, said: 'Gentlemen, I propose a toast to Carlos' birthday.'

'Seconded,' they all replied, also raising their glasses.

'Carlos,' the first guest continued, 'I drink to your twenty years. May you stir as many hearts over the next three hundred and sixty-five days as…'

'No long speeches, please! Let's drink!' cried a voice.

'What goes down the gullet is always so much more expressive than what comes out of the mouth in the form of words,' added someone else.

'And since we should always give precedence to the best-read member of the party, the best red I know is this wine we're drinking…'

'Oh, please, no more puns. You'll give us all indigestion!'

'Come on, let's drink!' said the chorus.

And they all drank to Carlos.

Carlos responded somewhat self-consciously. He could imagine Jenny eyeing him with amused displeasure; Jenny all alone with their father, who must have felt the absence of his son very deeply. And for the rest of the night, he could not shake off that painful image.

He was gripped by a single intense thought, something like remorse at being there, so much so that he listened only distractedly to the conversation in the room, and took no part in the discussions or the ideas aired by the others.

On such occasions, thought is rather like a blank photographic plate in a camera obscura. It records the images of external things, but they quickly dissipate once the objects motivating them are gone.

This explains the rather distracted, indifferent tone of the few remarks Carlos made during the rest of the evening, as well as the impatient note in his voice when he was obliged to give an answer.

Among the many other things said in the room, this is what he heard without really listening, and these were all topics he would have enjoyed had he been in his usual high spirits, happily joining in the banter.

The journalist sitting next to him asked why he was looking so glum. Any remark made by this journalist inevitably degenerated into a long literary ramble, which was very hard to interrupt.

'What's wrong, my friend? That letter seems to have had an almost apoplectic effect on you. Cheer up. Is it some affair of the heart? Some blonde, pale-skinned Miss, eh? Ah, those English girls! The bright innocence of their gentle flirting, which Garrett, finding no better Portuguese word, quite rightly, describes as "flirting".'

And then he was off.

'Have you read Garrett, Carlos? What do you think of his *Voyages Round My Country*, eh? It's definitely his best book. Frankly, I prefer him to Xavier Maistre, because, I must confess, I really don't share what seems to be the universal admiration for Maistre.'

There followed a pause during which he took a sip of sherry. After such an outspoken comment, a pause was essential.

Carlos, as we know, did not respond. During that interval, he heard a man on the other side of the table saying: 'What I really need is three hundred *contos de réis* – minimum. That would be enough for me to leave here and go to Paris and then...'

The journalist went on: 'Xavier Maistre clearly took his inspiration from Sterne, that much is clear, but he's nowhere near as good. Now *A Sentimental Journey* really is a good book. It's delicately seasoned with certain unique philosophical spices, which combine so well with that kind of light literature. Yes, humour died with Sterne.' Pause. 'Too much philosophy has a dire effect on literary inspiration. Think only of Pope. He's cold, arid, marmoreal.' Pause. 'The French poets don't tend to "foolosophise" if you'll forgive the neologism. Well, Victor Hugo does sometimes... Who do you prefer, Carlos, Lamartine or Victor Hugo? Victor Hugo is more Byronic. And yet interestingly enough it was Lamartine who envied *Childe Harold*! The attraction of opposites! What do you think of *Childe Harold*? In my opinion, it's the only truly romantic poem ever written.' Pause. 'I even forgive him the fawning stanza that begins "Poor, paltry slaves", the one in praise of Sintra. And I'm not even a huge admirer of Byron.'

Another longer pause, during which he lit a cigar.

Carlos still said nothing.

He heard someone in a neighbouring group say: 'Now I'll tell you who has a really fine carriage and pair and that's the Visconde de Custóias.'

'Manuel Galveias has a better one though.'

And elsewhere: 'I'm sorry, dear boy, but, for me, synthesis

doesn't just involve a proper consideration of the analytical facts. Synthesis precedes analysis, and provides the latter with the energy it seeks in the inner world, imbues it with all the immutable, necessary principles. Kant…'

The journalist was still speaking: 'I never take any notice of what the critics say. I have my own criteria. I'm never content merely to echo other people's opinions.' Pause. 'For example, I'm honest and brave enough to admit that I don't really see the point of Dante.'

An even longer pause.

'Father Manuel,' said another guest, at the far end of the table, pointing to the glass the priest was raising to his lips. '*Ecce Deus qui laetificat juventutem meam.*'

Father Manuel smiled, but said nothing. He was still too busy eating.

'Because after all,' continued the journalist, 'I'm sure you'll agree with me when I say that, like Homer, Dante is a rhapsode. After all, what is the *Divine Comedy* but a compendium of the religious beliefs of its day?'

Pause.

'Any news about the Carlist revolution in Pamplona?' Carlos heard someone ask.

'No, nothing new, or only that a few sergeants, corporals and civilians are now implicated,' said another voice.

And on and on went the literary dissertation: 'Dante's great triumph is his form. You can see that in the very first line: *Nel mezzo del cammin di nostra vita…* Personally, I think Boccaccio is more gifted, but then what can you expect? He had a large mind in a rather lesser body… Have you read *The Decameron*? Oh, you must. It's an astonishing book. There's something about it that endures beyond the century in which it was written. And that's a sure sign of genius. La Fontaine's imitations really pale into insignificance. But then La Fontaine was a contemporary of Louis XIV, and there was nothing in his court to inspire anything. I loathe the literature of that period. Yes, I detest Louis XIV and his entire century.' Pause. 'Molière is an exception, but why? Because the comic genre has a special quality. It's governed not by inspiration, but by analysis and philosophical thought.'

'I bet,' bellowed a politician, 'that if the allies attack Sebastopol, there won't be a man left alive.'

'Don't be so sure,' argued another. 'If Omar Pasha holds the road from Sebastopol to Sinferopol, it could be a whole other story. He disembarked in Yevpatoria with 40,000 men.'

The journalist went on: 'There's only one man I admire more than Molière as a comic writer, and that's Rabelais. He's the absolute tops. I have three books that are always on my desk and which I always take with me whenever I go travelling.'

'I know: the Bible, *The Lusiads* and *Paul et Virginie*. That's what everyone says,' Carlos said at last, getting to his feet, having lost all patience and wanting to remove himself from this torrent of questions, answers, critical opinions, comparisons and quotations that flowed so categorically from his neighbour's wordy mouth.

'No, not at all,' said the journalist, also getting up and taking Carlos' arm. 'They formulate the soul's three great emotions – religion, patriotism and love. I know that, but, temperamentally, I'm more drawn to authors who paint a picture of society and analyse the passions, and only three men did that well: Lesage, Richardson and Rabelais, who is famous, of course, for his creations Pantagruel and Gargantua!'

'Pontagruel?' exclaimed a music-lover, turning to face them as they passed his chair. 'You must mean Ponti. What a woman! What a voice! Such feeling!'

'You're not on about Ponti again, are you?' said the old-young man, a known adversary of the *prima donna* and one of a large sect who spend half the year longing to go to the theatre and the other half heaping scorn on the companies who do finally visit. 'You even think she makes a half-decent Norma. Ah, but if you'd heard Rossi-Cassi…'

'Rossi-Cassi! Oh, please! You'd need to give her a good dusting off first! I'm talking about now. You talk about Rossi as if you'd actually heard her sing, but that's tantamount to producing a birth certificate dated around 1800.'

'How dare you?' roared the old-young man, cut to the quick.

'*Parce sepulto*,' said the priest.

'*Lascia la donna in pace*,' sang a fellow music-lover.

Carlos and the journalist had moved on, and the journalist was now talking about libretti, about Felice Romani, Manzoni, about *Ei fu!* from Manzoni's *The Fifth of May*… etc, etc, etc.

A young man grabbed Carlos' arm.

'Here's someone who'll know,' he said. 'Tell us, Carlos, do you know Laura Viegas?'

'No, I don't,' answered Carlos vaguely.

'You must know her. She's the daughter of Viegas, that Brazilian who bought the Pedroso estate.'

'What about her?'

'So you do know her. Anyway, what kind of dowry do you think she'll have?'

Carlos shrugged, indicating that he had no idea, and was preparing to move on, when another man, equally preoccupied with dowries, grabbed his other arm.

'It doesn't matter, Viegas could only give her nine *contos* at most.'

'Multiply that by three and you'd still fall short,' said

the priest from the other end of the table, managing to make himself heard above the various disparate debates going on around him.

'There, you see!' said the two disputants, taking his word as proof positive.

The priest was calmly wiping his lips and filling his glass with malmsey.

'So you're saying that…'

'Viegas has at least…' began the priest, holding his glass up to the light to savour the clarity of the wine, and then, before completing his sentence, putting it to his lips and drinking it down in one.

Then he went on: 'He's worth at least… at least…'

He again dabbed at his lips and finally said: 'Sixty-seven *contos de réis.*'

'No!'

Carlos was now on the other side of the table, still followed by the journalist, who was saying: 'That's all people think about now. Money. And literature suffers as a consequence…'

And then he went on to talk about Alexandre Dumas *fils*, about Emile Augier, Ponsard, etc. etc.

'Oh, please,' a beardless youth was saying, 'Emília Vitorina is in another league entirely. I met her yesterday at the house of Barão de Tavares. She was dressed as Mary Stuart. She made a perfect queen, so distinguished, so splendid.'

'Oh, she was certainly splendid once, but not now. She was beginning to age when you were still teething. Age…' said his neighbour.

'What do you mean "age"? A woman is only as old as she looks.'

'I agree, but after the age of forty or so, a woman looks the age she is.'

'No! What do you think, Carlos?'

'I agree,' said Carlos, who wasn't even listening.

'This young upstart is saying he prefers Emília Vitorina to Mariana Prazeres.'

'Because I do.'

'You heretic! Who doesn't admire Mariana's lovely face?'

'Not to mention her hands. Those long, slender, blue-veined hands, truly artistic, aristocratic hands.'

'Speaking of hands, I beg leave to mention the most beautiful of all hands, at least here in the north, those of Clementina Rialva,' said an individual apparently roused from sleep.

'Seconded!' said many other voices.

'Speaking of Clementina Rialva,' exclaimed a chronicler of the day's gossip, 'did you know that Chico from Lousã is still hoping to marry her?'

'Really?'

'Yes, Brito told me yesterday, and, as you know, he and Chico are very close.'

'What a catastrophe!'

'Nonsense. What Chico wants is a job. And her father has influence, and once they've made their peace…'

'Yes, the kind of peace you get in the fifth acts of tragedies.'

'What influence does Rialva have?' asked a failed political candidate with a shrug.

'Lots. His brother-in-law has a job in the secretariat for internal affairs…'

'And the ministry owes him a few favours.'

'No, you're wrong. There used to be a lot of talk about Rialva helping people get votes, but I'm telling you, he didn't even manage to get four votes for Roboredo.'

'What do you mean? How did Roboredo get in then?'

'The person who helped Roboredo was...'

'I'm telling you, Pires, he did once have some influence in the ministry, but after he failed to get a post in customs and excise for his nephew, he gave up...'

'Which nephew is that? The one we used to call the giant Polyphemus when we were at university? He's a complete idiot.'

'He somehow always managed to pass his end-of-year exams and yet he could never accept the existence of the Antipodes. He said it made him feel quite ill thinking how uncomfortable it must be for the poor devils living upside down like that, if that is, they existed...'

'And then one day...'

A wave of raucous laughter coming from a group standing at the other end of the room interrupted the story.

All attention and all eyes turned in that direction.

Four young lads were laughing so much that tears were rolling down their cheeks. Standing next to them was a fifth lad, looking rather awkward and embarrassed.

'Oh, he's just priceless!' said one of the lads who was laughing.

'What happened?' asked those who weren't part of the group, but were already laughing in anticipation.

The embarrassed lad said: 'Oh, take no notice, they're all as mad as hatters.'

'No, what happened? Tell us,' insisted everyone.

'Cláudio Pires here has just made one of his great discoveries.'

'All I said was...' Pires said, trying to interrupt.

'Silence!' roared everyone.

'Cláudio,' said one of the lads who had been laughing loudest, 'overheard Lourenço here speaking in praise of how farmers abroad use compost, and he said he thought this an excellent thing, because nothing settles the stomach better after supper than a spoonful of compost.'

'Fruit compost is what I said.'

This justification was drowned out by a general chorus of laughter.

'No one's compost bin would be safe!'

'And all to save Cláudio's digestion!'

'Thus do great empires founder!'

And so the *bon mots* and epigrams continued to flow, with the noise growing ever louder.

Finally, a voice managed to make itself heard above the tumult.

'I would just remind you that it's eleven o'clock and time to make our grand entrance at one of the masked balls.'

It was the old-young man, who, rising from the table, filled his glass and cried: 'To tonight's conquests!'

'Seconded!' they all cried, also raising their glasses. 'To tonight's conquests!'

And the sound of chairs scraping on the floor was like the roar of thunder.

After a few minutes, the jolly companions emerged from the Golden Eagle after a supper that had lasted eight hours, and many of them, having spent a third of the day there, were slightly the worse for wear.

One of the company, who had been mostly silent throughout the meal, took Carlos' arm then, and leaning heavily on it, walked rather unsteadily with him across Largo da Batalha, and in between long puffs on his large pipe, he spoke these confidential, rather tearful words: 'Carlos, you're my friend, possibly the only friend I have, which is why I want you to be the first to hear my latest verses. I only like to talk about my poetry with someone who understands me. We poets need another heart to act as echo. The heart of a sensitive soul.'

These words were spoken very softly, but many of the others heard them and drew closer, because the poet in question had a certain reputation as an ingenious improviser of verses.

Others, though, had already met various stray carnival-goers on their way back from the theatre. Two were still belting out the duet from *Lucia di Lammermoor*:

Ó sole più rapido a sorger t'apresta...

The confiding poet began to recite enthusiastically, almost wildly, a hymn in praise of tobacco, which, we must confess, was likely to find an echo in many hearts.

In the midst of these
Circling clouds of smoke,
I feel like a god,
A god on an altar!
No other incense
Pleases as much
As the smoke from this
Vast exemplary pipe!

On magnificent divans,
Legs casually crossed,
The ardent sultan
Sits smoking for hours,
And the magical aroma
So goes to his head
That he forgets Mahoma,
Houris, and the Koran.

An English Family

It's so superior to opium
Which delights the dreams
Of that pitiful sect,
The Turkish Theriakis!
Cursèd be that vile narcotic
Of base poppies born!
And cursèd, too, the dreadful stuff
Cooked up in a saucepan
By the local Qasis*!*

Let the gentile race
In the world's hottest zones
Consume the beans
Of Arabica coffee.
Empty your cup
Of that vile brown beverage
The colour of the natives
Of sweltering Guiné.

And what of that exotic leaf,
The delight of the Chinese,
And, unhappily for us,
Now brought to us here,
And served en famille,
In a lukewarm concoction?
A curse on the use
Of those wretched tea leaves!

Not even you, alcoholic brew
Fresh from the wine press,
Will merit my songs,

An English Family

My hymns of praise.
Despite your gift,
When poured into glasses,
For making the silent loquacious.

And you, beer of Britain,
So furiously foamy,
Of what possible use
Are you to me?
Hearing Englishmen
Wax lyrical about
The wonder of hops,
Makes me laugh out loud.

And ignore all talk of camphor
And its marvels
From the famous inventor
Of cigarettes himself.
For while Raspail is heterodox,
I am orthodox
And care nothing
For his bizarre paradox.

I sing of America,
Land of tobacco,
Where Bacchus himself
Lay down his sceptre.
Europe, Asia, Africa,
The whole wide world
Is now covered in smoke
From that fashionable hero.

Even the diminutive natives
Of Lapland smoke,
As people do by the Seine,
By the Tiber and the Po,
By the Volga and the Vistula,
By the Tejo and the Douro,
What a treasure we owe
To Jean Nicot!

Let my poor arid lips
Inhale more smoke!
Let the foolish sigh
For kisses by the thousand.
I want no other kisses,
No other lover either,
For what could be more intoxicating
Than that subtlest of smokes?

Turned into human Vesuviuses
Mouths now spout smoke,
Vomit great clouds
That obscure the sky.
Ah, smoking! Such pleasure!
Worthy of a Nabob!
The Devil take
All other worldly passions!

'Bravo!' cried all those listening, filled with genuine admiration for the poet's muse. Even Carlos smiled, less preoccupied now, for the cloud hanging over his head was beginning to dissipate.

An English Family

'Who needs a ticket?'

'Anyone need tickets for the Teatro de São João?'

'Only twelve *vinténs*, my masters, twelve *vinténs*!'

Uttering these and other similar cries, a band of street-sellers fell upon the new arrivals from the Golden Eagle, who were keen to get the best ticket they could. Then they plunged into the theatre, where hundreds of others were dying of heat, asphyxia and tedium, and where they were trampled and squeezed and very nearly crushed by other masked carnival-goers, all caught up in a vertiginous gallop.

The reader, who doubtless finds Carnival as boring as I do, will, I'm sure, allow me to dispense with describing it all again, recalling the many dull hours to which we subject ourselves each year on the pretext of taking part in Oporto's Carnival and doing what everyone else does, which is always one of the most powerful motivating forces behind all our actions.

My apologies for having kept you so long over this scene, doubtless quite alien to your normal peaceful habits, but I did so only to show our hero in action and to exemplify his style of life and the company he usually kept, but since such scenes neither console nor amuse, I will now withdraw to quieter and less agitated scenes.

IV

The Angel of the Family

On the morning after the scenes just described, it is already late, gone eleven o'clock. Carlos is still sleeping.

He returned home at that critical moment when the stars are beginning to fade in the firmament, the birds to stir in their nests and the streets to echo with the hammering of some early-rising workmen. Is it any surprise, then, that he should still be sleeping and perhaps dreaming of a happy ending to some pleasant but inconclusive adventure at the previous night's ball.

The location of Mr Richard Whitestone's house definitely helped with this gross infraction of the rules of daytime, a time normally made for wakefulness and work, not sleep and dreams.

I need hardly tell any reader from Oporto that the Whitestone family lived in the area known as Cedofeito.

Our city – for those who may not know it well – divides naturally into three zones or *bairros*, the east, the centre and the west, each with its own distinctive physiognomy.

The centre is Oporto proper; the east is Brazilian, and the west is English.

The first of these areas is dominated by shops, offices, houses with lots of windows and large balconies, and other architectural indignities inflicted in a misplaced zeal for modernisation; there are entries and alleyways independent of any municipal diktats and entirely at the disposal of the inhabitants; narrow streets closely watched by policemen; street corners where carters wait for customers; these are the roads most commonly used for processions and therefore usually the muddiest; and the streets where most buying and selling is done, where people work by day and sleep by night. Despite its seemingly modern dress, this area still has the feel of the long-ago days when the bishops ruled.

The eastern area is mainly Brazilian, being the part of the city most popular with men returning to Portugal having made their fortune in the Americas. It is dominated by vast granite constructions known as *palacetes*, with wide doors, tiled walls – blue, green or yellow, both smooth and in relief – roofs with blue-painted eaves and blue and golden balconies; geometrical gardens measured out with compass and ruler and adorned with ceramic statues representing the four seasons; wrought-iron gates bearing, in gilt lettering, the name of the owner and the date the house was built; gothic windows and rectangular doors, rectangular windows and gothic doors, some even have battlements or a Chinese mirador. The streets there tend to be dusty. And if you peer through a window, you'll likely see some capitalist idling away the day.

The western zone is the English part of the city, because that is the chosen habitat of our English guests. The houses there are painted dark green or terra cotta or light brown or grey or black, yes, even black! The architecture is unpretentious but elegant; rectangular windows, with a preference for windowsills over balconies, which is itself a sign of a more secluded life, a windowsill being far more discreet than a balcony. Some houses are built in gardens shaded by acacias, lime trees and magnolias, and full of winding paths; the street doors are always kept firmly closed; and there is nearly always smoke billowing from the chimneys. The shutters and shades are the despair of the curious. No one is ever seen at the windows. In the streets, though, you will often meet some ringleted Englishwoman herding along a band of fair-haired children wearing white pinafores.

Those are the principal characteristics of Oporto's three main *bairros*, although it should be added, perhaps unnecessarily, that, as with all generalisations, there is nothing absolute about these classifications. By describing what is typical, we are neither drawing any definitive lines nor refusing to admit other, possibly numerous, exceptions, exceptions that are even more numerous now than they were in 1855.

Needless to say, the illustrious Mr Richard Whitestone and his family lived in the last of those zones. However, to avoid the kind of indiscretion frowned upon in places where everyone knows everyone else, I will not divulge the name of the street. I can, though, describe the house, albeit with due artifice so as not to encourage any reader with too much time on his or her hands to go looking for it.

It was one of those dark-painted houses – dark, that is, apart from the window panes framed in white wood – and it was set at the far end of a garden, whose surrounding railings were so thickly grown with evergreen climbers and the flower-laden branches of giant camellias, that the paths meandering across that lawn worthy of an English garden were safe from prying eyes.

The house was all on one level, apart from the mirador. A kind of pavilion or annex ran along one side of the garden, and its three ample windows gave onto the street, which was one of the quietest in the city. Here Carlos had his bedroom.

The whole house had about it an air of comfort, to use that

comfortable English noun. And it was far from the discordant voices of industry and commerce so fatal to the enchanting visions of morning dreams.

All this seemed as if designed to protect Carlos' restoring sleep, which was taking up the whole morning, at least according to the way of counting time still used by the few who, even today, start saying 'Good afternoon' the moment noon has passed.

Jenny could never go to sleep until she had heard her brother return safely home, although, not wishing to inhibit his pleasures, she never told him so or only when she thought a little inhibition was needed.

Knowing how late he had come home, she was leaving him to sleep now, so that he could recoup the energies expended that night and which he might need for yet another late night.

Like a young mother watching anxiously over her first child's sleep, she had been careful to keep the servants away from his door all morning and to fend off any noise that might wake him.

Since dawn, that gentle young woman had been pacing lightly up and down the broad corridor separating Carlos' room from the rest of the house, as if she were the guardian angel of her madcap brother, who was blissfully unaware of the wings protecting his sleep.

She would sometimes pause outside Carlos' room and press one ear to the door, listening for the slightest sound announcing that he was awake.

Then she would move off and slowly make her way to the room opposite, where she would inspect and direct the preparations for Mr Richard's lunch, the time for which was fast approaching.

Returning from one of her visits to her brother's room, she

came across a servant, a mere boy, leaning in the doorway leading into the garden, and apparently so weighed down with painful thoughts that he didn't even hear Jenny approach.

She looked at him kindly and asked: 'How's your mother, José?'

He turned, startled, then answered respectfully: 'I don't know, Miss, but when I left her yesterday, she was in a very bad way.'

'You don't know?' exclaimed Jenny, glancing over at the clock in the corridor, according to which it was half past eleven. 'But it's nearly midday!'

'Yes, but Senhor Carlos is still not up and...'

'Go and see her now, José, go on. You can't leave her alone in that state. She may need you.'

'But...'

'Off you go. Don't worry about Carlos. I'll tell him what's happened. Now go.'

'Thank you, Miss,' said the boy, touched by the kindness of his young mistress.

Jenny resumed her pacing.

When she passed the steps up to the mirador, she noticed something untoward. Going up the steps, she bent down to look more closely. It was a feather blown there by the wind. Jenny frowned.

Her scrupulous love of cleanliness – embedded deep in her character and in English habits in general – meant that she could not let this go unremarked.

'Have the steps been swept today, Pedro?' she asked a servant who happened to be passing.

'Yes, Miss,' he replied.

'Well, to be honest it doesn't look as if they have,' said Jenny. 'There's dust on the banister.'

62

'It's the wind, Miss.'

'Maybe, but that doesn't mean you can't dust it again.'

'Of course. I'll do it now.'

'And run a damp cloth over those glass panes too,' added Jenny, indicating the door leading out into the garden, 'they're all smeared. And give the metal handles a polish while you're at it.'

'Yes, Miss, and I'll tell the gardener to put some more gravel down after last night's rain,' said the servant who, like all servants, was far more zealous about other people's tasks than about his own.

Jenny nodded and walked on into the dining room.

She glanced at the table where the best glasses and the finest English china stood glittering on the spotless white linen cloth.

She spent some time carefully scrutinising every detail, and her face occasionally betrayed the fact that she had spotted some defect.

'Pedro,' she called, resting one hand on the back of Mr Richard's chair.

Pedro, who again happened to be passing, came when called.

'Where's the mustard?'

'Oh, sorry, Miss, you're quite right.'

And he ran to the sideboard to fetch that indispensable ingredient of British cuisine.

'And that napkin is creased.'

Pedro hastened to correct this imperfection.

'And this isn't the bread my father usually has with his lunch. You know that.'

'You're quite right, Miss.'

The bread was replaced with truly English speed.

'And move those flowers more into the centre. No, not so

close to the meat. Move the plate more over here. Now that knife is crooked. That's right. And put *The Times* beside it. That's fine. You can go now.'

Once alone, she herself made a few further adjustments, knowing the kind of small detail that pleased Mr Richard and which only she knew. Childish needs, but needs nonetheless, and which we all have. She drew the curtains, leaving the room in a discreet, very English half-light, then went back out into the corridor.

She had only gone a few steps when a maid, still quite new, came over to her, eyes lowered and looking distinctly embarrassed.

'Whatever's wrong, Luísa?' Jenny asked.

'I've come to say goodbye, Miss Jenny, because I'm leaving today.'

'What do you mean? Who told you to leave?'

'No one, but…'

'Aren't you well?'

'Yes, but…'

'So what is it?'

'As you know, my sister was working as a maid outside the city. Well, the work got too much for her, and she, poor thing, is so frail. Anyway, she kept it up for as long as she could, but then she fell ill. She's gone to live with our mother now, but how is my mother going to cope when she herself is half-crippled and blind? My brothers are out working all day, and we can't afford a nurse. So what's to be done? I'll have to go and take care of my sister until she's better, and then if you want me back again…'

'You can't possibly leave us now, Luísa.'

'But…'

'Listen, if you want to look after your sister, bring her here.'

'Oh, Miss…'

'You can make up that other room on the mirador.'

'Oh that would be perfect, Miss…'

'Another thing, Luísa,' Jenny broke in, 'see if you can have those cuffs ready for me today. Off you go.'

'I'll do it straightaway, Miss,' said the girl, her heart beating fast with contentment.

At this point, shrill, dissonant, piercing cries were heard. Jenny stopped in her tracks and a cloud of sadness passed over her serene face. The cries were coming from up above.

Luísa said in a voice that was half-pitying, half-amused: 'It's Senhora Catarina. She's been in one of her impatient moods since yesterday.'

'Poor Kate!' murmured Jenny with a sigh, then went lightly up the stairs to the mirador.

Catarina or Kate was a maid – now in her eighties – who had once been Mr Richard's nanny. Paraplegic and demented, she lived in one of the rooms that gave onto the mirador. She was affectionately cared for by the Whitestone family and, rather more impatiently, by the servants. On some days, she grew intensely angry, and her imprecations, in a mixture of Portuguese and English, and her spine-chilling screams disturbed the whole household. It was very hard to calm her down when she was like that. Her gestures were so violent that it took many pairs of arms to keep her from harming herself.

'Dogs!' she was shouting now, in that strange linguistic imbroglio impossible to reproduce here, and which provoked sniggers from the maids attending her. 'Dogs! They're holding me prisoner here! They want me to starve to death! Just wait until Dick comes, though, and he will, he will. Let me go! Dick! Dick!' This was her name for Mr Richard. 'Dick! Is this how you intend to kill me? Is this how you want to see me

die? Have you no pity, Dick? I carried you in my arms, I…
It's me, poor Kate Simpleton. Dick! Dick! Free me from these
demons. They're trying to suffocate me. What did I ever do to
you that you should let me die like this? Let me go!'

Clasping Jenny to her breast, she began rocking back and
forth, singing the same melancholy Scottish tune, with which,
fifty years before, she had lulled Dick, now Mr Richard
Whitestone, to sleep.

Here is the song she was singing:

Baloo, my boy, lie still and sleep
It grieves me sore to hear thee weep
If thou'lt be silent I'll be glad
Thy moaning makes my heart full sad.

Jenny made no attempt to pull away. The old woman was
weeping as she sang, and her voice gradually began to fade.
Finally, she fell into one of those deep sleeps, which, in people
at her stage in life, seem to take on the character of the final
sleep, which was clearly not far off.

She fell asleep singing in the faintest of voices:

If thou'lt be silent I'll be glad
Thy moaning makes my heart full sad.

Jenny gently extricated herself from Kate's embrace, smoothed
the bedclothes, closed the window and, hushing the maids,
went back downstairs. There she found the gardener sitting at
the bottom of the stairs, sobbing, his face in his hands.

'Whatever's wrong, Manuel?'

The old man leapt to his feet.

'Oh, Miss Jenny, look…'

And he pointed to the step outside the door to the garden where a china flowerpot containing a precious begonia lay shattered.

'How did that happen?' asked Jenny.

'Your father instructed me to take the pot from his room to the greenhouse and told me to be very, very careful. And then I, well, it was just bad luck really. I slipped going down the steps and... oh dear God!'

'Calm down. My father won't be that angry.'

'But he will. He told me to take particular care, and it's one of his favourite pots too. Oh, what a way to start the day!'

Jenny was touched to see how upset the old man was and how afraid he was even to tell Mr Richard what had happened.

The kind girl bent down and, picking up the two fragments still containing the soil and the begonia, carefully pieced them together and, going out into the garden, headed straight for the greenhouse.

'Where are you going, Miss?' asked the gardener, mystified.

Jenny didn't answer.

The old man followed her.

When she reached the greenhouse, where Mr Richard was labouring away at his gardening, Jenny said: 'I didn't want to entrust the pot to anyone else because... oh!'

The pot fell from her hands and broke into still more pieces on the ground, right outside the door to the greenhouse.

'Oh, no!' said Mr Richard, rushing to the aid of the begonia.

'You see,' Jenny said, pretending to be shocked. 'God is punishing me for my presumption.'

'Yes,' said Mr Richard, still crouching down. 'And it was such a pretty pot too. Really, child, just look at the state of this poor begonia!'

'You were quite right, Manuel,' Jenny said. 'I didn't trust

you to carry it, and now...'

The old gardener was dumbstruck, and while Mr Richard was examining the damage done to the begonia, Manuel seized her hand before she could stop him and covered it with kisses.

It was midday.

'Come along,' Jenny said to Mr Whitestone, 'forgive me and come and have lunch.'

Mr Richard looked fondly at his daughter and stroked her cheek, then, with a sigh, he left the begonia where it lay and followed her up to the house, murmuring and smiling: 'Butterfingers!'

The spilled soil on the steps into the house did not escape his sharp English eyes, but Jenny, seeing this evidence of Manuel's crime, quickly explained: 'Oh, that was me repotting those cuttings from England...'

'Ah, well, I don't even know if they'll take. We'll see.'

'Yes, but not now, now it's time for lunch.'

Mr Richard did not insist, and a few seconds later, he was preparing himself for his first meal of the day.

V

Mr Richard's Morning

Mr Richard was rigorously punctual in his daily domestic routine. First thing in the morning, having read a few pages of the Bible and reviewed his precious collection of British birds and insects – made after consulting books by Yarrell, Shuckard, Rennie and other experts in the field – he would then stroll out into the garden to enjoy the beauty of the morning and to exercise his passion for flowers, digging, weeding and sowing his well-stocked beds. It must be said that, despite his very best intentions, Mr Richard's morning labours were not entirely beneficial to the garden.

In his study, books on botany and horticulture lay open on his desk, from Curtis' *Flora Londinensis* and the complete works of Lindley to the publications of various horticultural societies in London, but Mr Richard liked to do things in his own way. Scorning both the recommendations of theoreticians and old Manuel's many years of experience, he would sometimes experiment with procedures not mentioned in any gardening manual to the detriment, alas, of the mimosas and the rare plants he acquired, regardless of price, from the best sources in Europe, mainly Covent Garden and the Pantheon in Oxford Street.

Nature always had her work cut out when remedying the results of his meddlings.

Fortunately for the garden as a whole, Mr Richard was only interested in flowers. At every season of the year, he would lavish all his horticultural care on one particular kind of flower. His favourites at the time were begonias. However, all his love and care had proved so disastrous that Manuel, who truly loved plants, became quite concerned.

Mr Whitestone had tried out a kind of fertiliser on the poor things, and a large number had died as a result. He believed that the artificial, highly indigestible liquid he had made would bring together all the elements he deemed essential for them to flourish.

'It'll scorch their leaves!' warned Manuel, as he watched Mr Richard concocting this potion.

'Nonsense, man. They'll thrive on the stuff.'

When he saw the results, though, he was obliged to abandon the process, while still refusing to admit failure.

'It's these pots, they're not porous enough. I'll send for some better ones from London.'

This was Mr Richard's usual way of getting out of tricky situations. Like the true Englishman he was, he always turned to London.

And this is how he passed the time until lunch, when he would return to the house. His lunch was a veritable hecatomb of oysters. The market in Oporto could barely cope with the demands of the molluscivores in the English colony, among whom Mr Richard occupied an eminent position. Roast beef, ham, mustard, potatoes, crackers, beer, and Cheddar cheese were also present at these lunches, tailored to satisfy that robust Anglo-Saxon stomach, a descendant of stomachs, which, according to Alexandre Herculano in his book *Jersey to Granville*, had still been cannibals in the fifth century.

Carlos normally joined his father at this morning repast,

and Mr Richard enjoyed having his son by his side at such solemn moments, even though he barely addressed more than a dozen words to him; for, after an initial exchange of greetings, he would open his copy of *The Times* and read that interminable newspaper as he chewed, interrupting his reading with an occasional short utterance either praising or criticising one or other of the dishes.

And Carlos' absence that morning was the cause of the deep frownline of discontent on Mr Richard's forehead – a discontent that the garden air had managed somewhat to dispel – and also the reason why he stopped gaily humming (or, rather, mangling) a cheerful tune the moment he entered the dining room.

The tune in question was a popular melody by Henry Russell, an extraordinarily popular English composer and singer of the day, whose eager, enthusiastic fans would flock to his London performances to hear him sing his own compositions, which he himself accompanied on the piano. The newspapers were full of reports of this notable musician's songs being sung in salons and in theatres, in the streets and the fields, both in England and America, songs greatly influenced by the Italian music of the day, but still resolutely British nonetheless.

Out of the collection of melodies or popular tunes published that year in London and excitedly sought out by amateurs all over the world, one was a particular favourite of Mr Richard's. And this was the tune he was humming when he came into the room.

His choice was more than justified both by the style of the song and the words, written by Charles Mackay, which encapsulated so much of the English character.

It's a song intended to encourage the many bands of emigrants leaving from all over Great Britain to cross the seas in search of a better life and who, without shedding so much as a tear, are bidding farewell to their native land, which they still love passionately. If, in society's present-day battles to garner wealth, there is still a glimmer of the epic glory that once surrounded the labours of that mythological figure Jason, then the English are definitely the heroes of those modern epics. The cool detachment with which they leave the two things to which they are almost fanatically devoted, namely, nation and family, the stoical courage that keeps them going in difficult times, the determination that, in victory, keeps them from sliding into a mood of dangerous complacency, all this lends these argonauts of commerce a respect and a prestige that no absurd external characteristics can erase.

As a complement to this study of Mr Richard Whitestone's character, we give here the words of that song by Mr Mackay, because the idea they embody is so in keeping with the sentiments of that honest businessman.

This was the song that the English soldiers sang in Crimea during the campaign there, and which, when the military band struck up the first notes, thousands of spectators sang along with them as the soldiers set off for foreign shores:

Cheer, boys, cheer. No more of idle sorrow,
Courage true hearts, shall bear us on our way
Hope points before and shows the bright tomorrow,
Let us forget the darkness of today
So, farewell England! Much as we may love thee
We'll dry the tears that we have shed before
Why should we weep to sail in search of fortune?
Farewell England! Farewell for evermore.
Chorus: *Cheer, boys, cheer! For England, Mother England*
Cheer, boys, cheer! The willing strong right hand

Cheer, boys, cheer! There's wealth for honest labour
Cheer, boys, cheer! For the new and happy land.

Cheer, boys, cheer! The steady wind is blowing
To float as freely o'er the ocean's breast
The world shall follow in the track we're going
The star of Empire glitters in the West
Here we had toil and little to reward it
But there shall plenty smile upon our pain
And ours shall be the prairie and the forest
And boundless meadows ripe with golden grain.

This, then, was the tune that Mr Richard stopped humming when, on entering the dining room, he saw that the table was only set for one.

'Is Carlos still in bed?' he asked Jenny in a slightly ill-tempered tone of voice.

I should advise readers now that, for your convenience and mine, I will have Mr Richard speak in fluent Portuguese, even respecting the rules of grammar whose authority he never acknowledged.

Jenny felt she needed to defend her brother from the disfavour of their father, who, already greatly upset by Carlos' absence on his birthday, was now full of disapproval for his son's excessive indolence.

As a great admirer of the beauties of this Earth, Mr Richard thought of sleep as an envious creature intent on stealing from us a few hours of life's pleasures and, obliged though he was to give way to sleep, he always regarded it as the enemy.

Jenny answered her father's question with a succinct 'Yes'.

'Oh!' added Mr Richard, resorting to his usual guttural, monosyllabic expression of displeasure, accompanied by all

73

the other usual noises.

Jenny added: 'Charles didn't get home until late last night.'

'He certainly chose a good day for it.'

'He forgot.'

'Oh really!'

'He said he was quite sure that he wouldn't have forgotten had it been *your* birthday.'

Mr Richard sat down and started reading *The Times*.

Jenny sat opposite him, but away from the table.

'And because he went to bed late,' she went on after a moment, 'I was worried that a lack of sleep might make him ill, and so I gave instructions for him not to be woken.'

'So he came home very late, then?'

'Yes, at about two o'clock, I think,' stammered Jenny.

The servant who had begun serving Mr Richard, helpfully corrected her: 'Forgive me, Miss Jenny, but it was after four.'

'Oh!' said Mr Richard again.

Jenny shot the servant a glance that made it clear that she did not appreciate the correction.

'Charles had promised to get together with some friends of his,' she said, 'and he only realised what day it was when it was too late to say No.'

Mr Richard didn't need to hear any more, and his disapproving comments ended there. He had long since lost the habit of disagreeing with his daughter, which is why, still reading *The Times*, he said: 'Fine, fine. It's his choice…'

Then bounding into the room came one of those small, hairy, black and brown dogs, who are the true Attilas of mice and the rivals of all the other exterminators of that persecuted race.

'Good morning, Butterfly! How do you do, sir?' cried Mr Richard, greeting his favourite dog, who held out his paw to be shaken. This was a clear request for a piece of ham, and Mr Richard duly obliged.

The small quadruped then hopped familiarly onto the chair beside his master, and did due justice to his share of the leftovers.

Jenny kept getting up to serve her father, and attending to the kind of detail too minor to be noticed by a servant or anyone other than a daughter.

On one such occasion, Mr Richard, as if picking up the thread of their previous conversation, said in a low voice: 'He hasn't been to the office for over a week, you know, and that's not good.'

Jenny didn't answer.

It was clear that they had both been thinking the same thing.

On this occasion, the journalists on *The Times* had, I fear, failed to hold their reader's attention.

Mr Richard finally left the table.

While washing his hands and gazing out at the flower beds in the garden, he was still murmuring: 'No, it's not good. He's getting into bad habits.'

And with that, he left the room and went to his study.

Jenny followed behind.

'I'm not asking much of him,' he was saying.

Putting on his overcoat and taking his hat and cane from Jenny, he continued in the same tone: 'People will talk... people will notice...'

Pulling on his pale kid gloves, which, on some patriotic whim, he'd had sent directly from England, he said: 'I don't understand what is so very difficult about spending a few minutes at the office.'

Then again: 'It looks bad, very bad.'

He seemed about to leave, but Jenny, who knew his every

mood, saw that he was hesitating, as if torn between two conflicting choices.

'I'll see you later, Jenny,' he said, but still he didn't leave.

'I'm sure I've forgotten something...' he muttered, clearly perplexed.

Jenny looked around the room.

'Your handkerchief?' she asked, holding out one she spotted on the dressing table.

'Ah, yes, my handkerchief...'

But it was clear that he was still not satisfied.

'Right, I've got everything now. Goodbye, Jenny.'

And this time, Jenny thought that he really would leave.

'Oh, I know,' he went on, stopping again.

Jenny looked at him interrogatively.

'Now what was it? Oh, I know. So is Carlos simply not getting up at all this morning?'

'Do you want me to wake him?'

'No, no, it's just that...'

Then, breaking off: 'No, it's nothing.'

'Do you want me to give him some instructions?'

'No... but... no, there's time enough.'

'Tell me what it is. Charles is sure to make an appearance sooner or later.'

'It's...'

And looking somewhat embarrassed, Mr Richard went over to his desk, opened it and took out a magnificent pocket watch complete with chain, which he had ordered specially from London to give to his son on his birthday.

Carlos' absence the previous evening had prevented him from making this fond gesture.

Now it seemed as if he felt ashamed that his affection should have survived that filial betrayal, and that he lacked the strength to repress such feelings.

'There you are,' he said to Jenny as brusquely as he could, trying to remove any hint of affection from his voice. 'You can give it to your brother if you like, after all, I bought it for him, and if, yesterday…'

Jenny took the watch and thanked him with a warm smile.

Mr Richard went on: 'I don't know if Carlos will want it, of course, although it's very valuable…'

'The most valuable thing about it is that you chose it.'

Mr Richard made some mumbled monosyllabic response and pulled a rather unconvincingly sceptical face.

Jenny added: 'It would be even more valuable if you gave it to him yourself.'

'Do you want me to go and wake Carlos up, so that he will do me the great favour of accepting my gift?' asked Mr Richard rather sourly.

'Why not give it to him after supper?'

'If, that is, he honours us with his company.'

'Oh, if Carlos knew…'

'Don't worry. You give it to him, if you like.'

And with this, he left the room, crossed the garden and, shortly afterwards, left by the main gate.

The servant he passed in the corridor heard him muttering: 'Yes, it looks very bad indeed.'

However, once out in the street, he seemed quite content. He walked with the briskness peculiar to people for whom time is money, spoke cordially to his favourite dog Butterfly and continued to hum that popular tune: 'Cheer, boys, cheer!'

VI

Carlos Awakes

After saying goodbye to her father, Jenny lingered a while by the door. She was looking at the objects around her, but her thoughts did not accompany her gaze.

Her face, a mysterious combination of stern maternalism and child-like candour, now took on an anxious, melancholy air, one of those shadows that serious thoughts seem to cast over the features of those who have not yet learned to disguise them.

Jenny sensed that once again she was going to have to bring her conciliatory, angelic influence to bear in order to drive away the clouds – however tenuous – that were gathering on the domestic horizon.

She had already worked her magic on one of the parties, having managed to soften Mr Richard's acerbic feelings towards his son; now she had to complete the task, and work her magic on Carlos too.

And Jenny, who knew her brother well, believed that her efforts would not be in vain. A ray of confidence broke through the gloom of her disquiet. And it was in this frame of mind that she summoned André and asked him to wake her brother up.

André was the household's oldest servant, a kind of butler, who had worked for Mr Whitestone ever since the latter moved to Oporto, and who had known both children since they were small.

'Tell Charles I'll wait for him in the library,' said Jenny.

When old André entered the bedroom, Carlos was still sleeping peacefully. His deep, slow, regular breathing indicated a sleep entirely free of nightmares and other troubling dreams.

For a while, André stood listening to this sound, which was the only sound in the room, apart from the ticking of the nearby clock, then – rather unnecessarily since he had come on purpose to wake Carlos up – he cautiously tiptoed over to one of the windows and opened it just a crack.

The room filled with a kind of half-light, sifted through the long curtains which, once liberated from their gilt hooks, brushed the carpet.

Then André could see the utter disorder in which the room lay.

Although rather less felicitous than the light summoned by the *fiat lux* in Genesis – let there be light – that light could, however, have been accurately described as illuminating a chaos, simply because it would be hard to find a more appropriate word to describe the state of that room, the sight of which made the look of studied seriousness on André's face and lips dissolve into a smile.

Indeed, the scene almost defied detailed description.

It was as if, during the night, all the room's contents had been engaged in some fantastical dance, and dawn had found them still dancing and far from their designated places.

The chairs, in an untidy pile in the middle of the room, had taken on the duties of the wardrobe, and the latter, its doors flung wide, revealed a disorderly, almost empty interior, like a house after the sacking of some conquered city.

Jackets, waistcoats, trousers and cravats of every colour and style were draped over tables, sofas and armchairs or strewn on the floor, in fact, everywhere except where they should be.

An English Family

On the floor were objects too numerous to count; here a pair of gloves, worn for the first time the previous evening and already discarded as redundant; there a posy of flowers, its leaves and petals limp and faded, but whose possession had doubtless been won only after tireless pleadings, then quickly thrown down and forgotten; and elsewhere, half-smoked cigars, the fragments of a precious Indian vase, a book that had committed the sin of not having aroused his curiosity, a fallen chair weighed down by the load placed on its back; letters, collars, paintings, handkerchiefs and horsewhips. A pair of spurs stood in place of the clock, which was now balanced on the marble edge of the stove; on the bed, a satin domino cloak; hanging on the bedhead, the evening paper and a long pipe with a gutta-percha stem; at the foot, a powder flask for hunting, a damask dressing gown and a saddle blanket for his favourite horse; on the bedside table, a silver inkwell transformed into an ashtray; a hat hanging from a hook on the back of the door; the oil-lamp on the floor, and a few books and maps peeking out from beneath the bed. A painted cardboard lampshade decorated with exotic Chinese figures in various Chinesey poses served as a beret for the bust of Shakespeare, his neck diplomatically festooned with a bow tie; opposite him, Byron, sporting a wide-brimmed felt hat tipped elegantly over his left ear, seemed to be gazing impertinently at his illustrious compatriot; while, in another corner, stood the grave, kindly figure of Sir Walter Scott, peeping rather shyly out from beneath a fez, an item made rather fashionable by the Crimean War; and, finally, a fourth bust wearing a black satin mask, which concealed the look of candour and long-suffering sadness of that singer of battles between devils and angels, the sublime Milton.

It was as if those great figures of English literature had

heard the call of Carnival and poked their pale heads up out of the grave in order to take part in a very strange masked ball.

In the midst of all this confusion, a huge Newfoundland dog, with leonine nostrils and the build of a bull, was languidly ensconced on the cushioned comfort of a sofa, his large, hairy paws resting on a magnificent album of engravings, showing no respect at all for such a precious object, which served him as both headrest and dais.

You may imagine the rest.

André, methodical André, was smiling and shaking his head at the sight of such disorder. It took him a few moments to take in the whole chaotic scene, which resembled the aftermath of some recent battle; then he walked over to the bed, slowly and rather reluctantly drew back the white curtains surrounding it and, still disinclined to wake Carlos from his tranquil slumbers, he instead bent low and regarded Carlos' smooth brow.

Carlos had a very pleasant, expressive face, which had all the best qualities of the classic Anglo-Saxon type: short, fair, naturally curly hair that parted to reveal his broad, prominent forehead; the delicate white skin of a Northern European; a very straight nose; fullish lips, gently curved into a smile, half-ironic, half-affectionate, and which could easily go in either of those two directions; large eyelids marked by a network of tiny blue veins, and the very faintest of dark shadows under his eyes, evidence of many a late night; these were the main features of that attractive, candid physiognomy which, in some respects, bore a certain resemblance to Byron. When awake, his eyes were as lively as the mind that animated them, his features alert and eloquent – something else he had in common with Byron, at least according to the latter's biographers.

Finally, André spoke to him, but in a voice that seemed

reluctant to be heard.

'Senhor Carlos,' he said.

Although spoken in a soft, almost fearful tone, this was enough to wake Carlos.

He immediately opened his eyes, fixed them on André, and reaching out his arms in the almost involuntary gesture with which, each morning, we cast off the chains binding us to sleep, he let them fall about André's neck, as if to rest them there, then said in a very hoarse voice: 'Good morning, André. What time is it?'

'Midday.'

This answer was accompanied by a meaningful smile.

'Save us!' exclaimed Carlos, imitating the English house-keeper – who often used that expression – and turning to look at the clock opposite, which, as if in response to his silent question, very slowly and deliberately struck twelve.

'Well, you could have fooled me,' said Carlos, once he had counted off each chime. 'I was surprised to see you up so early. And what about my father?'

'He's left.'

And… what did he say?'

André shrugged and said: 'Nothing.'

Which meant that he had said something.

Carlos understood this, but asked no further questions.

'It's time to get up, it's late!' said André, picking up a few of the objects from the floor.

'Oh cruel, inhuman one, must you remind me?' said Carlos as if reciting some tragic poem.

'Come on, lazybones.'

Carlos again opened his mouth, as if about to bid an almost sentimental farewell to fast departing sleep; with one hand he stroked the huge Newfoundland dog, which had come and placed its head on his knees, and with the other he opened at random the book nearest to him, a novel by Dickens, from which he distractedly read a few lines.

'So?' asked André, seeing that Carlos was in no mood to get up. 'Are you staying in bed?'

'Bring me some breakfast, man. No, just coffee. I feel as if I'm still digesting last night's rather turbulent supper.'

'So you want to eat your breakfast in bed?'

'Yes, a most praiseworthy decision, I think.'

'But...'

'But what? What are your objections? Speak.'

'Miss Jenny is waiting for you in the library.'

Carlos sat bolt upright and swung his legs around so that he was perched on the edge of the bed.

'Why on earth didn't you say so before, you fool? Quick, hand me that dressing gown, no, that's my Carnival outfit! Quick, hurry. Give me that handkerchief, no, the other one. Right. Go and tell Jenny I'll be with her in two ticks.'

And after performing his very swift ablutions, Carlos went into the library, where Jenny was waiting for him.

In this library, the two siblings had often sat reading together as children, when they studied the same books, their charming fair heads close together, a sight that Mr Richard Whitestone would watch as if rapt and full of silent blessings.

'Good morning, Charles,' said Jenny, holding out her hand, which he squeezed affectionately.

'Have you been waiting long? Forgive me, but that fool André neglected to tell me...'

'Yes, I'm sorry to wake you, but...'

'No, you were quite right. I would have slept all day otherwise.'

'You came home very late last night, Charles,' said Jenny,

surreptitiously bending down to stroke the Newfoundland dog, which had lain at her feet.

'Oh, so you heard me?'

'I did.'

'Did I wake you, Jenny? I tried not to make any noise, but then I'm always such a clumsy oaf!'

'No, you didn't wake me. I wasn't asleep.'

'You weren't asleep? At four o'clock in the morning? You weren't feeling ill, were you, Jenny?'

'No, but…'

Carlos looked at his sister with what was intended to be a stern expression.

'You mean it was because of me? I've told you before, Jenny. I'll get annoyed if you insist on sitting up like that, to the point…'

'I didn't sit up waiting for you, it's just…'

'It's just that you're very stubborn and what you deserve…'

'Let's not talk about that. Tell me, will you be coming home earlier tonight?'

'Tonight? On Carnival Tuesday? Oh, Jenny, at least let's get Carnival over with, and then… then, you'll see, I'll spend night after night at home with you and with… Have you been very bored here alone, poor thing?'

'I'm not talking about me, Charles, but all these long suppers, all these late nights will make you ill.'

'Me? Nothing makes me ill, besides…'

'And… Look, Charles, it's been such a very long time since you spent an evening with us… I'm not speaking for myself, as I said, but for Father. You know what he's like, old habits and all that… he likes to see the three of us together… at certain times at least. Poor love! I don't mean all the time, but now and then, if you wouldn't mind…'

'Of course, Jenny, of course. But in the summer. I promise. Then I'll do as you ask. Often. But on winter nights... despite what Thomson says in his poem about winter, winter nights are just too long to spend at home!'

'Yes, but in the summer, I know what you'll say, you're sure to find the nights so beautiful that...'

'No, really,' said Carlos, smiling, 'how could I when I've promised you? Look, Jenny, you're such a good person, and I know you're going to tell me off for what I'm about to say, but you must agree that, at least for a young man my age, it's really not much fun the way Father chooses to spend his evenings. That eternal *Times* of his just terrifies me, Jenny. I respect and admire the Bible, for example, but I tremble slightly to hear his paraphrases of our worthy men of letters, I do, I tremble. I know *Tristram Shandy* by heart, and as for *Tom Jones*, even before I'd read it, I knew every chapter just from hearing him quote great chunks from it; and to be honest, having to spend a night listening, yet again, to what he has to say about one or other of those books, with which, in his inexhaustible enthusiasm, he's sure to torture us... to be honest...'

'Charles!' said Jenny in a reproving voice.

'And to top it all,' Carlos went on, 'having to live under the permanent threat of a visit from the splenetic Mr Morlays, or the no less dreadful, jovial Mr Brains, who are, respectively, an English Heraclitus and Democritus, and even harder to digest than their Greek originals. That's what makes me seek out those places where, as Thomson says "...the city swarms intense. The public haunt, full of each theme and warm with mixed discourse, hums indistinct."'

Jenny couldn't help smiling at her brother's thoughts, but to cover up this moment of weakness, she hurriedly said: 'Yes, but not to be here yesterday of all days. Really! On your birthday!'

85

'What can I say? I completely forgot. Honestly. The fact of my birth hardly seems to me a reason for celebration!'

'But those who love you think differently. Wouldn't you even give them the pleasure of saying so?'

'I would, if I remembered.'

'Father had a surprise for you. Poor love. I felt so sorry for him when, a little while ago, he gave me this watch,' said Jenny, handing Mr Richard's gift to her brother.

'Really! Oh, poor Father! And I deprived him of that pleasure! Ah, this madcap head of mine, Jenny! But you at least know that I have a good heart, don't you, Jenny?'

'Yes, Charles, I do.'

'Other people though...'

'They all think so too, it's only you who...'

'But this is a truly magnificent watch, Jenny! Well, Senhor Carlos, it's time you did something to reciprocate. That's it: I won't wait until Summer. Carnival is nearly over, and once it's done, I will do penance all through Lent.'

'Oh, Carnival! Those masked balls must be tremendous fun, Charles, for you to find them such a draw!'

'No, Jenny, you're wrong, and... you won't understand this, but it's true. They're somehow dull and irresistible at the same time.'

'Oh, come now.'

'It's true. There's hardly a night when I'm not bored rigid, when I don't almost die of boredom in the midst of that infernal tumult, and then, when I think of you and your quiet evenings and your silent nights in your lovely mauve-painted bedroom, I ask myself why I stay away from home, what drags me from the doors of this paradise, which I have voluntarily lost. I must be mad. I don't deserve to be your brother. Then, I feel like uttering a lament, like Eve, about having to wander down into a lower World, right next door to yours, Jenny, but obscure and wild, and having to breathe in another air less pure, isn't that what Milton says? And I don't have the excuse of some archangelical power forcing me into exile. Do you see what I mean?'

'Are you joking, Charles?'

'No, I'm not. Others would say the same.'

'And is that what kept you out until four o'clock this morning?'

'This morning? Ah, forgive me, Jenny, but there's an exception to every rule. Last night, I must confess, left no unpleasant memories.'

'Meaning?'

'Meaning… that I have something to tell you, as long as you have the patience to hear me out and promise not to scold too much.'

'Ah, so we're feeling guilty, are we?'

'I really don't know. I have so little confidence in myself that I hesitate to say whether I behaved well or ill. See what you think.'

Jenny smiled.

'We're listening,' she said, preparing his lunch, which a servant had just brought into the room.

VII

A Review of the Night's Events

'As I was saying, Jenny,' Carlos began as he launched into that improvised breakfast, at an hour when many people were setting about the serious and important task of digesting their lunch, 'last night turned out to be far more enjoyable than usual.'

'Why is that? What happened?'

'I'll tell you. We finished supper at about eleven o'clock. It was a very long supper, with endless toasts to keep us all cheerful. I arrived at the theatre feeling slightly dazed and a little sad, dazed by the stimulating effects of all those libations and by the general chatter...'

'And sad...'

'Oh, because of the feelings of remorse your letter aroused in me.'

'Remorse!'

'Yes, really. In that mood, the theatre felt like an inferno, with all those tedious masks as the demons and the scraping of the orchestra imitating the cries of the damned.'

'But you stayed.'

'I did. I stayed, longing for the fun to end and allow me to leave. I know you can't understand these things, but that's how it is. May I continue?'

'Please do,' said Jenny, leafing through a book of English

engravings on the table. 'But you certainly have an odd way of having fun... by torturing yourself.'

'I agree, but I'm not alone in that.'

'All right, let's move on,' said Jenny, fixing her eyes on the gold lettering in the book.

'I left my companions and sat down, feeling absolutely exhausted. I didn't even want to see or take in what was going on around me. In the end, though, just to do something, I decided to take a look at the people I was sitting cheek by jowl with, and among whom fate had thrown me.'

Jenny looked up at her brother with sudden interest.

'On my right was a fat man, fast asleep. Since the happiness of others brings us no comfort when we ourselves are plunged in gloom, I resentfully averted my gaze from such good fortune and instead turned it upon...'

'The person to your left?'

'Exactly.'

'And what did you find on that side of your heart, Charles?' asked Jenny, smiling.

'Ah, my poor sister Jenny! Prepare your saintly patience, for I am about to confess to you that I've lost my heart yet again.'

'I could see it coming. I could somehow tell from the look on your face. So you're really in love?'

'I'm afraid so.'

'Oh, poor Charles! What bad luck!'

'Are you making fun of me?' said Carlos, smiling and holding out his empty cup to be refilled. 'Just listen. To my left was a woman in mask and domino costume, looking at me in a way, well, I hardly know how to describe it, and with such eyes, oh, Jenny, such beautiful eyes!'

'The eyes on her mask, you mean?' asked Jenny, pouring

him some more coffee.

'No, the masked woman's own eyes, which I could see through the holes in the elegant black satin mask she was wearing. Her head was slightly tilted towards her shoulder in such a languid, melancholy posture, and, in that position, the silk mask revealed one corner of her mouth and the beginning of a shapely neck, and I just couldn't take my enraptured eyes off her and... Why are you smiling, Jenny?'

'I'm just admiring the speed with which you fall in love and become enraptured.'

'You can't imagine the lovely curve of that cheek, you really can't! I'll tell you something, Jenny. I know all the tricks played by women and their satin masks, which they apparently carelessly lift just a little, just enough. Because most faces have their minor flaws, which the mask artificially hides, leaving only the perfections on show. I know how easy it is to be fooled and to take the part for the whole and so on...'

'Enough, Charles. It's just such a shame that all this knowledge of yours is of so little use to you, given that even yesterday...'

'No, yesterday, there were no tricks. Definitely not. That head wasn't one of those fidgety heads, always shifting about like aspen leaves, one of those heads that is just dying to be noticed. It was a thoughtful, melancholy head, full of feeling, terribly embarrassed to think that it might allow someone a glimpse of its beauty...'

'A most unusual head!'

'Besides, there are certain extremes of perfection that Nature, when she created them, wouldn't go wasting on any old face, where such perfections would be out of place. And that was the case with what I glimpsed of my charming

90

neighbour's profile, indeed, I even spoke to her.'

'You spoke to her!'

'Yes, what's so extraordinary about that? At a masked ball, you don't need introductions, which, besides, are one of those silly inventions of etiquette, which, I suspect, has its roots in our English diplomacy.'

This historical note changed Jenny's look of surprise into a smile.

Carlos went on: 'And you'll see how everything I said could easily have been repeated to the most ingenuous of lady guests at one of our family dances. You see, dear sister, while I may have somehow acquired a reputation for being rather forward, I can be as awkward as even the most timid fifteen-year-old.'

This confession, in which there was some truth, provoked a momentary look of doubt on Jenny's face, but her affectionate smile quickly softened any hint of scepticism.

'It's true,' said her brother, 'and if you don't believe me, just listen. As I said, I spoke to my charming neighbour and asked if she was feeling tired. You see, what could be more innocent, or even ridiculous? Do you disapprove?'

'Not at all. And then what happened?'

'She said: "I'm much more tired of all this than I expected when I came, Senhor Carlos."'

'Senhor Carlos?'

'Yes, the mysterious stranger knew my name. That, as you can imagine, made me even more curious. We talked some more, and I learned that she had come there with some other ladies, whose rather more festive mood was in marked contrast to her own melancholy seriousness. We sat talking in the same friendly, innocent way in which I'm talking to you now. And do you know, she even spoke a little like you, had some of the same mannerisms, and that was perhaps why I felt a certain constraint, which I couldn't shake off. You can't imagine the grace and good sense and wit she revealed in that dialogue with me. She seemed to know all about me and about our family. There was even a moment when she seemed to want to talk about you, but I quickly changed the subject.'

'Oh why?' asked Jenny, pretending to be put out.

'Because...' stammered Carlos, clearly embarrassed, before adding more confidently: 'To tell you the truth, Jenny, I hold you in such respect and so venerate your name that I would hate to hear it mentioned in such places, and on lips... regardless of the favourable impression that unknown young woman made on me... on lips that I cannot yet be sure are worthy to pronounce it. She and I spent possibly two hours engaged in harmless conversation, then some of the lads who'd gone to the ball with me suddenly turned up, having grown tired of adding to the general ruckus. Their presence made me feel distinctly uncomfortable, and I was even more put out by the flirtatious remarks they addressed to my fellow conversationalist and the jokey comments they made about her to me.'

'Poor girl!'

'Poor girl? Don't feel sorry for her just yet, or you'll spoil my story.'

'Why's that?'

'Listen. At first, she didn't seem shy at all, and held her own in the banter, triumphantly parrying and fending off those flirtatious remarks. But the battle proved unequal, because in that duel of words, they had weapons in reserve that she did not. When she saw this, she became extremely uneasy and got up to leave. We followed and, at the door, she and her companions turned and seemed genuinely frightened when they saw us in hot pursuit. She spoke to me and asked for my protection, appealed to my generosity, and I…'

'You did do as she asked, didn't you?' said Jenny, clasping her hands together and looking pleadingly at her brother. 'You did, didn't you?'

'Oh, yes, I was a regular Don Quixote of hapless maidens. What do you expect? Didn't I just say that I still have a lot of the wide-eyed fifteen-year-old in me?'

'Oh, don't apologise, Charles, never apologise for being generous.'

'I managed to get her away from my colleagues, which was no small achievement. I insisted on my rights as the one who had discovered her, and promised to reveal her identity later, as was my duty. Then I followed her and her companions. At first, they were all gratitude for my nobility of spirit, for my kindness, my sensitivity, etc., but once we had left the more central streets and their fear of being pursued had passed, everything changed and they asked *me* to leave them alone too. I found such ingratitude offensive and refused… Then. Oh, but you're looking very serious again!'

'I am indeed, Charles. You mean that they asked you, but you… That's not generous at all. And, who knows, they may have had their reasons.'

'Forgive me, Jenny, but you know nothing about these matters. They were the ones lacking in generosity. Besides, were those requests to leave them genuine? The rule is always to refuse, and a refusal almost never offends.'

'On this occasion though…'

'No, Jenny. You have your own imagined idea of what these masked balls are like. You assume that all those ladies were – I don't know – princesses in disguise or Jennys like you.'

'Well, now that you mention it, just suppose that it had

been me.'

Carlos saw that he was on dangerous ground if he allowed this hypothesis, which is why he interrupted his sister and said: 'No, I can't suppose anything of the sort, because... because no one has ever seen a Jenny in such a place. Besides, I haven't yet done anything to deserve such stern looks. As I said, I did insist on following them, although I would have stopped had they taken off their masks, but they refused to do so, especially the one whose identity I most wanted to know. At half past three we were standing here, outside the house, where they had clearly brought me, hoping I would go in. I wasn't to be tempted, though, and so walked straight past my own front door and continued to follow them. The unknown lady's companions took it all as a joke and would, I think, eventually have revealed their faces, but she either seemed or was pretending to be genuinely upset. She actually pleaded with me to leave.'

'And what did you do?'

'I refused.'

'Oh, Charles!'

'Listen. She insisted, saying I could do her great harm if I didn't go away, but I insisted too...'

'You can be so cruel sometimes!'

'But I wasn't convinced she really was afraid, even now... but then in a tearful and utterly sincere voice, she said: "Please, do this for..." and said a name, can you guess whose name?'

'No.'

'She said: "Please, for your sister's sake, for Jenny's sake." Yes, she mentioned you, and clasped her hands together with such innocence and such sincerity when she said those words, that I... Well, I need hardly say, I hope, that, this time, I relented.'

Jenny held out her hand to her brother.

'Thank you. Good always triumphs in your heart. I knew it would.'

Carlos bowed his head as if mortified by his sister's words of praise, which seemed to fill him with remorse rather than console him.

After a brief pause, he said, greatly embarrassed: 'Look, Jenny... I really don't deserve such praise... that would be rank hypocrisy. I hate to say this, but I have to tell you that I am unworthy of your applause.'

'Why?'

'Because of what happened. I haven't told you the whole story yet. It's true that I did relent, but not without first demanding or, rather, stealing... by way of compensation...'

'What?'

'A kiss, and the poor girl didn't manage to pull away from me in time, and was thrown into a kind of despair. Of course, she may have been pretending, yes, but she did it very well.'

Jenny pulled a disapproving face, and Carlos was quick to add: 'But don't condemn me out of hand, Jenny, because I still didn't see her face, and I'm probably now doomed never to find out who she is. And I kept my promise and stopped following her, which was really hard for me. I still keep thinking about those eyes, that voice, and I almost regret... But don't look at me like that. You're refusing to forgive me when...'

'To be honest, you don't deserve to be forgiven, but since you relented in my name, you've almost deprived me of the right to tell you off. But what you did in the end... really.'

'But you see what a hardened sinner I am? For me, that kiss was the sweetest part of the whole adventure.'

'No!' cried Jenny, gently hitting him with the book she was holding. 'Do you want me to withdraw my forgiveness alto-

gether? What else do you have weighing on your conscience?
You might as well make the most of my benevolent mood.'

'I don't think I have anything else on my conscience.'

'Well, there's a soul with a very high opinion of itself!
Have you then done all your duties?'

'What duties?'

'What a question! Don't you know your duties? That's
a very bad sign! Your duties as a Christian, a citizen, a son
and...'

'Hang on, Jenny, hang on! Let's just take those things one
at a time, otherwise...'

'I just want to talk to you about some of them, the ones you
seem to have been neglecting.'

'Go on.'

'Tell me, have you been to the office lately?'

'Ah, the office!' said Carlos, laughing. 'So that's what you
wanted to talk to me about. That was the last thing on my
mind.'

'So have you been there?'

'No.'

'No?'

'No, I haven't been for a while now, but do you consider
that a great sin?'

'How can you ask? Isn't work a duty?'

'Real work would be, yes.'

'Meaning?'

'There's a difference. Have you any idea what I actually
do at the office? It's another of those social impositions that
would be funny if it wasn't so tedious. You should know, my
dear Jenny, that all the real work, the useful work, the work-
work is embodied in the person of Manuel Quintino. He does
everything, resolves everything, and he seems to me to be

the only one capable of doing that. I'm supposed to go there, but not to work; all I do is annoy the good man, distract the other clerks and get all the paperwork in a mess. I only go there in order to pretend that I care, to play the part of the businessman, even though I understand none of the secrets nor what transactions the company's involved in. One day, it will occur to someone to mention the beginning of some particular deal, but they never feel the need to tell me the result, just as I don't feel the need to ask. The next day, they might tell me, but only in part, the result of some other deal, which I didn't even know about. That's the kind of businessman I am. Father likes to see me there, as a representative of Whitestone & Co., but that's all. I arrive at the office, open the window, show myself to the public, like a kind of signboard; I take a couple of turns around the square outside, talk about everything but business and then leave. That isn't work.'

'But since you loathe such idleness, why don't you do some proper work?'

'Because that just isn't the custom. Work is for book-keepers. People like me are like godfathers; we give the child a name and pay for its layette, but we don't take on the wearisome task of actually bringing the child up. Once or twice, I have tried working, just to ease my conscience, but this was greeted with outright laughter by Manuel Quintino and furtive smirks from the other clerks. It seems I committed a complete *faux pas*.'

'Yes, but it's precisely because so little is demanded of you that you should be more assiduous.'

'But it's so monotonous! You have no idea. I hate the place, Jenny, I loathe it!

'And so you prefer to disappoint your father, when a small sacrifice…'

'Don't call it "small", but, however large the sacrifice, I will make that sacrifice just to please you. Tomorrow…'

'Tomorrow!' said Jenny with a shrug.

'You don't expect me to start today, do you?'

'Why not?'

'It's too late…'

'It will be later still if you delay any longer.'

Carlos fell silent.

'And at the same time,' Jenny went on, 'you could find out about that poor English widow, who I haven't seen for days now. I didn't want to send a servant to ask after her, because, however much I tell them not to, they like to goad the poor thing, and that just upsets her all the more. If you go to the office today, you could drop in and see her, it's on the way…'

Jenny knew that any generous action would encourage Carlos to make a sacrifice, which is why she mentioned paying a charitable visit to one of the poorest of the many people supported by the Whitestone family.

'Right,' said Carlos resolutely. 'Today, I'm going to work. Manuel Quintino, the great engine of that commercial machine, doesn't know what's in store for him. He may not give two hoots for my help, but he has you to thank for that, Jenny. Send José to help me dress. I haven't seen hide nor hair of the rascal today.'

'Ah, José,' said Jenny, placing one hand on her brother's shoulder. 'The poor boy's mother is really ill, and I took pity on him and sent him off to be with her.'

'That's fine. You were quite right. I'd completely forgotten. We'll cope without José, and we'll cope very well.'

Jenny embraced her brother and left the room feeling pleased.

As a consequence of this conversation, Carlos appeared

in that centre of commerce, Rua dos Ingleses, at around two
o'clock in the afternoon.

VIII

Rua dos Ingleses

When Mr Richard Whitestone's son finally arrived in the broad street known as Rua dos Ingleses, the place was full of hustle and bustle.

Commercial life was at its busiest; assorted groups jammed the pavements, even the street itself and the doorways of the old houses on either side. On such occasions, the place invites closer observation.

From their postures, gestures and other external signs you can tell quite a lot about the position on the commercial ladder occupied by the individuals who make up these groups.

There are men of a grave demeanour, slow, considered movements, measured words, who are listened to, here and there, by a silent, attentive, open-mouthed audience, whose heads, nodding like china dolls, comment approvingly on the words of these oracles; they are the managers of banks or businesses of some kind, of good or bad repute, and are the prime movers in the street; the shareholders, always uneasy about the future of their capital, ponder their every word as if it were a message from Napoleon III at the opening of the French parliament.

Elsewhere, other men, with a self-confident air, pay no heed to what those prime movers are saying, but instead greet them with fraternal familiarity. They are followed by a far smaller cortège, and yet every head in the street turns to them and nods; their presence provokes affable smiles and low deferential bows, not dissimilar to what Sterne called 'the true persuasive angle of incidence', which requires the speaker 'to bend forwards just so far as to make an angle of 85 degrees and a half'. These men do not administer other people's money, but possess their own vast wealth; the great multitude of small capitalists may depend on them the least, but their fate influences pretty much everyone. And, besides, they enjoy the prestige of being rich, which impresses even those who have no expectation of benefitting from that wealth.

Occasionally, one does see a situation, which, at first sight, is very hard to interpret. A bearded gentleman, humbly dressed, grim-faced, and head bowed, is surrounded by a circle of the most resplendent members of the commercial world, all listening intently to what he has to say, as if anxious not to miss a word. Now and then, he makes some murmured comment and wipes away a tear, and the other men raise their hands to heaven, fold their arms, shrug their shoulders, scratch their heads, or go for a brief stroll as if to drive away their sorrows, only to return to him, as if he were the focal point for those disparate elements, and then the whole scene starts again. What does this mean? He is a recently bankrupt businessman surrounded by his creditors, and, in his humiliated state, he both dominates and, now and then, terrifies, as he calculates in a doleful voice the tiny repayments he would be able to make. Every social position and situation in life, however abject or precarious it may seem, has its aristocracy. Even thieves have their all-conquering monarchs; homicides have duellists and warriors; the poor, the oppressed and the wretched class of debtors have great failed businessmen.

Any eye experienced in studying the physiology of the

street might be able to distinguish the businessman whose debts have never been known to be cancelled from those whose remote financial 'fractures' have been miraculously 'mended' thanks to a dowry from their wife. However, the confidence and candour of both species is so very similar that it is, in our view, impossible to tell them apart.

In contrast, you can see an equally numerous tribe rushing up and down the street, always in a hurry, boys mostly, carrying papers, sacks or samples; they dash from one doorway to another; they head off down the Calçada do Terreiro towards the Alfândega, to the harbour or to board some merchant ship; they consult individuals in one of the above-mentioned groups or wait patiently to be noticed and asked what they want; they speak then, although not without first doffing their hat – a courtesy not always reciprocated. They are junior clerks, so-called 'runners', trainees, bill collectors and even dispatchers; they are, in short, those who bear the heaviest burden of a life in commerce and benefit the least. They can be easily identified by how quickly they walk; indeed, it is almost painful to see the speed at which dispatchers run.

It is worth noting, too, the positions adopted by those who engage in the brief dialogues constantly taking place in the street between the representatives of the various social hierarchies, namely, clerk and boss. The clerk stands clutching the brim of his hat, his eyes fixed on the lips of his boss; the latter answers while looking away, sometimes smiling at a colleague who waves to him from afar – a dangerous distraction for the clarity of the orders being given, and whose consequences will be attributed to the person receiving the orders; the more approachable bosses are 'kind' enough, while issuing their instructions, to tug at a button on a clerk's jacket or even undo a button on a subordinate's waistcoat. When the clerk is describing the result of whatever errand he has run, he is then permitted to speak, especially if, in carrying out the errand, he succeeded in overcoming the resistance of some now ex-debtor, and then he can even attempt a witty comment, knowing that his boss will be pleased. However, when the clerk looks more modest and the boss more impertinent, this means that the latter is being told by the former of some shameful and hitherto unconfessed error.

There is yet another class, equally harried and tireless, although they show little of the reverence of the class described above. There is something artificial about their deep bows, which fool no one, and their respectful façade is sometimes replaced by a less ceremonious familiarity. They are terrifyingly tenacious in their pursuit of merchants and traders, who try in vain to escape; they assail them now from the right, now from the left; they block their path; they follow them into the building and up the stairs, invade the inner sanctum of the office, breach the barrier of the counter, lean casually on desks, clap their prey on the shoulder, place before them bottles, rolls of fabric, price lists, samples of every kind, with which they always come supplied, and they release their chosen victim only very reluctantly. These are the salesmen and agents who work for foreign companies.

The head book-keepers are the aristocratic portion of this commercial bureaucracy or officeocracy. They can occasionally be spotted at first-floor windows, taking a break from their book-keeping duties. Normally, they keep their pen between their fingers, as if to indicate that this is only a momentary pause, although this is not always the case. Since they are more necessary, and, therefore, more appreciated and respected, they enjoy certain freedoms and privileges that others of the same class do not. They are permitted to call down from the window to address a colleague or friend passing in the street below, and some are even allowed to go out onto the balcony to smoke a cigar and absent themselves from the office without first asking permission; in the street, they are far more casual about greeting their bosses and receive a less absent-minded response.

Add to these classes the idle progeny of the large capitalists, honorary businessmen, whose commercial life, like that of Carlos, is a matter of strolling around in the street until about four o'clock in the afternoon; then there is the retired wealthy returnee from Brazil, who spends his time as a spectator of other men's labours, rather like an old sailor who sits by the sea watching the waves from which he no longer makes his living; then there is the customs officer, smoking a cigarette during the frequent breaks he takes after a hectic morning; the carters waiting on each corner; the office boys leaning in doorways; the children of company directors entrusted to the care of some lowly employee; imagine this hotchpotch of red-haired Englishmen, blond Germans, swarthy Brazilians and Portuguese gentlemen of every hue, and you will have a picture of Oporto's main business streets at the hour when Carlos Whitestone arrived that day.

Carlos was walking past the different groups as if he were equally familiar with them all and was as at ease there as he was everywhere. Naturally averse to etiquette, his social position meant that no one was ever offended by such familiarity.

He took the arm of one of the more sensible businessmen, whom he called by his first name; then, suddenly, he left him to light his cigar on the cigarette of an assistant clerk enjoying a furtive smoke, and with whom, right there and then, he agreed to go hunting. He joined a group of capitalists and barons engaged in a heated discussion about some company report, and quickly diverted their conversation onto some cheerier and more frivolous subject; he then abandoned them and embraced some equally industrious lads his own age, who were discussing the previous evening's dance or else yawning out of sheer boredom; from there he went over to greet a scrawny Englishman passing by on an equally scrawny horse, and examined with a connoisseur's eyes the physical qualities of the quadruped in question and the resources required to master the art of horsemanship; he stopped an office boy who was racing across the square and, who, even though he was in a hurry, paused to listen to him; he addressed the bootboy on the corner by name and got him to clean the mud off his boots, idly tapping the boy's hat with his whip as he did so. He would occasionally listen, apparently attentively, to a man wanting to discuss some matter pending at Whitestone & Co., but if the exposition went on too long, his interlocutor, when he least expected it, would find himself alone, because Carlos had abruptly gone off to talk to his friend the book-keeper whom he had spotted up at the first-floor window. He would as easily strike up a dialogue with a beggar asking for alms as he would with a pretty young girl.

This is how Carlos Whitestone spent that day, hoping to achieve his one aim: to be seen by his father.

Mr Richard, however, was at the English Assembly, where he was an assiduous visitor.

One of the many groups that Carlos Whitestone approached was made up of some of the city's most eminent individuals.

Carlos put his arm around the shoulder of a baron, linked arms with a Brazilian merchant, and nonchalantly greeted an elderly Englishman who was part of that group.

'There's nothing in Europe to compare with Oporto's stock exchange,' said one well-intentioned merchant, who had the very Portuguese defect of wanting to place anything Portuguese on the very pinnacle of perfection.

The Englishman shuddered.

'What?!' This was uttered with the violence of an explosion. 'Nothing in Europe! What are you saying, sir? Have you never travelled?'

'No, I've never left Oporto, but people in the know say…'

'Oh, really! What about the London Stock Exchange… or, rather, the Royal Exchange, because the first Royal Exchange dates from the reign of Queen Elizabeth, built by a man called Gresham in 1500 and something; it burned down in 1666. Two years later, the second one was designed by a Mr Jerman, and that burned down in 1838. I was in London at the time. In 1842, the foundation stone was laid, following a plan by Tite, and within three years it was complete.'

'And when did they burn that one down?' asked Carlos.

The Englishman smiled, but did not deign to answer, and was about to launch into a detailed description of the whole building, when Carlos interrupted him again: 'It seems to me, Mr Lyons, that there is a marked tendency in London to burn down stock exchanges.'

The baron and the Brazilian found this remark hilarious, and clapped him on the back and called him 'wag', 'card', 'joker', and other affectionately insulting terms, and lost all interest in what the Englishman was about to tell them, and he then found himself obliged to swallow all his historical and architectural knowledge.

Carlos then joined another group, in which the cautious owner of five shares in a certain company was saying to one of the directors of that company: 'I won't mince my words, sir – why should I – but I really don't like the way things are going. Doing business with the government is never a good thing,

106

I mean who *is* the government? The government never feels under any obligation to anyone, that's why I vote…'

'Yes,' said the director with exemplary patience, 'but the guarantees offered are as safe as houses; the government has made a commitment…'

'Huh!' retorted the other man. 'That's the problem, because, as I say, who *is* the government? I don't know who they are. A bunch of wastrels, here today and gone tomorrow. You make a deal with one set of people and tomorrow you're dealing with some entirely new faces. I can't be doing with it. Oh, they can charm the birds from the trees, all right, but when it comes to taking responsibility for what's theirs… and for our capital…'

His capital consisted of one hundred *mil réis* at most.

So as not to fall out with the stubborn fellow, the director prayed to God for patience, and Carlos appeared like a messenger from Heaven. He simply took the argumentative shareholder by the arm and, ignoring his attempts to pull away, led him off, muttering: 'Do you realise what's going on here today? They're setting up a huge company.'

'Yes, yes, but I have more to say to that gentleman over there…'

'Listen,' said Carlos, 'shareholders will earn forty per cent, at the very least.'

The man, who was known among his colleagues as an ingenuous fool, eyed Carlos with an expression that was half suspicious and half intrigued.

That forty per cent rang in his ears though!

Carlos' face took on a look of utter certainty.

'Yes, but just now…' the man stammered.

Carlos insisted: 'I'm serious. Some English businessmen are interested, and my father has been charged with setting the whole thing up. That's why I…'

'But what kind of company?' asked the man, brimming with curiosity.

'They're hoping the government will provide a subsidy...'

The man was tempted to asked who *was* the government, but resisted.

'But what's it for?' he asked instead.

'Commerce in Oporto will benefit enormously too,' Carlos went on, genuinely caught up in organising this non-existent company.

'But what is the aim of the company?' bellowed the man.

'The aim? A great aim... constructing a new route for commercial traffic between the upper city and the lower.'

'What? A new street?'

'No, sir, it aims to take advantage of an as yet unexplored source of wealth right in the heart of the city.'

A swarm of wild ideas fluttered about in the shareholder's imagination, and, burning with curiosity now, he asked: 'But what is it? How?'

'Nothing less than making the River Vila navigable.'

The argumentative shareholder gazed for a few moments at Carlos, then, disappointed, abruptly turned his back on him and went in search of the director he had been interrogating earlier. The director, however, had seized his chance and disappeared, thus avoiding having to answer the difficult question the man had launched at him: Who *is* the government?

Any readers from Oporto, please allow me to explain to non-natives that the grand name of River Vila is given to a little stream of murky water that flows through certain hidden and equally murky places before trickling furtively, almost shamefacedly, into the Douro.

The next person Carlos approached was an important businessman who was listening politely to a colleague who was asking him to ask someone else to ask someone else and for that someone else to ask the minister if he could give a post in the customs and excise office to the son of the brother-in-law of the man making the original request. This tangled skein of requests – which inevitably put quite a strain on the preceding sentence – seemed perfectly clear to the object of the entreaty, for, without demanding any further explanations, and as a man who clearly went straight to the heart of the matter, he promised to bring all his influence to bear and to be positively importunate in trying to help his friend.

Carlos arrived in the middle of these very cordial promises. We should explain that Carlos happened to know that the important businessman had, that very morning, received a letter from Lisbon assuring him that the aforementioned post in customs and excise had been given to a relative of his. Jenny's honest brother was truly horrified at the shameless way in which the businessman was lying to a friend. In the grip of the highly unfashionable frankness which was, as we said, one of Carlos' characteristics, Carlos could not hold back and said: 'But Senhor F., be careful what you promise. Have you forgotten that, only yesterday, your relative, C. was appointed to that very post?'

The two men exchanged grimaces and a few awkward words, then, tiring of these meaningless utterances, they parted coldly.

The businessman told Carlos off in no uncertain terms, but Carlos, in turn, told him off for his lack of honesty.

And yet they remained friends. There is something about frank, generous natures like Carlos' that somehow dissipates any feelings of resentment in even the most reserved and egotistical of people.

Then Carlos finally made up his mind to go into the office.

As he was walking there, he saw a short, fat, red-faced man coming towards him and bowing in anticipation.

After the usual exchange of greetings, he stopped to listen to the man, who said: 'I've just been to your office, but I didn't see either you or your father. I'm not sure if you know who I am.'

'No, I don't, sir,' said Carlos, absorbed in studying the other fellow's bow tie.

'My name is Anastácio Rebelo, and I made that shipment of oranges last year.'

Carlos nodded distractedly and directed his gaze at the flower in Senhor Anastácio's buttonhole.

'As I'm sure you know,' said Senhor Rebelo, 'two months ago... a customer of mine in Braga asked... I don't know if your father told you... perhaps he didn't...'

'No, perhaps he didn't,' echoed Carlos, not really listening.

'Well, it's a simple enough matter. This customer of mine, who is also a friend, or, rather, I'm godfather to his rather delicate thirteen-year-old son, who stayed with me for a few months, taking the waters at Foz...'

By now, Carlos was whistling.

'Anyway, this friend of mine... look, here's the letter he wrote to me,' the man went on, rummaging around in his jacket pocket. 'I'm sure I had it with me... And that will give you an idea...'

And he began pulling out all kinds of papers, letters, documents, invoices, bills, accounts, receipts... saying as he examined each and every one: 'No, that's not it... that's the order demanding I be paid some fifty or so *mil réis*, and not before time either... Now where the devil did I put that letter? No, that's not it. That's the lease on the house I'm renting out in Forno Velho. And this, what on earth is this? Ah, a letter from Maranhão… and this, this is a request from Bragança. You wouldn't happen to know where I could buy an engraving of the Crimean War, would you?'

'I'm afraid not, sir,' said Carlos, taking two steps in the direction of the office.

'They asked me to buy one and I…' said the man, following him. 'Ah, I've found it, here's the letter!' he exclaimed, grabbing Carlos' sleeve. 'Would you care to read it?'

'No, I'd rather not,' said Carlos, trying to escape.

'"Dear Friend and Colleague,"' the man began to read. '"Thank you for your letter of the thirteenth and for the recommendations you make. My wife sends her best regards to Senhora Dona Maria do Carmo," that's my wife, "and Juca", that's my godson, "sends his love to his godfather…"'

'That's you,' said Carlos, growing impatient now.

'Exactly,' said the man, pleased at how quick Carlos was on the uptake.

'Good, but I really must be going now,' said Carlos, making another attempt at escape.

'But that's of no interest,' said the man, 'further down he says… "The festival of the Baby Jesus this year promises to be a particularly spectacular affair, and I do hope that you…" You see, they want me to…'

'Forgive me, but I'm in a hurry.'

'No, that's not it either. Here it is: "As you know, the municipal council was re-elected, and the opposition suffered a bad defeat that…"'

Carlos could stand it no longer.

'My dear sir, what does any of this have to do with me?'

'You're quite right. It's just that I thought… "The insurance company is refusing to pay for the damage caused by the fire in my house in Rua do Souto", no, that's not it either…'

'Goodbye,' said Carlos, finally breaking free.

'Ah, here it is,' the man exclaimed triumphantly. 'The order I sent to England…'

Just when Senhor Anastácio reached the part of the letter he had been looking for, having first waded through that sea of shallows, Carlos spotted a pretty young seamstress hurrying across the road and unceremoniously abandoned the gentleman to speak to her instead.

'Hello, my dear.'

The young woman answered: 'No one would have recognised you yesterday at the ball.'

'Oh, so you were there too, were you?'

And they continued in this vein, even right under the noses of the cream of the commercial classes, for they would forgive Richard Whitestone's son anything.

Anastácio Rebelo folded up his friend's letter and stalked off in disgust.

Then some other young men approached, and the seamstress fled.

Finally, after a few more such encounters, Carlos went into the office.

This was how he did business out in the street. Let's see now how he fares in the office.

IX

In the Office

It was there, in Mr Richard Whitestone's office, in that old room with its grey walls and worm-eaten floorboards, that Senhor Manuel Quintino had spent the last twenty years, writing, adding, subtracting, multiplying and dividing, muttering, humming and coughing; he was the same age as the century and was the company's chief book-keeper, a man whose habits were as beneficial to his bodily health as they were to maintaining his peace of mind.

Manuel Quintino was the soul of the place. After his long years of experience, he was the only one who could find order in the chaos of papers he had to deal with each day – correspondence, invoices, current accounts, bills of sale, letters of acknowledgment, first, second and third drafts of bills, insurance policies, receipts and other commercial documents. He himself boasted of this, and it was no vain boast.

When asked out of the blue for even the most insignificant letter, he could go straight to it; he had, however, devised a method of filing known only to him. Even Mr Richard found the office filing system a labyrinth, one that he could navigate only with the help of his book-keeper's ball of thread.

Manuel Quintino was a man of the most regular habits, and as soon as the clock chimed seven in the morning in summer and eight in winter, Manuel Quintino would be turning the key in the office door, and, half an hour later, would be at his desk immersed in his work. At three in the afternoon in winter and at four in summer, he would turn the key again, this time in the opposite direction, except on the few rare occasions when there was a greater than usual influx of work and he was obliged to stay late.

Manuel Quintino was neither quick nor expeditious, the kind of man who can instantly resolve several matters at once. He liked to take his time, and was always saying: 'I'm not a man for rushing things'; however, thanks to his patience and regularity – for he never missed a day – the work somehow always got done, and it would have been hard to find an example of him ever getting behind.

He was a great believer in the old adage, *festina lente*, more haste, less speed, and was living proof of its efficacy.

Manuel Quintino loved that office exactly as it was, shabby and bare. Mr Richard and, more especially, Carlos, had occasionally tried to carry out certain improvements that would make the place more comfortable. However, they had always been obliged to give in to the old book-keeper's objections, for he found the very idea repugnant, and, as the most interested party – since he spent much of his life there – he easily won the day.

And thus he continued to delight in those four grey walls, in the wood-panelled ceiling blackened by time, in the rough, worm-eaten floorboards, the old-fashioned casement windows adorned with locks, latches and hatches, the fortress-like front door with its creaking hinges – a sound that, to Manuel Quintino, was like the pleasant albeit unharmonious voice of a friend – in the desks, the benches, the coat-racks, the washbasin, and all the other furnishings made in the fashion of offices of old. These furnishings had witnessed his hair growing grey, and he loved them for that.

The other staff consisted of two junior book-keepers and an office boy, all of whom Manuel Quintino was constantly accusing of being sluggards and yet, so keen was he to do everything himself, that he almost prevented them from getting on with their own work.

Moments before Carlos arrived, Manuel Quintino had given the book-keepers two insignificant letters to copy out, while he applied all his five senses to the task of writing the letters to be sent to London.

One of the book-keepers, having completed his easy task, took advantage of Manuel Quintino's absorption in his own work to cautiously open his desk and take out a novel by Paul de Kock, which he then began reading with the urgent curiosity of any seventeen-year-old; the other book-keeper filled the time writing a love letter to the lady of his dreams, a letter which, incidentally, included a few epigrammatic allusions to Manuel Quintino, whom he described, among other things, as 'a Pitiless Argus'; the office boy, who was also left with nothing to do, was meanwhile amusing himself swatting flies on the window or breathing on the glass and tracing large letters with his finger. All three of these quiet occupations maintained the hushed silence that Manuel Quintino found so pleasing.

Indeed, he was the only person to disturb the silence, because of the constant murmured monologue he kept up with his pen, for Manuel Quintino was under a most singular illusion.

Having spent all those years writing with a pen and feeling that the pen was indissolubly linked with his own fate, he had ended up endowing it almost with a degree of intelligence, and he would talk to it as if it were a frisky horse, encouraging, scolding, and reining in any wild impulses.

'Come on, come on,' he would say. 'Oh, you are slow

today! Look, we haven't time to dawdle. Now, what is it? Oh, you want more ink, do you? You soon drank the last lot! There you are. Nice R! I wasn't expecting that of you. Oh, mind that hair! Now I've got ink everywhere. Clumsy thing! No, don't sulk. Come on, come on! No, wait. You forgot the D. You need more space between those two letters. That's it. No, don't touch the double S. Fine. On you go, but be careful. No, don't stop. Just let... Oh, no!'

A blot had fallen in the middle of the page, ruining the letter just when he had nearly finished it.

'Tra la la la la la...'

He would then tra-la-la his way through the national anthem, as he always did at such critical moments. And then, without another word, he would put the inkblotted paper to one side, prepare another sheet and begin again, first putting the pen down and replacing it with another, saying as he did so: 'You have a rest. You're obviously having one of your off days,' and saying to another pen. 'It's your turn now. You behave yourself, mind!' before adding: 'Hm, you're not looking too good. Let's see. Come on now, I have got other things to do, you know. Spread that nib of yours. Yes, good. Bravo! Who would have thought it! Goodness!'

And with these encouraging words, he continued to applaud the excellent work the pen was doing, almost as if he thought that, in response to this stimulus, the pen was actually working harder.

It was then that the door to the office burst open, and Carlos' Newfoundland dog invaded that silent, tranquil retreat, immediately knocking over a pitcher of water placed in one corner of the room.

Seeing the mess caused by the impetuous hound, Manuel Quintino – who had shuddered when it first irrupted into the room – stared silently at both dog and door, as if expecting a second, no less subversive invasion. Carlos did not keep him waiting.

'Good morning, Mr Manuel Quintino!' Carlos bellowed, bowing very low.

'Good morning, Mr Charles,' answered Manuel Quintino with a shrug and a look of patient resignation and kindly ill humour.

I should mention here that, after his long association with those of Her Majesty's subjects resident in Oporto, Manuel Quintino spoke English, but his English was rather like the Portuguese spoken by his boss, and it was particularly startling to hear him pronounce English words with an authentically Portuguese accent and inflection. You might say that Manuel Quintino spoke Portuguese in English.

'Well, you're a sight for sore eyes!' he said to Carlos. Then he spoke to the office boy – 'Mop up that water, will you?' – before turning to Carlos again with a wicked look on his face: 'So, have you been ill?'

'Me? No, I'm positively bursting with good health,' answered Carlos.

'It's just that you've not been here for a while.' Then to the office boy: 'Come on, come on, jump to it!'

'I was much missed, then, was I?'

'Hm!' snorted Manuel Quintino.

With the arrival of Carlos, the junior book-keepers had hidden away their respective novel and letter, and both of them smiled and exchanged knowing glances.

'How have you managed here without me, my flower?' asked Carlos, picking up various bits of paper. 'You're getting handsomer and happier by the day.'

'Away with you! And leave those papers alone! What do

you want?'

'A light for my cigar. Has no one got a light in this place?
Really!'

'I should have known. All you think about is smoking. Wait
there, wait, and leave that alone, will you? I'll give you a light.
There you are. Now go away.'

Carlos lit his cigar and offered one to each of the book-
keepers, who gazed at them greedily, not daring to accept.

'Have a smoke, go on,' said Carlos.

Manuel Quintino looked up and gave the two lads a hard
stare.

Under the sway of those eyes, they still hesitated.

Carlos, however, made them take the cigars, offered them
a light and meanwhile turned to Manuel Quintino, and, seeing
his disapproving frown, went over to him: 'What's the matter,
Manuel Quintino? Let the lads have a smoke. Don't be such
an old dinosaur.'

'If your father comes in, he'll be sure to... Besides, you're
keeping them from their work...'

'What work? Look how hard they were working!' he said,
then, turning to the persecutor of flies, he added: 'Boy! Go to
Rua de Santo António and find out if my jacket is ready and,
on the way, look in at the Teatro de São João and tell the box
office clerk that you've orders from me to reserve six seats for
the performance on Thursday. Got that? Six seats, then...'

'And when exactly is he going to deliver my letters?'
Manuel Quintino grumbled.

'I don't know. Go on, off you go.'

'But...'

'You can send someone else to the post office. Go on, quick
now.'

The boy raced off.

Manuel Quintino shrugged.

Carlos went over to the window, which he flung open, letting in a gust of air that sent Manuel Quintino's paperwork flying.

'Just look at the mess you're making!' exclaimed Quintino. 'Now what am I going to do?'

Carlos roared with laughter.

'That's right, laugh all you like. And what are you two gentlemen doing?' Manuel Quintino asked, unleashing his annoyance on the two junior book-keepers. 'Sitting around chatting and smoking while I work, eh?'

'Don't worry, I'll pick everything up,' said Carlos, still laughing.

And the four of them started picking up the papers, which were scattered everywhere.

'And how, may I ask, will you know where to put them?' Manuel Quintino went on. 'I had them all in order too. Look at the state of this letter to our man in Liverpool. And these bills for the upkeep of the English chapel! They're in a fine state. And these policies. And that wretched dog of yours has trailed that draft document through the water. Out with you, you rascal!'

Then returning to his desk, he once again began putting the papers to rights.

'Manuel Quintino,' Carlos said from his place by the window, 'who's that girl opposite, on the third floor. I haven't seen her before.'

'How should I know, man? Look, just leave me alone.'

'Who is she, Paulo, you must know, a lad of your age,' said Carlos, familiarly addressing one of the junior book-keepers.

This particular lad was still pale and beardless, and as was only right in someone who had not yet turned eighteen, there was a touch of melancholy about his otherwise cheerful smile. In response to Carlos' question, he went over to the window.

'I don't know,' he said, 'I've no idea. Ask Pires.'

Pires was the name of the other junior book-keeper, who was, in turn, summoned to the window.

As a result, all three stood leaning there, chatting about matters of equal moment.

Manuel Quintino, who had now restored order to his paperwork, would occasionally glance over at them and again begin humming the national anthem.

Having wreaked havoc on his paperwork, the wind was now directing its fury at his sinuses, for Manuel Quintino began to sneeze.

'Bless me!' he said after each explosion.

After the fifth sneeze, he could not help but say to Carlos: 'Now, really, sir. What on earth are you doing, standing at the window with such a devil of a wind blowing? Why, I…' and he sneezed again, 'I've caught a cold already!'

'In that case, I will close it,' said Carlos, closing the window and going over to lean on Manuel Quintino's desk, where the book-keeper had already gone back to composing his letters.

'Ah, Senhor Manuel Quintino,' said Carlos, exhaling a great cloud of smoke, at which the old man grimaced. 'Are you any relation to the Quentin Durward of whom Walter Scott speaks? You do know who Walter Scott was, don't you, Manuel Quintino?'

'No, I don't, sir,' answered the old man, continuing to write.

'Walter Scott was a novelist. You do know what a novelist is, don't you? Tell me, have you ever read a novel?'

'No, I haven't. I have better things to do.'

'I'll have to lend you some.'

'Most kind.'

The first will be *The Chevalier*...'

The two junior book-keepers were smothering their giggles.

'...*D'Harmental*,' concluded Carlos mischievously, then added: 'I'm sure I don't know what those two gentlemen are laughing at.'

'It's because they lead such exhausting lives,' said Manuel Quintino.

'Then I'll lend you *Mademoiselle*...'

The junior book-keepers continued their muffled laughter.

'*Mademoiselle de la Seiglière*, a delightful confection by Jules Sandeau,' concluded Carlos, eyeing them with mock severity.

'Oh, no, now you've made me go wrong!' exclaimed Manuel Quintino. 'I wrote "conform" instead of "confirm".'

'That's easily put right.'

'Easy for you to say.'

'Yes, look, you just have to make that "o" into an "i"...'

'No, it's no use.'

And with exemplary patience he began a new letter.

'Oh, really, you're not going to start all over, are you?'

'Thanks to you, yes, I am.'

'You certainly do have lovely handwriting. I envy you. If only you could teach me to write like that.'

'What would be the point?'

And to focus his attention, he began speaking out loud the words he was writing: 'Thank you for your letter of the 14th inst...'

'What do mean "what would be the point'?' said Carlos. 'The young lady I write to...'

'In reply, our price for...' Manuel Quintino was saying, at the same time addressing Carlos. 'You talk to me about young ladies, but what I'd like to see is a little conscientiousness!...

121

the product in question is…'

'So you find the matter unworthy of consideration, do you? Now tell me, Manuel Quintino, when you were a lad, didn't you also bore the old men of your day with such talk?'

'Including the usual commission. No, when I was a lad, I had more important things to think about. In view, then, of the orders received… Do you think I could lie in bed until midday thinking about girls and that I went to bed in the small hours because of them too?'

'What did you do then?' asked Carlos, picking up a pen and idly drawing a figure in the margin of the newspaper.

'With a likely profit… Oh, I can remember the late nights I had when I was twenty…'

'Late nights, eh? Say no more.'

'No, I was working. Not everyone enjoys your easy life, you know; if only… The bankruptcy of Rodrigues & Co…'

'Oh, yes, I have a great life!' Carlos went on. 'Could there be anything more boring? The precious hours I've wasted in this gloomy room.'

And as he spoke these words, not even thinking what he was saying, he almost began drawing on the letter Manuel Quintino was writing.

'Stop!' cried the old man, pushing away his hand. 'What are you doing? Were you going to ruin another letter for me?'

Carlos stepped back, laughing, and started pacing up and down.

'Has my father not been in today?'

'Hours ago.'

'And will he be back?'

'God willing, yes.'

'You should close up earlier today,' Carlos said. 'These gentlemen need to go out and enjoy Carnival.'

'The whole world's a Carnival!'

'What time is it?'

'Twenty past two,' said Manuel Quintino, without even looking at the clock and not so much as half a second out.

'If my father...' began Carlos, but was interrupted by the creak of Mr Richard's boots on the stairs.

Order was restored in the office. The junior book-keepers began writing furiously, and even Carlos picked up an English newspaper and pretended to be scrutinising the business section.

Manuel Quintino hunched still lower over his desk and moved his pen more nimbly over the paper.

Mr Richard came into the office smiling and whistling one of his favourite English melodies, although, since he had no ear for music at all, the tune emerged from his lips so transformed that not even the composer himself would have recognised it.

Butterfly, with the lightness that justified his name, ran across the room to greet his colleague the Newfoundland, who, sitting down now with his tongue hanging out, received him with benevolent, circumspect majesty.

Everyone stood up when Mr Richard entered the room, and any experienced eye would have noted on his face a certain air of contentment, prompted by his son's unexpected presence.

Jenny's plan had worked.

Mr Richard went straight into his private office. Carlos followed him in order to ask his blessing and, at the same time, take the opportunity to thank him for the watch and apologise for missing the family supper the night before.

Mr Richard Whitestone now harboured not a shred of resentment towards his son. Carlos' arrival at the office was enough to drive away the slightest hint of ill feeling.

'I was sure you'd like it,' he said several times, interrupting

Carlos' long string of excuses, 'yes, I was sure you'd like it, because it comes from a very reputable watchmaker, who tells all his customers that it won't lose so much as half a minute in five years! Although that might be a case of over-confidence!' he added, beaming.

'Or fatherly indulgence,' said Carlos, laughing with him.

'Yes, fatherly indulgence,' Mr Richard agreed, beaming still more broadly and himself experiencing the effects of that indulgence.

He then opened two bottles of Bass, took a large packet of biscuits from the cupboard and, with his son for company, celebrated his third meal of the day.

After a few minutes, they both returned to the office in the best of moods.

How pleased Jenny would have been to see them!

Mr Richard went over to Manuel Quintino's desk, and Carlos sat down at the desk opposite and pretended to read some commercial journals.

Mr Richard asked his head book-keeper about certain matters pending, to which Manuel Quintino responded laconically, but promptly.

Mr Richard then consulted a few letters, handed some to Manuel Quintino, made a few notes, issued orders, examined the books, opened the correspondence file, then suddenly turning his back on Manuel Quintino and addressing Carlos, asked affably: 'Have you read this letter from our correspondent in London?'

'Not yet, sir, no.'

'Why ever didn't you show it to him?' he said, turning to Manuel Quintino, before again addressing Carlos. 'It contains important news and suggests that this could be a most advantageous year for us, if…'

'Mr Leeson is a very diligent fellow,' remarked Carlos, wanting to say something, but, alas, he confused the name of their man in London with that of their man in Liverpool.

'What do you mean "Leeson"?' cried Mr Richard, mortified. 'Leeson in London?!'

Carlos realised he had made a great mistake, but the worst of it was that he couldn't correct it, because he had completely forgotten the name of their London correspondent.

'Oh, London,' he mumbled. 'I thought… yes, London, it's just that I…'

Mr Richard was waiting to hear his son say the right name, but in vain.

Manuel Quintino had very good reasons – reasons that the reader can easily divine – for not keeping Carlos Whitestone up to date on the latest news; he nevertheless opened his desk, removed the letter in question, and took it over to Carlos, unable to suppress a smile, to which Carlos responded with a slight shrug.

Instead of saying the name of the correspondent, Carlos began reading the letter.

'Mention the business of the rum,' whispered Manuel Quintino before withdrawing to his own desk.

Mr Richard had started pacing up and down, rubbing his hands, and occasionally stopping by the window, on which he tapped lightly. He hadn't quite recovered from his disappointment at finding his son so ill-informed about the names of the company's correspondents.

Carlos was still staring at the letter, but not, I think, actually reading it. He was wondering how he could make use of Manuel Quintino's not entirely crystal-clear advice and talk to his father about the problematic matter of the rum, which, for him, was a complete mystery.

If he just blurted something out, he was afraid he would only make his situation worse, not better.

Manuel Quintino had resumed his writing, casting a mischievous smile in Carlos' direction whenever he dipped his pen in the ink.

Carlos put the letter down.

His father was looking at him out of the corner of his eye, as if awaiting his thoughts on the matter.

Carlos looked again at Manuel Quintino, who nodded almost imperceptibly.

Carlos said tentatively: 'As for the business of the rum, nothing...'

The effect was miraculous.

Mr Whitestone spun round and, making no attempt to disguise the deep satisfaction it gave him to find his son so well informed, he exclaimeed: 'Ah, you noticed that too. Those were exactly my thoughts. I was afraid you might not agree.'

Encouraged by this result, Carlos proceeded more confidently: 'Since it was a major deal...'

Manuel Quintino, however, pulled a face that made Carlos correct himself: 'Well, not major perhaps, but...'

'But that might well become so in the future... yes, exactly,' said Mr Richard, interrupting him.

'Exactly,' said Carlos.

Manuel Quintino was smiling.

'I was wondering, though,' Mr Richard went on, 'if market conditions in London might have an effect. The price might rise and exceed the maximum indicated in our letters.'

'Possibly,' said Carlos, looking at Manuel Quintino in the hope of receiving further inspiration.

Manuel Quintino mouthed a word, which Carlos thought

was 'interest', and so he blurted out: 'And the interest too…'

He stopped, because he really had no idea what he should say about the interest, nor why or whether it should go up or down.

Manuel Quintino raised his head ceilingwards, indicating the first hypothesis.

'The interest might go up,' Carlos concluded.

Clearly pleased, Mr Richard leapt on his son's words and said briskly: 'Well, the interest rates are very high in London.'

'They haven't been so unfavourable to us for a while,' Carlos said, this time without a moment's hesitation, since he was simply repeating what he had said before in a slightly different way.

'That's true. They're the highest they've been for ten years.'

Carlos saw Manuel Quintino shake his head and so added: 'I don't know about ten years, that seems a bit much…'

'Believe me, it's not,' said Mr Richard, really impressed by how well informed his son was. Then, having thought for a while, he turned to Manuel Quintino and asked: 'When did Blackfield's in London go under?'

'In October 1847,' Manuel Quintino responded, not even glancing up from his writing.

'In 1847? So you're right, that's only eight years. Because I remember the rate was at eight per cent at the time.'

'And then,' said Manuel Quintino, 'the exchange rate was less favourable than it is now.'

'Indeed, indeed.'

This conversation went on for some time, to Mr Richard's visible satisfaction, albeit with some awkwardness on Carlos' part, and thanks to Manuel Quintino's superior diplomatic skills, for he had proved himself to be Jenny's able collaborator in her mission to restore domestic harmony.

Then the bell on the Church of São Francisco struck three o'clock, and, after a final look at the books and after making a few more recommendations, Mr Richard left the office, bidding Manuel Quintino goodbye and giving Carlos a wave that was slightly less brusque than usual, and, more importantly, patting Carlos' dog as he walked past, something he only ever did when he was on very good terms with his son.

Barely had the sound of his footsteps on the stairs vanished along with the delighted yapping of Butterfly – impatient for freedom – than the letter from the London correspondent performed a parabola and landed back on Manuel Quintino's desk. Carlos lit another cigar and prepared to follow his father's example.

'Until the hour of redemption sounds!' he cried, putting on his hat.

'Leaving so soon?' asked Manuel Quintino mischievously.

'Don't you think I've had a large enough dose of commerce for one day? And in the middle of Carnival too! Have you no pity?'

'And what about that business with the rum, eh? The interest rates are high, I believe...'

'Yes, I got in a real pickle with that rum!'

'But you wriggled your way out.'

'Thanks to your help.'

'Do you have anything to say to the London correspondent?'

'Tell him to go to the devil! I simply could not remember the wretch's name. I still can't.'

'It's Woodfall Hope. He works for one of the most important companies in London, and as for that business with the rum...'

'No, Manuel Quintino, enough is enough,' said Carlos, interrupting him, 'I don't want to hear another word about it. Good afternoon. Goodbye, gentlemen. Stop work and take yourselves off to one of the masked balls. Goodbye.'

'Goodbye, Mr Charles…'

Shortly afterwards, they heard Carlos going swiftly down the stairs and the street door slamming shut.

Silence returned to the office. The square outside was almost deserted. Since it was Carnival Tuesday, the hustle and bustle of commerce had finished earlier than usual The junior book-keepers were yawning, and the scratching of Manuel Quintino's pen only added to the soporific atmosphere.

Suddenly, though, the silence was broken by loud tra-la-las from Manuel Quintino.

Having finished his letter, the good man had discovered various omissions and mistakes, which meant he would have to rewrite it yet again, and he set to with exemplary patience, laying all the blame on himself.

'I really should have more sense. I'm as bad as a child, letting myself get distracted like that. I deserve a good spanking.'

Then, remembering Carlos, he said: 'And he's another naughty boy! Goodness me!'

Then, turning to his juniors, he said: 'You can go now. Off to those masked balls with you, but be sensible and don't ruin your health. Off you go. I'll stay here.'

'If you'd like us to help, Senhor Manuel Quintino…' they said deferentially.

'No, off you go, both of you. Goodbye.'

The junior book-keepers did not need to be told twice.

'Now settle down,' Manuel Quintino told himself once he was alone. 'Settle down, otherwise I won't get home until dark, and Cecilia will be getting tired. What a wasted day! I'd hoped to finish this earlier, because I was in good time, but… Why did he have to come to the office today of all days?

He's a good lad, though, with a heart of gold, but such a giddy head... And that conversation about the rum, goodness, that was funny. And his father was completely taken in... But then we poor parents all have a soft spot for our offspring. I should know. And his father really does love him. It's just so painful to him that the boy has no taste for business. That could change though. He's still young. No, he's a good lad really, and from fine stock too, because his father's a decent man through and through... and his mother was a saint. And as for his sister, well, she's an angel! And they're not even Catholics! But with Protestants like them, St Peter couldn't possibly turn them away.'

As a consequence of Carlos' visit, Manuel Quintino only finished his work and closed up the office at half past three, returning home with an empty stomach and a clear conscience. As you see, dear reader, Carlos was quite right when he said he had no head for business.

X

Jenny

As soon as Carlos left for the office, Jenny went to her mauve-painted bedroom, a delightful place, revealing a good taste and an unaffected elegance that combined beautifully with a certain English austerity, not enough to spoil the light, gracious touch appropriate in a twenty-year-old woman's bedroom, but enough to make it seem uncluttered by the kind of ornaments of which certain childish rather than feminine minds are so enamoured.

It certainly didn't fit the description made by a French novelist of his heroine's boudoir, so abundant in tapestries and rugs that not an inch of wood was left uncovered, and with walls so soft and padded that any bird caught in that perfumed cage could fly fearlessly from wall to wall and be in no danger of damaging its wings.

Such flaccid Parisian elegance fitted very ill with Jenny Whitestone's serious, unpretentious nature. There is a little of the Puritan in all Englishwomen; even in the gentlest among them there is always something which, from the moral point of view, corresponds to that innate inflexibility, so different from the indolent, almost delicate nature of southern women.

None of the objects in Jenny's room were of the kind you might find in the almost doll-like boudoirs fashionable at the time, all *papier-mâché*, rosewood, and gilt, the niceties of an art whose love of delicacy can easily tip over into the effete and ridiculous.

There, elegance retained a certain rather rare dignity, and there was none of the usual artifice one expects of modern industry; everything was what it seemed to be; the marble was marble, the bronze was bronze, the damask was damask, and the lace was real lace. There were no veneers masking cheaper wood with more expensive varieties, none of the marvels of imitation achieved with varnish and paint, no metals embellished with falsely noble titles. There was not a single mendacious object in that room.

People of good faith love objects of equally good faith.

The room's predominant colour, one that artists would have found pleasing, perfectly set off the chastely drawn milk-white curtains.

The only louder colours were those of the camellias which, arranged in simple biscuit and porcelain vases, adorned the dressing table and the fireplace.

The space given to those poor flowers remained unusurped by the profusion of knicknacks so fashionable nowadays: bottles containing perfumes, pomades and oils, boxes of all sizes, porcelain or jasper figures, flowers made from feathers or parchment or leather or onion skin paper, all considered preferable to the real thing; portraits of kings and queens, bars of soap of various shapes and hues, and an infinite number of other small objects that give any room the appearance of a bazaar or a market stall.

At most, there were a few bronzes, some exquisite cut-glass from England, a few pretty vases, and the occasional literary or religious text bound in inimitable English fashion.

The walls were bare of any ornate coloured lithographs depicting little girls hiding a smile behind a fan, playing with a cat, smelling a flower, peering at us through a magnifying glass and other equally affected and unappealing poses; instead of that adornment so common in other rooms in Oporto, there were a few notable British etchings and some watercolours, faithful copies of English landscapes.

The light entered the room through discreet Venetian blinds and curtains, appropriately adjusted to Jenny's needs.

Everything about the room had the air of a peaceful retreat, perfect for the thoughtful, slightly melancholy spirit of Carlos' adorable sister.

There, with the shutters and curtains closed, she would sit alone in silence, her face cupped in her hands, as she was now, immersed in thoughts blessed by God, and from which gentle joys emanated out to all those around her.

At that moment, her heart was stirred by still vivid, poignant memories, for she was gazing with almost religious fervour at the portrait of her mother, a faithful, tender miniature, which she guarded as the most precious of her jewels.

That image, which so moved her and seemed to be regarding her with a kindly smile that not even death had erased, always made a powerful impression on Jenny.

Sometimes, by sheer force of looking, it seemed to her that those beloved features came to life, that her mother's lips moved slightly, that a glimmer of life flickered briefly in those eyes so full of pity and sadness.

What joy this brought to poor Jenny's heart! She convinced herself that her mother's soul, summoned up by her daughter's love, had momentarily illuminated that lifeless image in order to bless her daughter, who had been orphaned of her loving caresses when she was still so very young.

Jenny kept this illusion to herself. It was one of those intimate secrets of the human heart that can be divulged to no one. However proven a friendship, however deep the love, the soul, however expansive, does not reveal everything. There is an obscure part of our inner world that remains ever inaccessible to others' eyes, in which lie hidden those private secrets, at which even we would laugh were our lips one day to put them into words, except that we would never dare. Some perfumes are so subtle that, once the bottle is opened, they dissolve almost instantly into the air; so it is with those inner mysteries, the insubstantial food of our imagination; they, too, are lost if we attempt to communicate them.

We all keep that part of our mind to ourselves, the baseless superstitions and childish beliefs that cannot be separated from us, unless we deny them and join others in making fun of them, poor things, born to live imprisoned in our soul, on which they seem to feed.

They are like certain types of delicate seaweed, which expand in the water into exquisite branched shapes, deluding those who fall in love with such beauty and remove them from their natural environment, the sea, only to see them quickly shrivel and shrink.

Jenny was a very rational being, and yet, in her inner world, she cherished the illusory belief – illusory to me at least, an outsider – that the look on her mother's face in that portrait did, in fact, change.

I would like to say that this was felt rather than thought by Jenny, but I'm not sure philosophical rigour would allow this, and yet I can find no other way of describing that common psychological phenomenon: the persistence of certain irrational beliefs even in the strongest and most logical of minds.

There were days when Jenny thought she could see happiness in those features, a happiness that immediately entered her own heart; on other days, though, she saw shades of sadness that made her tremble, as if they presaged some misfortune.

Were these merely reflections of her own presentiments? Perhaps, but does that help us understand the mystery any better?

Presentiments! What philosophical mind will allow that such things exist?

Jenny was still a child when she lost her mother; that blow to the heart came while she was still absorbed in childhood games and toys; the terrible, threatening evil had been growing there beside her, but she, in her innocence, had only realised this when the victim fell prostrate into her arms. That carefree age is fortunate in many ways, but then, in a single moment, her whole life became something utterly different from the life she had foreseen. From a very early age, that weak and fragile child was invested by her dying mother with a grown woman's sacrosanct mission; in her final moments, she bequeathed to her the blessed task that she herself had unceasingly performed.

Clasping in her already cold hands the hands of her tearful daughter – who only then saw the death that had so long been threatening her deepest affections – her mother laid upon her the heavy burden of the family; and with trembling voice and eyes clouded with the shadows of that final sleep, she told her that she was entrusting to those hands the inner peace and happiness of those she loved most, along with the treasure and balm of fond affection with which hearth and home can cure the many sorrows and disillusions we bring from our struggles in the outside world; then, clutching her daughter to her breast, as if to make one final urgent plea for which she now lacked words, she died kissing her daughter's cheek, anointing her with her final tears and making such a deep impression on her child's mind that, after weeping over her mother's grave, that poor orphan rose up a woman, despite her scant twelve years, a woman in her common sense and in her lively, fervent consciousness of her new mission in life.

Misfortune is a very good teacher! From that fateful hour, it was as if Jenny's eyes had opened to see more deeply into the hearts of those it was her duty to make happy. Only then did she begin to realise that, even among the noblest and purest of hearts, there are sometimes contradictions, which can bring about painful conflicts; that the misfortunes and miseries of life do not always spring from the baleful influence of some evil that has been allowed to contaminate a whole human soul; that a storm more often begins with a clash of two essentially generous emotions. On the high seas, a prevailing wind can decide the direction and course of a ship, but only an extremely violent wind can, on its own, capsize it. However, if a vessel falls into one of those whirlpools whipped up by contrary winds, then disaster will almost certainly follow.

And so it is in life.

It isn't enough for the people involved to be large-hearted and kind, to be bound together by family ties or society, for harmony to prevail. If contrary winds begin to blow around them, then fatal collisions and troubles can ensue.

Nature also teaches us that strong poisons do sometimes arise from a combination of otherwise inoffensive elements.

Once she had bidden an early farewell to the spontaneous, unforced joys of childhood, which had ended with her mother's final breath, all these things became apparent in young Jenny's mind by dint of deep thought.

This was very early indeed for an English girl who – at an age when other girls are beginning to aspire to being ladies – would ordinarily be playing happily and without a care in the world in parks and gardens, running, jumping, laughing, and not worrying about getting the hem of her dress wet on the grass.

This cheerful expansiveness of spirit in young English girls is perhaps why they become so unaffectedly serious when nature, rather than premature artifice, turns them into women.

In Jenny, though, the laughter proper to her age ceased, the irrepressible giggles that can be triggered by a word or by the tiniest thing, just as the orange tree rains down its fragrant, snow-white petals onto the grass at the slightest breeze.

She grew used to thinking and to devoting herself wholly to the happiness of her loved ones, doing her best to insinuate herself into each person's little secrets in order to guide them, painlessly, through the sphere of action, the circle, in which they had to live.

From that point on, Jenny's sway over the whole family began to grow rapidly – a very benign subjection, which was as pleasing to her subjects as a blessing from heaven.

Until then, Jenny had been loved as a sweet child, whose cheerful nature could distract others from more serious preoccupations; however, that love soon took on a different, more respectful character.

Mr Richard Whitestone's protective affection for his daughter acquired a kind of deferential, almost reverential quality; in Carlos, the familiarity bred by their closeness in age and by their shared games and studies gradually changed to become a feeling of respect and docile submission that became apparent in all his actions.

Armed with that double advantage, Jenny devoutly carried out her mother's legacy, her thoughts and eyes always fixed on her mother's image, in which she thought she saw the mingled feelings of joy and sadness that her family's fate must stir in that kindly soul looking down on her from Heaven.

That oracle, mute to all others, spoke eloquently only to Jenny's heart, and Jenny consulted it with an ardent faith whenever she shut herself away in her room, where the light and noise from outside penetrated only very discreetly, as befitted a place of pious mysteries.

Did the picture look sad today?

Why?

If Jenny's lips were to give voice to the ideas absorbing her then, they would have said this: 'Poor mother! Why are you so sad? Surely this morning's cloud has passed over now? It was such a small, light cloud, and didn't even trouble *me* very much. What are you thinking, mother?' These were her thoughts as she kissed the portrait. 'Cheer up. Carlos will be at the office now. Poor love, he has such a good heart! How he would love you and embrace you, Mother, if you were still here with us. Not many people really know him. But why are you still sad? They'll come back home firm friends, you'll see. Those two fond hearts are easily reconciled. However many clouds pass between them, they still adore each other. The sight of Carlos in the office would have been enough to banish any resentment... the resentment proper to someone who genuinely cares. Do you not trust your daughter? You can see how everyone here loves me. They must see in me something of your spirit, Mother, for them to be so obedient to a poor girl like me. They're really obeying your soul, which accompanies me at all times. Stay by my side, Mother, and I will be strong; don't abandon me, and you'll see that all your fears are baseless. Still sad?' She kissed the portrait again. 'Still? Still?' She kissed it over and over.

Then reason tried to drive away those pious illusions.

'I must be mad,' thought Jenny, 'how can a portrait...'

She moved into the light.

The illusions returned, like a swarm of bees that the wind carries away from the flowers.

'I don't know how it's possible, but your expression is definitely sadder than yesterday. Why so sad? Was it the way he talked about the ball yesterday or was it that masked woman he spoke to? But what of that? Oh no, you look even sadder now! I have no alternative then but to think…'

Just then, she heard steps outside the door.

The spell was broken! And to the semi-hallucinatory senses of that visionary of the emotions – if I dare to call her that – all expression vanished from the portrait, and she quickly put it away.

Luísa, the maid we have already met, appeared in the doorway.

'What is it, Luísa?'

'It's Senhor Manuel Quintino's daughter.'

'Ah, so Cecília has finally arrived! Show her in, Luísa, show her in. I don't know why you didn't send her straight up,' said Jenny brightly.

Cecília was one of her dearest friends.

XI

Cecília

After a few moments, in came Manuel Quintino's daughter, light as a swallow and as cheerful as any child. She was all the family he had in the world.

Jenny fondly held out her hand… and then, the reader will assume, they kissed each other on the cheek. But, no, they didn't, for Englishwomen are far less free with the gift of their lips than women from other countries; a friendly handshake, a smile, a few affectionate words… and nothing more. Is this so that when any kisses are finally granted, they will be appreciated all the more?

Cecília was the very model of Portuguese – or even Oporto – beauty at its finest.

When we writers want to give our readers an idea of how beautiful a woman is, we tend to compare her to the Spanish, the Italians, the Germans, the English, but never to the Portuguese, and our female compatriots, with the sublime resignation of martyrs, have suffered this flagrant injustice for many years.

It's as if our homegrown beauty were unworthy of mention, and that only when, by some caprice of Nature, it takes on a foreign quality does a woman merit the usual high-sounding, hyperbolic formulae of our admiration.

One is always hearing: 'She's so beautiful! There's a kind

of diaphanous, Germanic look about her!' – 'What a woman! She just oozes Spanish style!' – 'Such majesty, such languor. She's the perfect Italian *madonna*!' – 'So poetic, so dignified! She's like a real English lady!' What you don't hear, at least I have yet to hear it, is this: 'What a lovely girl! A perfect Portuguese beauty!'

The reason is that we are a small, rather unfashionable nation, shy and new to the great, glittering society of Europe, which is kind enough to allow us in; and we consider ourselves truly flattered when those foreigners benevolently let themselves be admired by us!

We are inexperienced in the ways of society, which teaches everyone to know their place. When we are not exaggeratedly over-valuing all things Portuguese, like that man we met in one of the groups in Rua dos Ingleses, we go to the other extreme and don't even talk about them, as if we simply took them for granted.

Painful though it may be to our national vanity, it has to be said – since we're all family here – that we do share the defect of those provincials who, when they visit the capital, always shamefacedly suppress their deep love of their home town and instead, rather comically, praise to the skies the pleasures and excitements of life in the big city, which they have barely had time to enjoy and savour. They talk of the theatres, the balls, the new diva, the latest scandal, without daring to say a word about the trees and landscapes, the local traditions and customs, the cosy domesticity of their own province, which others might find far more interesting, and thus they end up seeming even more absurdly provincial.

So it is with the Portuguese, the shrinking violets of European society, who never confer certificates of excellence on anything that belongs to them; they are embarrassed to speak of their own national treasures, but speak openly of all sorts of trifles that foreign vanity vaunts as being wonders of the world; they take modesty to extremes, if it is modesty, almost afraid that those foreigners might ask how things are where they come from, and are then effusively grateful for the smallest crumb of praise that those same foreigners might deign to bestow on their country.

If we dare to speak of Camões in the same breath as Tasso, Dante and Milton, if we dare to place port wine on the same level as sherry, Château-Lafitte and Tokay, that is only because they, the foreigners, have given them the stamp of authority, whereas if it were left to us, we would say nothing, reading one and drinking the other without really appreciating the value of what we are reading or drinking, or else feeling ashamed that we think one sublime and the other delicious.

You may think one of these similes lacking in delicacy, but it's the same with feminine beauty. We are more than happy to exclaim: 'Ah, those Spanish women!' – 'Ah, those Italian women!' – 'Ah, those German women!' – but we would consider it in bad taste to declare in public: 'Those Portuguese women!' even without the preceding incremental 'Ah!'

And even those who have never set foot outside Oporto, where there is hardly a superabundance of such exotic beauties, even they do the same.

I, however, intend to raise the puritan flag in this glorious campaign. And I'm sure my readers will not mind.

I do not wish, in any way, to decry the traditional reputation of the types of beauties that have already been studied and classified, agreed upon and exalted as such by the whole world. I embrace them all, but I simply wish to create a space for our own beauties, who certainly deserve that distinction.

You may say that there is no one type of Portuguese beauty.

It is simply a variation on the much vaster species. I just wish you could have met Cecília, and then told me to which of the permitted, sanctioned female types she belonged.

If there were a single formula for feminine beauty, then describing as beautiful just one of the two women here before you would be to condemn the other, for they were so different, so dissimilar! But that isn't necessary, for there are so many ways of being beautiful, so many ways of arousing in us those mysterious vibrations that make our hearts flutter, that it would, as in everything, be madness to argue over which is superior.

If the orchards of Minho are beautiful, does that make the verdant banks of the river Vouga or even the alpine landscapes of Trás-os-Montes less beautiful?

Cecília was neither fair nor dark, nor was she pale in the way that sets poets dreaming and doctors worrying; her delicately oval face was of a complexion for which, to put it poetically, no word had yet been created.

If, though, for lack of the right word, we were simply to call her pale, we should add that it was a paleness beneath which one could sense her lively blood, which sometimes transformed her pallor into the diffuse pink of a child's cheek; her naturally curly hair fell back to reveal her smooth forehead and was a shade somewhere between black and dark brown; her eyes, though, were dark verging on black and – unusually – were impenetrably discreet. Imagine that, discreet eyes! For, normally, our eyes are the first to betray both us and our silent lips! Eyes that dare to look at you without letting slip a secret or turning away for fear of betraying themselves. Discreet, but full of sympathy and kindness. You cannot imagine the charm of such eyes. And don't go thinking them incapable of eloquence, for when filled with trust and love, you will see the dazzling rays they emit! But what they don't do – and quite right too – is wander around squandering their eloquence, like one of those implacable, constantly declaiming talker. Cecilia was completely without affectation, and there was such naturalness and frankness in her lips, her smile, the tilt of her head, her every movement and gesture, that one's gaze lingered on her with gentle, candid pleasure.

But how does one recognise what I describe as a typically Portuguese beauty? It happens when you stand next to a beautiful woman, feeling totally at ease and untroubled, with no need to flatter, with none of the usual poetic emotions fluttering in your heart; it happens when, under the gentle influence of an unflirtatious gaze, you're able to hold an affectionate, sincere, loyal conversation, much as you would with a friend or a sister; it happens when, on parting, you shake her cordially by the hand, without yours or hers trembling when they touch, and take away from that conversation a pleasant impression that warms you rather than disturbs your dreams; then you can be sure that you have met such a beauty.

I would, however, warn you not to consider such beauties entirely innocuous, nor be taken in by those first mild effects; if you value the freedom of your heart, then escape while there's still time, because if you continue to enjoy that intimate, natural, engaging relationship, you run the risk of gradually becoming caught, and when, one day, you try to end it, you will find yourself truly in love, and only then will you realise, from the pain that you feel, what deep roots love has put down in you.

In my view, these passions are the most irresistible, whereas those that grow rapidly and evolve rapidly, often fade rapidly too.

If, as some do, you see such passions as a kind of disease of the soul, it would perhaps be possible to make an analogous distinction to that made by doctors. There would, then, be acute passions and chronic passions; some, as with acute physical illnesses, would be sparked by sudden impressions, quick to advance and quick to end, while others, acquired more insidiously, from everyday encounters, without you even noticing, would labour away in secret, revealing themselves only when the territory was won and victory assured.

Just which of these two diseases most perplexes the medical arts, only doctors and patients can know.

But to return to Cecília: her conversation, enhanced by the timbre of her rich, vibrant voice, had a vivacity and a vigour, almost, you might say, a natural eloquence, that was a pleasure to listen to; it was notable that, in the course of any conversation, the expression of her voice and face was constantly shifting between joy and sadness, just as, in the fields, light and shade alternate when the north wind drives the clouds swiftly across the sky.

So it was that, even when describing sad events, some circumstance or other would prompt a smile or a humorous comment, and, in the middle of the most jovial of anecdotes, the faintest trace of another very different emotion would surface and, suddenly, the smile would vanish from her lips, and her eyes would fill with a look of generous melancholy.

One day, for example, she was almost tearfully telling Jenny about a poor centenarian whom her father had helped. This unfortunate old man was living in a hovel, abandoned by everyone, and would have slowly starved to death had Manuel Quintino not taken pity on him and saved him from that terrible fate.

'If you had seen the poor man,' Cecília said, her voice breaking, 'if you had seen him! The way he welcomed us, weeping and laughing, how he clasped my hands and kissed them! How he raised his eyes to heaven, eyes that were almost blind from age and misfortune! It was heartbreaking. He was so frail and bent.' Then, smiling, she could not resist adding: 'And yet despite his great age and the wretched conditions in which he lived, the poor man still took enormous pride in his pigtail!'

On another occasion, she was recounting, and laughing as she did so, the grotesque story of a workman, a neighbour of hers, who had returned home one night blind drunk, and kept the whole street awake with his spontaneous outbursts of joy, talking, singing and playing into the small hours. All of this had drawn smiles from her, but, the next moment, her face became profoundly sad, and, sighing, she took Jenny's hands in hers and went on: 'But do you know what happened? Just when this man was at his most joyous, someone brought him the dead body of a dog, a dog he had loved and who, that very night, had been poisoned in the streets. I can see him now. For a long time, he stood in silence, just looking at the poor creature, then he burst into tears and embraced the dog, calling him his friend, his companion and even,' and here she smiled again, 'even his brother. It was tragic. And the people round about just laughed. Was that something to be laughed at?'

Such keen powers of observation, such a talent for appreciating every facet of human feelings and actions, are rare, and yet they came naturally to her.

As we said before, you couldn't describe Cecília as being as passionate as an Italian, as pensive as a German, as serious as an Englishwoman, as languid as a Spaniard, as coquettish as a Frenchwoman, because she was none of those things; she was Portuguese through and through, and to describe that type of beauty I know only one phrase, which will perhaps make the reader laugh, but it's one for which I feel an inexplicable fondness. My mind associates it with such a bundle of physical and moral qualities that, whenever I hear it spoken, it replaces any need for long descriptions, and, were I to analyse it, I would doubtless fail to find in it the meaning I instinctively attribute to it. If the reader feels the same, then he or she will understand what Cecília was like as soon as I say it.

Cecília was what we might spontaneously call 'a dear girl'. I know there's nothing in that expression to make one assume that the person in question is beautiful, nor does it imply any superior moral qualities, which is why I don't like to analyse it too closely.

And yet, whenever I hear a woman I don't know described like that, I do, for some reason, imagine her to be beautiful, beautiful in the Portuguese sense and endowed with a kind heart... like Cecília's heart.

And here we have Jenny too, who could easily stand comparison with her friend as regards charm and kindness, but while I have called Jenny an angel and a good fairy, I would hesitate to call her 'a dear girl', as I do Cecília.

I will be accused of making Manuel Quintino's daughter seem too bourgeois by using that bourgeois turn of phrase. However, I don't believe such a criticism is valid, because – and here comes another brave confession – I feel more sympathy for bourgeois types than for aristocratic ones – especially when it comes to women. In my eyes, a bourgeois girl, who has no ambitions to be anything else when she sits sewing by candlelight, has far more poetry about her than the elegant frequenter of salons, who fritters away her powers of imagination on fussing about her hair and clothes. Sewing, the simple, modest act of sewing, the useful and blessedly female task of wielding a needle, pleases me far more than any futile, but reputedly more noble, behind-the-scenes prettification;

the woman who combs her own hair seems to me far more deserving of the artist's gaze than the indolent creature who reclines in an armchair while she leafs through a fashion magazine and lets a maid or a hairdresser tend to her coiffure. Were an artist to paint such a woman, all he would need as canvas would be a fan or a biscuit box.

No, Cecília had nothing of the aristocrat about her; in that sense, she was a true native of Oporto, a city whose main claim to glory is that, in the days when having a noble title was all-important, it realised that, in order to be its own proud self, it could and should do without such things.

XII

Another Testimony

'Are you feeling unwell, Cecília?' asked Jenny, taking her friend's hat.

'No, why do you ask?'

'I'm not sure, I seemed to see it in your face and, besides, you're late.'

'Ah,' said Cecília, smiling and smoothing her hair, left slightly dishevelled by her hat. 'How did you guess? Today, I've been playing the fine lady. I didn't get up until gone eight o'clock.'

'You lazy thing! Does that mean you've forgotten to bring those collars you were telling me about?'

'Not at all. I've brought those and a few other things too…'

'Oh, do let me see,' said Jenny, full of curiosity.

And the two young women went and sat side by side on the sofa by the window.

'Did you walk here alone?' asked Jenny a moment later.

'Yes.'

'And you weren't afraid to do so on a Carnival day?'

'No, not at all. From my house to here, the roads are almost like village roads that take you past gardens and fields. I met a few little girls coming from school, and I talked to them the whole way.'

And still rummaging about in her green morocco leather

149

bag, Cecília went on in a slightly different tone of voice: 'Don't go thinking I'm about to show you some marvel or other, it was just something I made when I had a free half hour on Saturday night. I've had so much else to do this week, and, as you know, I don't have a lot of time just to play. Look.'

And what she showed Jenny was a perfect example of womanly art; it was simply a collar, but, if I had the necessary technical vocabulary, I could launch into a description as long as Homer's description of Achilles' shield.

However, my female readers are so knowledgable and my male readers so ignorant regarding this matter, that none of them will be any the wiser if I don't.

'I was just about to say that I think this one is even prettier than the one you showed me a couple of days ago,' said Jenny, studying the collar.

'Yes, it is more delicate, but... oh dear!' Cecília added with a sigh, rubbing her eyes and smiling: 'Do you know, I'm so tired I can barely see.'

'Tired? Even though you got up so late? Is there something you're not telling me, Cecília?'

'I went to bed very late too.'

'Were you working?'

There was a brief silence while Cecília got up the courage to answer. Jenny asked again and looked at her. She saw that her friend was blushing and seemed to be concentrating very hard on a pin.

Pins are a woman's main accomplice when she's trying to conceal something. Whenever a woman needs to hide a smile, an awkwardness, a blush, she is sure to find one of these obliging friends to serve as a pretext. There's always a pin that needs pinning or unpinning or repinning.

Making a visible effort at self-control, Cecília responded

in a voice that struggled in vain to seem natural: 'No, Jenny, I wasn't working.'

Jenny sensed a secret in her friend's perplexity and hesitation, but made no attempt to probe further. Setting aside her suspicions, she said: 'What was that lovely bit of crochet you just put down?'

Cecília showed it to her, without saying a word.

And for some time, a mutual silence reigned, until, at last – as if eager to give expression to a good thought before any subsequent thoughts surfaced to suppress it – Cecília took one of her frequent sudden decisions and, rather impatiently, set aside the work she had spread out on her lap, and taking Jenny's hands in hers, fixed her lively, dark eyes on her friend's slightly melancholy and somewhat bemused blue eyes.

Cecília remained silent and indecisive for a few more moments, then, finally, blushing still more deeply and in the grip of a nervousness no smile could disguise, she said in a voice trembling with emotion: 'You're my friend, Jenny, and so I think it's best if I tell you everything...'

'Whatever it is you have to tell me, but are afraid to tell me because you doubt my friendship, then I can assure you, Cecília, that...'

'No, I would never doubt you,' said Cecília, and in one quick impulsive movement, and before Jenny could react, she raised Jenny's slender hands to her lips.

'What are you doing?' said Jenny, laughing.

'Oh, let me. You know how fond I am of you, and you know I have complete confidence in you, it's just that some things are hard to say.'

Jenny smiled knowingly, for she saw in Cecília's embarrassment the imminent confession of some new romance.

Cecília understood the meaning of that smile, because she

was quick to add: 'No, no, it's not what you think, Jenny. If it was, I wouldn't hesitate for a moment, really.'

Despite the certainty with which Cecília spoke, I doubt she would have found it so very easy to confide something of that nature, of the sort that makes even the bravest of us quake in our shoes. However, since we have no choice, let us take her at her word.

'Whatever it is,' said Jenny, trying to give her courage, 'there's no need to have any scruples about telling me. Why should you? After all, we're both young women. And almost the same age too.'

'Yes, but you're so different from the rest of us! You're so sensible that you're bound to feel bemused by the things we featherbrains so thoughtlessly get up to, only to regret them later on.'

'You're being unfair to me and to yourself, Cecília. You're no featherbrain, and I'm not as sensible as you say I am.'

'All right,' said Cecília, 'I'm going to confess all, but you must promise me that, afterwards, you'll tell me frankly what you think. I'll be annoyed if you don't tell me the truth, however unfavourable.'

'It won't be unfavourable.'

'I think it will.'

'Cecília, please, you're frightening me,' said Jenny cheerily. 'There's such genuine terror in your face and your words, I feel quite afraid. Have you committed some crime?'

These words, and still more the tone in which they were spoken, made Cecília laugh and helped diminish the doubts she had been struggling with up until then.

'What I want you to do,' she said, 'is to let me carry on doing the edging on this collar while I'm talking. Somehow I feel more at ease if I'm busy doing something.'

'As you wish, but let me find something to do too, by seeing what else is in this bag.'

'I didn't bring anything else, apart from...'

'Don't worry, I'll find something. Now begin.'

With each of them busy at their chosen tasks, Cecília began: 'Have I ever mentioned Major Matos' daughters? They've been my neighbours for several years, as well as my classmates.'

'Yes, you've often spoken of them.'

'They're very good girls and very fond of me, but...'

Jenny looked up at Cecília when she felt her hesitate, then Cecília continued: 'More than that, though, and this is just between you and me, Jenny, they're even fonder of having fun. They've inherited their father's outgoing nature, because he's as sprightly as a twenty-year-old, and they're always coming up with ideas for new amusements.'

'It's a great joy to have such a nature, don't you think?' said Jenny, examining a small piece of embroidery.

'Oh,' said Cecília, noticing what Jenny was looking at, 'that one's no good at all. I don't know why I even brought it.'

Jenny put the object in question to one side and indicated to Cecília to continue.

'But as for my friends,' Cecília said, 'they're really hard workers, poor things, but whenever they have a little free time – at the end of the day, for example – all they can think of is what they're going to do the following Sunday, and then they'll ask their father if they can go for a boat ride upriver, or have supper in Pedra Salgada or in Fonte da Vinha, or lunch in Leça or in Foz, or a night at the theatre, and their father, who adores them, rarely denies them such outings, which, it must be said, he enjoys too. They often invite me to go with them, and I must confess they've given me hours of fun. They're a lovely family, and my father is perfectly happy for me to go anywhere with them.'

'I was expecting some shocking confession that would set me trembling, and yet what you're telling me is all so healthy and natural that I have to say I'm almost disappointed,' said Jenny, pulling a face and closing the leather bag, having put away all the pieces of embroidery.

Cecília smiled, then added: 'Don't be impatient. Don't be too quick to judge, because you might have to change your mind later. Ages ago now, well, ever since last year really, the girls have been putting together a plan that was rather more difficult to carry out than any of their other plans, and they wanted me to join them. At first, I said No, but they kept nagging me and telling me there was nothing to fear, and so, in the end, I said Yes. Now this, Jenny, is where the bad bit of my story begins. The plan was…'

'Let me see – to set fire to the city?'

'No!'

'Start a revolution?'

'Don't be silly.'

'Set off to join the troops in Crimea?'

'Jenny!'

'Well, given how reluctant you are to tell me…'

'The plan was to go to the theatre wearing Carnival masks.'

'Oh!' said Jenny, unable to conceal a flicker of disapproval. Looking up, Cecília saw that flicker.

'Didn't I tell you? You see you're already starting to…'

'No, really, go on,' said Jenny, feeling curious now and not taking her eyes off Cecília.

'This plan,' Cecília said, 'was fraught with difficulties. The Major, usually so happy to grant his daughters' every wish, wouldn't hear of it. They, however, could think of nothing else.'

'And so they went?' asked Jenny.

'They'd been waiting for a chance for a long time, and Carnival was slipping away. However, about three days ago, the Major had to leave the city on some military business.'

'And so?'

'The girls were left alone at home with an aunt, who's a very nice woman, but she can't bring herself to refuse them anything. What more could they want?'

'And so they went?'

'They did. Yesterday. It was as if everything had worked out exactly as they had planned.'

'And what about you?' asked Jenny, increasingly worried by what she was hearing.

'They had invited me to go to their house in the afternoon. And once I was there, without my knowledge, they sent a message to my father saying I would be home late, because I would be going with them to visit some good friends of theirs.'

'And then…'

'It was already dark when they presented me with my Carnival costume and told me their plan. I raised a few objections, but…'

'You went?'

'Yes, I did. Oh, don't look so serious! I did warn you?'

Jenny couldn't disguise her feelings on hearing Cecília's confession, not only because of the nature of that confession, but also because it was so very similar to what her brother had told her only a few hours before.

'I promised to be honest with you, Cecília,' Jenny said, clasping her friend's hands, for Cecília had stopped her sewing. 'And I would be breaking my promise were I to deny that your decision seems to me to have been somewhat foolish. A few young ladies alone in a place like that, where apparently all kinds of people go, whole crowds of them! I really don't know, but tell me what happened next and then I'll have a better idea whether or not my fears are unfounded, as I'm sure they are...'

'No, they're not, Jenny. To be honest, I was quite curious at first. The only thing that bothered me was having to deceive my father, but since he had no idea I would be going to a masked ball, I was eager to see what it would be like, and, besides, the Major's sister was coming with us...'

'And then?'

'We arrived at the theatre at around ten o'clock, all of us in fancy dress and wearing masks. And I had to laugh when I saw the mask the Major's sister was wearing. It was extraordinary! It was the very first one she chose, and it really did look like her, in the same way a caricature resembles the person caricatured.'

Cecília was almost distracted by this incidental resemblance, but Jenny brought her back to the matter in hand.

'Yes, but tell me what happened.'

'Ah, yes, you're right. First of all, we went to visit a few of the boxes where my friends knew some of the ladies and we spoke to them without once being recognised. That did make me laugh. One rather ancient lady got it into her head that we were her relatives from Braga and kept calling me her Joaninha! The poor thing was so upset when she saw my hair and realised she'd been deceived, and then I did feel sorry for her! "Oh, it's not you, oh, how sad!" she said and in such a heartfelt voice that I couldn't help but embrace her and kiss her. I risked being unmasked, of course, and giving away the identity of my friends, and they did tell me off afterwards, but I couldn't help myself!'

'I know,' said Jenny, smiling at her friend's kind response. 'And what happened after that?'

'Ah, after that, Jenny…' said Cecília with a sigh, as if she found it very hard to go on. Then she said: 'We went into the main room. Have you ever been to a carnival ball? Well, you haven't missed much. The heat! The noise! Just fifteen minutes after going in, I was already longing to leave, but the others wouldn't hear of it. It was midnight perhaps when, tired and fed up with the crowd and the hubbub, I found a place to sit.'

At this point, Cecília stopped, as if she were deeply troubled by what she had to say next.

Jenny couldn't help but smile at how similar this part of her confession was to her brother's.

'Soon afterwards,' Cecília went on, 'someone came and sat down next to me.'

A pin suddenly demanded her full attention, and Cecília could never refuse the demands of her pins.

Occupied then with pinning or possibly unpinning, she said: 'It was someone I knew, but they didn't recognise me and spoke to me anyway. I responded, and we sat there talking for a long time.'

But when Jenny, perfectly naturally, asked: 'What about?' Cecília paused before replying. Then, after a few moments, she said: 'I don't really know. About all kinds of things, and it was really very pleasant. Then some others joined us, and they were far less polite than him…'

'Than *him*? Oh, so it was a man you were talking to? I didn't realise,' Jenny remarked slightly mischievously.

'Yes, didn't I say? Oh, that's right, I said "they". Anyway, yes, he was a man. And the other young men who joined us showed me just how foolish we had been.'

Now Jenny didn't lose a single word or inflection or change in her friend's colour; Cecília, though, was oblivious to this, because her pins had grown so demanding of her attention that they wouldn't allow her to attend to anything else. Nevertheless, she added: 'My friends felt the same, and so we prepared to leave the ball. When I saw that we were being followed, I appealed to the chivalry of the man who had spoken to me, and that saved us.'

'Ah!'

'He served as our guide and protector through the streets, which were still full of people in masks and costumes, but then he insisted on accompanying us right to our door. This worried me more than it did the others, because he knows my father and if he realised this, well... However hard we pleaded with him, he wouldn't leave us, and I was so frightened, I prayed to God for inspiration. Inspiration came, and it worked. He finally left us, and we went in. By then, it was four o'clock in the morning.'

Jenny could easily have filled in any gaps in Cecília's confession; however, she carefully averted her gaze so that she appeared to be thinking what to ask next, then said: 'All that's lacking, Cecília, is for you to tell me who this man was and what form that heaven-sent inspiration took.'

This time, it was Jenny's pins that seemed to demand all her attention, and she immediately obliged.

Clearly embarrassed, Cecília stammered: 'Who he was? I don't know, I mean... he was...'

Jenny took her hand.

'You can be absolutely frank with me,' she said warmly. 'That man was my brother.'

Cecília gazed in astonishment at Jenny.

'How do you know that?'

'I know everything,' answered Jenny, squeezing her hand affectionately, 'and I also know the nature of that inspiration, and I thank you for it.'

'You know? But how…'

'Carlos is in the habit of telling me everything, and this very morning… he told me…'

'*Everything?*' asked Cecília urgently, blushing.

'Everything,' said Jenny, laying particular stress on the word and smiling, which only made Cecília blush all the more.

As the reader will have noticed, Cecília had omitted something important from her confession, an omission that Jenny's 'everything' revealed to have been futile.

'And what did Senhor Carlos have to say about me?' asked Cecília, genuinely troubled.

Jenny grew serious again and thought for a while before responding.

You can't imagine how extraordinarily beautiful Jenny looked when she adopted that pensive air, which so often filled her eyes and traced the faintest of lines on her forehead.

Cecília studied that expressive face with evident alarm.

'Look, Cecília,' Jenny said at last, 'as you yourself acknowledged, what you and your friends did was very foolish. The fact that you had to conceal it from your father is proof enough, and that was before anything else had happened to provide still further proof. Carlos behaved both well and badly; well in protecting you and your friends, and badly afterwards. As I told him, he should have considered the possibility that the person he had first protected and then pursued might be a respectable young woman, who really did want to conceal her identity. I said this to him just a short while ago, and do you know what he said?'

'What?'

'If I tell you, Cecília, it's only so that, in future, you'll trust what your kind heart tells you, and believe that it always gives you excellent advice. When I asked Carlos to imagine that it could have been me behind that mask and being pursued by a group of young men, he said that this simply wasn't possible, because, women who...'

'Don't say any more, Jenny,' said Cecília, breaking in and almost sealing her friend's lips with her hand. Then true to her impulsive, expansive nature, her eyes filled with tears that ran, one by one, down her cheeks.

'As you see, Cecília,' said Jenny fondly, 'Carlos was quite wrong, and it was all entirely his fault. So don't upset yourself any more. There's no need. It was just a girlish escapade, with no unpleasant consequences, except for the one that not even that heaven-sent inspiration could save you from. And if that makes you cry, what tears will you have left when you experience some real misfortune?'

'Jenny, promise that you'll never tell anyone that it was me...'

'Don't worry, very soon even I will have forgotten.'

'Oh, just the thought of it!'

Jenny quickly managed to calm the sudden storm clouding Cecília's thoughts, and to divert her attention onto other matters.

By the time Cecília left Mr Richard's house, she and Jenny had enjoyed a good laugh together, and when Cecília entered her own house, her mind was at rest and she breathed with the ease of her eighteen years and her naturally tranquil nature.

A fortunate age, and a fortunate heart!

XIII

Oporto Life

Manuel Quintino lived in a street near the west end of the city, safely removed from the worst of the hurly-burly, a hurly-burly which, from three in the afternoon until six in the morning, he always found unbearable. Indeed, Manuel Quintino's tastes were of such diurnal regularity they resembled a meteorological instrument.

As soon as the sun rose behind the hills visible in the distance through his bedroom windows, he would grow impatient with the quietness of the area in which he lived and be seized by a feverish desire to work; he was never tempted to stay and listen to the morning chirruping of the birds in the trees in the garden, unless, of course, it was a Sunday or a public holiday; it was as if he found more harmony in the cries of the vendors filling the streets in the centre of town. However, as evening came on, his heart would begin to be filled with domestic longings; he would start to loathe the office, Rua dos Ingleses, the hubbub in the squares, and to sigh, like an expatriate, for the joy of returning home, where, from his dining-room balcony, he would watch ecstatically the magnificent spectacle of the setting sun sinking into the ocean with all the pleasure of someone in a box at the theatre transfixed by the glorious final act of some sacred drama.

The interior of Manuel Quintino's house had an air of well-being and comfort that seemed almost about to cross the line into outright luxury.

This was made possible by the salary that Manuel Quintino, as chief book-keeper, received from Mr Richard, who often added a few extra crumbs to the agreed amount.

We should add that Cecília's economical spirit and intelligent management of funds were also a major contribution. In her capable hands – accustomed to managing domestic affairs from a very young age – their incomings and outgoings were so scrupulously regulated that what he earned was sufficient not only for life's necessities, but even for what one might term certain superfluities.

It hardly seems necessary to add that Manuel Quintino idolised Cecília, who was the focus of all his affections. She was only six when her mother died, leaving Cecília entirely in his care, and he still mourned his wife's passing; while surrounding his innocent child with assiduous care and affection, in a truly maternal fashion, his love for his daughter had grown so strong that it had become the criterion for all his other emotions.

Nothing was too good for Cecília.

He had worked hard to bring her up well and took immense pleasure in watching that lovely child grow in life, intelligence and kindness, the child beside whose cradle he had watched during many nights, pondering her future.

Gradually, he had allowed himself to be overtaken by a feeling of respect and veneration for his daughter, a feeling that bordered almost on idolatry.

He always carried with him, like a miraculous talisman, a lock of Cecília's fair hair; and he filed away the briefest and most mundane of notes she sent to him while he was at the office as if these were relics that it would have been sacrilege to lose.

Manuel Quintino had his childish traits, but these would have provoked laughter only in those who did not share them. For example, he could be moved almost to tears by some affectionate phrase in that trivial correspondence. It filled him with joy to read at the beginning of a note: 'Dearest Father' or 'My dear Father' or, at the end, 'Your loving daughter' or 'Your obedient daughter'. On an irresistible impulse, he would press his lips to those words and kiss them fervently.

As we have seen, he carried out his work in the office with such composure and regularity that he appeared to be a man little given to emotional outpourings, and yet if, in the middle of his daily tasks, he happened to think of Cecília, he would become like a child again.

He would put down his pen, abandon the accounts or the letter he was writing or whatever it was he was busy with, and gleefully rub his hands together, like a schoolboy suddenly remembering that the holidays will soon be upon him.

Sometimes, he could not resist striding up and down the office, humming, then walking over to the window, his pen behind his ear, to gauge the height of the sun in the sky.

When he returned home, Manuel Quintino never lingered in the streets, but always took the emptier lanes and alleyways, to avoid any chance encounters that might make him late for his usual afternoon chat with his daughter.

When anyone mentioned some epidemic about to threaten the city, he would be filled with genuine terror, as was more than evident from the look on his face, and this had given him a reputation among his younger colleagues as somewhat pusillanimous; indeed, they even made fun of him, deliberately prompting such panic reactions, not realising how cruel they were being.

It wasn't the thought of any risk to himself that made him grow pale; he had only one fear, one tormenting idea, and that was the potential risk to Cecília's life.

You cannot imagine the madness that ensued when she did once fall ill. For the very first time, the smooth working of the office was disrupted, and the letters, on whose immaculate appearance Manuel Quintino so prided himself, frequently left his hands all stained with tears. On the day that the beaming doctor told him that Cecília was on the mend, Manuel Quintino could not help but fling himself, laughing and crying, into the doctor's arms, calling him his benefactor, and even kissing him.

This crisis had only exacerbated his already intense fatherly devotion.

Manuel Quintino was perhaps too frugal as regards himself, which is why, among his friends, he had acquired an undeserved reputation as a miser, and yet not a Saturday passed without him returning home without some treat, some gift for Cecília, despite her tenderly disapproving comments and her rather unconvincing tut-tutting.

He would often turn a blind eye, as the saying goes, to the threadbare elbows or gaping seams on his own jacket, to his sadly battered silk hat, purely in order to save a little money and buy a shawl, a new armchair or a new dress for Cecília!

Only after repeated hints, requests and even affectionate threats on the part of his daughter, only after she had exhausted all her eloquence, would Manuel Quintino decide, at last, to look to himself and attend to his own needs.

Cecília's most effective ploy was to ask him to accompany her to some public place. Since he could refuse her nothing, he would promise and think and scratch his head and examine his ancient suit, screw up his nose and grumble, but, on the appointed day, he would duly appear in a brand-new outfit, to serve as escort to his daughter.

What worked this miracle and overcame his modest repugnance was the mere idea of embarrassing her in public.

Cecília knew she was the object of his worship, and repaid him by heaping him with fond attentions, and this, for her father, was supreme happiness.

Any reader accustomed to spending the evening at the theatre, at balls or at social gatherings will find it hard to imagine the deep pleasure with which Manuel Quintino would watch darkness fall and the first pale stars appear in the sky.

He was preparing himself for one of the quiet pleasures unfamiliar to those who lead more turbulent lives, but to which all human temperaments and characters could easily succumb were they ever to enjoy an extended period of such delights.

It is easier and far more common for someone to make a transition from a tumultous, frantic, vagabond life to the monotonous pleasures of domesticity than the other way round, as if the latter were mankind's natural inclination.

Manuel Quintino's evenings, his beloved evenings, were so uniform that, if I describe one, you will, with a few rare exceptions, know them all.

The evening and night of the day we have already told you about provides a perfect example.

After supper, Manuel Quintino would sit on his west-facing balcony and watch the spectacle of the dying day and feast his eyes on the gardens, mansions, houses and avenues of that vast panorama bordered by the silvery sea.

It was a rainy afternoon, but the southwest wind had succeeded in breaking up the thick mantle of cloud covering the sky, to reveal a little blue in the heavenly vault, thus allowing the setting sun to tinge with gold the few remaining clouds hugging the horizon.

Cecília's domestic duties only occasionally allowed her to join him on the balcony, but when she did, she would rest one arm on the back of her father's chair and point out some particularly beautiful detail of that vast picture, which he, with his unanalytical brain, could only appreciate as a whole.

'Look at that pink cloud. Doesn't it remind you of a bird with its wings spread?' Cecília would say, indicating a cloud touched by the fiery light of the sun.

'A bird?' Manuel Quintino would exclaim, staring at the chosen cloud. 'In what way does it resemble a bird, my dear?'

'Look, there's the head, there's one wing and the other wing. It's even more like a bird now, because you can make out its tail.'

'Well, to be perfectly honest...' murmured Manuel Quintino, still unable to see the resemblance.

'Honestly, Pa! Can you really not see? Where are you looking?'

And Cecília would place her lovely head next to her father's, so close that he would seize the opportunity to plant a kiss on her forehead.

'That one over there. Doesn't it look like a bird to you?' Cecília insisted.

'Ah, yes, now I see it,' he would cry, having at last seen the resemblance. 'Yes. And what a long beak it has! Who'd have thought it!'

'Could you come and help, Miss?'

This was the maid Antónia requiring Cecília's advice on some tricky domestic matter. Antónia was such a typical maidservant that there seems no need to describe her.

Cecília withdrew from the balcony. Manuel Quintino remained, his eyes fixed on the place his daughter had shown him, until the pink cloud lost all colour and shape.

He then sat quietly and pondered his happiness.

A few moments later, Cecília crept up behind him and covered his eyes with her hands, asking: 'Guess who it is.'

'That's easy enough!' answered Manuel Quintino. 'I'd recognise those hands anywhere. It's the water-seller.'

'Oh, really!' Cecília exclaimed, laughing. 'But what is it you find so fascinating that you didn't even hear me creep up on you?'

'I was looking at some building work going on over there. If I'm not mistaken, that's Counsellor Arantes' place.'

'Look at those trees and those houses. Don't you fancy sitting in the shade of those oak trees?'

'It's not impossible. If you'd like to…'

'So you promise to take me there?'

'I'll promise you anything you want.'

'Be careful what you say! I might ask for something difficult.'

'Oh, I'm used to your demands.'

'Are you? Well, then, there is something I'd like you to do.'

'It has to be something big.'

'Oh, it is, and will you promise you'll do it?'

'What is it?'

'Do you promise?'

'Tell me what it is first.'

'No, you have to promise.'

'You know I never refuse you anything.'

'So why not promise, then?'

'All right, I promise.'

'Do you give me your word?'

'Yes, I give you my word,' said Manuel Quintino, laughing.

'Well, what I would like you to do,' said Cecília, stroking

her father's white hair, 'is to buy a new umbrella, because the one you've got is just...'

'Oh, I thought it would be something bigger than that!'

'It doesn't matter, because you promised.'

'Yes, but listen...'

'No, I have things to do.'

And she rushed off to avoid any possible excuses he might make, saying: 'I'm not listening. You promised.'

Shortly afterwards, it was her father's turn to call to her: 'Cecília, Cecília, come quickly! There's a steamship.'

Cecília ran to the balcony.

'Do you see it?'

'Now I'm just like you were with that cloud.'

'Can't you see? Look, there, to the right of that chimney, in the gap between the pine trees.'

'Ah, yes, now I see it. Is it arriving or leaving?'

'Arriving, and with the river as high as it is too! It's an English ship. Bring me my telescope.'

'No, it's nearly dark, and you won't see a thing. Besides, it's getting cold. Perhaps you'd better close the window and come downstairs. I've got work to do and need to light the lamps a little earlier than usual.'

'In that case, let's go downstairs.'

There then began an even more agreeable pastime for the worthy book-keeper.

They went down to the room next to Manuel Quintino's bedroom, a modestly furnished room, but every detail of which revealed Cecília's good taste. Nothing in it was showy or expensive, but nor was there anything vulgar or excessive or jarring. Everything was clean and comfortable and a pleasure to contemplate.

Manuel Quintino sat down at his desk in a very patriarchal

armchair; Cecília brought a lamp, closed the windows, took up her sewing basket and came and sat next to her father.

Manuel Quintino would tell her about something that had happened at the office, and Cecília would reciprocate, telling him what had happened in the house in his absence.

That evening, he spoke a great deal about Carlos, about his pranks, his idleness, the blunders he'd caused him to make in the letter he was writing, the business with the rum, Mr Richard's love for his son, and, above all, the lad's good heart.

Cecília listened attentively, never asking any questions, and never looking up from her sewing.

At this point, the door bell rang.

'Ah, there's my man,' said Manuel Quintino.

'Antónia, take a lamp and show him up,' cried Cecília.

Antónia's heavy footsteps could be heard going down the stairs, then there was a brief exchange of words at the front door, the footsteps of two people coming up, and, finally, the man for whom Manuel Quintino seemed to be waiting entered the room, taking off his hat and greeting those present with his usual words: 'A very good evening to you, Senhor Manuel Quintino, and a very good evening to you too, my dear.'

'My man' was a neighbour and friend of Manuel Quintino's, one who had, for many years, been in the habit of visiting each evening to read the newspaper, drink tea and hold the most soporific and rambling of conversations imaginable with the book-keeper, until, at the stroke of nine, he would wrap himself up in the woollen shawl he took with him everywhere as a precaution. His name was José Fortunato, and he had once been a dealer in cereals; now he was an owner of several properties, an issuer of credit notes, a fellow of quiet habits and conservative ideas, modest in dress, discreet in manner, whose favourite supper was a hearty stew, and whose greatest extravagance was the occasional purchase of a lobster to eat with salad.

He was a strict observer of commercial laws and rigorous in his accounts, to the point where one might even paraphrase a line from the Lord's Prayer: May they repay their debts to us, Lord, as we repay our creditors.

This daily visit to Manuel Quintino had become a necessity for Senhor Fortunato, and his presence and conversation, although hardly enlivening, were equally necessary to Manuel Quintino, who had reached the age when old habits rule and we are far less inclined to shape our lives to the demands of new habits.

After the usual exchange of greetings, José Fortunato sat down next to Manuel Quintino, and they launched into a dialogue which, as the reader will appreciate, had very few variations, and went more or less like this: 'Awfully cold, Senhor Fortunato,' said one.

'And rainy too,' replied the other, making himself comfortable. 'Were you in town today?'

A pointless question.

'I was.'

'So, what news?'

'Oh, nothing much.'

'Is the river still very high?'

'It seems to be subsiding a little.'

'Terrible weather.'

'And the chaos it's caused!'

'Mind you, I prefer the cold,' Manuel Quintino would add a few moments later.

'To be honest, so do I. I don't really mind the winter at all. My appetite's better then. But I can't shift this bronchitis.'

And to demonstrate this, he would cough.

This, more or less, is what they said each and every day.

'Terrible for the farmers, though.'

'The prices are through the roof.'

'And the meat!'

'They've sold all our cattle abroad! There should be a law against it.'

A piece of economic advice that remains fashionable today.

'Things are going from bad to worse!'

It was with this golden key that they almost always closed their dialogue. Then they would both fall silent.

Cecília, who was waiting for that silence and knew what it meant, would then go and fetch the day's newspaper and prepare to read, while the two old gentlemen prepared to listen.

They both took an indefinable pleasure in hearing Cecília read.

She read with such grace and intelligence that Senhor José Fortunato confessed that he often understood things that, despite his best efforts, he had entirely failed to grasp when reading on his own.

It was a curious scene.

Out of fatherly compassion, Manuel Quintino would let her off reading the small ads, and so that compliant young woman would read the editorial somewhat reluctantly, the foreign news more intrepidly, the local news with a certain curiosity, the *feuilleton* rather more willingly, and everything else as fluently as possible, so as not to spoil her listeners' pleasure.

Cecília's nature did not always allow her to proceed without making some comment on what she read. She would interrupt a high-flown apologia from the government with an aside that would have provoked a ministerial crisis had it been spoken in parliament, a violent, acerbically oppositionist diatribe that challenged ideas neutralising the antigovernmental contagion that was beginning to gnaw away at Senhor José Fortunato's profound belief in order.

The reader will be aware, I'm sure, that, at the time, public curiosity was monopolised by what was happening in the Crimean War.

Cecília was obliged to read the descriptions of the carnage that filled the newspapers every day, and she always did so with a frown of displeasure.

Manuel Quintino was on the side of the allies, while José Fortunato supported the Russian cause, although neither of them knew quite why. Cecília was always on the side of the dead and wounded.

One day, she stopped in the middle of a description of one of the bloodiest encounters between the two armies to ask her father what had triggered that implacable war.

Manuel Quintino was considerably embarrassed by this question and glanced at Senhor José Fortunato as if hoping that he might help; however, all Senhor Fortunato could say was this: 'The war started because of certain… things.'

Cecília did not press him further, but that evening, she read: 'During the night, the Russians fire on the allies' camp, but the latter do not respond.'

'They're afraid,' said Senhor José Fortunato with a smile.

'No, it's a strategy!' said Manuel Quintino with the air of someone privy to a mystery.

'However,' Cecília read on, 'the allies respond during the day with great success.'

'You see, didn't I say so? It was a strategy,' exclaimed Manuel Quintino.

'Pure luck,' retorted Senhor José with a scornful shrug.

'The soldiers,' Cecília continued, 'are begging the general in charge to go into battle,' and when she finished reading this, she pulled a face.

'Let them!' said Senhor José Fortunato, like a man who knew everything there was to know about the army's resources.

'In Sebastopol, there are 2,000 cannon,' Cecília read.

José Fortunato looked at his friend with a provocative, triumphant expression on his face, almost as if he were urging him to attack and putting himself forward as the defender of those auxiliaries.

Then Cecília read that Vasif Pasha had taken command of the Asian army, and it was the turn of Manuel Quintino to repay his friend's arrogance, as if he had great confidence in Vasif and the field operations of the Asian army. This triumphal look only grew when he heard that, on 30th January, Ulrich, of whom he had never heard, had left for Crimea with the French imperial guard. To compensate for his alarm at this assault, José Fortunato could only cling to the news that there were 6,000 Russians in Pruth.

Local news, however, was neutral territory where her audience's curiosities were free of conflict.

One thing that Cecília could not forgive was the frivolous way in which the local reporters treated certain very serious matters, for example, a poor man being put in jail, a domestic disturbance, a suicide attempt. She grew impatient with this and proposed a vote of censure, which was seconded by both Manuel Quintino and José Fortunato.

The newspaper at the time was full of descriptions of disasters caused by the flooding of the Douro.

It was with great consternation that Cecília read these tales of misfortune. She was moved most of all by a truly tragic incident, which some Oporto residents may still remember. The brother of a pilot on one of the ships overwhelmed by the flood waters had completely lost his reason when, having failed to rescue his brother, he was obliged to watch him drown, a double tragedy that proved a death blow to their elderly father. Manuel Quintino, who knew all about fatherly love, furtively wiped away a tear, but José Fortunato, even though he was basically a good-hearted soul, would sometimes make dismissive comments about such stories, comments that would have tried the patience of a saint.

Hearing Cecília read that story, he said: 'Oh, it's all made up. Sometimes the people who write those stories...'

'Made up? Oh, please, Senhor Fortunato!' cried Cecília impatiently. 'Remember, it was one brother trying to save another and then having to watch him drown, and a father losing both his sons. Isn't that reason enough to die or go mad?'

'Well, the other brother shouldn't have put himself in danger, he should have thought...'

'He should have thought? Who can think anything at such moments? Really, Senhor Fortunato, you do have some odd ideas!'

Senhor Fortunato was already regretting having spoken.

'On a slightly lesser scale,' added Manuel Quintino, 'some time ago, Carlos, my boss' son, risked his life in Foz. He spotted a small rowing boat adrift in the river, with two small children in charge, one of whom didn't even know how to swim; and Carlos, who was on the beach, trying to catch seagulls with some other English friends – something he still likes to do – didn't hesitate. He dived in like a fish and saved both children. Then he continued his hunting, soaked to the skin, and he was there for ages, and could easily have caught his death of cold.'

Cecília was so absorbed in reading some other item in the newspaper, which she was holding really close to her eyes, that she didn't seem to be listening to her father's story. And yet, as soon as Senhor José Fortunato, having heard the tale, said in his usual abrupt way: 'Ridiculous!' Cecília immediately raised her head and, blushing, looked daggers at him.

I don't know quite how to explain that look in someone who was apparently so distracted, a look that had no consequences either, because she immediately went back to reading the *feuilleton*.

Manuel Quintino listened to this with eyes drooping, but any writers of *feuilletons* should not take this amiss. José Fortunato, on the other hand, listened with passionate attention, for Cecília's way of reading had given him a taste for novels. He now felt a real passion for those adventures. It was a point of faith with him that everything described there had really happened and all the various characters had really existed or were still alive. This is why he criticised those imagined heroes with the same violence and praised them with the same enthusiasm as if they were real members of society.

Once she had read the *feuilleton*, Cecília passed the newspaper over to Senhor Fortunato and went to make the tea, while Senhor Fortunato read the small ads and Manuel Quintino drifted off to sleep.

Afterwards, the two would begin a dialogue full of highly infectious yawns, unsurprising given the subjects under discussion. Here is the programme for that evening:

Part One: – Fortunato opens the conversation with a deep sigh. – Manuel Quintino responds, saying that Fortunato has nothing to complain about – 'Neither have you for that matter,' says Fortunato – 'Oh, I have more than enough reasons to complain,' replies Manuel Quintino. Two long yawns on both sides, then a pause.

Part Two: – Manuel Quintino mentions that he keeps getting headaches. Fortunato attributes it to the weather and rubs his eyes. Manuel Quintino says he's more inclined to think it's his stomach. Fortunato advises him not to drink coffee in the morning. Reciprocal yawns.

Part Three: – Looking up, Senhor Fortunato remarks that the room has a very low ceiling. Manuel Quintino responds by saying that, given the size of the room, it's fine. Senhor Fortunato makes some remark about the advantages of stucco. Manuel Quintino agrees and tries to move the conversation on to the vexed subject of landlords; Fortunato responds with a diatribe against housekeepers. A yawn appears in Manuel Quintino's mouth and is instantly transmitted to José Fortunato.

Part Four: – Fortunato comments that Carnival is nearly over. – Manuel Quintino replies that he won't mind in the least. – Fortunato agrees. – Manuel Quintino takes a dim view of the arrival of Lent, because this will mean having to go to confession. They discuss who are the most indulgent confessors. Manuel Quintino wonders who invented confession. Fortunato blames the Romans, which is as far back in history as he can go.

This time, their yawns are interrupted by the arrival of Cecília and Antónia bearing the tea tray.

Fortunato is positively transformed, cheered by the sight of the toast and the hot milk. But what do you expect? It wasn't that he needed to eat, but the sight stirred his gustatory sensibilities and, thanks to the mysterious links between the physical and the moral, he was finally at one with his soul.

That inner satisfaction revealed itself in compliments addressed to the domestic Hebe serving that ambrosia – Senhora Antónia.

'You look younger every day, Senhora Antónia,' he said.

'Really, Senhor Fortunato, I'm fast nearing the end.'

'The end? Why you've barely started...'

I don't know if it was Senhor Fortunato's intention to end his sentence there, since the sense remained somewhat obscure. And the reason I don't know is because, at this point, Cecília interrupted him, saying: 'Have you got enough sugar, Senhor Fortunato?'

'I do, but perhaps just another little spoonful... that's it, one more, and that's it.'

After they had all resumed their respective positions, Senhor Fortunato began to speak, mixing the words in his mouth with tea and milk, with toast and cakes.

'I'm dying to see if that delinquent escapes from prison.'

'Who's been put in prison?' asked Manuel Quintino, who, having briefly dozed off, didn't know his friend was talking about the novel being serialised in the newspaper.

'Didn't you hear?' said Senhor Fortunato, swiftly devouring another cake. 'She was well and truly taken in, that's the fact of the matter. Because the man, it seems, didn't know that the stranger was the girl's father, so he was astonished when the other fellow turned up, all dressed in black, and said...' – And here Senhor Fortunato put on a gruff voice: – "I am the last of your victims!" And then the son found out, because he'd known nothing about it until then. He discovered that the sister of the *comendador*'s friend had provided the money they'd given to the scribe's brother-in-law's widow.'

Manuel Quintino was mechanically stirring his tea, staring open-mouthed at his friend and not understanding a word he said, despite all Senhor Fortunato's dramatic gesturings.

'I haven't the foggiest idea what you're talking about.'

'Weren't you listening?' said his friend. 'They had agreed that, as soon as the ship left, the boy would be accused of stealing the *comendador's* money, which is why they told the dead man's aunt and uncle that the jewels were found in trunk of the stranger's squire, but…'

'Who the devil are this ragbag of people?' exclaimed Manuel Quintino impatiently.

'You obviously weren't paying attention,' said Senhor Fortunato, whose natural lack of eloquence became even more marked when it came to setting out the tangled plot concocted by a French novelist.

Cecília, who hadn't initially been listening to this comic dialogue, could not resist bursting out laughing.

'But where did all this happen, man?' asked Manuel Quintino.

'In Paris, of course…'

'Senhor Fortunato is talking about a novel, Pa.'

'Oh, I see.'

'What did you think he was doing?'

'I have no idea. I don't understand novels. But now that I think about it, that rascal Carlos was saying he would lend me some to read. He's such a card.'

'And a wastrel too!' said Senhor Fortunato, who was of the party who believed Carlos to be a dangerous man.

'No, he's not. He's a very kind soul!' said Manuel Quintino. 'What could anyone possibly have against him? He'd give the shirt off his back to help a beggar. Once, in broad daylight, I saw him leading his horse into the city and, sitting on the saddle, was a poor old lady he'd met on the road and who had broken her ankle; and there was another occasion… Cecília, are you daydreaming or something? Senhor Fortunato has been sitting there with an empty cup for ages now.'

'Oh, I'm sorry,' said Cecília, blushing at her own absent-mindedness.

I don't quite know why she was blushing, but she was.

Senhor Fortunato, who, for some time, had been coughing

and sighing to attract her attention to both himself and his cup, said politely: 'Oh, there's no hurry.'

Manuel Quintino continued to heap praise on Carlos.

'As for that business with the old lady,' said Fortunato, taking another cup of tea from Cecília, 'that was just him showing off...'

'More sugar?' said Cecília rather sharply, and again I don't quite know how to explain this sharpness, since it was so contrary to her usual mild manner.

Senhor Fortunato noticed.

'Thank you, my dear,' he said. 'Just another little spoonful. That's it.'

'It was nothing of the sort, Senhor Fortunato,' said Manuel Quintino. 'You obviously don't know Carlos. He's never been one to show off. Even as a child...'

'Have one of these cakes, Pa,' said Cecília in such an affectionate way that her father could not help but feel touched.

'Don't worry about me, my dear, I'll help myself.'

'Then again,' Manuel Quintino went on, 'he has got into some bad habits, that's true.'

'Antónia, pour Senhor Fortunato some more tea, will you,' said Cecília brusquely, an order that surprised everyone, and again, I don't know how to explain it.

'Oh, that's just the folly of youth,' said Manuel Quintino. 'But he has a very good heart.'

'But a man who has no direction in life...'

'There are plenty of heartless people at the head of large establishments, Senhor Fortunato. Having a career is no guarantee of probity!'

'I know that, my dear, but...'

'But, my friend,' said Manuel Quintino, 'what no one can deny is that he's a good man. Many young men do far worse

179

things and with far less justification…'

The conversation continued, and Carlos was mentioned frequently. Cecília, however, chose not to participate.

Tea was over. The talk grew less heated. Manuel Quintino could feel sleep beckoning, and José Fortunato could feel his food digesting. Cecília was sewing and sometimes sat staring at the lamp, as if the light were offering her new qualities worthy of examination. The clock struck nine.

'Right, time to go home,' said José Fortunato, getting up.

'Wrap up warm,' said Manuel Quintino.

'Antónia, bring a lamp, will you,' said Cecília.

And having said his farewells, Senhor Fortunato went down the stairs, chatting about chilblains to Antónia on the way. Then he walked back to his own house, where his imagination would insist on recalling Cecília's sweet face and everything she had said to him.

'She seemed in rather an odd mood tonight,' he thought as he got into bed, for a perfidious passion had, for some time, been eating away at the poor man.

Manuel Quintino had to get up early the next day, and so he went to bed shortly after Fortunato had left.

This time the dialogue between father and daughter went like this: 'Senhor Fortunato can be a bit of a trial sometimes!'

'He's certainly a stick-in-the-mud.'

'The things he comes out with… Anyway, goodnight, Pa.'

'And a very goodnight to you, my dear. God bless you.'

Cecília then went to her room.

As the reader knows, Cecília had gone to bed very late the previous night, and yet she wasn't sleepy at all. She appeared to be still dazed after the ball. She was going over and over in her head everything that Carlos had said to her as well as what he had later told Jenny. Then she thought about Senhor

180

Fortunato's comments, about her father's words and the stories he had told about Carlos. Finally, she succumbed to sleep, not that this helped. Sleep can sometimes be more exhausting than lying awake. Our dreams engage in a kind of battle that leaves us drained of energy.

Cecília imagined she was in a boat on a river being swept along by the rushing current down to the sea. She was in real danger, and the boat was full of people in fancy dress, dancing. Cecília was screaming, but couldn't hear her own screams. The oarsman was Senhor Fortunato, and somehow he was managing to row and drink tea at the same time. Then Carlos arrived, leading a horse, but even more surprising was that he was walking across the water. Carlos was trying to save her and pull her out of the boat, but Senhor Fortunato and the passengers in fancy-dress wouldn't let him. Except that Senhor Fortunato was no longer Senhor Fortunato, but one of the characters in the novel that had made such an impression on him, and the sea wasn't exactly the sea, because it was surrounded by boxes as if they were at the theatre. And yet the danger continued, although she didn't know exactly how or why, and now she was running away from Carlos.

Finally, the dream turned into a jumble of all the elements of the various events and matters that had been preoccupying Cecília all day.

Much to Manuel Quintino's distress, Cecília woke the next morning, looking pale and tired.

XIV

A Crisis Looms

While Cecília was spending that evening quietly at home, Carlos was eagerly doing the rounds of all the theatres and dance halls in search of the masked woman he had met the previous night.

Jenny had noticed the impatience with which her brother waited for night to fall, and when she saw him about to go out, she said rather pointedly: 'Goodnight, Charles, I don't imagine you'll be coming home at four o'clock in the morning again.'

'Who knows, Jenny.'

'I can sense it.'

In fact, it wasn't yet two o'clock when, grown weary of looking in vain for that unknown woman, Carlos Whitestone returned home in a distinctly bad mood.

Jenny heard him come in and smiled to herself, thinking: 'Thank heavens Carnival is over. In a couple of days' time, his mind will be on other things.'

Carnival had indeed ended, and those days devoted to unbridled madness and folly gave way to a time of penitence and sermons.

As to which of the two contains more truths concealed behind false appearances, I will leave it to the moralists to decide. The time for wearing veils not masks was about to begin, and, on Fridays, piety and fashion would lead the crowds to the church of São João Novo, and on Sundays, half the city would spill out into the suburbs to watch the procession of the Stations of the Cross and hear the closing sermon.

Carlos spent almost the whole of Ash Wednesday morning at home.

Contrary to expectations, he was still haunted by the memory of that mysterious woman in a mask; his annoyance at having allowed her to escape, leaving him with not a single clue as to how he might one day find out who she was, would not let him rest. He kept racking his brain for some solution to the problem, but none came to the aid of his tormented imagination.

In the end, he left the house with no idea why or where he was going; instead of seeking out the most crowded parts of town, where he could usually be seen and heard, he headed aimlessly off in the opposite direction and, after a while, found himself walking through the pine woods surrounding the far end of Rua da Boavista, which had not yet been built on.

Given his essentially urban life, he so rarely found himself among trees and away from people, especially at that hour of the day, that it made a very singular impression on him.

It was like a new world, and such a short distance from home too!

He plunged into the woods and fields, until he lost sight of the road. Then he stopped. In his current state of mind, it did not take one of Nature's great spectacles to arouse in him the kind of thoughts to which poets are so often prone.

The vastness of the sea, the broad horizon viewed from atop a mountain, the roar of a waterfall cascading down into a valley can overwhelm and give food for thought even to those least inclined to abstract ruminations.

If, however, the mind of a man is already filled with a

ferment of poetry or in the grip of melancholy, which is another form of poetry, it takes very little stimulus to produce great effects.

A crawling insect or a worm snaking along through dried leaves, a fallen acorn being swept downstream, a ray of sunlight glowing on the marvellous web woven by a spider on a gorse bush, the slavish opening and closing of sea anemones in rock pools on the beach, and other such phenomena – which make no impression on anyone who sees them while his mind is on other things – are nourishment enough for more refined imaginations.

Carlos' imagination was currently predisposed to such subtle impressions and, since he rarely experienced them, he received them with redoubled intensity.

It was about three o'clock on one of those rare beautiful February afternoons. There was a freshness about the countryside, the sense of life reborn we always get when bright sunshine follows long days of rain. There wasn't a cloud in the sky, the blue undimmed by so much as a transparent veil of mist. The pine trees were silent, as if, in the belief that it must already be Spring, they were listening to the birds; the wind was so gentle that it barely stirred the shifting leaves of those trees untouched by Winter. So peaceful was it, that the smoke from the nearby rustic houses rose in slow, straight columns, with not a breeze to trouble them, until they dispersed into the upper air.

From where he was, Carlos could clearly hear the voice of country girls calling in the cattle, laughing or singing.

Those voices came from far away, but, given the silence and stillness of the hour, they reached him clearly and distinctly.

Carlos felt utterly charmed by all this.

'I must be mad,' he thought, 'to think that I'm making the

most of my youth by spending my days as I do. People would usually say of a young man leading my kind of existence that he was enjoying life to the full. But how exactly do I spend my time? In the suffocating atmosphere of a café, in the stalls at the theatre, where people talk and think of everything except the beauty of art, in tedious social gatherings, hanging about on street corners or in fashionable shops. Oh, yes, what could be better! And the mind that we feel beating and stirring in us when we're young grows dull and lethargic, becomes incapable of giving us certain pleasures for which our senses were intended. And then people say of someone who has voluntarily deprived himself of these most pleasing of sensations that he really knew how to enjoy life!'

Carlos was saying or, rather, thinking this as he ventured further into the pine wood, breathing in great lungfuls of the balmy air.

'I'm not even sure,' he thought, 'how it is that I can still feel such pleasure at finding myself alone here. When you lead the kind of life I lead, you lose the ability to savour solitude, and yet it's possible that here the imagination is at its most subtle…'

You can see, dear readers, where the attractions of this rustic solitude were leading Carlos!

His ideas really were undergoing a transformation, for they seemed to be racing along, under full sail, seduced by the pleasures of the reclusive life. However, a less misanthropic, more sociable thought made them change direction.

'No,' he decided, 'it isn't enough just to feel, we need to communicate our feelings to others, and tree trunks are hardly the most appropriate of confidantes. Everything needs to be reflected back if it is not to be lost in the immensity of everything; in a vast space, light dissipates and sound fades, feelings, too, seem to grow weaker if there is no other heart to reflect and reinforce them. That's why the presence of a friend... ah, but what friends do I have?'

Seeing him preparing to answer this question, I tremble for Carlos' supposed friends.

'Take F., for example,' he went on, 'whose friendship wouldn't survive me pointing out to him the first *non sequitur* in a serialised novel; or C. who would break off his friendship with me if I were foolish enough to criticise some minor fault in his riding technique; or L. who would abandon a friend as soon as he saw him setting off along a path that might put him at risk of muddying his patent-leather boots... and the others are just the same. I certainly wouldn't choose one of them as my companion on these sentimental journeys.'

There he broke off to observe a small, nimble lizard, which fled in terror at his approach, and then, with bright, glittering eyes, continued to watch his every move from the hole where it had taken shelter. Carlos found this ordinary event absolutely fascinating. Then he walked on, still deep in thought: 'If I were to say to one of those friends that I had paused to observe a small reptile running through the ferns and over the mossy stones of that wall, they would laugh at my innocence, would call me downright soppy... There are certain kinds of sensibility that you simply can't confide to anyone else, unless... unless you do so to a feminine heart. Women do have a certain sublimely child-like quality, but, no, they're as bad as my male friends. When I think of some of the women I've been in love with, what do I see? S. is so highly strung she would faint at the mere sight of a lizard... hers is the sensibility of the dressing-table; C. is as hard as nails, and the only thing that would move her is an earthquake, like the one that shook Lisbon; and E. is a drawing-room beauty, who rises at midday and admires Nature... in gardens, of course, and her only regret is that there's no one around to *see* her admiring Nature; and the same is true of all the others and of me as well, but perhaps if I were to look elsewhere...'

At this point, his meditations took a different turn. Just a few steps further on, he was thinking: 'By laughing, in company, at real, disinterested love, at happily married couples, at family life, I have almost allowed myself to be persuaded that my laughter was genuine. And yet, when I think about it, if I make the most of these rare moments when I'm being frank and open with myself...'

The reader doubtless knows where such thoughts can lead when you follow the path Carlos is taking; especially, if, like him, you're in the middle of a wood and far from the hurlyburly of the city; if you do know this, then you won't be surprised to find that, just moments later, Carlos was thinking this: 'Real life, living in close communion with a woman whom you love like a lover, respect like a sister, venerate like a mother, protect like a daughter, is clearly man's natural fate, the completion of his mission on earth...'

Carlos Whitestone had just emerged on the opposite side of the wood when he formulated this thought, this profession of faith, which every twenty-year-old mind, however given over to wild living, must have come up with time and again.

The countryside there was less obscured by trees, and occupied instead by cultivated fields, vineyards, estates and their respective houses, some close together, others more scattered, and all rather lovely.

Carlos sat down on the low wall surrounding the wood. The horizon that lay before him was vast, but his gaze fixed on one of the most distant of those houses, even though his mind took no part in that apparent act of contemplation.

An English Family

That house had two floors, and what he could see from there was the rear of the house. The balcony on the first floor was all twined about with climbers growing up from the garden below. Between the two downstairs windows grew what appeared to be a large camellia bush. Some washing had been hung out to dry on a line that extended the length of the upstairs balcony.

As I said, Carlos' eyes lingered on the house quite unaccompanied by his thoughts, which were still absorbed in his meditations on man's purpose in life.

Moments later, though, something happened that provided a kind of link between the object of both his visual and mental contemplations, which met and fused in his examination of that modest house, on whose windows the sun had taken on the guise of a blazing fire.

It was nothing very extraordinary. A woman appeared on the upper balcony, that's all, but this woman, even though he could barely see her, was clearly still young, given her elegant figure and lively movements. And needless to say, his twenty-year-old imagination assumed she was also beautiful.

She had come out to check the washing, now blush-pink in the sun, removing some and replacing it with what she had brought out from indoors or else turning a sheet around to catch the sun's rays; now and then, she would interrupt her labours and look out at the fields, shading her eyes with one hand; at other times, she would turn round and appear to be talking to someone inside. She came and went, always intent on her work.

Carlos enjoyed watching that woman's comings and goings, and even though he could barely make out her appearance, he did not for one moment think she could possibly be a servant.

Having been dreaming of the charms of domestic bliss, he took pleasure now in imagining that house to contain one of those modest little worlds he felt so drawn to.

'She must be the wife, probably a newly-wed, taking great pains over her household duties,' he thought. 'It must be so indescribably pleasurable to feel cared for by such a person, to have someone devoted entirely to your happiness…'

At this point, he naturally thought of Jenny, albeit briefly; his imagination smiled affectionately at that sweet image, then abandoned it. His heart was not in a state to be satisfied only with the fond, sisterly smile that lit up Jenny's kind face. To his regret, he found himself aspiring to something more than that.

It was getting late, and still he lingered on, captivated by the sight of that house and that delightful balcony.

Finally, the windows were closed. It would not be long before the sun sank into the sea. Carlos realised then that it was time to go home.

He gave one final, almost yearning look at the balcony. His imperfect knowledge of that part of the city meant he couldn't even guess which street the house was in. And our natural discretion prevents us from supplying that detail.

Retracing his steps, and walking more briskly now, Carlos returned home.

When he was almost at the door to his house, he felt a hand on his shoulder. Turning, he saw that it was one of his friends.

'Where are you going, man?'

'Home.'

'Where have you been?'

'In the countryside.'

'Oh, so you've become a cultivator of the bucolic, have you, pastoral poetry and all that?'

'Occasionally, yes.'

'My condolences. Of the pastoral poets, Salomon Gessner

grew old, and Florian is sleeping the sleep of the inoffensive. By the way, have I ever shown you the essay I wrote about Serrão's book?'

'No, not yet.'

'Come to the Café Guichard tonight. The book is just a pretext really. What I'm trying to do is to describe modern literature, separating out the fields of romanticism and classicism, which have become rather confused. My approach is always to look for great revelations in small details, you see. And that is what I did this time too. And so, in this study, I used as my starting point just two words, one taken from Racine's *Berenice*, and the other from Victor Hugo's *Ruy Blas*. They are the final words of each of those two tragedies. Antiochus sees Berenice leaving and cries: *Hélas*! Ruy Blas dies in the queen's arms, murmuring *Merci*! That's all I need. *Hélas!* is the cry of pain and despair, of cowardice in the face of misfortune; it is the last word of a literature that has no confidence in the future, a literature that lives only in the past. *Merci!* on the other hand, is a cry of acceptance, hope, the reduction of suffering to the intoxicating essence of personal pain, which almost becomes pleasure, and is, therefore, the word worthy of a living literature with its eyes on the future...'

The lecture continued, and Carlos saw in his own feelings of impatience that he was in no mood to enjoy the company of his friends that night. He parted company with that particular friend as quickly as he could.

'I won't be going to the Café Guichard tonight. This time I will bow to Jenny's wishes, and I will stay at home,' he said to himself, as soon as he had managed to make his excuses and leave.

And he entered the house at precisely the moment when the bell for supper was being rung.

Seeing him come in and noticing his grave air, Jenny thought to herself: 'It's still too early to expect a complete recovery. We must be patient.'

XV

English Life

At first, supper passed in silence, as it usually did.

Despite his apparent air of satisfaction, Mr Richard set the tone for the evening, using only monosyllables and never taking the trouble to formulate a complete sentence when a single word would get his meaning across.

'Beef? Salami? Ham? Oysters?' This was his way of asking Carlos or Jenny which dish they would like to help themselves to.

'Mustard… Cheese… That… This… Bring… Remove… Take away.' Those were the orders issued to the servants, who all worked with an essentially British promptitude, seriousness and silence.

Carlos was no more talkative. As well as his natural disinclination to speak in his father's presence, he was not at all himself that evening, and in any other company his taciturn mood would doubtless have been thought strange.

In a very soft voice, Jenny also issued a few orders to the servants, and they diligently bent low to hear her; in the same soft voice, she made the occasional comment to Carlos and even ventured to ask her father a few questions, but without ever succeeding in sparking a general conversation.

All these things, the regular, efficient service, the servants' grave demeanour and immaculate uniforms, as well as the rather dim lighting, lent the whole affair a somewhat funereal air.

However, as the wine flowed and the various libations took their effect on Mr Richard's brain, he began to slough off that mood of glum gravity, and his tongue loosened, bringing to an end the reticence imposed on him by the rules of British etiquette.

This provided support for a view expressed by Fielding, a writer who rivalled Sterne as Mr Richard's literary favourite. According to the author of *Tom Jones*, wine brings out a man's true nature, a nature which, when sober, is often concealed by artifice. As we have said, Mr Richard was only superficially gloomy and was, basically, a rather jovial fellow, and, as supper progressed, that joviality rose to the surface.

Even with Jenny still present at the table, he began trying out a few jokes, retailing certain anecdotes from his life in London, describing childhood pranks and boyish japes.

Carlos did mischievously try to catch his sister's eye, but she discreetly avoided his, because they both knew these stories by heart, recurring as they always did in certain circumstances.

Whenever, over supper, Carlos saw that turkey was about to be served, he knew to expect the story of how, as a boy, Mr Richard, or Dick as he was known then, had, along with a few schoolmates, managed to steal a turkey from their teacher, Reverend Jackson, and had then, secretly, made a truly disgusting roast dinner.

A sirloin steak would inevitably evoke the apocryphal tale of the English king who, in an access of good humour, dubbed that delicious comestible a knight, hence the name Sir Loin.

A plate of hazelnuts always brought with it the story of a famous hazel tree in a park on the outskirts of London. As a boy, Mr Richard had often successfully climbed this tree, until one day, he slipped and was left dangling from a branch for several minutes.

Pudding was a pretext to speak of the monstrous pudding made in England at some popular celebration or other, and this, in turn, summoned up a whole long list of other national customs and notable festivals. Of these, the one given the most detailed description was Lord Mayor's Day, which was observed by the whole City of London as a holiday, on which the person elected to that lofty office was carried in procession to see the Lord Chancellor, in order for his election to be confirmed. Mr Richard knew and described every detail of the ceremony, as well as all the many officers who make up that remarkable corporation, from the Lord Mayor down to the most modest parish beadle.

As with the river pageant on the Thames held on that same day, Mr Richard was sometimes in danger of drowning, as the meticulous description of that event led on to another incident on the occasion of the riots that greeted George IV's plans to divorce, and this was followed by the story of that whole scandalous process, with the addition of various unedifying details about Queen Caroline and her favourite and secretary Bartolomeo Pergami.

Carlos would hear all this in silence, with an air of resignation and filial deference; Jenny managed to look interested, even if her mind was not as attentive as her face.

Jenny was the first to leave the table, according to the discreet custom that most people have adopted now, but which was originally British.

Then Mr Richard's libations only grew in number.

He would light a cigar and grow positively chatty, which he never was in any other situation.

Carlos would usually also become less constrained with his

father and, lighting a cigar of his own, would enter more easily into that dialogue.

On that evening, however, he remained rather withdrawn, almost distracted, in the face of Mr Richard's mounting garrulousness.

At some point during that rather drunken conversation, Mr Richard would infallibly mention his favourite book, Sterne's *Tristram Shandy*.

He loved everything about that eccentric book. He knew it almost by heart and, however many times he read it, it always made him laugh, even though it held no surprises for him.

Even before Carlos had read the book himself, he knew it through and through, thanks to his father's habit of quoting from it daily. Carlos, however, was obliged to listen as if it were all new to him.

Tristram's father's philosophical dissertations, Uncle Toby's military inventions and mad escapades, Corporal Trim's clever exploits, the wild, interminable ramblings of Tristram, the supposed autobiographer – Mr Richard would mention all these things with enthusiasm and vivacity.

He never skipped over any of the racier, not to say Rabelaisian, episodes or speeches, capable of offending more innocent ears. Indeed, the episode detailing Uncle Toby's encounter with Widow Wadman and the amorous encounters of his faithful comrade were among his favourite passages and the ones that made him laugh most heartily.

Lamps were brought in, and the conversation continued, sometimes in ribald fashion.

When they left the table, they would take up their respective positions at the fireside, and still the talk went on, but, by then, the peak of Mr Richard Whitestone's loquacity and jollity had passed.

During this early period of decline, he quoted mainly from *Tom Jones.*

Mr Richard never wearied of praising Fielding's brilliant pen portraits nor the judicious thoughts with which he interspersed the narrative.

Later, his closeness to the heat of the fire, the fumes given off by the English coal, the thick smoke from their cigars, and, later on, the punch, depressed his spirits still more.

He then went on to speak of politics, quoting from *The Times.* That night, he told Carlos that Lord Palmerston was determined to dissolve Parliament if he did not have the support of the House of Commons.

This was said in a very gloomy voice. Carlos, needless to say, couldn't care less what happened in the English Parliament.

Then Mr Richard spoke of the main manoeuvres and attacks made by the allied army in Crimea and about the probable success of the campaign; and from there he moved on to his thoughts about the state of commerce in London. Carlos, meanwhile, was heroically struggling to suppress his yawns.

By then, it was dark, and Mr Richard's voice was already growing somewhat hoarse and this, combined with the chiming of the clock, had an irresistibly soporific effect on Carlos.

When Jenny heard silence fall – a sign that things had reached a critical point – she would return to the room, and it was then that her brother usually seized the opportunity to leave.

That night, though, he stayed.

Jenny regarded him with some surprise.

Carlos responded with a shrug, as if to say that, this time, he had resolved to cooperate by staying.

His sister thanked him with a look, but she was thinking: 'I know. You still haven't got over your disappointment at last night's failed adventure. Patience!'

As we said, Carlos had returned home feeling reconciled with domestic life and convinced that he was ready to enjoy the pleasures of an English evening at home, which is why he chose to stay, but Jenny's suspicions were, nonetheless, very well-founded.

Discouraged by the lack of clues as to the identity of the mystery woman in the mask, about whom he was, regretfully, still thinking, he didn't really feel like going out when there was so little hope of solving the puzzle.

However, domestic life, as exemplified by that fireside scene, where Mr Richard was now almost dozing off, was hardly enough to satisfy him.

The idea of enjoying a home life, whose charms Carlos thought he had grasped earlier that day, was merely an accessory to something much closer to his heart, something he was beginning to feel as a necessity. He was drawn to cosy domestic bliss, but of a kind warmed and lit by flames other than those licking the fender of that particular hearth, and enlivened by more ardent feelings than those of fraternal affection, however close he was to his sister, and than those of filial respect, however fond and deep-rooted.

This is why he was feeling so disappointed, comparing the monotony of that English evening with the pleasure he imagined he could enjoy in some other home, and this disappointment made him even more silent and sombre than he had been on other nights spent at home.

When Jenny joined them, Mr Richard, as usual, expressed a desire to hear her play. With this in mind, they went into another room where the fire was also lit. Mr Richard sat by the hearth, and Carlos took a seat nearby, while Jenny took up her position at the piano.

An English Family

Jenny knew her father's favourites and so she opened her copy of Russell's *Popular Songs* and looked for a poem by George Pope Morris, which both father and brother always listened to piously and thoughtfully.

The reason for this lay above all in the words, which seemed written on purpose to awaken, in the whole family, a yearning for the past. Jenny sang softly, but with real feeling, a poem entitled *My Mother's Bible*, which went as follows:

This book is all that's left me now!
Tears will unbidden start,–
With faltering lip and throbbing brow
I press it to my heart.
For many generations past,
Here is our family tree;
My mother's hands this Bible clasped,
She, dying, gave it me.

Ah! well do I remember those
Whose names these records bear;
Who round the hearth-stone used to close
After the evening prayer,
And speak of what these pages said,
In tones my heart would thrill!
Though they are with the silent dead,
Here are they living still.

My father read this holy book
To brothers, sisters dear;
How calm was my poor mother's look
Who leaned God's word to hear!
Her angel face – I see it yet!

What vivid memories come!
Again that little group is met
Within the halls of home!

Thou truest friend man ever knew,
Thy constancy I've tried;
Where all were false I found thee true,
My counsellor and guide.
The mines of earth no treasures give
That could this volume buy:
In teaching me the way to live,
It taught me how to die.

Once Jenny had finished singing, the talk naturally turned to various passages from the Bible. Mr Richard quoted one verse after another, until he stumbled over one and asked his daughter to check the exact wording.

Jenny immediately opened the Bible, a copy of which was to be found in every room, and began to read.

Carlos loved to hear his sister reading from those simple, sublime pages.

People speak very ill of the English language, and it's true that on hearing certain sons of Albion, one does immediately recall those familiar lines:

All the world says that the British mumble,
And the British insist that the world's a liar.

And yet a voice like Jenny's, tender, melodious and intelligently, gracefully modulated, seems to transform that ungrateful language into something akin to birdsong, which everyone likes, even if they can't understand what's said.

The thoughtful way in which Jenny read the most beautiful episodes from the Old and New Testament only enhanced the sweetness of her voice.

Unfortunately, a simple reading of the text with no commentary was not enough to satisfy Mr Richard Whitestone's fervent Anglicanism, which is why he kept interrupting her with the interpretations of some of the reverend doctors at his episcopal church, or with recent remarks made by the English cleric during the Protestant mass in Campo Pequeno.

Jenny would look at her brother, urging him to control his feelings and at least pretend to be listening. At ten, tea was served, and Mr Richard revived a little and spoke of the importance of the East India Company, about the great service it had done for commerce, about its history, the difficulties it had faced and the wealth it had accrued. Then he set out his own theory on the expansion of the British colonies, made a few acerbic comments about the Portuguese colonial system and ended with an outright condemnation of the French policy in general.

Mr Richard cordially loathed France. Well, he wouldn't be English if he didn't.

At eleven o'clock, Mr Richard finally stopped talking; his eyelids were beginning to droop, the fire to burn down, with no one adding more coal to keep it alive.

Half an hour later, the family headed off to bed, and Carlos had barely spoken a dozen words all evening.

Jenny walked with her brother along the corridor that led to their respective bedrooms.

'So what do you think of my conversion, of the prodigal son's touching, miraculous transformation?' Carlos asked Jenny, when they reached the door to the library, which is where they would go their separate ways.

'I'm not sure how long it will last,' she said.

'How could it last, Jenny? You saw the narcotic delights of that fireside monologue. I mean, sleep is very pleasurable, but not at my age!'

'Charles, really!' said Jenny, giving him a disapproving look.

'Look, Jenny, believe me when I say that, today, I was absolutely genuine in my desire to be reconciled with our domestic fairy godmother, the one who protected Cinderella in the story we were told as children. I came home filled with dreams of domestic bliss only to find they were illusions. I saw all that blue and gold turn to grey.'

'Perhaps you expect too much.'

'No, I don't, but how can I possibly summon up the courage to hear tomorrow and the next day and for ever after the tale of Reverend Jackson's turkey? Or about Lord Mayor's Day? Or the riots in favour of Queen Caroline? Is it any wonder I want to run away when faced by the theological subtleties of our church scholars or...?'

'Yes, you're right. Before you can transform your heart, you must first educate it.'

'My heart? What do you mean?'

'You come to spend the evening at home as if you were going to the theatre, expecting to be entertained. It's clear that family life isn't enough for an imagination like yours, if, that is, you're only here to keep your imagination amused. And I realise that all this must be unbearable for you if your heart has closed its doors to the only pleasures we can offer you.'

'I'm not so hard-hearted that I can't appreciate the tender pleasures of family life, Jenny. Do you really think I don't understand the value of your love and even of our father's? Bear with me, and don't be too severe with me. While Father was rambling on just now about the East India Company, I was thinking…'

'What?'

'I was thinking that certain charming ideas I had while walking in the country this afternoon were entirely false…'

'Walking in the country? You?'

'Yes, in the country… it gave me certain ideas. I see things more clearly now, and I think we shouldn't live so closely bound to the family, as has been the custom in patriarchal societies. The modern tendency to loosen family ties a little is quite right, or at least excusable, although without doing away with all the feelings that feed and foster familial love. It's a matter of living more independently. What's to be gained from binding two or three people with different natures and different tastes together to the point of impeding their movement and freedom to act, simply because they're blood relatives? All that happens is that none of them then has full use of his faculties, they get in each other's way because they're so tightly bound together, and the inevitable consequence is, I wouldn't say loathing, but irritation, minor quarrels, and, when you least expect it, even bitter disagreements.'

Jenny was shaking her head and looking hard at her brother.

'You're full of some very sad philosophies today,' she said at last. 'I find you harder and harder to understand, Charles.'

Carlos burst out laughing.

'But why, Jenny? What do you find so incomprehensible?'

'A few days ago… the morning after one of your many late nights on the town, and when what you've just said would have made much more sense, you spoke eloquently and convincingly about the joys of family life. You could have persuaded the most dissolute of men. And all because of a poem a friend of yours had written in your scrap book. Now though…'

'It's all perfectly explicable, and for precisely the reasons I've just given. I tried to bind those ties tightly around me, seduced by the promises of certain moralising novelists, but I found the ties cut into me, as they would... But what poem was it that awoke in me such salutary ideas? I don't remember.'

'Do you want me to read it to you?' Jenny asked, placing one hand on the key to the library door, as if about to open it.

'Of course I do.'

They went into the room, whose walls were lined with rosewood shelves crammed with magnificently bound English editions. In the middle of the room stood a very solid old-fashioned rectangular table with embossed metal handles, exquisite carving, and stout spiral legs – a perfect example of the beautiful furniture that has seen a revival lately, thanks largely to the predilections of the English population; indeed, they have become so keen on it that it is now quite hard to find. On the table were various recent publications, newspapers, both foreign and local, as well as engravings; around it were comfortable armchairs and upholstered footstools that invited one to take a seat and read.

Jenny put down her lamp and, picking up a scrapbook from among the other books and periodicals, she began leafing through it, while her brother sat beside her.

'If my memory serves me right,' she said, 'it's the translation of a popular legend from Brittany, entitled... *Amel and Pennor*,' she said, having alighted on the very page she was looking for.

'I have no idea what that is.'

'Listen then.'

And Jenny, with inexpressible tenderness and grace, began to read the following legend, falsely or accurately attributed by a contemporary French writer to the popular muse of Brittany.

An English Family

Far off, in the land known as Brittany,
Whose coast is washed by a sinister sea,
There lived, years ago, a poor fisherman,
Called Amel by name, with his wife Pennor.
They had a fine son, a fair-haired child –
An angel, the garland and gold of their world.
One day, when the three were a-sailing home,
They were just reaching land as darkness was falling,
And the sea, it turned fierce and was loud and was strong!
And the tide arose quickly, and there on the waves
Lay Death, so pitiless, so very cruel.
Amel looked at his wife and he said:
'Death is close by – look and see the waves rise!
But you must outlive me! Climb onto my shoulders,
And, yes, O be brave, my dear wife, and hold tight,
And when I go under, then think on me!'
She obeyed, but when Amel, still standing firm,
Sank at last 'neath the o'erwhelming waves,
His wife cried: 'Poor friend, my dearest Amel!
Who is it who feels the most grief, you who die
Or I, who am fated to witness your death.'
As the waters continued to mount, wave by wave,
And the poor woman's body was drawn ever down.
She looked at her son and she said unto him:
'O child, death's approaching, see the tide's ever higher!
So climb on my shoulders, be brave and hold tight!'
Yes, be brave and hold tight, and when I'm gone,
Remember me and your poor dear Papa!'
And as the waves washed over her, the child wept,
And little by little he went down too, until
All that was left, adrift on the tide, was one fair lock of
hair...

Then a fairy flew over those turbulent waters,
And, seeing that one tress of blond hair adrift,
For the sake of pity, she reached out a hand,
And snatched up both hair and the pale child himself.
Then smiling, she said: 'What a great weight you are!'
But she soon saw the reason; for holding on
To the trembling child's ankles
Was his poor frightened mother,
Who also began to rise up to the surface.
The fairy smiled then to see them both there,
And said yet again: 'What a great weight you are!'
Then up came the husband, still holding on tight,
Still clasping the ankles of his dear wife.
And the fairy, on seeing him, laughed once again,
And flew swiftly to shore with her still living bundle,
That human chain with its links made of love.

Putting the book down, Jenny went on: 'There are about four more lines, which give the moral of the tale, although I probably don't need to read them out.'

'Indeed. The allegory hardly requires any further comment. But tell me something, Jenny, what would the good fairy say or do if, flying over the beach one day, when the tide wasn't rushing in and the sea wasn't threatening to devour the whole dear family... what would she say or do if she found the three beings forming that human chain to be as ridiculous as they are touching in that legend? The fairy would doubtless smile again, but this time would add: "My, what mad creatures you are!" Shall I add something similar to those four moralising lines you didn't read?' said Carlos, stroking Jenny's cheek and with a triumphant smile on his face, to which she responded with another smile, saying: 'No, there's no need, but don't forget, Charles, storms at sea can sometimes appear out of nowhere. And no one can foresee when danger might strike. You saw how those fisherpeople were coming home, all three of them happy and trusting in the sea. What would have happened if they hadn't stuck together? When the tide came in, Amel wouldn't have tried to save his wife and she wouldn't have tried to save their son, and the lock of hair floating on the water wouldn't have caught the eye of the kind fairy, giving her the chance to save that human chain. Do you see what I mean?'

'Am I so far away that I can't still offer you my shoulders to stand on if the tide should come in one day and place us in danger?'

'No, Charles. And you're not the Charles I'm telling off, it's the Charles that you sometimes like to pretend you are. It's odd, some generous souls suffer from the opposite vice to hypocrisy, and actually try to appear to be bad! Why lie with your lips, saying what you don't feel?'

'All right, I was being a bit cruel, but...'

Jenny placed a hand over his mouth.

'Let's leave that "but" for tomorrow. For the moment I still don't put much trust in it.'

'So you won't give me the chance to justify myself?'

'As you see, my confidence in you is doing a better job of that than you are?'

'Goodnight, Jenny.'

And with that they parted with a cordial handshake.

Carlos was once again more reconciled to the pleasures of domestic life, for that dialogue had left too pleasing an impression on him for it to be otherwise.

XVI

At the Theatre

Some days later, posters were being put up on street corners, announcing a production of *Lucia di Lammermoor*.

Mr Richard Whitestone was not an assiduous theatre-goer. However, there was one exception that would, infallibly, take him there, at least once.

Having despaired of ever hearing the music of English composers in Oporto – composers such as Handel, Gray, Arnold, Bishop and others, names that were always on his lips – he had resigned himself to soothing his deeply patriotic feelings by going to any operas based on some British masterpiece.

Othello, Macbeth, The Capulets and the Montagues, Imprisoned in Edinburgh, The Two Foscari, Marino Faliero or others of the sort, won out over love of his own fireside and thus brought to the public gaze that physiognomy, radiant with contentment and oozing good health, with which the reader is already familiar.

He would prepare himself the previous evening by re-reading the work that had provided the basis for the opera, and he would then happily go to the theatre.

It was not Rossini, Verdi, Bellini, Ricci or Donizetti who drew him and entranced him, but Shakespeare, Byron and Walter Scott, whose looming figures he seemed to see there on stage, like the characters their genius had once summoned into life. The music was a mere accessory. Mr Richard was not applauding the conductor, but his famous compatriots.

Among those operas, he included *Lucia di Lammermoor*: a Scottish subject from the pen of a Scottish writer, who so brilliantly portrayed souls moral and immoral. How could Mr Richard resist? He had to go.

And so he reserved a box for the night. He never liked sitting in the stalls. A box provided him with more privacy and allowed him to be alone with his own people, and that, for him, was a necessity.

On these occasions, Mr Richard always invited Manuel Quintino, much to the latter's displeasure, although he did not dare refuse. He accepted the invitation and even thanked his employer, while secretly regretting having to deprive himself of one of his sweetly pleasurable evenings at home, of Cecília's attentive care, and even the monotonous opinions of his friend José Fortunato, who was equally sad to have to change the habit of a lifetime and be deprived of his neighbour's tea and yawns. Left with no choice in the matter, Manuel Quintino would dutifully go to the theatre.

Once this decision was made, he then became aware that it was his duty to arrive on time, for he was punctuality personified, believing that it is always better to wait than be waited for; and although it was highly unlikely that they would wait for him to begin the opera, the fact is that, shortly after dark, he could be seen, as he was that evening, pacing up and down in the theatre foyer, waiting for the inner doors to be opened.

As soon as they were, he bought the libretto, because he could never resign himself to not understanding what someone was singing. He then went up to the box reserved by Mr

Richard and, in the still dim lighting, began to read.

There he would watch the candles being lit, the orchestra tuning up, the stalls, boxes and circle gradually filling with people, and that, for him, was one of the more intriguing parts of the evening. This innocent delight slightly calmed his anxiety about the late arrival of the Whitestone family, fearing, as he did, that they might miss the start of the opera, a fear that would not let him rest, until, finally, he heard the door behind him opening. It was Mr Richard and Jenny.

Mr Richard greeted him familiarly, and Jenny affectionately shook his hand.

'I didn't expect to see you here,' Jenny said, taking off her cloak and repairing any slight faults in her *toilette*.

'Yes, Mr Whitestone was kind enough to invite me.'

'And Cecília?'

'Ah, Cecília!' cried Manuel Quintino with a shrug, 'I didn't even bother asking her, since she always refuses to come.'

While Jenny was smoothing her hair and her attire, Mr Richard went to the front of the box to cast a quick eye over the auditorium.

'And what about Carlos?' Manuel Quintino asked Jenny as, with passable gallantry, he helped find a place for the cloak she had just taken off.

'He may well be here,' said Jenny.

'Where? In the stalls?'

'Probably.'

'When he has a box at his disposal! How wasteful!' thought the economical Manuel Quintino.

Once they had taken up their respective positions, and finding himself sitting next to Jenny, Manuel Quintino felt he should strike up a conversation.

'Whenever I come to the theatre,' he said, 'I always

remember seeing that celebrated actress, Josefa Teresa Soares! Now she really was remarkable. And there was Grata Nicolini too, whom you may have heard of. To be honest, though, I used to enjoy the plays they put on then far more than I do the ones they put on now. Even the costumes and the scenery were better. Now it's all drawing rooms and tailcoats. It's always some father wanting to marry off his daughter to a rich old man, and the daughter wanting to marry a poor youth, who is a poet, and the young man turning on the old man, and the young woman dying... and yet people think it's wonderful. I don't like it at all. I wish audiences now could have seen *The Emperor Joseph II visiting the prisons of Germany* or *Camilla or the Subterraneans* or *Hariadan Barberousse* or *Sixteen Years Ago or the Incendiaries*, *The Seven Princes of Lara*, *Inês de Castro...*'

And Manuel Quintino was about to continue this review of past plays, when Jenny interrupted him, thus missing a golden opportunity to inform herself, among other things, of the merits of the celebrated Josefa Teresa, still fondly remembered by ex-theatre-goers, whose legitimate successors are the dilettanti of today.

'Did Carlos go to the office?' Jenny asked softly.

'Yes, he came in on Tuesday – unfortunately,' said Manuel Quintino, remembering the mistakes Carlos' visit had prompted.

'Why "unfortunately"?'

Manuel Quintino was about to tell Jenny about the kind of 'help' Carlos had given him at the office, but, sensing that Mr Richard was showing signs of listening in to what he was saying, he thought it wise to change direction.

'It's just that, at the grand old age of fifty-five, I'm very easily distracted, and once I get chatting, I don't get any work done and neither…'

He paused briefly, because what he was about to say seemed far too flattering, then concluded: '…and neither does Carlos.'

Mr Richard bit his lip to keep himself from smiling.

Jenny also struggled to keep a straight face, but thanked Manuel Quintino for his generous intentions with a smile.

She felt it best, though, to change the subject, which is why she said: 'But you still haven't told me why Cecília didn't come.'

'I have no idea. She didn't come because she didn't want to. It's always been a struggle to persuade her to accept any invitation you're kind enough to extend to her. She's very much her own mistress, and has been since she was a child, but more especially now. There's something worrying her. She's doing her best to hide it, but…'

Manuel Quintino adopted a mysterious air and continued more quietly: 'I don't know. She's been behaving a bit strangely for a few days now. I haven't wanted to say anything to her, because I know what she's like, and I'm afraid of making her feel self-conscious, but…'

'What makes you think she's worried?' asked Jenny, genuinely interested in what Manuel Quintino was saying.

'She seems sad. A father's eyes aren't easily deceived. Others might be, but not mine. Cecília isn't usually like that, as anyone who knows her will agree. She still laughs and jokes, but there's something not quite right. You know her well, surely you've noticed too…'

'No, I haven't noticed any change in her.'

'Ah now, let me think. She hasn't been back to your house since Tuesday, is that right? And it's only since then that I've noticed this change.'

Jenny was listening with growing curiosity.

'And so today,' he went on, 'after I got home… but please, don't say anything to her about this, it might make matters worse…'

'Don't worry,' said Jenny, not wanting to miss a word.

'Well, this evening, I noticed that she hardly ate any supper, and at her age, any loss of appetite is a bad sign, don't you think?'

Jenny nodded, although I'm not convinced that she entirely agreed with Manuel Quintino as regards appetite.

'And then?' she asked.

'Afterwards,' he said, 'she shut herself up in her bedroom, which is something she never does. I was quite alarmed, and so I called to her. She didn't answer at once. I thought perhaps she was feeling ill and I was just about to go downstairs to see what was wrong, when she appeared. Unless I'm very much mistaken, though, she'd been crying. Oh, she was smiling, but I…'

'You must have imagined it. Why would Cecília be crying?'

'That's precisely what worries me. I really don't know. Sometimes I wonder if I'm the cause. You know, I would rather slave away my entire life and have not a mouthful of bread to eat, than give her any reason to shed a single tear.'

And there was a tremor in his voice that touched Jenny.

'Don't worry,' she said to reassure him. 'I'm quite certain you're not the cause of any sadness in her. What more could you do for her than you do already?'

'And she deserves it all, and more if I could give her more. She's an angel. You can't imagine.'

'I certainly can. After all, she's my dearest friend.'

At this, Manuel Quintino could not resist clasping her hands fondly.

Then the orchestra launched into the overture, and silence fell.

Manuel Quintino's thoughts took another direction, and forgetting all about the confidences that had left Jenny so sunk in thought, he instead listened to the music, fixing his eyes on the curtain, waiting for it to be raised.

'Of course, the story of this opera,' he was saying while he waited, 'is very pretty, but very sad too. It's about a nobleman, I can't remember where he's from now…'

Then, after thinking for a moment, he added: 'From Spain, I think, yes, from Spain…'

Mr Whitestone may have been distracted, but no amount of distraction can stop an Englishman correcting some inexactitude that touches, however lightly, on his nationality, which is why he immediately interrupted Manuel Quintino: 'From Spain! He's from Scotland. It's set in the Lammermuir Hills and is based on Sir Walter Scott's *The Bride of Lammermoor*. Everyone knows that.'

'Ah, yes, you're quite right. He's from Scotland. I forgot. Anyway, this nobleman, it seems, has fallen out with one of his neighbours, who is also a nobleman, but a penniless one. It's an old feud. I've known such things myself. Then St Peter goes and makes him fall in love with the other man's sister, as always happens.'

At this point, the curtain went up

Having surveyed the stage, Manuel Quintino continued: 'Those men in skirts over there are the servants of the nobleman. They're spying on the lover, who has come to the garden to speak with the young woman.'

Manuel Quintino kept up this rambling commentary, although neither Mr Richard nor Jenny paid any attention.

After the arrival of the baritone and during his recitative, Manuel Quintino insisted on translating any Italian phrases he understood, which were, of course, the ones least in need of translation.

'*Mortale nemico*' sang the baritone on the stage – 'Mortal enemy' said Manuel Quintino. '*Di mia prosapia*' said one, 'He himself admits he is of noble lineage' – he said, mistranslating wildly – '*Io fremo*' – added the singer shortly afterwards – 'He says he's trembling,' said Manuel Quintino.

And so on and on, until, when the baritone launched into the aria '*Cruda funesta smania...*', Mr Richard put an end to his book-keeper's brilliant explanations with a faint 'Shh'.

Manuel Quintino immediately fell silent, intending to continue his translations after the first interval.

Before the end of the act, there was some kind of disturbance in the stalls, something that has, alas, become a fairly common event in our theatres, and a trial and tribulation to our impresarios.

When the *prima donna* came on stage, and before she had even sung a note, there was much hissing and booing from one side of the theatre.

Most of the audience knew nothing about the backstage politics that were the cause of these sudden storms, and found it odd that someone who, only a few days before, had been greeted with wild applause, possibly too wild, should now be booed.

The two rival camps made so much noise that the performance had to be interrupted for a few minutes.

Confusion broke out on stage; in the boxes, men leaned over to get a bird's-eye view of the human storm taking place beneath their feet, and some more impatient types shouted bitter words of censure, which were lost in the air; ladies almost fainted with fear; others, more courageous, observed the brawls through their opera glasses; the orchestra stopped playing, got to their feet and themselves became spectators;

the singers folded their arms and did the same; the inhabitants of the upper circle, possibly the only genuine lovers of the art, howled indignantly; the manager stood up in his box and demanded to be heard...

In the midst of all this tumult, Mr Richard gave clear signs of his displeasure, which took the form of much harrumphing and tut-tutting, a lot of headshaking and drumming of fingers.

Manuel Quintino was equally scandalised and rather more verbal in expressing his indignation.

He talked and railed and gesticulated, he rounded on the authorities, concocted absurd plans to form a police force just for the theatre, and did all this while leaning out of the box and watching the dark mass of people in the stalls, whose protests were growing ever louder.

Jenny was looking in the same direction, but for different reasons.

In the box along from theirs she had heard someone speak harshly of the mutineers, and among the names mentioned was that of her brother. Jenny trembled and immediately took to scrutinising the mob.

Meanwhile, Manuel Quintino was shouting: 'If I was in charge, I'd pack the whole lot of them off to jail. This is outrageous. A person comes here to enjoy himself and...'

He stopped talking because something had caught his eye.

'Aha,' he said. 'I should have known he'd be here. The party wouldn't be complete without him.'

'Who?' asked Jenny, fearing his answer.

'Why Carlos of course. Over there.'

'Where? Where?' asked Mr Richard urgently.

Manuel Quintino felt Jenny clutch his arm as if urging him to be discreet, but he had already realised the need for prudence.

'Over there!' and he pointed in precisely the opposite direction from the spot where he had seen Carlos.

'Where, man? I can't see him.'

'Isn't that him? Near that fellow in the white hat. Can't you see, sir? There he goes. No, he's gone.'

'That wasn't him.'

'It was. I even thought I saw him gesture to me like someone who's had enough of such impudence.'

Manuel Quintino was beginning to damage the very cause he was defending, by, as was his wont, taking his defence too far.

Carlos had indeed been caught up in the tumult, although with the praiseworthy aim of trying to calm down two friends who were about to resort to fisticuffs over this theatrical dispute. Glancing up occasionally at the box, though, he saw the supplicant, anxious expression on Jenny's face, and while Mr Richard's eyes, treacherously drawn away by Manuel Quintino, were looking for him elsewhere, he allowed two other pacifiers to take his place and abandoned the stalls.

Manuel Quintino, who was following his every move, breathed more easily then, and said: 'Here he comes. He won't be long now, sir. And he's quite right to join us up here in the box rather than stay down there with people like that.'

Carlos was not long in arriving. He looked first at his sister, who was able to reassure him with a reciprocal look that told him precisely what role he needed to play before his father.

Carlos understood and was severely critical of the rioters, which, of course, pleased Mr Richard.

Meanwhile, calm had been restored, and the first act finally ended, the only novelty being that the *prima donna* was then enthusiastically applauded by the very people who had booed her entrance.

Mysteries of the theatre, which I have never been able to fathom.

Mr Whitestone left the box in the interval, and Carlos stayed.

Manuel Quintino then launched into a sermon on the perils of getting into bad company. Carlos listened, laughing and responding to his pompous words with various jokey comments, which prevented Manuel Quintino from maintaining the serious demeanour required by such weighty matters.

After a while, Carlos began to study the different female types and outfits adorning the other boxes, and was not always kind in his criticisms. On one occasion, so as to continue his scrutiny, he decided to clean the lenses of his opera glasses and drew from his pocket a woman's dainty, lace-edged handkerchief, which he regarded with surprise.

Then he held it up by two corners to show it to his sister, saying: 'I'd completely forgotten I had this, Jenny.'

'What's that?'

'Something else that I stole, in the hope of finding out more, and I'm so forgetful that it had completely slipped my mind.'

'What are you talking about?'

'Don't you remember what I told you about what happened on Carnival night?'

'Ah!' said Jenny, immediately glancing across at Manuel Quintino, who appeared to be studying the handkerchief with growing interest.

'Give it to me,' said Jenny, holding out her hand.

'No, I won't,' retorted Carlos, snatching it from her, laughing.

'May I see it?' asked Manuel Quintino, also holding out his hand.

'What, so that you can give it to Jenny afterwards?'

'No, I just want to see it.'

'Of what possible interest can this handkerchief be to you?' asked Carlos.

Jenny was becoming visibly uneasy.

Manuel Quintino was now examining the handkerchief closely.

'How very odd,' he said. 'It's exactly like one of the handkerchiefs I gave to my daughter on her birthday.'

'What?' said Carlos, glancing at his sister.

Jenny's unease redoubled.

'No, it's exactly the same, the lace, the embroidery on the corners, all that's missing, ah, there it is, the initial C! This handkerchief belongs to Cecília! But how is that possible?'

Jenny thought it was time to intervene.

'You're getting all worked up over something very simple,' she said, laughing. 'This handkerchief does belong to Cecília, you're right. She accidentally left it at my house a few days ago, on Tuesday it was. This light-fingered fellow here is always taking things from my room without telling me, and so, thinking it was mine…'

'I *knew* it was the handkerchief I'd given to Cecília. That's why I was so surprised.'

Carlos was looking first at Jenny and then at Manuel Quintino, as if not knowing quite what he should make of it all.

'Will you give it back to me,' said Jenny, 'since I'm the one who should return it to Cecília.'

Carlos was about to make some possibly reckless response, but a gesture from his sister both silenced him and explained everything.

The name of the unknown young woman at the ball was no

longer a mystery to him!

Taking the handkerchief from Manuel Quintino and giving it to his sister, he said knowingly: 'Yes, you're quite right, Jenny. You're the person who should return it to her. I'd completely forgotten to mention that "theft" to you, and I'm rather glad I did.'

'Why's that?' Jenny asked, growing serious.

'Just to see the look of surprise on our friend Manuel Quintino's face.'

'I just found it very odd,' said Manuel Quintino.

Jenny adroitly changed the subject.

Carlos remained thoughtful though. He returned to the stalls when the second act began, and everyone found it strange that he should now be so distracted and so indifferent to the ongoing dispute over the earlier ruckus.

He was equally indifferent to the singers and the opera.

Jenny was watching him from the box, and could see this same indifference in the fact that he did not once move or change position during the next two acts and during one whole interval, as if oblivious to everything going on around him.

'What will come of all that deep thought?' she wondered.

At the beginning of the final act, Carlos returned to the box.

Unable to resist the force of habit a moment longer, Manuel Quintino had fallen fast asleep. Mr Richard, meanwhile, was deep in conversation with a compatriot, a gentleman with snow-white hair and whiskers, a cravat of the same colour, and a rosy complexion; they were discussing the lyrical triumphs of the celebrated *mezzo-soprano* Malibran, whom both had heard in London when they were lads, as well as the singing technique of that rarest of tenors, Rubini, whom they had admired in 1831, at the Queen's Theatre, in Mozart's *Don Giovanni*, music of which the British ear never tires, and in

Gray's *Beggar's Opera* – a very British riposte to the Italians, which went entirely unnoticed in Italy.

Sitting down beside his sister, Carlos sensed that it was now safe to talk.

'So the lovely stranger in the silk domino…' he began.

Jenny eyed Manuel Quintino nervously.

'Don't worry,' said Carlos. 'He's sleeping so soundly he might even start snoring.'

'Are you now convinced, Charles,' said Jenny softly, 'of the truth of what I said the other day.'

'About what?'

'About your adventure on that Carnival night. Cecília is a well-brought-up young woman of very delicate feelings. It was very foolish of her to go there, and who knows what trouble it might have caused her if your generosity had not ultimately prevailed over your folly, and as it will, I hope, continue to do. Weren't you about to consign her to the ranks of women you don't respect because you don't know them? Are you now filled with remorse?'

'But Cecília…'

'On the same day that you told me about that evening, she came to see me and told me everything, for I am *her* confidante too. And if you had seen how frightened she was to tell me! If you had seen how she interrupted me with genuine tears in her eyes when I was about to reveal what you thought of women who frequented such places, alone and masked!'

'You told her that? Oh, Jenny!'

'I told her enough to put her off doing such things again, given that she might not always find a protector endowed with at least a few generous impulses…'

'Good heavens, Jenny! I still can't believe it. So it was Cecília! I admit, Jenny, that I never imagined she had such wit, such intelligence, such…'

'That isn't what I want you to repent of, Charles, but, rather, the assumptions you made about Cecília, the way you treated her, simply because you met her in a place where you wouldn't even have dreamed of finding your own sister…'

'Nor would I!' said Carlos spontaneously.

'That's all very well, Charles,' said Jenny in a placid, but rather reproving voice. 'All I'm saying is that Cecília's qualities and the way she lives her life give her the right to expect as much consideration and respect as you say you feel for me. She *is* my best friend, you know.'

Carlos looked at his sister, surprised at the serious tone in which she spoke.

We should say here that he had never thought of Cecília as anything more than a pretty girl, whom he had often given admiring looks, then forgotten as soon as he left her company.

I believe I mentioned earlier that Cecília's beauty was of the kind that did not immediately make a deep impression.

Carlos had never considered her moral qualities, and why should he? And that is why the suddenly serious expression on Jenny's face so impressed him.

'Your words, Jenny,' he replied, adopting an equally serious demeanour, 'would restore the honour even of those whose honour needed restoring. And I firmly believe that Cecília is not of that tribe. I am the only one deserving of censure in this whole affair. And I will prove to you that I mean this.'

Jenny held out her hand to him.

'That's the Charles I know and love. Thank you.'

Then, pointing to Manuel Quintino, she added: 'Needless to say, he knows nothing about this.'

'And he will continue to know nothing.'

Manuel Quintino was dreaming he was in the office, trying

and failing to add up a column of figures.

Not long afterwards, the carriage transporting the White-stone family home was rolling along the city streets.

Of the three people inside, not one spoke during the entire journey.

XVII

Carlos consults his Conscience

That evening's events had made such an impression on Carlos that when he returned home, he couldn't sleep. Instead, he sat down at his desk and casually opened a book.

As chance would have it, the book was Byron's *Hours of Idleness*, in which Carlos read:

Woman! Experience might have told me...

He read no further, for that first word – *Woman!* – was enough. Swept along on that magical noun, his imagination gathered speed and, leaving the other senses to read the lines that followed, it set off on its own path, travelling far faster and far further.

If he cares to look, the reader can probably find in his own library the path they took, so let us leave Byron in peace and follow Carlos' imagination as best we can.

His imagination began by remembering the purely chance revelation of only a few moments before. Did I say remember? To use that word in its strictest sense, such a discovery would, however briefly, have left the field open for him to think other thoughts, but did it? I think not.

Carlos then became engaged in another more active task, that of trying to evoke the image of Cecília, of whom he had only the vaguest memory, as if her face were veiled by a cloud he tried in vain to dissipate.

Any reader who has taken on such an enterprise will know how desperately hard it can be. The more urgent the desire to recall a face that we do not as yet have firmly fixed in our memory, the more pleasure some malign spirit seems to take in completely altering its features, combining the most disparate physiognomic elements, randomly inventing a profile, mendaciously bestowing the wrong colours on hair and complexion, and startling us with its gross misrepresentation of other curves and reliefs.

Carlos had often seen Cecília, although he had never paid her much attention, and now he simply could not dredge up a clear image of her.

In compensation, he could remember the warm tones in which she had spoken to him at the ball, her charming laugh, everything she had said, indeed, each tiny detail of that Carnival adventure, and so deeply did he immerse himself in these thoughts that, sitting there, head in hands, elbows on desk, eyes half-closed, he forgot all about Byron – whom he truly believed he was still reading – and was even unaware of quite where he actually was.

The dim light filled the room with a lugubrious glow, and it was so silent that Carlos could hear himself breathe.

He leaned back and rubbed his eyes, like someone waking from a dream. And then, having turned the lamp up a little, he once again fell into that same abstracted state.

This time, though, he rested his head on his left hand only, while his right hand picked up a pen and began drawing and writing at random on a blank sheet of paper that happened to be there.

Needless to say, his soul took no part in this.

According to Xavier de Maistre's theory, *la bête* or the *other*, which is quite different from our *I*, had grown weary of reading and was now writing, while the soul, still immersed in its earlier task, continued to think.

I would say, however, that what that *other* gets up to when it momentarily shakes off the yoke attaching it to its companion is often rather dangerous. Xavier de Maistre himself gives us examples of this.

One of the most perilous of such distractions is that of writing. The hand is indiscreet, and in a careless moment, can easily, unexpectedly betray the mind with those automatic, apparently insignificant movements.

Peer over the shoulder of a man absorbed in grave thoughts, but whose hand is busily, heedlessly scribbling on a sheet of paper, and some word or mark is sure to reveal, along with many other trifling things, whatever idea is currently gripping his mind.

That other engine or principle, which controls our actions when our consciousness does not, seems, like the soul, to have a memory too, and uses it to store away the insignificant details that accompany any important event in our life. Say we've heard some revelatory fact, well, while our reason is storing that away, the *other* memory will be noting down the clothes worn by the person telling us that fact, the colour of the walls of the room where we heard it, a comment made by someone who happened to be passing. Now, these accessory memories often still have enough bearing on the main event for some probing mind, by a process of deduction, to reach into the very depths of our thoughts.

That is why, at such moments, it is dangerous to trust any pen that is moved by that *other* will, which, being naturally indiscreet, will almost certainly leave traces on the paper of its own curious preoccupations.

This is what was happening to Carlos.

He began by absent-mindedly drawing a helmet, which might appear to have nothing to do with the likely drift of his thoughts at that moment. It falls to me, however, to explain that an individual in a Roman cloak and wearing just such a helmet had walked past him in the theatre at the very moment when he had first spotted Cecília.

After the helmet, he drew an eye-mask – and since the connection there is quite obvious, it requires no further comment – followed by a hand. He was perhaps thinking of Cecília's hand, whose beauty he had noticed when he clasped it in his to say goodbye. Then – and this really does seem out of place – a streetlamp! It's true, though, that just such a lamp had been shining down on his mysterious companion when, in her distress, she had invoked Jenny's name and, thanks to that name, had prevented Carlos from pursuing her further. And that is probably what lay behind that drawing, since his hand then went on to write, over and over, in various styles: *for your sister's sake, for Jenny's sake!* Then it was the turn of a church organ, which could only be considered irrelevant by someone who has forgotten the name of the saint whose emblem it is, namely, St Cecilia, but that isn't an idea that would immediately spring to a Protestant mind, if, here on earth, there were not some as yet unbeatified person of the same name. Then he wrote an absurd, unusual, impenetrable word: *Ailicec.* However, if the reader reverses the letters, any puzzlement will vanish; other no less peculiar words followed, made up of various combinations of the same seven letters, which finally appeared in their proper order: Cecília. Further down the page, in a very odd transition, he wrote very clearly the word 'Pope', then 'Calvin', and immediately afterwards, the name of a friend and compatriot who, months earlier, had married a Catholic lady. If you can interpret these signs, dear reader, would you not agree that the *other*, the soul's inseparable companion, was being extremely indiscreet.

Finally, very slowly and carefully, the hand wrote the following two words: Cecília Whitestone.

The mind seemed to wake up then and, alarmed at what had been done in its absence, made an attempt to put an end to such imprudence, with the hand immediately striking out the last two words as soon as it had written them.

Carlos stood up and paced about the room.

He began to persuade himself that he really had been most unfair to draw such hasty and unfavourable conclusions about his masked companion, and most ungentlemanly in his treatment of her. Jenny had scolded him for all these things, and Carlos thought he could hear his own conscience applauding Jenny. He even persuaded himself that he was filled with remorse and should find some way to remedy such gross faults.

While he was thinking this, he heard the clock strike two.

He lay down on his bed fully clothed, and it seemed to him ever more necessary and urgent to resolve the matter.

It was three o'clock before he began to feel sleepy. He lay down under the bedclothes and turned out the light.

Far from inviting him to rest, though, the surrounding silence grated on his nerves, one of those nocturnal silences so complete that you can even hear an invisible woodworm gnawing away somewhere. When our mind is troubled, when an idea will not leave us alone, silence and tranquillity seem to mock and jeer at us.

Less than a quarter of an hour later, the bedclothes were in a tangle and the pillow on the floor. Carlos again lit the candle, picked up a book and sat in bed for half an hour staring at the same pages.

Then he threw back the bedclothes and perched impatiently on the edge of the bed, convinced that he must have a fever.

This went on until five o'clock in the morning, and only then did he manage to fall asleep, or rather succumb to the exhaustion brought on by insomnia.

And what was the result of all that thinking? We will see shortly.

Let us go now to Manuel Quintino's house, where we will meet with some old acquaintances.

On returning from the theatre, Manuel Quintino had told his daughter not just the entire plot of *Lucia di Lammermoor*, which he had been prevented from doing while he was with Mr Richard and Jenny, but also the main events of the evening, apart, that is, from the handkerchief incident, which he had deemed unimportant.

Cecília listened in silence. It was almost as if it irritated her to hear Carlos' name mentioned so often, because Manuel Quintino did seem bent on talking about that wild young man, of whom, however wild, he was genuinely fond.

To judge by the slightly pained expression on Cecília's face at such moments, you would think she profoundly disliked her father's favourite. However, it would be best not to pay too much heed to the logical rigour of such physiognomical deductions, especially when applied to a young woman.

The following morning, when Manuel Quintino left for the office, his daughter appeared no less melancholy than she had on previous mornings, indeed, she looked even paler. Pale! God alone knows what deep and painful tremors that word triggers in a father's heart! For a father, his daughter's rosy cheeks are like the firmament for those overly impressionable souls who are filled with sadness when the clouds cover the sky, and filled with joy when the sky is cloudless and blue.

228

Imagine with what a heavy heart he set off to work.

How he racked his brain! The extravagant theories he came up with! How painstakingly he unpicked his own actions and words as he walked along, and all in order to discover the cause of that ill-disguised melancholy! But in vain!

At the office, he continued to worry away at the problem, and more than once found that his tireless companion, the pen, had come to a halt in the middle of a word, while he stared down at the sheet of paper, seeing nothing, and in a state of complete abstraction, and this in a man so little given to such states of mind!

It hadn't happened since the death of his wife – fifteen years before – and since Cecília's illness – six years before – and so he found it very odd.

In a way, Manuel Quintino was right to feel concerned.

Not that Cecília was *very* sad; her father's imagination, precisely because he so loved her, exaggerated her apparent sadness, simply because it troubled him; but she had definitely lost her naturally carefree, almost child-like air; she had grown suddenly tired of certain childish pastimes which, in the midst of the hustle and bustle of her domestic tasks, she had continued to enjoy; she had developed an unexpected taste for walking alone down the corridors and the garden paths, which was quite out of keeping with a character so little given to meditation, at least until then. Manuel Quintino was surprised, for example, not to see her playing with her very sweet, agile tabby cat, who had also noticed the change; nor to hear her singing to herself when she was working near the window that gave onto the garden, or making some innocently satirical remarks about the neighbours or asking the impertinent questions with which she would deliberately pester the maid; no one seeing her now would think she was someone of a naturally cheerful disposition.

On the morning that Manuel Quintino was struggling with the fears aroused in him by Cecília's altered behaviour, she was sewing in her room, and, unusually for her, she had the windows closed, and was so distracted that she would frequently stop what she was doing, her needle poised in mid-air.

More than once, Antónia came in to consult her on some domestic matter, but was obliged to repeat her question, because Cecília hadn't understood, and it should be said in Senhora Antónia's defence that this was certainly not due to any lack of clarity on her part.

Cecília was drawn out of one of those frequent deep abstractions by someone loudly ringing the doorbell.

Cecília started in surprise and glanced at the clock. It was just after one o'clock, so it couldn't be her father coming back, and it was rare for anyone else to ring the bell like that, still less at that time of day.

Her surprise grew and almost tipped over into disquiet and fear when Antónia entered with a look on her face that would have worried anyone, for the look on that venerable matron's highly expressive face was one of utter astonishment.

Seeing her, Cecília sprang to her feet and turned pale, as if expecting some dreadful news.

'Miss! Miss!' the maid managed to say, all out of breath.

'Goodness, what is it, Antónia?' asked Cecília, her heart beating so violently it seemed about to burst out of her chest.

'Oh, I still haven't got over the shock!' Antónia went on.

'Tell me what it is!'

'I'll tell you, but don't be alarmed. Although I must admit, I still am!'

'What is it? Tell me.'

'I will, I will, Miss, of course I will. That's why I came.'

'Well, it doesn't seem like it. Can't you see how alarmed I am?'

'Oh, there's no need to be alarmed. It's just that… oh, dear, let me catch my breath…'

Cecília clasped her hands impatiently.

'It's a gentleman,' Antónia said at last, 'a very smart, handsome gentleman. Oh, dear, I can feel one of my headaches coming on!'

'What does he want, Antónia?'

'He wants to speak to you.'

'To me? What do you mean? Is he still here?'

'Yes, he is.'

'But where?'

'In the parlour.'

'Good heavens! You invited him in?'

'What else was I supposed to do? He wanted to speak to you, and it always pays to be polite, especially with people who are also polite. And he has such lovely manners, saying Senhora this and Senhora that. He's not like those labourers who sometimes turn up and assume everyone was brought up in the same rough way they were. No, he's very refined…'

'But it's just not possible. There must be some mistake. It can't be me he's looking for. Did you hear him right?'

'I did, Miss, I did. Honestly, I'm not a complete fool, you know. I wouldn't let just anyone into the house, a stranger, without listening and asking. Really, Miss, you should know me better than that. What do you take me for? If I can't understand what's said to me, I might as well curl up my toes and die. Words were given to us so that we could understand each other, and the Good Lord gave us ears to hear, eyes to see and a mind to understand. Amen.'

'All right, all right. I clearly have no alternative but to go and see who the fellow is. And with Father away from home too!'

'We haven't been attacked by thieves. Besides, there's nothing so very odd about it. If you were alone, yes, but in the company of a respectable person like myself...'

Cecília still seemed uncertain.

Antónia insisted: 'Come on, Miss. It's rude to keep the gentleman waiting. What are you afraid of? If we're going to...'

'That's enough, woman. Be quiet. I know what you've been saying,' Cecília broke in, impatient now. 'I know I have to go. Now that the damage has been done.'

'What damage? Oh, don't say that, Miss. Did you expect me to...'

After hastily smoothing her hair in the mirror, Cecília turned her back on Antónia and went into the parlour where the maid had left the mysterious visitor whose presence was causing such a stir.

Antónia followed, still muttering to herself.

When Cecília went in, there was no one to be seen. The person waiting was standing on the balcony that gave onto the garden. He turned round, though, as soon as he heard the two women enter the room, but since he had the sun behind him, Cecília could still not see who it was.

She took a few hesitant steps, saying: 'I think there must be some mistake..'

'No, Senhora, there's no mistake. I came to see you.'

Cecília was dumbstruck. She knew that voice, and knew the person too.

It was Carlos Whitestone.

The alarm and confusion into which Cecília was thrown are indescribable, but easy enough to imagine for anyone who overheard that double confession of a few pages ago.

Cecília had to lean on the back of a nearby chair to disguise her troubled state; she blushed scarlet and just managed to say in a faint, tremulous voice: 'Senhor Carlos! What are you doing here?'

'I came to do my duty, Senhora.'

'Would you like to sit down?' Cecília said, almost too embarrassed to do so herself in case her legs gave way.

'Are you afraid to speak to me alone, Senhora?' asked Carlos, glancing across at Antónia.

Cecília had still not quite recovered from the shock, and so gestured to Antónia, who, stationed in the doorway, showed little desire to leave her post, which is why she pretended not to understand the order, even though she had heard what Carlos said perfectly clearly.

Cecília needed to shake off the spell she was under and was helped in this by the impatient way in which she repeated the gesture, this time adding rather brusquely: 'Leave.'

Antónia obeyed and went up the stairs, muttering resentfully: 'The jumped-up little dandy. Honestly, some people. As if I would reveal his secrets. Far better men than him have confided in me. Dr Raposo, now, he was a proper man of the law he was, and he never hesitated to talk to me about the clients and lawsuits he had to deal with. And during the three years I worked for Dr Dionísio, he was perfectly happy after supper of an evening to tell me about his patients and what he'd seen and heard in their houses. And I never breathed a word of it to a soul. The man hasn't been born who could accuse me of being a telltale. The fool, the milksop, the nincumpoop...'

And mocking Carlos' manners, she went on: 'Are you afraid to speak to me alone, Senhora? Yes, she is, and quite

233

right too. Or if she isn't, she should be… Fancy listening to a mere boy like him, whose face has barely seen a razor, and without a sensible adult on hand. And then she says to me: "Leave!" just like that. No, I won't, Senhora. Or only because, well, so as not to make a scene, but that's the only reason.'

This long palinode continued in the same vein, and Carlos sank still lower in Senhora Antónia's esteem.

As soon as the sound of Antónia's footsteps on the stairs had vanished, Cecília, tremulous and confused, went on: 'I can't imagine to what I owe the honour…'

Carlos did not allow her to continue: 'Forgive me, Senhora. You must know what has brought me here…'

'Must I?' asked Cecília, trembling.

'Yes, Senhora,' said Carlos. 'If you knew me, if you had learned to do me due justice, you should have realised when you saw me come into your house today, that there could only be one reason.'

'Which is?' murmured Cecília, almost afraid to hear the answer.

'To ask your forgiveness, Senhora.'

'My forgiveness?'

When she heard that word, Cecília felt as if she were about to faint.

'I know everything, Senhora,' Carlos went on, 'and please believe me when I say that I am filled with remorse not to have realised at once. Never have I been so painfully aware of the effects of my frivolous behaviour.'

'But… *what* do you know, sir?' stammered Cecília, as if still trying to doubt what she already knew for certain.

'Will you not spare me the pain of recalling the scene I am guilty of?'

'So Jenny told you…' Cecília cried, almost involuntarily,

as if speaking to herself; and her eyes filled with tears that threatened to spill over onto her cheeks.

Carlos interrupted her: 'No, Senhora, Jenny was the soul of discretion. Chance revealed everything I have so wanted to know ever since that night. My sister simply made me realise the rank indelicacy of my behaviour and the urgent need for an apology. And that is what I have come here to offer you. You have a right to that, just as Jenny would, and as I myself would demand from anyone who treated my sister as... discourteously as I treated you.'

'But, Senhor Carlos, it was entirely my fault...'

'Don't say that! Refusing to acknowledge my guilt is merely a polite way of refusing me the forgiveness I have come here to ask.'

Cecília did not respond, and so Carlos went on: 'You are Jenny's best friend, as she herself told me yesterday. I beg you not to consider me unworthy of your friendship too. I consider myself to be my sister's best friend too, and two people who merit the regard of an angel like her should have the same regard for each other, don't you think?'

'But, Senhor Carlos, I've never had any reason... I have no right to feel anything other than... than regard for you.'

'So you forgive me?'

Cecília remained silent for a moment, then, making a great effort, she said brightly: 'Senhor Carlos, let's speak no more about it, please. Let's forget the whole thing, as if it had all been a dream... a bad dream.'

And she lowered her eyes, as if exhausted by the violence of that inner struggle.

Carlos did not reply immediately. The intervening silence lasted a few awkward seconds, awkward for both of them. Then, looking at Cecília, he said: 'Forget?' in a way that seemed to suggest he didn't like the idea at all. Then he added: 'Yes, of course. Let's forget the whole thing, if that's what you want. But I must forget by repenting, as I already have, and you by forgiving. Why will you not forgive me? Do you forgive me?'

Cecília was again about to deny that he was to blame, but, looking up, she saw Carlos holding out his hand to her and, not quite thinking what she was doing, she held out hers too, murmuring: 'I forgive you.'

When she then tried to withdraw her hand and her words, it was too late.

As soon as he heard Cecília's words of forgiveness, which was the reason why he had come there, Carlos stood up.

'Thank you, Senhora,' he said. 'I have done my duty, and can leave contented.'

The poor girl could say nothing, indeed, it all still seemed like a dream to her.

'Just one other thing,' Carlos said, picking up his hat. 'When you entered the room, I was outside on the balcony. And I had just made a remarkable discovery.'

'A discovery?'

'Yes, a remarkable one too. A few days ago,' said Carlos, going over to the window where Cecília was now standing, 'I was walking in those pine woods... just over there. I was deep in thought – although I have no idea quite what I was thinking about – and for some reason, I felt my gaze, and then my imagination, drawn to a house I could see from there. The balcony was thick with climbing plants, and there was a camellia bush growing up between the two windows, and a young woman kept going back and forth on the balcony, busy with her domestic tasks, the kind of modest tasks which, in my eyes, surround the loveliest of women with the sweet perfume

236

of poetry.'

Cecília looked down, blushing, and appeared to be studying the bracket of a glass candleholder next to her.

'You can imagine my surprise when, on arriving here, I recognised the balcony, the windows and the camellia bush as being the very ones that had so caught my attention from afar. Which is why,' he added with a smile, 'it was easy to conclude who that lady was. Isn't that mysterious? It's as if that bush were telling me to take the step I took today? I'm certainly tempted to believe that, and, out of gratitude, may I take a souvenir? May I pick one of those camellias?'

Cecília could only smile in response and nod.

Carlos leaned over the balcony and broke off an as yet unopened bud, then stepping back into the room, he bowed respectfully and, after saying goodbye, left.

She saw him leave, but didn't move an inch, and for a long time remained in the same place and the same position.

Her mind was filled with a whirlwind of ideas, which one moment mortified her and the next, somehow or other, wrapped pleasantly about her.

Again, it was Antónia who put a stop to this abstracted state.

'So who was that very cautious, circumspect gentleman?' she asked, eager to assuage her curiosity.

'Didn't you recognise him? He's the son of Mr Richard, Papa's employer…'

'Really? Why, he's a grown man now. Last time I saw him, he was a child. But as for manners, well, he's clearly forgotten them.'

'Why do you say that?'

'Didn't you notice the impudence with which he asked you, in my presence, to send me away? And then you did as he asked. So what did the young upstart want?'

'Oh, nothing… but don't tell my father about his… er… visit.'

And seeing the startled look on Antónia's face, Cecília added: 'You see Jenny… and her brother… want to organise a surprise for my father… on his birthday… and they wanted to make sure I knew…'

Cecília clearly had no gift for lying; she spoke so hesitantly and blushed so deeply that no one would have been taken in.

As she herself would have put it, Antónia had eyes in her head to see, and witnessing Cecília's embarrassment and flushed cheeks, she said to herself: 'There's something odd going on here. I don't know whether I should say anything to Senhor Manuel Quintino or not… Not that there would be any point, since she can twist him round her little finger, and then I'll be the one in trouble. Oh, let them get on with it. A surprise for his birthday, indeed? Honestly! And then I bet I'll be the one who gets told off!'

Cecília shut herself up in her room to resume her sewing, but I can assure you that no further work was done.

Manuel Quintino was quite right: there was something troubling his daughter.

XVIII

Jenny consults Carlos' Conscience

When he left Manuel Quintino's house, Carlos was in pretty much the same agitated state as Cecília.

Viewed impartially, that visit – which, in his own eyes, he had tried to pass off as natural reparation for one of his many frivolous acts – could well have merited a different interpretation to him supposedly 'doing his duty'.

Had it been another woman, and not Cecília, one with fewer attractive qualities, but possibly with more right to expect some act of reparation, Carlos might not have been able to convince himself as profoundly and as quickly, as it appears he did, of the pressing need to take the step he took; perhaps he would not have spent all night thinking about it and would certainly not have acted on that impulse without first consulting Jenny, his counsellor in all things; but far from consulting her, he had carefully concealed his plan from her, as if afraid he might be dissuaded.

There are certain scrupulous respecters of the letter of the law, who will happily commit any plainly illicit act if they can find a way around the Code that will save them from being found out, for they care little about mangling the spirit in which the legislator wrote that law.

While a few may treat civil law in this way, there are many more who, every day and at every moment, do treat the laws of their conscience in exactly the same fashion. Rare are those who dare to face up to the punishment handed down by that rigid, all-seeing judge and bravely confess their crime; no, almost everyone protests against that punishment, tries to twist it, alter it and generally wriggle out of it, even if the punishment apparently fits the crime.

Pride often leads the criminal to refuse to defend himself in human courts; not even society's scorn or the severity of the law are enough to make him bow his head; he has the courage to adopt the crime, even calling it a crime, but that same criminal, alone in the tribunal of his conscience, will ardently plead the very case he refused to defend before the judges, who have the power to impose the death penalty.

Far be it from us to attempt to draw a close analogy between the perpetrators of heinous crimes and Carlos, who only has to justify himself to his conscience for one of those peccadillos that any hot-blooded twenty-year-old is bound to commit. But the conscience's jury is such that any case that comes before its court, is, by definition, bad, and no lawyers are needed.

Let us not delude ourselves, as Carlos did; we wouldn't want to doubt his good intentions, but there may well have been other reasons for the visit described in detail in the previous chapter.

What is beyond doubt is that, after his sleepless night, Carlos' one thought and one desire was to find a way of meeting Cecília and talking to her. And the result of that we already know.

The chance revelation at the theatre had already made a deep impression on an already susceptible mind, but it cut still deeper after that visit to Cecília.

It would seem that Carlos had found hidden meanings in the few words Cecília spoke during that encounter, and he could not stop thinking about them.

Once he became aware that he had been almost summoned by that female figure when, days before, he had distractedly fixed his gaze on a distant window, this now seemed to him like something much more than mere chance; he was almost inclined to believe that his eyes had been drawn there by some secret power.

Carlos' heart must be in a very serious state indeed if he is now inclined towards such superstitious beliefs.

It was two o'clock in the afternoon when Carlos arrived home. He walked along one of the garden paths to his sister's bedroom window and, pausing there, tapped very lightly on the pane.

Shortly afterwards, the curtains were drawn aside and Jenny appeared.

'What are you doing here at this hour, Charles?'

'Could we talk, Jenny?'

'Of course, come in.'

Carlos walked back down the path, in through the front door, and along a few corridors to Jenny's room.

Jenny was busy making a layette for the new-born baby of an impoverished family she was helping out.

Carlos sat down beside her, and Jenny went on with her work.

'What miracle is this? The magnolias in the garden must have been shocked to see you approach at this hour of the day!'

Carlos did not respond, but, playing with a coral necklace he had picked up from the dressing table, he said: 'Do you know where I've come from?'

'No, I don't,' said Jenny, without looking up.

'From Manuel Quintino's house.'

'Oh, yes, and why did you go there?'

'To ask Cecília's forgiveness.'

There was a silence.

Then Jenny turned suddenly, fixing Carlos with a grave, piercing look. Carlos seemed entirely absorbed in counting the beads in the necklace.

'Are you telling the truth, Charles?' asked Jenny, still with her eyes fixed on him.

'Why wouldn't I be?' Carlos replied and remained equally motionless.

'And did you talk to her?'

'I did.'

'What did you say?'

'I told her I was to blame for everything that happened on the night of the ball and asked her forgiveness.'

'And what did she say?'

'She…' began Carlos, finally putting down the necklace, 'after a little modest hesitation, she forgave me.'

'Oh, Charles, Charles! That wild head of yours!' said Jenny softly and in a benignly scolding tone.

'What?' said Carlos, slightly irritated. 'Did I do the wrong thing? Wasn't it my duty to do just that? I was expecting you to applaud my actions and yet you…'

At this, Jenny could not help rather impatiently setting aside her sewing, clasping Carlos' hands in hers and fixing him with those eyes as serene and limpid as a Spring sky; then, half-smiling, she asked: 'Tell me the truth, Charles, and only the truth. Why did you go and visit Cecília?'

'What a question! I've just told you. Wasn't it my duty to do so?'

'No, it wasn't. It would have been far better to pretend you knew nothing than make that poor girl blush in your presence. What you did – and which you say I should applaud – came not from your good, generous heart, but from that head of yours,' and she placed her hand on his forehead, 'that mad head of yours.'

'This time you're being unfair, Jenny.'

'No, I'm not. I'd like to believe you were deluding yourself, but, when you think about it, you'll see that I'm right. Yesterday, when we left the theatre, you were sad. I could sense it. And why were you sad? Was it remorse for your lack of respect for someone who merited only respect?'

'Yes.'

'No, it wasn't, Charles. Why are you trying to deceive me? It wasn't remorse. You were simply sad to see the end of an adventure you had imagined would last longer. The character of the person involved showed you, once you knew who she was, that your hopes were baseless, and then you...'

'Jenny!'

'Why deny it? I pride myself on being able to read your mind. I learned how to a long time ago, and you yourself helped me.'

Carlos lowered his eyes and began playing with his watch chain.

From that moment on, the victory was Jenny's. She sensed this and so went on: 'Then your imagination, that mischievous imagination of yours that we both know so well, set to work. It just couldn't resign itself to seeing that romance end so soon, when it had imagined it would go on and on, and so it fought really hard and even though you went to bed early last night, I bet it kept you awake for far longer than the entire episode at the Carnival ball. I'm right, aren't I? Admit it. And all the while your heart was quietly insisting that the truly generous thing would be to drop the whole thing, but your imagination kept coming up with problems, inventing obligations,

243

suggesting all kinds of tricky points of honour, and then your heart, your poor heart, which was fast losing ground, told you to at least consult your sister, but that naughty imagination of yours wouldn't even allow you that and even showed you the advantages of concealing everything from me, afraid I might dissuade you. And so you obeyed your imagination, got up and set off in search of Cecília to childishly ask her forgiveness, something that, in different circumstances, would have made you laugh, and the poor girl did forgive you, without really knowing what she was doing. Admit it, Charles, that's what happened, isn't it?'

Carlos couldn't help but smile, and kissing the hand his sister had placed on his, he murmured: 'You're a witch!'

Jenny smiled too, adding: 'That imagination of yours is clearly made of stern stuff, given what it manages to make you do! And yet,' she added, more seriously, 'and yet, I prefer to speak to your heart, which is made of equally stern stuff, because it's very sensitive and very generous and will eventually win out. Isn't that so? So I will speak to your heart, Charles, and hope it listens.'

'Speak, Jenny, speak. Advise me. You know I've long held you to be my good angel. Speak,' said Carlos fondly.

'Tell me, Charles,' Jenny went on, more and more earnestly. 'Can't you see what might come of your fantasy if you allow yourself to be carried away by it? Up until now, Cecília has been happy. She has never before had anything to feel sad or ashamed about, has never imagined some distant cloud threatening her future. It's been a life of utter tranquillity and serenity. But Cecília is eighteen, Charles, and has a trusting, imaginative heart... not unlike yours. I know her heart too. If an idea gets into that head of hers, if she starts nursing some illusion, it will prove very difficult and painful to root it out.

Wouldn't your good conscience come to hate your imagination if it seduced you into creating such an illusion, causing you to blight someone's entire future on a mere whim?'

'But how would I blight that future?' asked Carlos, looking up at his sister.

'How? Well, what if, following your visit, Cecília, who had forgotten all about the Carnival ball and its consequences, were to start thinking about you more? What if, having blushed in your presence out of shyness, she were, little by little, to begin blushing out of excitement... out of love?'

And when she spoke this word, Jenny herself blushed scarlet.

Carlos smiled to see this.

'Are you laughing, Charles? Is that because you find it odd to hear such words coming from me, or because you think my fears are unfounded? You're wrong on both counts. What I have failed to learn from personal experience, I've learned from other people, and most of all from you. I know how these things happen, how a whim becomes an *idée fixe*, and how that fixed idea becomes a passion. I know this, Charles, because I've seen it happen to you, and I know that Cecília, like you, has an imagination that could lead her to such extremes, with the difference that, in you, passion soon becomes forgetting, whereas in her... were she to love you...'

'What would be so wrong about that? I would love her in return, Jenny.'

Jenny looked away, trying to appear annoyed, then replied: 'Here am I talking to your heart, Charles, and you answer me with your imagination! Like a twenty-year-old child! I'm being serious. All right, children are allowed to play, but not with things they're not yet ready to cope with. You still haven't learned to cope with affections and with other people's hearts, not without endangering them. That's why I'm asking you not to continue with this game. You have no idea what might happen, what struggles you could find yourself embroiled in, if one day...'

'I have courage enough to struggle,' said Carlos somewhat wildly.

'Well, keep that courage for when the struggle becomes unavoidable, but don't yourself provoke such a struggle, which is always painful.'

'I don't understand.'

'All I'm asking, Charles, is that you abandon this mere fancy of yours, which I can see still has you in its grip. Stop it, Charles, if you want to avoid having to repent at some future date, when it will be too late. Stop now, if you want to spare yourself any feelings of remorse. It's your sister asking you this, and you always say how much you respect my judgement...'

'How could you doubt that now, Jenny?' said Carlos rather wearily.

'I don't, Charles, and I have complete faith in your ability to overcome this fanciful whim of yours.'

Carlos again bowed his head and remained silent for a moment.

'I don't know, Jenny,' he said at last, getting to his feet and pacing up and down the room. 'I don't know that this is just a whim.'

'So it's already developed into a passion, has it?' said Jenny rather mischievously, and taking up her sewing again. 'And after only two days! That grew very quickly! Please, Charles, don't be such a child. I just want you to question your conscience dispassionately, and what your conscience tells you...'

'Ah, don't trust too much in my conscience, Jenny. You've seen what it advised me to do this morning.'

Jenny gave him a look of utter incredulity.

'Oh, so it was your conscience that advised you to visit Cecília? Really?'

Carlos said nothing. He continued his pacing, all the while staring down at the floor.

Finally, he stopped, and gazing at his sister's image looking back at him from the mirror, he said in a rather tremulous voice: 'I'll try to obey you, Jenny, but I fear…'

'Don't talk to me about fear. Nothing can be achieved without faith, O incredulous one. Courage! Not long ago, you were boasting that you had enough courage to struggle.'

'I'll leave you now, Jenny. All I can say is that if the impression Cecília made on me ever does disappear… and I'm speaking to you frankly now, I will never again fear for my heart.'

'I remember you saying something like that before.'

Carlos was about to respond, but, as if wanting to escape a very awkward conversation, he rushed out of the room.

Jenny watched him leave and sat for a while deep in thought.

Moments later, Elisa came in with a letter.

'Who's it from?' asked Jenny.

'From Senhor Manuel Quintino's house.'

Jenny recognised Cecília's handwriting. She opened the letter and read:

My dear Jenny,

Forgive me, but I won't be able to visit you today. I don't feel well and think I may have to stay at home for a few days. My father is worried about my health and, even if only to reassure him, I will have to deprive myself of the pleasure of seeing you. Jenny, think of me and pray to God to give me your kindness of

heart and serenity of mind, because, given my character and
my head, I doubt I can be happy in this world.
    Your friend,
    Cecília

'Ah, so she feels the same!' murmured Jenny when she had finished reading the letter. She remained even deeper in thought than before, and a slight frown appeared on her brow.

The dismay apparently concealed beneath the words of that brief note, a dismay that Cecília had tried in vain to disguise as cheerfulness, explained the slight cloud that had settled over Jenny's usually serene countenance; accustomed to her friend's bright and breezy nature, normally so evident in her letters and her conversation, Jenny was understandably troubled by these signs of sadness.

Nor had she forgotten what Manuel Quintino had said at the theatre about his daughter's sudden changes of mood.

This is what she had been thinking about when Carlos came looking for her, and was what lay behind her possibly exaggerated feelings of apprehension when he told her about his meeting with Cecília, and her fears for the latter's future, so closely bound up with whatever Carlos did next.

She felt concerned, too, about Carlos' state of mind. In his presence, she had pretended a confidence she did not feel. She was concerned about what had happened, although without quite knowing why, and to her regret, she could think of nothing else.

To calm her thoughts, she tried to convince herself that her fears were baseless. She recalled her brother's previous passing fancies, all of which she had seen dissolve into nothing and with no unfortunate consequences for anyone. She struggled to find a thousand other reasons for Cecília's disquiet, apart from the one that an inner voice nevertheless continued to repeat.

She ended up in one of those moods when she felt the need to contemplate the beloved face of her mother, her counsellor from beyond the grave.

And so this pious daughter sat gazing at that portrait, sunk in a long, deep meditation.

Finally, she raised her eyes to heaven as if to offer up a silent prayer. Would the Lord look down on this angel's pleas and soothe her troubled mind? The fact is that, after a few moments, her features resumed their usual placid expression.

XIX

The Symptoms grow Worse

For all her innate kindness and her penetrating mind, Jenny had acted imprudently.

In not hesitating to confess to her brother her fears regarding what might result from his visit to Cecília, thus allowing him a glimpse of the possibility of arousing in the poor girl the kind of feelings to which young hearts can so easily succumb and which can sometimes quickly take on the force of a passion, Jenny, sensible Jenny, had merely given wings to the very evil she had thought to drive away.

As he listened to her, Carlos, far from reflecting on the serious consequences that such a nascent passion might bring with it, felt a wave of pleasure at the possibility; and that passion, however undelineated, was already smiling at him seductively, as the vague, future thing it still was.

One can never be too careful with imaginations like his, which are always ready to fly off into the realm of golden dreams.

You need to behave as cautiously as you would when spotting a child teetering on the edge of an abyss; often the shout you instinctively give in order to save them is the very thing that tips them over the edge; best commend them to Providence and not show them the danger until it is past. There are times when the heart, too, plays dangerously close to some precipice, and any advice is just as dangerous, and the alarm it causes can provoke a fall.

This is what happened with Carlos Whitestone.

It's extraordinary the importance we give, in matters of the heart, to other people's opinions! We spend ages trying to decide what name to give the feelings that a particular woman stirs in us, and which, however long we think about it, we still do not dare to call love. One day, though, we meet some hare-brained fool who thoughtlessly describes it as precisely that, and we bow to his potent authority. There are even examples of someone almost being convinced that he loves a woman simply because others keep telling him he does.

Carlos had more of an excuse, though, because Jenny was not one for making judgements lightly, nor of giving voice to unfounded suspicions and fears.

For all these reasons, he was in a far worse state when he left his sister than he had been before. And readers must forgive me if I use the words "worse state" to describe someone setting off along the road to love, and I would not do so were it not for the long cortège of misfortunes that usually accompany that emotion.

Carlos spent the rest of the day in his room, in a state of complete idleness.

Idleness! Can we give that name to those long intervals of apparent repose in which the muscles rest, but in which the brain engages perhaps in its most violent and exhausting exercises? As to whether or not this can be called idleness is a judgement I leave to any reader fortunate enough to possess one of those cool minds so ceaselessly absorbed in fulfilling its daily duties that it feels no need occasionally to throw off the yoke and run free through other more personal domains.

Carlos' life was about to enter one of those phases that throw up serious problems for the novelist determined to illumine his creation only with the light of reality. When a genuine passion fills a man's heart, the subjective life grows fiery and exalted, but the external life – which looms large only for those with no eyes to see and no heart to understand another man's heart – sinks down to the level of the puerile.

When manly dignity and masculine pride remain irreproachable and intact at the peak of such a passion, one should always doubt its sincerity.

For passion overturns all conventions.

A remnant of earlier days lies hidden in even the gravest and most sensible of men. The childish element never entirely dies in anyone. Our desire to conform works hard to conceal from others that legacy from childhood; the most sensible are the most successful at doing this, but a moment of distraction is all it takes for that childish streak to resurface.

This explains the proverbial candour of mathematicians and lovers.

It is also the reason why games were invented. People pretended to believe that whist, ombre, boston, etc. etc. were serious occupations, so that anyone could indulge in them in public without offending conventional ideas of seriousness, because if we didn't make these concessions to the child within – who can sometimes prove most impertinent – we run the risk of provoking far more scandalous rebellions.

As we were saying, though, a genuine passion – one of those ever rarer passions, in which the pleasure of loving vies in intensity with the pleasure of being loved – so absorbs the mind that it cannot exercise the necessary vigilance over that mischievous inner child.

And without some indulgence on the part of the person observing these breaches in seriousness, the victim of the passion runs the risk of being looked at askance.

This is why I shy away from chronicling what went on inside Carlos in the days that followed his conversation with his sister, because it will reveal little of what is deemed worthy of the hero of a novel.

I appeal, then, to the readers' own memories of their past behaviour, so that I can, if necessary, echo Christ's words in defence of the adulteress.

One of the first phenomena to manifest itself in Carlos was a sudden timidity, which was really most unusual in him, a truly childish timidity, in complete contrast to his former boldness, which had been evident even on his first visit to Cecília.

Now, for the first time, he felt shy.

Impelled by his heart to see Cecília again, he set out in the afternoon with that intention and headed for the street where she lived; when he had just turned the corner and was still some distance away, he thought he saw her at the window. What luck, eh? Or so one would have thought. However, he lacked the courage to walk past her door and so, unseen and feeling absolutely furious with himself, he took a different route.

Shortly afterwards, he appeared again at the same corner and, seeing no one at the window, he found the courage to walk past her house.

He felt simultaneously pleased and mortified that no one was there. I don't know if one cause can have such contradictory effects, but feel free to interpret this as you wish. I am merely recording the facts.

When he had almost reached the house, someone appeared at the window. It was Cecília, and Carlos guessed as much even before he recognised her face. He again experienced that same paradoxical phenomenon, feeling both mortified and pleased.

He immediately quickened his step and took on the air of a man in a great hurry, as if wanting to give the impression that he had just happened to be passing or was there on some urgent business.

"How very inconsistent!" the professional gallant will cry. And he would be right, but it's a very poor passion that knows nothing of inconsistencies. If syllogistic rigour resists such upheavals of the heart, why take such feelings seriously at all?

As he walked past the window, Carlos greeted Cecília shyly, almost awkwardly, and entirely lacked the courage to meet her eye or to look back as he continued on down the street.

Inside, he felt even more impatient and annoyed with himself. He, who had always been so bold, was now behaving like some self-conscious novice!

He paused at the end of the street. He couldn't get that thought out of his head. "What is happening to me?" he was thinking. "Have I reverted to being a fifteen-year-old schoolboy who doesn't even have the nerve to greet his cousin, with whom he thinks he is madly in love? Ridiculous!"

And after a few moments, he plucked up his courage and prepared to walk back, more brazenly this time.

Despite all this, though, his courage again began to fail him as he approached the danger point.

In one of those happy coincidences that once he would have known how to use to his advantage, but which he now almost resented, Manuel Quintino appeared at the door just as Carlos reached the house.

He was obliged to stop, having again, entirely unaudaciously, greeted Cecília, who was still standing at the window.

"What are you doing in these parts?' asked Manuel Quintino, surprised. 'What brings you here today?"

Carlos stammered out a few words, none of which constituted an answer.

Manuel Quintino smiled mischievously.

"I bet you're up to something, eh?"

Carlos blushed. Yes, he actually blushed!

"Really," he insisted, "I just happened to be passing and…"

"Oh, yes," Manuel Quintino said in the same knowing tone of voice.

Carlos was beside himself.

"No, seriously…"

"Yes, seriously… what man would say any different? Off you go now…"

Carlos was incapable of continuing the conversation, during which he did not once dare to look up at Cecília, or accept Manuel Quintino's invitation to go inside and rest a while.

He left, feeling even angrier with himself, as if his main aim had been to conceal from Cecília, not reveal, what he was beginning to feel for her.

And now a question: would Cecília have sensed all this? It seems rational to answer in the negative, but who knows how a woman's heart comes to know certain things, especially if…

But let us set aside such discreet "ifs", because it would be wrong to trespass so casually on Cecília's feelings.

Carlos spent the rest of the day in his room, reading.

There is something very particular about the way one reads when in such a state of mind.

Novels are the preferred reading matter, but not in order to be enjoyed from a literary point of view, but more as children and most women enjoy them – for the twists and turns of the plot. And if you'll allow me to say so, I imagine that they are precisely the readers any novelist would find most pleasing.

We eagerly follow the various phases of the passion described therein; we are filled with love for the heroine; we take on the character of the hero; and we never forgive the author when he ends the story with some catastrophe.

This is exactly the way in which Carlos was reading. A dangerous sign! He read a Walter Scott novel in a state of near intoxication, and afterwards sat for a long time thinking about what he had read; not so much about the wonders that abound even in that great novelist's least famous works, but about the happiness of the newlyweds; because in the final chapters of his books, Scott nearly always has hero and heroine joined in matrimony.

That night, Carlos again walked past Cecília's house. There was a light on in the front room, a light that could only be glimpsed through a crack in the shutters. It was time for tea and José Fortunato's nightly visit.

Carlos took an indefinable pleasure in observing that light. Experienced readers will understand why we should be worried about Carlos' state of mind.

At home, he avoided Jenny, fearing what she might say. For her part, Jenny thought it prudent not to provoke any further conversations on the subject. If only she had known that her usual gentle approach would not, this time, win the day.

On the first Sunday following these scenes – having first diplomatically gleaned from Manuel Quintino that he and his daughter usually went to mass at the Church of Cedofeita – Carlos abandoned his Protestant duties and, at a time when he knew the mass would be drawing to a close, he made his way to that ancient Catholic temple where he strolled up and down outside, determined to be seen.

However, when the first people started coming out of church, he was once more gripped by shyness, afraid now that he *would* be seen. With no time to go any further, he went and leaned on the wrought-iron gate of the adjoining graveyard.

A bad idea, well, good and bad at the same time, because Carlos was still caught between conflicting aspirations, as he had been for the last few days.

His fear of being seen coincided with a desire to be discovered. Illogical, but true.

And when Manuel Quintino came out of church, he made straight for the graveyard, for it was also the resting-place of Cecília's mother, and Manuel Quintino almost always went to pray beside his wife's grave after mass.

By the time Carlos had seen the direction father and daughter were taking, it was too late to escape. Manuel Quintino had already seen him, as had Cecília.

Manuel Quintino gave a friendly smile, and Cecília blushed in response to Carlos' awkward greeting.

'Have you come to pray for the dead?' asked Manuel Quintino mischievously.

Carlos attempted a number of lame excuses to explain his presence there.

'Well, if you did come to pray for the dead, you are in good company,' Manuel Quintino said, 'for I, alas, have someone to pray over too. Let me go and find the sexton so that he can open the gate for us.'

And he headed off towards the sacristy, abruptly leaving Carlos alone with Cecília.

Need I mention that this unexpected and involuntary meeting left both of them feeling profoundly embarrassed? Much has been made of the awkwardness of first encounters, and I would not deny it, but it seems to me that a second meeting is even harder to bear, when the first has been of any significance.

Carlos could not think of a single thing to say. He didn't even mention the weather! Cecilia was no more eloquent and silently fixed her gaze on the church door, through which her father had disappeared.

At this point, an old beggarwoman, of the kind always to be found at church doors after mass, came hobbling over to them.

'Kind sir,' she said in a mournful voice, 'have pity on a poor old woman who can no longer earn her daily bread.'

Carlos ignored her.

The old woman insisted.

'Please sir, give me something, and may the Good Lord see you do it.'

'No, I can't,' said Carlos distractedly.

The old woman then turned to Cecília.

'Sweet girl, ask him to give me some alms, and may the Good Lord make you both very happy, because you're obviously made for each other.'

Cecília tried to smile, but was so flustered that, instead, she stared down at the ground; no less disconcerted by the old lady's mistake, Carlos took a silver coin out of his pocket and gave it to her, saying: 'There you are, now off you go, woman.'

But the beggarwoman felt that further effusive words of gratitude were called for.

'May Our Lord God make you very happy and give you many years together, since you're obviously so well matched, poor loves! I'll pray hard to the Lord to bless you and keep you in His divine love. Goodbye, sir, goodbye. Goodbye, my dear. May our Lord Jesus look down on you from heaven and give you the happiness you wish for. Our Father who art in Heaven…'

Carlos and Cecília watched her leave and smiled, still not looking at each other or knowing what to say. Manuel Quintino returned and neither of them mentioned the incident, which would doubtless have amused him.

In my view, that silence is of great importance.

Carlos accompanied Manuel Quintino and Cecília to the modest grave, where a name, date and many flowers marked the place where lay the woman still so greatly missed by both. When they reached the grave, Cecília knelt down and, for some time, prayed devoutly. Manuel Quintino remained standing to say his prayers.

Their feelings filled Carlos' heart too. After all, he knew what it was to have lost one's mother.

Two souls who, as children, experienced that painful loss when they were far too young, can more easily understand each other, as if an invisible tie already bound them together. When in church, or beside a grave, one begins to pray, the filial piety of the other can sense the form that prayer is taking, can feel the anguish of that grief.

Silent and sad, Carlos gazed at the touching figure of that woman at prayer, and was almost tempted to kneel down beside her and pray with her.

When she stood up, Cecília found Carlos' eyes still fixed on her. There was such genuine compassion in that gaze, such sympathy, of the sort that banishes hesitation and inspires confidence, that, for the first time, Cecília dared to meet his gaze, saying with a look of genuine gratitude on her face: 'We've brought you to a sad place, Senhor Carlos. Forgive me for not sparing you the somewhat cheerless sight of a daughter praying at her mother's grave.'

'There are many kinds of happiness, Senhora,' answered Carlos. 'Melancholy feelings can sometimes bring with them a kind of pleasure too, a gentle, intimate, consoling pleasure, and I thank you for giving me such a pleasure.'

Then they fell silent again.

Having finished his prayers, Manuel Quintino was eager to leave that place of which he was far from fond.

The bitter-sweet quality of grief makes those for whom the sweetness predominates enjoy revisiting it, while others, who feel the bitterness more than the sweetness, are always in a hurry to escape. Manuel Quintino belonged to the latter category.

Carlos left the cemetery with them. Cecília went ahead. With his eyes still fixed on her, Carlos kept up a seamless conversation with Manuel Quintino on the most diverse topics. The old book-keeper spoke of agriculture, commerce, national politics, and public works, stopping several times in the middle of the street to give more forceful expression to his ideas. Carlos listened to him with such unparalleled patience and docility that even Manuel Quintino was amazed.

Sometimes, when they reached a street that would have allowed Carlos to take a more direct route home, Manuel Quintino would ask: 'Shall we leave you here, then?'

'No, no, I'll stay with you a while longer,' said Carlos.

'Yes, but…'

'No, it's fine, let's walk on.'

They had almost reached Manuel Quintino's house, and the book-keeper again insisted that Carlos should go no further: 'Unless, of course, you'd care to dine with me,' and only then did Carlos reluctantly agree to leave them.

He bade a fond farewell to Manuel Quintino and Cecília, at whom he looked rather less shyly than before, albeit with a shyness that would have shamed even the most timid of gallants. As he rounded the corner where he would finally lose sight of father and daughter, he summoned up the courage to turn and catch one last glimpse.

Manuel Quintino was already going in through the front door; Cecília, though, who had been walking a little behind, also chanced to turn round – at least I think it was chance – so that her eyes met Carlos'.

This very simple detail provided Carlos' imagination with enough food for the rest of the day, for the imaginations of those in love require very little sustenance. All it takes is the most trifling thing – a smile, a word, a look – and their imaginations will extract from that infinite riches for the mind. From then on, as chance would have it – and again I don't know if it was anything more than chance – Cecília was always at the window when Carlos rode past, heading out of the city; and in the evenings, when Senhor Fortunato was beginning to think that tea was rather late in being served, there was always a moment when Cecília would decide to go and see what the weather was like and would then linger at the window, contemplating the sky.

As chance would have it – again, always assuming this was a matter of chance – this was precisely the time when Carlos would be returning from his ride into the country. Since he could not possibly fail to recognise Cecília's profile in the lighted window, and he would, of course, bow to her, and since, at that moment, the light from the streetlamp always lit up his face, Cecília had no choice but to respond to his greeting.

The days that followed were full of equally significant events, but I would never finish this chapter were I to record them all. I will, therefore, leave it to you, the reader, to fill in the blanks, because this chapter is one that is common to all romances.

Jenny, meanwhile, was finding her brother's behaviour ever more confusing, and Manuel Quintino, for his part, became increasingly worried about Cecília's changes of mood.

Carlos had broken completely with his usual habits, and his absence was noted in cafés, theatres, meetings and at any gatherings of his friends.

He spent hours and hours in his room, and sometimes sat with his head in his hands, not reading or writing, or doing anything at all; at other times, the servants would hear him pacing up and down, smoking cigar after cigar, and filling the air he breathed with smoke.

He went out either on foot or on horseback, but he nearly always left the city behind him. He suddenly became very fond of a certain old Englishman, deemed the most boring man in the entire English community, and would even go and wait for him at the office and patiently accompany him to his house, which just happened to be in the same direction as Manuel Quintino's house.

If he did occasionally find himself in Jenny's company, she was always astonished at the change in him; if he tried to put on a cheerful front, she could see how much effort this took. All these things gave her a great deal to think about.

One day, Jenny saw him angrily throw down the book he was reading, and seeing that it was a volume of Byron's work, she asked with a smile: 'What's this? Why have you suddenly taken against an author you so admire?'

'To be honest, I sometimes get rather irritated with Lord Byron. There's so much sourness and sarcasm in some of what he writes that reading several of his admirable poems one after the other can have a very depressing effect. His poetry may be sublime, but it's disquieting too. It both dazzles the mind and pains the heart. The instincts of an eagle may be loftier and more heroic than those of a dove, but whereas we're all perfectly happy to have doves living near the house, having an eagle as a neighbour would be rather less consoling, even though the sight of one always excites our curiosity.'

Instead of smiling at her brother's words – which revealed in him a very different way of thinking – Jenny regarded him seriously for a moment, then said: 'Look at me, Carlos,' and Carlos raised his eyes. 'Do you really mean that?'

'Yes. Why do you ask?'

'Because I wanted to know.'

And then she said nothing more and resumed her sewing.

On another occasion, he went over to his sister, who again was sewing, and took out the Bible she always kept in her sewing box. Opening it at random, he read for a while in silence. Then, setting it down on the table, he said in a jocular tone: 'Whenever I read about the simple customs of the patriarchs as described in Genesis, I can't help but think what lengths mankind appears to have gone to in order to make the path to happiness ever more fraught with difficulties. Think how simple it was for Isaac and Rebecca, for example, to get married, and then compare that with the thousand and one absurd obstacles you have to overcome to do so now, and all in the name of social custom...'

Jenny responded in the same tone.

'So what are you saying, Charles? Would you really like to see a return to those customs? If, like Abraham, a father sent a servant to the land of his forefathers to get a wife for his son, would a modern rebellious Isaac accept her, even if the servant had, as in the Scriptures, asked and received from God the necessary inspiration for making that choice?'

Carlos burst out laughing, then, after a pause, answered: 'At least in those days the people who meddled in the futures of others took their inspiration from a good source. Now, it would take more than an encounter with a kind woman drawing water from a well to quench the thirst of the servant and his camels to prove that she was God's chosen one. Nowadays, the servant wouldn't bother giving her gold nose rings and bracelets, he'd want to know how much money her family had and her social class…'

These words gave Jenny much food for thought. For her part, Cecília was proving equally baffling to her father. All the symptoms Manuel Quintino had noted before had grown still worse.

Cecília was in the overwrought state so frequent in women of a nervous disposition, which means that even the most trivial of reasons can make them burst out laughing or burst into tears. A grey, rainy morning, a flower unpetalled by the wind, a butterfly damaged by the frost all loom like major tragedies; a clearing sky, the first shoots of a plant, the first swallow of summer, the first dawn chorus all unleash a joy more appropriate to some great celebration.

A single word can prompt an angry response; a single look can overcome deep-seated antipathies; a mere nothing can be enough to destroy some project long in the planning; while new resolutions spring up easily and inspirations of the moment are met with blind belief, long-pondered resolutions are cast aside; in short, nothing in a woman's mind is fixed and stable. In such a state, there is no logic to emotions. The heart beats irregularly, virginal cheeks are constantly blushing then turning pale – evidence of mysterious inner struggles.

Unversed in the phenomena of the heart, Manuel Quintino saw only the symptoms, and this was quite worrying enough. No one could dissuade him from the idea that his daughter was about to fall ill, that her mother had passed on her disease to her daughter. And yet, consumed by this fear, he was the one who was in danger of becoming ill.

XX

Manuel Quintino seeks Distractions

The first of April 1855 fell on a Sunday.

We mention this fact, which the reader may check if he or she so chooses, only because it proved not insignificant for the destinies of the various people caught up in the story we are writing.

These are precisely the things that make our human plans so fallible; amazing consequences can sometimes spring from one tiny, inconsiderable event, and can upturn the fate not just of one man, but of whole empires.

Since the abovementioned circumstance would not occur were it not for leap years, it follows that, because of this, the fate of the characters in this story is linked to such distinguished men as Julius Caesar and Pope Gregory XIII, who, at different times, were the ones who ruled on this matter and gave us the calendar we have today.

Having made this point of philosophy-cum-history, let us continue.

As it was a Sunday, Manuel Quintino lunched earlier than usual, and seeing that his daughter's mood had still not lifted, he insisted on the need for her to get out of the house. He suggested that she go and visit Jenny, an idea that Cecília greeted with evident distaste.

A sense of delicacy prevented her from seeking out her

closest friend, because Carlos lived in the same house, and, as the reader will have noticed, without me actually having said as much, Mr Whitestone's son was hardly a matter of indifference to Cecília.

Manuel Quintino urged her, though, to 'get a breath of fresh air and some company' and he did so in such a way that Cecília decided to do as he asked and go and see Major Matos' daughters, who lived just a few houses away.

'Yes, do that,' said Manuel Quintino, 'that will be much more fun than spending the rest of the afternoon with me.'

'Does that mean you're going to be left alone?'

'Me? Yes, but I'll be fine.'

'No, I'm not having that,' retorted Cecília. 'I'll only go out if you promise you'll go for a walk as well.'

'All right, all right. I'll find something to do, but don't let that stop you.'

'You'd better get dressed then.'

'Let me have a rest first.'

'No, I'm not going out until you do.'

Manuel Quintino was obliged to give way. He was sure that it would be good for his daughter to spend the afternoon in amusing company, because he himself was feeling so low in spirits that he didn't feel capable of providing her with such company.

And so, in order to encourage Cecília to leave the house, he went out as well, also in search of some distraction.

Manuel Quintino was an excellent fellow, but lacked the insight needed to probe the enigma of an eighteen-year-old girl's sadness. As a doting father, his almost excessive love for her got in the way. He saw in everything a sign of illness, and that *idée fixe* meant that he didn't have the necessary coolness of mind to see these things clearly.

When he woke each morning, what first filled his mind was this same black thought: 'Will Cecília have succumbed to the sickness?'

Every afternoon, when he came home from work, instead of trembling with anticipatory pleasure at the thought of seeing and embracing his daughter, he trembled with fear that he might find her ill.

However hard he tried, he couldn't rid himself of that thought. When he slept, he was troubled by dreams, when he ate, the food tasted as bitter as gall, when he was working, he couldn't concentrate on the task in hand.

His friends eyed him anxiously and talked about him behind his back.

'There's something bothering Manuel Quintino, poor man.'

'He's not long for this world, I reckon.'

'If he goes on like this, Mr Richard had better start looking around for another book-keeper...'

But once the human mind is in the grip of an *idée fixe*, it struggles in vain to free itself, to divert its thoughts onto other topics; a kind of natural bent always brings it back to that one idea. You might compare it to a loaded dice which, however, you throw it, always lands the same way up. States of moral equilibrium seem to be ruled by laws similar to those governing physical equilibrium. Stability of mind is intimately linked to the relative intensity of the ideas acting upon it, which will often set a particular thought in motion, then leave it to its own devices, with no new demands being made upon it; the weightier idea will determine the mind's equilibrium; only if the ideas all make equal demands will this be a matter of indifference, and that only happens in the most fatuous of minds.

As we have seen, at the time, Manuel Quintino could think

of nothing but his daughter's sadness, which he interpreted as a prelude to illness, which would soon come to vie with him for her love. All afternoon, regardless of any thoughts prompted by the things he saw, they all arrived at the same conclusion.

Whenever Manuel Quintino went for a walk in search of distraction, he always chose the same route. He had done so since time immemorial, and it did not even occur to him to change it. He let himself be guided by habit, as he did in everything else. He walked through the city to the riverside quarter of Ribeira and then continued along the right bank as far as Campanhã; then, on reaching Esteiro, he headed uphill to the Jardim de São Lázaro, and from there began the walk home.

This is what he did that afternoon too. He crossed the city, still grappling with the same sad thought with which he had left the house, and the first diversion occurred only when he came to the fish market in Ribeira.

The fishing boats had just that minute arrived at the quay. The market was filled with the hustle and bustle of vendors and customers and the fishermen selling their wares.

Manuel Quintino always enjoyed this lively spectacle, the noise and the hubbub; he studied with an expert eye the various types of fish, and enquired about the current prices. When he left, he was thinking: 'There's nothing better for domestic order than hake. It's the most innocent fish there is. It's hardly surprising that we Portuguese call it the chicken of the sea. There's the sardine, of course, which is delicious, but less healthy somehow. Sardines from Espinho are another matter, but the local ones... I wonder why they're so different? After all, it's the same fish. Perhaps it's because the beaches here are stonier and so the fish get more of a battering, because the coastline here is very rocky. Well, you just have to think of the danger to shipping. Why, only the other day, there were those eight fishermen whose boat was wrecked! Cecília was terribly upset when the newspapers explained that a little child had been orphaned. Poor Cecília! She has such a big heart, poor love. She's an angel. And when I think about how sad she's been lately...'

And there was his *idée fixe* again! It was as if the idea itself had composed that string of associated ideas in order to lead him back to that one thought.

The positive impression the market had made on Manuel Quintino vanished completely, and he continued on his way, once more sunk in melancholy.

Further on, having passed the last house blocking his view of the river and the opposite shore, he naturally turned his gaze on the bare sombre shape of Serra do Pilar, crowned by its ruined monastery and its round church. The sad vestiges of past civil wars are too much in evidence there for the memory of them not to rush in upon anyone studying them for any length of time.

Like nearly all natives of Oporto of a certain age, Manuel Quintino had been more than a mere spectator of those tragic scenes from those all too memorable times.

'Twenty or more years ago,' he was thinking, 'it wouldn't have been so peaceful around here. Nor would a stroll by the river have been advisable. There were more dangers then than just the mist coming off the river. What a time that was, and what I went through! It feels like only the other day, and yet it's more than twenty years ago! Oh, but the joy when the siege was lifted! At the time, Cecília's mother was no more than a girl, and it wasn't until four years later that she began to fill my thoughts... Poor lass! I can see her now. So thin and pale, but always so kind and hard-working too. That's why I'm so worried... Oh, dear God, there I am thinking about Cecília again.'

And thus from the Serra do Pilar and the days of the siege that obsessive idea had once again managed to insinuate itself into his mind, and this time it seemed to have brought in its train even more sinister omens.

When he reached the Fonte do Carvalhinho, he climbed the stone steps and drank a little water from the basin of the fountain itself, something he always made a point of doing, because he had great faith in the medicinal properties of that excellent water.

'Ah,' he said, 'it does one good to drink such water! Oporto's the place for that! They say the water in Lisbon's bad, but good water is vital for our health. Then again, there's a lot of illness about in Oporto too, despite the good water. Young people nowadays are so scrawny, so puny. Not good at all. That's what I fear when I look at Cecília. She's so delicate, so...'

And there he was again, sunk in gloom for quite some time.

He came to the so-called Quinta da China, a favourite haunt of the working classes.

A few small groups of people were there, in festive mood; laughing and singing, they were walking down the slope that leads to the river. The women from Avintes were bringing their boats in to shore to welcome them; others, still some distance away, were calling to them with all the force of their strong lungs. Propelled by the vigorous arms of those graceful, cheerful rowers, the boats came and went, laden with people out to enjoy the rustic pleasures of Areinho and the fishing. Everything on the river was laughter and song.

Manuel Quintino saw all this and listened idly to what one of the female rowers was singing:

An English Family

All the wealth of the world
Is as nothing to me.
For in your loving arms,
I'm rich as can be.

And he started thinking: 'How contented these poor people are with their hard life! Out in all weathers, and heavens knows what they have to eat at home. And yet they sing and laugh with such gusto. It's wonderful to see these fifteen-or-sixteen-year-old girls rowing so vigorously. It would exhaust a fellow like me. There's nothing like good fresh country air and the outdoor life to toughen people up. Indeed, if I thought it would help Cecília...'

And his thoughts returned to their usual place, from which they had, for a moment, strayed.

He reached the point along the river called Rego Lameiro. There the Douro undergoes one of its sudden and surprising transformations. The hills fall away from the shore to reveal a delightful valley full of thick, lush vegetation and streams rushing down the nearby slopes. One appreciates these rare moments when the stern Douro actually smiles, as one appreciates a flicker of joy on a usually glum face.

Here the river widens and the current slackens, creating, at low tide, little islands, where the fishermen's children go to play. The tortuously winding banks, which make the actual route of the river hard to follow, gave this area the appearance of a small, picturesque lake. On one side are the sandy shores of Quebrantões, beyond which lie green meadows, fertile plains, thick groves of trees and, hidden among them, the charming houses of small rural settlements; further on, there's the house and estate of Pedra Salgada and, in the hazy blue distance, the

271

delightful town of Avintes; on the other side lie the palace of Freixo with its towers and balustrades and the gardens and riverside paths of Valbom and Campanhã. And if, at the end of the day, when the whole scene is gilded by the sun, leaving fiery reflections in any west-facing windows, and the gentle evening breeze fills the white sails of small boats, and the sky is blue and the water clear, then the landscape more than compensates those unable to visit the more celebrated beauty spots praised by travellers and poets, the equivalents of which we are sometimes too blind to see, even though they are just two steps from our own front door.

Manuel Quintino always sat here for a few minutes, on a rock near the shore.

'How lovely!' he thought. 'There's no other walk like it around Oporto. And the evening is so serene and quiet that you can almost hear what people are saying in Areinho. If I had the money, this is where I would buy a house and some land. I would leave the office on a Saturday, hop in a boat or even go on foot, after all, it's only a short walk. It might be rather far for Cecília, of course, although she never gets tired. Well, perhaps now she does...'

And the black idea, that stubborn black idea, once again took hold of Manuel Quintino! And as the evening advanced, growing ever blacker, it was as if the shadows were also thickening around that idea.

From that point on, his thoughts did not alter. A tannery, some children to whom he gave some money, a few warehouses, everything he saw, all plunged Manuel Quintino back into his earlier anxieties. And that walk, which was supposed to distract him, only exacerbated his ills.

He was walking up the steep incline that led from Rua do Esteiro de Campanhã to Padrão. The afternoon had grown suddenly colder. Whether as a result of continually dwelling on sad things or something else entirely, Manuel Quintino began to feel unwell. His head felt heavy and slightly dizzy; his knees gave way beneath him, and he was overcome by a general weariness that made the walk home much harder; and then there was that sense of melancholy weighing on his heart, which felt now as if it were in the grip of an iron hand.

Feeling discouraged and sad, he almost had to drag himself up that steep slope.

When he reached one of the taverns where, on Sundays in Spring and Summer, a few jolly Oporto residents got together for lunch, he heard singing and laughing, which rather jarred with him in his current muddled state. In the midst of all the loud chatter, he seemed to hear someone say his name, but, too distracted now to hear what they were saying, he continued walking.

Suddenly, a colleague from the office appeared at the tavern door and called out to him.

Manuel Quintino turned slowly, without saying a word.

'Where have you been, Senhor Manuel Quintino?'

'Down by the river,' he replied in a faint voice.

'Didn't you meet anyone you knew along the way?'

'No.'

'Well, someone was here asking for you not long since.'

'Asking for me?'

'Yes. So you have no idea what it could be about?' said the man, who spoke in rather grave, measured tones.

Manuel Quintino's heart began to beat wildly.

'No, I…'

'Well, they were here just a few minutes ago, saying you should go straight home because…'

'Why?' asked Manuel Quintino, and a shudder ran through

him, and his mouth went dry, as if he were burning up with fever.

'Well, given what he said, it seems your daughter's rather ill. He said he'd called in at the office already, but...'

Manuel Quintino was no longer listening. Dredging up strength from his love for his daughter, and still shocked and anxious, he now almost ran rather than trudged up the hill.

Seeing him race off like that, the man who had spoken to him, burst out laughing.

'Come and see this! Just look at him go!' he said to his companions.

One of the other men joined him at the door.

'Poor man. Call him back. He might have a heart attack.'

'Hey, Manuel Quintino! Don't forget it's April Fool's day today! Manuel Quintino!'

But the poor old man didn't even hear them and was running even faster now.

Those men had had their April Fool's fun by cutting to the quick a father's heart. And they were laughing!

The world is full of such pranksters.

'Someone will soon put him out of his misery,' said the joker. 'Leave him be. Think how happy he'll feel when he gets home.'

And he laughed again.

In the meantime, Manuel Quintino continued his rapid, furious onward march, as if he wanted to eat up the distance still separating him from his daughter, and all the while he was muttering to himself: 'Cecília... my poor daughter! Oh, dear God! How dreadful...how dreadful! Whatever possessed me to go for a walk? No, it can't be... But why else would someone come looking for me. Who knows... She must be in grave danger, yes, grave danger. Oh, holy Mother of God. And it's so far too. She's probably desperate for me to get home. Oh, my poor daughter…'

And the tears streamed down his face.

The dizziness was getting worse; the brief burst of physical energy the news had given him was subsiding now into the utter exhaustion that had made his knees turn to water. Realising this, the poor man felt terrified. Trembling, he kept repeating to himself: 'Oh, Lord, please give me the strength to get home quickly! My poor daughter!'

And the buzzing in his ears was growing ever louder; reddish spots and specks and clouds of blood passed before his eyes; he could hear the pounding in his temples and his carotid arteries; the ground seemed to be slipping away from under him; he was walking, but without knowing he was walking, no longer able to regulate his increasingly uncoordinated movements.

Some passers-by stopped to stare at him, and Manuel Quintino heard them say: 'Look at that poor soul! He'll be lucky to get home in one piece!'

These words made him feel even more anxious. He had reached the little Senhor do Padrão chapel.

'Oh, Holy Mother of God help me!' he murmured.

He leaned for some time against the chapel door.

He said a fervent prayer, of the kind that could only possibly fail to reach the throne of God if the gates to Heaven had been closed for ever to humanity's pleas. Never has there been a more heartfelt prayer.

He appeared then to summon up a little energy. He managed to walk on, but more slowly and uncertainly. However, the dizziness soon returned. His heart was gripped by a deep sense of foreboding, a mysterious sense of imminent danger.

The light from the streetlamps seemed to him tinged with

red. His vision became more clouded; everything about him was spinning; objects became blurred, and he felt as if the ground were suddenly dropping away, so rapidly that he had to stop walking in order not to fall. He leaned in a doorway, where he heard a voice say: 'Are you all right, sir? Come in and rest a while.'

'No,' he said rather abruptly, as if that offer of help cruelly destroyed the illusion he was struggling to maintain. Then he tried again to walk. He was near the public cemetery now, the so-called Place of Rest; he took a few more steps, but experienced the same symptoms, only more violently this time; the dizziness became vertigo, and the ground seemed to give way beneath him.

He managed to murmur: 'Oh Lord, please, for pity's sake! Am I to die here without seeing my daughter?'

And he sank down onto one of the stone benches in the esplanade outside the cemetery.

XXI

The Importance of being Decisive

Thinking that her father's walk would not take long, Cecília returned home when it was still light.

However, dusk began to fall, and there was still no sign of him. It was now dark out in the street, and the sky above the sea was turning flame red... and still no sign of him!

Cecília's heart began to fill with a vague mist of fears to which she avoided giving any definite shape, but as night came on, that mist became a fog, and still no Manuel Quintino! Her imagination began to invent a thousand obscure explanations for that otherwise inexplicable delay.

Unable to rest, she kept going over to the window hoping to spot his familiar figure at the top of the road, and then, feeling sad and frightened when he failed to appear, she came inside again.

She spoke to Antónia, hoping for some reassurance, but far from reassuring her, Antónia, who was equally alarmed at her master's continued absence, merely terrified her with theories dreamed up by her own fertile imagination.

'I can't understand why he's so late. He's usually so punctual,' she said. 'Unless, of course, something's happened to him...'

'But what could possibly have happened to him, woman? How can you say that?' said Cecília, horrified at her maid's vague insinuation.

'What do you mean?' Antónia went on. 'Accidents can happen anywhere. You can break your leg while lying in bed. Just look at that old man who used to walk past here every day on his way to the customs house. One day, he tripped over the step at the front door, only as big as this it was, and he fell so badly that a week later, he was dead and buried.'

Cecília turned pale at these words.

'But if something had happened to my father, someone would have told us.'

'Hm, that depends. Sometimes these things happen in places where you don't know a soul, and if he can't tell someone, well…'

'I know, it could all go horribly wrong, but it's not as if my father had gone into a jungle inhabited by savages. Honestly, the things you come out with!'

'All right, but if he was simply delayed for some entirely innocent reason, he would have sent word, wouldn't he? He'd know how worried and alarmed you'd be.'

Exasperated by this Cassandra of the kitchen, Cecília went back to the window.

The streetlamps were lit now, but the shadows of the night seemed to creep into Cecília's own heart.

'Shall I bring a lamp, Senhora?' asked Antónia.

This question obliged Cecília to notice the lateness of the hour and sounded a funereal note in her ears.

'No,' she said, her voice shaking. 'Why light the lamps so early?'

'Early? It's gone seven o'clock. He's clearly not coming.'

'What do you mean "not coming"? Are you mad, woman? Of course he'll come,' Cecília exclaimed, feeling even more exasperated and almost angry now as she leaned further out of the window.

'There's no point waiting there. It won't make him arrive any sooner,' Antónia added rather foolishly.

'That's none of your business. Now leave me alone,' said Cecília curtly.

'Who'd have thought it, eh?' the maid went on. 'But then these things always happen when you least expect it. A person leaves his house with not a care in the world, and for some reason… I mean where can he have got to? Who's to say what's happened to him? Gone! I remember that one day, my father…'

'Go and fetch a lamp, go on,' ordered Cecília, to stop Antónia launching into that anecdote, doubtless with the pious intention of drawing from it some discomfiting conclusion.

Antónia left the room.

Cecília was by now beside herself with fear and had no idea what she should do.

She imagined that any figure appearing at the top of the road must be her father, and she would follow whoever it was with an eager curiosity that soon became despair as she watched the figure walk straight past their house.

Cecília was close to tears when Antónia returned with the lamp.

'Still no sign?' she asked.

Cecília didn't even reply.

'Shall I close the windows?'

'No.'

'It's not like him at all. Your father always comes home early and he'd be sure to send a message if, for some reason or other, he couldn't come. I can't help thinking that something must have happened to him.'

The clock struck half past seven.

An English Family

'Half past seven! It's late. Shall I get the tea ready?'

'No! What do I care about tea? Have you gone mad?'

'It's just that Senhor José Fortunato will be here soon…'

'Well, if he comes, he comes. I've got more important things to think about than Senhor José Fortunato! Just leave me be.'

Antónia was the sort who never loses sight of her daily duties however worried she might be. Her mind might be troubled and her mouth give voice to her problems, but her hands, independent of the imagination, would still get on with their usual tasks.

Cecília was different. Being of a passionate nature, she was entirely possessed by that one thought. The indecision into which she had been plunged by this state of anguished doubt made her incapable of any task.

She didn't want to talk about anything or hear anything or be told anything.

She waited nervously, impatiently, feverishly, she walked from window to window, came back into the room, went out onto the landing, then ran to the window again.

On one of those occasions, she heard two women talking in the street below. One of them was saying: 'It was such a tragedy! No one got out unscathed. Some died, while others were left crippled for life.'

Cecília's heart beat still faster when she heard this, and, unable to help herself, she called down to the women to ask what tragedy they were talking about.

And she waited with bated breath to hear their answer. They told her that the day before some workers had been caught in a landslide at a quarry. She breathed again.

Another time, a man came running all the way from the top of the road and stopped right in front of the house and hovered there like someone trying to identify one house in particular. Cecília wanted to ask him who he was looking for, but so intense was her fear when she saw him that her voice almost failed her.

It seemed impossible that he was not some messenger of doom.

Finally, she managed to speak, and it turned out that the man was looking for one of her neighbours.

Still barely recovered from her fright, Cecília pointed him in the right direction, and going back into the room, she heard the doorbell ring.

A shudder ran through her, a mixture of hopes and fears. Could it be him?

Antónia came down the corridor and announced with great aplomb: 'It's Senhor José Fortunato.'

Sadly, haughtily, Cecília turned her back on Antónia, feeling almost resentful of their nightly visitor.

'Good evening, my dear. How are you?' asked José Fortunato when he came into the room.

'I'm worried sick, Senhor José Fortunato,' Cecília said.

'Really?' he asked, setting down his various accoutrements – umbrella, cape, scarf, gloves, hat, cigarette case – before finally sitting in his usual chair.

'Haven't you heard?' asked Cecília. 'My father went out for a walk this afternoon and he's still not back. And it's getting late.'

'That certainly is most... most unusual. Do you think something has happened to him?'

A very stupid question.

José Fortunato rivalled even Antónia in the clumsy way he intervened in the present crisis; far from being reassuring, his words had the effect of increasing Cecília's disquiet and fear.

281

She responded to his unsettling words by returning to her post at the window in the grip of an even greater anxiety, saying in a quavering voice: 'Whatever can have happened to him?'

Placidly seated at the table, José Fortunato went on: 'Senhor Manuel Quintino hasn't been quite himself for a few days now. I told him so just the day before yesterday "You should go and see someone about it before it gets worse." He wouldn't hear of it, though, but then that's the kind of man he was.'

His choice of the past tense only redoubled Cecília's fears. *Was!* This, however, was typical of José Fortunato. It was as if, for him, Manuel Quintino no longer deserved to be spoken of in the present tense! Not content with this, he went on:

'This changeable weather can be very dangerous especially for those of a certain age. I know a lot of people who've come down with sudden illnesses. That Gamboa fellow, who worked for the Council, he had an attack of apoplexy yesterday and dropped dead on the spot.'

'Please, Senhor Fortunato, don't talk of such things,' Cecília cried in an anguished voice. 'Surely if some misfortune had befallen my father, someone would have come to tell us, wouldn't they? He's just been delayed for some reason…'

'I'm not saying that… but disaster can strike at any time… And your father had another bad habit, which I'd often warned him about. He was always going down to meet the English steamships, and although he's quite a big man, he's no spring chicken, and he could be quite reckless when boarding the ships as they were mooring, because that's a dangerous business, you know. Especially for someone who doesn't know how to swim…'

José Fortunato's words rang in Cecília's ears like a death knell.

'Senhor José Fortunato,' she said, almost raising her hands to fend him off, 'don't you see that your words are killing me? Besides, it's Sunday today, and my father wouldn't have been boarding any steamships. I told you, he just went for a walk.'

'Calm down, my dear. That was merely a manner of speaking. Like you, I very much hope no misfortune has befallen him. God is good and he knows how much Senhor Manuel Quintino is needed here. It just doesn't bear thinking about. And although he's always been very careful managing his finances, I don't believe he had entirely sorted out his will. Oh, I know that everything he has would be left to you, but there were still a few outstanding loans... and it's always a good idea to keep up to date on such things...'

Cecília could no longer hold back the tears filling her eyes after listening to these lugubrious thoughts.

'Don't upset yourself,' said José Fortunato in the same tone of voice. 'What's the point of getting upset? That won't get us anywhere. Besides, if it's God's will that some misfortune should have befallen him, you certainly wouldn't be left alone. You have friends and protectors... You would lose an excellent father, that's true, but...'

'Please, Senhor José Fortunato, don't talk to me like that. It's too cruel.'

'I don't mean to upset you, but, in the circumstances, it's always wisest to think the worst.'

And with the best of intentions, Senhor José Fortunato continued with this homeopathic approach to comforting her.

Cecília was becoming more and more distressed.

'Antónia!' she shouted, seeing the maid passing in the corridor. 'I'm sorry, but I can't help myself. The uncertainty is killing me. Go to the office, will you, and see if he's there. Now that Senhor José Fortunato's here and... Please go.'

'But it's pitch-black night out there, Senhora. A woman on her own can't just walk down into town like a flibbertigibbet!'

'Why ever not?'

'What do you mean "why ever not"?'

'It wouldn't be decent,' said José Fortunato, making himself more comfortable at the table.

Cecília said nothing and again ran to the window.

The street was deserted.

'Don't catch cold now,' warned José Fortunato. 'It sounds to me as if you've already got a bit of a sore throat. You need to be careful, an ordinary cold can easily turn into something far worse. You need a hot drink.'

'Ah, Senhor José Fortunato,' said Antónia. 'I sense a touch of egotism. You're thinking it's high time they brought in the tea. How the flesh is weak!'

'I don't know what's wrong with me, why I don't just go myself!' exclaimed Cecília returning from the window. 'If this continues much longer, I won't answer for my actions. Oh, what I'd give to be a boy!'

José Fortunato didn't know quite what he should do at this stage, and this betrayed not so much an unwillingness to help as a lack of understanding.

He was always a little slow on the uptake, and the appropriate response tended to occur to him too late, when it was no longer relevant. And that is why all he could say was: 'That would be quite some miracle, if you were to change into a boy! But don't worry, my dear, if something has happened to your father, you'll find out soon enough.'

'Thank you for your consoling words!' Cecília said, unable to conceal her irritation.

'I once went to a celebration, near Cruz da Regateira it was, and on the way back…'

Senhor José Fortunato felt that this was the perfect moment for an anecdote.

Antónia settled down to listen.

Cecília returned impatiently to the window.

At the very moment she looked out, she saw a man on horseback approaching from the opposite direction she was expecting her father to come from.

It was Carlos, returning from his usual country ride.

When Cecília saw it was him, she had an idea.

He had still not quite reached the house, when Cecília turned and said: 'So neither of you is willing to go and look for my father, is that right?'

That angry 'neither of you' tugged at Senhor José Fortunato's rusty intelligence, and, for the first time, it occurred to him that he could actually be of some service.

'It's pitch-black night out there, Senhora!' Antónia said again.

Senhor Fortunato was still mentally digesting his recent discovery, but Cecília did not wait for the result of that digestion process.

Carlos Whitestone had stopped beneath her window to bow to her.

Cecília did not hesitate.

'Senhor Carlos,' she said in a nervous, tremulous voice.

Surprised to hear himself addressed in this way, Carlos drew his horse closer to the window.

'Yes, Senhora?'

'Forgive me for asking,' Cecília went on, 'but my father left the house this afternoon and still hasn't come back and I've no news of him at all. You can imagine how worried I am. Do you happen to know…'

'Where did he go when he left?'

'He just said he was going for a walk, but…'

'And he hasn't come back?' Carlos said, interrupting her, for he was equally nonplussed by her father's delay.

'Whatever can have happened to him?' cried Cecília, catching the note of alarm in Carlos' voice and immediately transforming it into utter terror.

Carlos was as quick to act as José Fortunato was slow.

'Don't worry, Senhora. I'll go and find out, and I promise I'll bring your father home soon.'

'Oh, thank you, thank you so much, Senhor Carlos!' said Cecília, her voice brimming with gratitude.

Carlos bowed again and left at a gallop.

Seeing him leave, the consolation of hope entered Cecília's heart for the first time.

For her, Carlos was one of those men who if, one day, he were ever to attempt the impossible, he would be sure to succeed.

Turning round, Cecília found Antónia and Senhor José Fortunato standing just a few feet from her, staring at her in blank amazement.

'What have you done?' they both asked almost in unison.

'What you obliged me to do. If I could, I would long since have gone myself, rather than sitting here pointlessly racking my brain for some explanation and finding only alarming conclusions. If I'd had anyone else to ask, I wouldn't have had to bother someone who…'

'But why, then, didn't you ask me? I was here, after all,' said José Fortunato with utter candour.

Cecília gave him an angry stare and didn't even respond.

'To be perfectly frank,' said Antónia, 'I don't know what to think! What do you mean by talking to that gentleman from the window?'

'What if the neighbours had seen?' added Senhor José Fortunato, peering out to check whether the aforementioned neighbours could have seen anything. 'And to ask him, of all people, a young fool like him... the son...'

'That's enough!' said Cecília, unable to hold her tongue a moment longer. 'This would not have been necessary if other people had shown the necessary kindness and consideration. You've watched me for a whole hour now getting more and more upset, and all you've done is offer me "consolations" that would make anyone laugh who wasn't going through what I'm going through. And then you come with your talk about what the neighbours might say. Why should I care about them when they can't help me one jot?'

José Fortunato was truly sorry not to have understood sooner what he should have done, but then that was his nature.

'Senhora Antónia, bring me a lamp, will you,' he said, picking up the accoutrements required for his 'crusade'.

'Where are you going?' asked Cecília. 'What's done is done. By the time you get to the end of the street, Senhor Whitestone will have ridden round the whole city. You'd better stay here.'

José Fortunato stayed.

The ease with which he abandoned any resolutions was another of his 'qualities'.

Meanwhile, Carlos was flying through the city, crossing it from end to end in no time at all.

It was a miracle he didn't knock someone down. Many of those who escaped his impetuous advance, comparable to that of a meteorite, were left muttering angrily under their breath at this reckless horseman.

Within a matter of minutes he had reached the office in Rua dos Ingleses.

The silence that reigned there was in stark contrast to the lively atmosphere that prevailed on weekday mornings.

Carlos pounded on the front door, causing the whole house to shake.

A few neighbours came to the window.

The caretaker hurried to receive orders from his youngest boss.

Without dismounting, Carlos asked if he had seen Manuel Quintino that afternoon.

The caretaker said that he'd seen him walking through the fish market heading towards Campanhã, and that, since this was his favourite walk, it was likely that…

Carlos did not wait to hear the end of the sentence, but set off at a gallop again in the direction indicated.

'Goodness!' said the caretaker to himself. 'You'd think the very devil was after him!'

Carlos rode at the same speed down the whole right bank of the river, along which Manuel Quintino had walked just hours before. Only a really excellent horseman could have done this safely, especially at that time of night and at that speed.

Carlos made for the wine warehouse owned by the Whitestone family in Campanhã. Nearby lived the master tanner, who rushed out to discover the identity of this nocturnal horseman who seemed determined to break down the heavy oak warehouse doors with his fists.

He was amazed to see that the rider was Carlos, and when Carlos asked if he had seen Manuel Quintino, he replied that, late that afternoon, he'd noticed him going up the road towards the chapel in Rua de Direita, and that he should have arrived home hours ago.

Carlos resumed his race against time, leaving the tanner in the same dumbstruck state as the caretaker.

En route, he passed a group of men who were returning, singing, from the tavern, where they had spent the whole afternoon eating and drinking in the shade of the vine trellis.

Carlos knew them. They were some of the idler members of the commercial classes, and most would have been acquaintances of Manuel Quintino.

He was about to ride past when he thought to ask if they had seen the book-keeper.

They laughed and told him about the practical joke they'd played on him, because these were the same men we met earlier. They were still laughing at the memory of Manuel Quintino racing up the hill from Campanhã.

'What a stupid joke!' said Carlos, preparing to go on his way.

'Why?' retorted one of the men. 'Think how happy he'll be when he arrives home and sees that…'

'If he hasn't died first,' cut in Carlos, spurring on his horse and leaving at a gallop.

'The man's mad,' said one.

'He'll come a-cropper if he's not careful,' said another.

'Well, what's one Englishman more or less. He can go to the devil for all I care.'

And they resumed their singing and laughing.

Carlos soon reached the aforementioned chapel.

From there he continued at a more moderate pace, asking here and there for any further sightings of Manuel Quintino. However, he gleaned very little information until he happened to ask the woman in whose doorway the old book-keeper had paused.

She gave him alarming details about the state he had been in, and clearly held out little hope for him.

Genuinely worried now, Carlos rode on until he reached

the cemetery.

Thinking he could make out the dark shape of a man on one of the stone benches, he went closer.

With a feeling of real joy, he recognised Manuel Quintino. However, that initial feeling of joy was swiftly followed by one of alarm.

The old man was lying motionless and his features were distorted, as if he were already a corpse.

Carlos grabbed one arm and shook it hard.

'Manuel Quintino! Manuel Quintino!' he shouted.

The only response was a hoarse, inarticulate groan.

Carlos called his name again, more loudly this time.

Hearing that familiar voice, Manuel Quintino slowly opened his eyes and fixed Carlos with a distant gaze.

'Whatever happened, Manuel Quintino? What are you doing here? What's wrong? Tell me, what happened to you?'

After a few attempts, the old man managed to give him a rather garbled account of events.

'I... I was walking... and I suddenly felt unwell... When they told me... about Cecília's illness... I tried to run... and... then I felt dizzy... I wasn't feeling right at all... The cold... I think it was the cold... Every time I tried to move... Even now...'

'Don't worry. Your daughter's fine, she's just very worried about you not coming home. See if you can sit up.'

'But... down there... they told me...'

'That was just some stupid prank played by certain so-called gentlemen who, judging other people's feelings by their own total lack of delicacy, thought they should celebrate April Fool's day in that cruel fashion.'

'Well, God forgive them if that's so...'

'They admitted it themselves. Anyway, let's not make your

people even more worried than they already are.'

'My poor daughter! I'm coming, but I don't know if…'

Manuel Quintino tried to get up, but his legs gave way beneath him and he sat down again.

Carlos wasn't sure what to do, how best to proceed.

'Do you think you have the strength to get on my horse?'

Manuel Quintino again tried to stand, with the same result.

Carlos was growing increasingly desperate.

He was just wondering if he could somehow haul Manuel Quintino up behind him on the horse, when a hired cab passed, heading back into the city. The coachman was letting the horses trot along at their own pace and he himself was whistling. A kind of postillion was sleeping at his side. Carlos knew the coachman.

'Gonçalo!'

'Who's that?'

'Is your cab empty?'

Then the coachman recognised Carlos.

'Oh, it's you, sir. Yes, it's empty.'

'This man is ill. Help me get him home, as fast as you can.'

The coachman hastened to do as asked.

'And you,' said Carlos, to the impromptu postillion, 'get on that horse and take him back to my house. Off you go!'

Carlos was instantly obeyed, thanks to his reputation as one of the most generous customers in the city and the promptest of payers too.

'And another thing,' he said to the postillion, 'on the way there, call in at Dr F.'s house and ask him to go and see Senhor Manuel Quintino at home – urgently. Tell him I sent you. Go on.'

The lad was off like a rocket.

Carlos and the coachman helped Manuel Quintino into the cab, and, whipped along by the coachman, who was in turn driven on by the prospect of a very large tip – the horses' hooves were soon striking sparks from the cobblestones.

Carlos had kept his promise to Cecília.

Cecília, whose fears had only grown in the meanwhile, gave a gleeful whoop when she saw the cab stop outside the house and her father step out, with Carlos supporting one arm.

Those first moments were entirely taken up with feelings of joy.

She ran to the front door and welcomed her father with open arms, while shedding copious tears. All her feelings about that painful episode found expression in the form of random, incoherent phrases, exclamations, questions, kisses and smiles.

Manuel Quintino went up the stairs supported on one side by Cecília and on the other by Carlos. And that is how they entered the living room, where Antónia and José Fortunato, while offering congratulations, questions and even words of advice, kept shooting wary glances at Carlos, who hadn't even noticed their presence.

After that first explosion of incoherent, unreflecting joy, Cecília had room in her heart for two opposing feelings.

The first was of gratitude towards Carlos, and she held out her hand to him in friendly fashion and, with a look, a tone of voice and blushing cheeks that filled her rather hackneyed words with meaning, she said: 'Thank you so much.'

An insignificant phrase, which, on this occasion, proved more eloquent than any speech.

Then, she became concerned again about her father's condition. His altered features, his pallor, his unusually sombre mood, revived anew the fears that his arrival had assuaged.

She then asked for a detailed account of what had happened. Carlos gave her a brief explanation. Cecília listened with horror and with grateful tears. Antónia and José Fortunato offered various prudent words of advice, but these went unheard by anyone but them.

Cecília redoubled her attentions towards her father, who accepted them all with a certain unnatural coolness, which frightened her.

Carlos sometimes joined the tender, young nurse in her efforts, and did so with such intelligence and solicitude that he received frequent grateful, approving smiles.

When the doctor arrived, Carlos was still there.

The doctor said that Manuel Quintino had suffered one of the eight forms of cerebral congestion described by Professor Gabriel Andral, and one of the most benign. He described the symptoms and the causes, prescribed treatment, then bled the patient and left.

Manuel Quintino was already feeling better.

Reassured, Carlos said good night and promised to return.

On the way out, Cecília squeezed his hand affectionately.

Antónia mumbled disapprovingly.

José Fortunato returned home at around midnight, feeling most unhappy with himself.

XXII

An Education in Commerce

During the days that followed, Manuel Quintino was obliged, by force of circumstance, to keep to his bed.

The doctor attending him insisted, Cecília begged and Carlos demanded, as did even Mr Richard Whitestone, who came to visit him in the morning.

The hardest thing of all for Manuel Quintino was the enforced idleness. He imagined that work at the office would go completely off the rails without him; he was tormented by the thought of the chaos into which the office would inevitably be plunged should his illness last much longer.

'Goodness knows the state things will be in,' he would say, genuinely terrified by the idea, when, in the presence of Cecília and Carlos, who had stayed rather longer than Mr Richard, he was eating his meagre bowl of gruel, the only food the doctor would allow.

'You're worrying unnecessarily!' said Carlos, trying to reassure him. 'You'll soon be better, and the firm of Whitestone will gain nothing from you trying to rush things. After all, the other book-keepers are all there.'

'Oh, yes, the other book-keepers. That's easy enough to say…'

'But what else can you do, Pa? When the Good Lord restores you to health, you'll be able to do double the work.

For now, though, just finish what's left of your soup…'

'I don't even want to think about the mess the accounts will be in, all out of date! Oh, please, Cecília, that's enough soup for now.'

'Just a couple more spoonfuls.'

'Why shouldn't Paulo do the accounts?' asked Carlos.

Manuel looked at him in horror.

For him, the science of book-keeping was a matter of such complexity and such transcendent importance that Carlos' question grated on his nerves like some unforgivable heresy.

'Paulo?! Are you mad?' Do you think keeping the books is the same as drawing up a laundry list?'

'I'm sure he might find it hard initially, but after three days or so…'

'Why not three hours? Goodness me! Oh, Cecília, I really can't finish this soup. Take it away, will you?'

'Just one more spoonful,' said Cecília, so meekly that Manuel Quintino's could not resist.

'All right, give it here.' And closing his eyes, he drained the bitter cup to the dregs, grimaced, then gave a sigh of relief, as if a great weight had been lifted from his shoulders.

Not long afterwards, he was again worrying about not going to the office. He foresaw serious complications for certain pending negotiations, and his fertile imagination went so far down this particular path that it only stopped at the point of imminent bankruptcy.

As a man who had never missed a day's work, he exaggerated the consequences of his absence; and as a book-keeper who had acquired his commercial know-how from long, hard experience, he assumed it would take years to train another mind to acquire that knowledge and organise the keeping of accounts.

This is why he listened with horror and not a little mockery to the extraordinary proposal Carlos ended up putting to him, after a prolonged discussion during which, with Cecília's help, he had managed to assuage Manuel Quintino's fears.

'Don't worry,' said Carlos. 'Keep to your bed for as long as you want and need to, because I will take charge of the books.'

For some time, Manuel Quintino stared wide-eyed at Mr Richard's son; he knew precisely what he thought of Carlos' commercial experience, and this promise seemed to him so outrageous that he could think of no immediate response.

Cecília was equally taken aback by the offer. They both thought Carlos was joking. And yet the look on Carlos' face was so serious that Cecília immediately began to believe that it wasn't a joke at all.

Manuel Quintino took longer to convince.

'*You* take over the accounts?' he asked, unable to suppress a smile, the first that had appeared on his lips that morning.

'Yes.'

'What great good fortune for the company! Now it's sure to prosper!'

'Are you doing me the injustice of assuming that I would be incapable of applying my mind to a task when that would be a way of helping a friend?'

When Carlos asked that question, Cecília immediately espoused his cause: she not only believed in the sincerity of his offer, she even – such confidence! – believed in the possibility, no, the probability that he would be as good as his word.

Manuel Quintino was not so easily convinced. However, he, too, had been moved by Carlos' words, albeit for another reason.

'No,' he said, his voice full of emotion, 'I don't for one moment doubt your good will, nor your willingness to make sacrifices. I have more than enough proof of that. Indeed, I'm aware that I may well owe you my life. Please don't think me ungrateful, but how do you intend to take charge of the very work you've always shunned? It would be like me jumping in to save someone drowning in the river. Wouldn't all my good intentions be in vain if he dropped like a stone to the bottom before I even reached him?'

'Do you really think the work is so complicated that, with your advice and help, I wouldn't be able to grasp it in a matter of a few days?'

Manuel Quintino shrugged.

'You obviously don't think much of my intelligence!' Carlos responded. 'Besides, I did learn a thing or two at school that could possibly be of use. Maybe I could dredge up some of what I learned there, even though, I admit, I haven't made much use of it since.'

'And pigs might fly! Now he comes out with what he learned at school!'

'Why can't we at least try? We lose nothing by trying. You won't be able to go back to work this week or, possibly, next week either.'

'Don't be such a gloom-monger!'

'No, you won't and mustn't go to the office. I'm determined to put my aptitude for commerce to the test. Who knows, I might even acquire a taste for it.'

'If only!'

'Well, I might. Will you agree to give me lessons? Three will do.'

'You're not going to learn much in three lessons.'

'Do you want to bet on it?'

'No, just go and get on with your life. Have fun. This isn't a hobby, you know…'

Carlos put on a grave face.

'So, Manuel Quintino, do you really think me so frivolous that I can't be serious once in a while?'

'No, but…'

Cecília timidly came to Carlos' defence.

'Why not accept Senhor Carlos' offer of help?'

'Oh, not you as well! What has got into you two today? This young man is deceiving himself. As I said, I don't doubt his good intentions, but…'

'But,' Carlos cut in, 'just say the word. Would you give me a few lessons in book-keeping? You don't stand to lose anything.'

'They'll be very odd lessons.'

'That's all right. Yes or no?'

'All right, "Yes".'

'I'll see you this evening then, teacher,' said Carlos, picking up his hat and about to leave.

'Yes, I'll see you then,' said Manuel Quintino, amused by Carlos' determination, in which he had little faith, but which nevertheless made him laugh out loud and almost forget his worries about the office.

As he left, Carlos said goodbye to Cecília, saying: 'In three days' time, I promise to be an efficient, conscientious clerk. My word on it.'

Cecília smiled and held out her hand to him.

'Thank you so much for your generosity, Senhor Carlos.'

'Do you think it's only generosity?'

'What else?'

Carlos did not answer. He merely shook her hand, smiling and feeling a deep inner sense of contentment as he uttered the trivial words: 'I'll see you later.'

Cecília was left wondering what lay behind Carlos' decision

apart from generosity. But she spent the rest of the day in such a good mood that her father found far fewer reasons to be concerned about her health, and that was no small guarantee to him that his own health would also improve.

Carlos went straight from there to the office.

It was a cause of some surprise to Mr Richard to see Carlos sitting at Manuel Quintino's desk poring over the accounts books, the day's correspondence and that of previous days; the other clerks were no less amazed by this rare phenomenon; and they were even more amazed when Carlos questioned them about the progress of certain negotiations, and when they saw him speaking to clients, who came to ask for information, and whom he answered very knowledgeably.

Indeed, this caused such a stir in the world of commerce that soon the whole street was talking about it. The occasional nosey parker even invented some spurious business deal in order to witness this change with his own eyes.

Carlos' quick intelligence – aided by his upbringing – allowed him to grasp the rules of book-keeping very easily, whereas less agile minds would have struggled to do so.

He remembered or understood the main points merely after mulling them over a little, and Manuel Quintino was able to clear up any minor doubts or difficulties in a matter of minutes.

It should be said that these doubts and difficulties mainly had to do with the usefulness of the complicated, old-fashioned approach to accounting scrupulously followed by Manuel Quintino. Carlos could see simpler, more efficient ways of doing certain entries and procedures and when he saw the more tortuous methods adopted, he felt confused and assumed there must be some reason for this that he could not fathom.

When he left the office, Carlos had already made great progress in his commercial education. He hadn't had such a busy morning in a very long time!

That night, when he was about to go off to see his 'teacher', he met Jenny in the corridor and she jokily asked: 'Is it true what I've heard, Charles?'

'What have you heard?'

'That today you worked tirelessly as a book-keeper and that everyone in the office was astonished at your sheer application to the task.'

'Yes, it was a momentary whim.'

'A whim? So is it only a whim this sudden feverish desire to work?'

'What else could it be?'

Jenny said nothing for a moment, but kept her eyes fixed on her brother.

'You're right. It must be a whim. I'm sure it is, but perhaps not as innocent and unimportant as you would like to make out.'

'Now you're the one being inconsistent, Jenny.'

'Why?'

'You've been nagging me for days about my lack of interest in the office, and now you seem to be scolding me for working too hard.'

'Only because I suspect some ulterior motive.'

'An ulterior motive?'

Jenny changed tack.

'May I ask you a question?'

'Of course.'

'Where are you off to now?'

Carlos was clearly troubled by this question.

'To Manuel Quintino's house.'

'Ah!'

'As you know, the poor man is ill...'

'I just heard that he's feeling much better. We sent someone to ask. So if you don't have time to visit him…'

'But I promised…'

'Ah, you promised!'

'Look, Jenny. I'll be honest with you. In order to reassure the poor man, who couldn't bear the thought of leaving the office unsupervised, I promised I would take it on. But you know, or can imagine, the limitations of my knowledge in that sphere. If I'm to keep my promise, I need information that only Manuel Quintino can give me, and so…'

'And you're not worried that, given how ill he is, you might make him worse by asking him all those questions?'

'I don't have that many.'

'Why couldn't you ask your father?'

A slight impatient frown appeared on Carlos' face.

Jenny added with a sigh: 'I see you have forgotten your promise to me.'

'What do you mean?'

'You know what I mean. What if I asked you not to go to Manuel Quintino's house today?'

'I would say that you were being as capricious as any other mere female! You weren't born for such feminine caprices, my dear, clever sister.'

And clasping Jenny's hands and kissing them, he hurried off so as not to hear any more.

Jenny watched him leave with a sorrowful look on her face.

'There's nothing I can do now,' she said bitterly. 'Heaven knows how this will all end.'

Senhor José Fortunato was most displeased to find Carlos Whitestone at Manuel Quintino's house that evening. He saw in this evidence that his daily habits were about to be disrupted.

He received this news first from Antónia, who viewed this

intrusion equally unfavourably.

Antónia and José Fortunato were zealous allies as regards their privileges and influences vis-à-vis Manuel Quintino.

'That man's here again!' Antónia had whispered to Senhor Fortunato when she opened the door to him.

'Who?' he asked, pausing at the bottom of the stair.

'The man who was here yesterday. The Englishman.'

'And what's he doing here?'

'I know why he's here. And it doesn't please me one bit. It's certainly not because he's been sent by his father…'

A dark shadow fell across Senhor José Fortunato's heart.

The room where they were to meet for the evening was Manuel Quintino's bedroom, since the doctor had advised the patient to stay in bed.

Manuel Quintino and his daughter responded to his greeting in the usual way, but it seemed to him that they did so rather more absent-mindedly than usual.

This bothered him. Carlos acknowledged him with a brief nod, then returned to whatever it was he was doing.

He was engaged in his first lesson in business.

José Fortunato couldn't comprehend what he was seeing.

Sitting up in bed, Manuel Quintino wore the grave expression of a professor, tempered by a smile that revealed a slight scepticism regarding his pupil's good intentions and abilities.

On one side of the bed sat Carlos Whitestone, who was attending not only to Manuel Quintino's lecture, but also to the attentions of the plump tabby cat that kept rubbing up against him – a show of affection it had never afforded José Fortunato, despite the many years he had been coming to the house.

There was a further object demanding Carlos' attention – possibly the larger and more precious portion – and that was Cecília.

From her position on the other side of the bed, she was busy with her sewing, which she frequently neglected, instead following with interest her father's lecture and the occasional objection raised by Carlos, although she, too, was unable entirely to suppress the laughter aroused by this remarkable scene.

The arrival of José Fortunato did nothing to alter the arrangement of things or people, for he was not a man to make his presence felt in any way.

'Right, let's get down to work,' Manuel Quintino was saying, 'to tell you the truth, I don't quite know where to begin.'

'I would say…' Carlos began, but Manuel Quintino stopped him.

'Now don't start interrupting me, otherwise, we'll get nothing done. Let me see…'

And after thinking for a while, he went on: 'In accounting, we use four main books…'

This very elementary beginning did not please his student, who cut in saying: 'Yes, I know that.'

'You know? How?'

'How could I not? This morning, at the office, I went still further.'

'You don't say!'

'Yes.'

'Well, if you already know, I don't need to…'

'I know that there are four books used in accounting, called the general journal, the general ledger, the cash receipt and cash disbursement journals, plus the auxiliary ledgers.'

Manuel Quintino was genuinely surprised that Carlos knew so much!

'Why are you so surprised, Pa? Even I knew that,' said Cecília.

Manuel Quintino looked at her and shrugged.

'What clever people I live with!' he said, then added, addressing Carlos: 'Why don't you tell me what it is you don't know, and I'll explain.'

'I just need clarifications of certain points I'm still unsure about. The actual process of keeping accounts is not so complicated that it won't yield to a little close study, especially if my memory comes to my aid. But I do think the process could be far simpler.'

'Oh no, it couldn't. Don't come to me with your modernising ways. All those ledgers are necessary...'

'Not really. There are two types of book-keeping, aren't there? Single and double entry accounting.'

'That's right.'

'And they differ...'

'Let me explain,' said Manuel Quintino, interrupting him. 'Let's suppose that Senhor Fortunato buys ten barrels of wine from us...'

'What would I want with so much wine?' grumbled Senhor José Fortunato, just to say something.

'Those barrels,' Manuel Quintino went on, 'cost two *contos de réis*. You write this down in the journal in large letters – always in large letters. For ten barrels of wine at 200 *mil-réis* José Fortunato owes two *contos de réis.*'

'Yes, I know that, but...'

'You seem to know everything, but that is the single entry method.'

'Forgive me, but I understood that the single entry method was more involved than that...'

'If that's all it is, then it isn't much more complicated than my household accounts,' said Cecília, laughing and straightening the sheet that Manuel Quintino had rumpled.

'Believe me,' said Carlos in the same jovial tone, 'many of our book-keepers should embrace that same simplicity because it's far better than the confusing, mysterious methods you find elsewhere, which are impenetrable even to the keenest eye. Or so it seems to me.'

'So you think it's all nonsense, do you?' said Manuel Quintino, who was growing impatient with these frivolous criticisms of an art he considered to be as important as it was perfect.

José Fortunato was yawning.

'Anyway,' Manuel Quintino went on, 'would you like to know how you would deal with the same sale in a double entry ledger? If, when he bought the wine, Senhor José Fortunato were to accept a bill of exchange or if he were to endorse one, payable on demand, you would write in the journal: Bill of Exchange for Wine... Remember the names of the creditor and the debtor are always written in large letters. Do you see?'

And he went on to explain how to fill in the other entries.

Assuming that my readers are not all versed in book-keeping, I will not transcribe in its entirety Manuel Quintino's lecture, during which the teacher's practical mind, his respect for the old ways, and his years of experience were in constant conflict with his pupil's innovative verve, his drive towards simplification and his aversion for unnecessary complications.

In short, the eternal struggle between theory and practice, with, on the one hand, Carlos and his young man's instincts, his desire for change and his love of the future and progress, and, on the other, Manuel Quintino's staid maturity, a tendency to the prosaic and the conservative, faithful to the past and suspicious of the unknowable future, sternly impatient with wild, new ideas. One, like a child, playful and looking forward to the morrow, the other, like a grandfather, protesting and sighing for yesteryear; one, like Don Quixote, in love with ideals and a righter of wrongs, the other, like Sancho Panza, loathing utopias and content with the established order of things. These two contenders are to be found in all fields of human knowledge. While the new method is based on ideas and diagnoses of recent physiological discoveries, the old practices shrug these off with a smile, and carry on as before; while the young graduate develops theories on social science and transcendent views on the philosophy of law, the lawyer, grown old and grey in the courtroom, examines the articles of the code, picks apart the letter of the law, deals out advice and issues writs.

In the examples given above, Manuel Quintino was the representative of conservative ideas and Carlos was the apostle of progress.

Sometimes, the book-keeper's steadfast rock of experience was rudely shaken by the objections launched at him by Carlos' lucid intelligence. However, like that rock, Manuel Quintino did not repel them, but let them wash over him.

For example, Manuel Quintino had explained to Carlos how to write the entry for, say, a shipment of wool to Liverpool.

Carlos protested about the length and complexity of the process, setting out a way in which he felt it could and should be simplified; it seemed to him that too many things were recorded in the books, in this case even amounts that were simultaneously credited and debited. Why even mention them if they were instantly gone.

You can imagine Manuel Quintino's reaction!

However, he was not a man to break with old habits and renege on the old system to which he had remained faithful during his many years in commerce just because some upstart objected to it; all of which explains his rather tart response:

'That's simply how it's done.'

'Maybe, but couldn't you also do it in the way I'm suggesting?'

'You could... no, you couldn't... you could, no, you couldn't.'

'Why not?'

'Because.'

'But it's so much simpler.'

'That's as maybe. All right, it's simpler... you're right, but let it be. It's not a matter of being more or less simple. It's just the way it is. We were clearly all waiting for you to arrive and make these new discoveries. Up until now, we've been groping in the dark. What we needed was Senhor Carlos with his simplicities! There's nothing wrong with that, it *would* be simpler, but we don't want things to be simple. It may be a bad method, but many a good company has sworn by it. You just try applying your simple methods and see what happens. Theories! I never trust them. They come to no good. A businessman with theories is a bankrupt in waiting. Yes, it's simpler! Simpler still would be to make no entries at all.'

Carlos burst out laughing. He understood how hard it must be for Manuel Quintino to give in and he respected that. By generously retreating from the field, he advanced on another front, namely Cecília's gratitude for showing such delicacy towards her father.

Manuel Quintino was eager for revenge, and he found it.

During the previous discussion, there had been much talk of invoices, and the old man suddenly turned to Carlos, asking him *ex abrupto* if he knew how to write an invoice. Carlos did not respond at once.

The practical man sensed victory. To be absolutely sure, he would not allow verbal explanations, but ordered paper, pen and ink to be brought, then said to his pupil: 'Go on then, let's see you draw up an invoice.'

Carlos hesitated, and Manuel Quintino savoured the sweet taste of victory.

'You see!' he exclaimed. 'That's theories for you. Some people can talk like an expert, but put them to work and you'll find out that, actually, they've no idea. Come on, find a way out of this particular problem. I'm waiting. We only know who the real soldiers are when they come under fire. Just lighting a firework isn't enough. Go on, write down what I tell you to write and put all your theories to one side. Don't be ashamed to learn something new. We're all learners unto the grave.'

And he began by showing Carlos how to rule the necessary lines, add the various headings and the sums to be recorded, without omitting a single detail.

Carlos obeyed so meekly that it made Cecília laugh.

'At the top write "Invoice for..."' Manuel Quintino said, 'and put whatever product you like...'

'How about patience, which is the thing *you* most need for putting up with this.'

'Are you joking? If I do need patience it's for putting up with you.'

'Oh, you don't want to give my father patience!' said Cecília. 'He can be very careless when it comes to merchandise.'

'Now, you're both making fun of me, and I have *two* children to put up with.'

Had Manuel Quintino known anything about the mysteries of the human heart, he wouldn't have lumped Carlos and Cecília together like that, especially not under the heading of 'children', a most imprudent thing to do given the current state of their feelings.

He continued his instructions on how to draw up an invoice,

and the lesson ended there.

At this point, tea was served, but that evening, it tasted unusually bitter to José Fortunato.

Manuel Quintino, for all his apparent impatience, was privately amazed at how much Carlos knew.

'The lad's so bright!' he said to Cecília, when everyone else had left and she was getting him to drink his last bowl of soup for the day and plumping up his pillows for the night. 'It's astonishing. He's never taken the slightest bit of interest in the business and yet he picks things up so quickly. He could run rings round someone less experienced than me. It's as if he had an instinct for it. The man's made for commerce. Give him a few years on the job and then you'll see.'

Cecília said nothing.

XXIII

Diplomacy of the Heart

Carlos' commercial education continued, and he made swift and auspicious progress. On only the second evening, he astonished Manuel Quintino by presenting him with the impeccable entries he had made that morning and which required no correction at all.

It was only with some difficulty that Manuel Quintino managed to convince his enthusiastic student that he should not himself write in the ledgers, since the normal practice was for just one individual to do so. It was enough, he said – and this was no small thing – for Carlos to help him out and leave everything ready so that, once Manuel Quintino had recovered, he would only have to transcribe the transactions made during the time of his illness.

After three or four sessions, Manuel Quintino had nothing more to teach his student. He knew everything!

And so the lessons came to an end, but Carlos' visits did not, as would have seemed natural. Those evening gatherings merely changed in character.

Now it was Carlos who read out loud from the newspapers, much to the chagrin of José Fortunato, who much preferred it when Cecília read.

Increasingly, Carlos began to have fun at José Fortunato's expense. Having learned from Manuel Quintino that Senhor

José owned shares in various companies, Carlos, when reading the papers, would often invent news that seemed to foretell an imminent collapse in value and even possible bankruptcy. In response, José Fortunato would then fulminate bitterly against governments past, present and future.

When the two old men got into some heated discussion, Carlos would seize the opportunity to talk to Cecília, and those dialogues became increasingly dangerous for both their hearts. Let's listen in.

One evening, Cecília was sewing a shirt she had made for her father.

'What do you call what you're doing?' asked Carlos, bending over her work.

'It's called sewing,' said Cecília with a smile. 'Have you not heard of it before?'

'Yes, of course I have, but that isn't what I was asking. What I meant is what do you call that stitch?'

'This? Backstitch.'

'Ah, backstitch. Is that the same as overstitch?'

Cecília burst out laughing at this question.

'No, it isn't. They're completely different things.'

'I suppose they must be, since backstitch goes backwards and overstitch goes over.'

'Exactly.'

'But why use one and not the other?'

'Such curiosity! You're obviously very interested.'

'Why shouldn't I be? As you've seen, I'm eager to widen my knowledge. After all, you must have noticed how meekly I listened to all those lessons on book-keeping.'

'But they'll be of some use to you.'

'So if what you're doing is backstitch, what is overstitch?'

Laughing, Cecília looked for an example of overstitching

on the shirt she was making and showed it to Carlos, saying: 'That's overstitch. Can you see the difference?'

Carlos examined it with apparent attention and seriousness.

And Cecília stopped her work.

'Satisfied?' she said mischievously, when Carlos appeared to have finished this examination.

'I can see that they're different things, but I couldn't really say why.'

'And that must be a cause of great concern to you.'

'Tell me,' said Carlos, who seemed determined to get to grips with this business of backstitching, 'do you use backstitch all the time?'

Cecília could not help but laugh at this unexpected question.

'No,' she replied, 'the type of stitch depends on the type of work you're doing.'

'So backstitch *is* a stitch.'

'Of course it is. Look, this is how you do it.'

And matching action to word, Cecília began to sew very slowly, while Carlos watched with all the grave attentiveness of an eager pupil. Although it did seem to me that he spent rather more time admiring the perfect shape and delicate colouring of the hand holding the needle than watching the movements of the needle itself.

'Look,' Cecília was saying, 'you make the first stitch, which is larger or smaller depending on the delicacy of the work. Then you go to the end of that first stitch and pull the needle through to make another stitch the same length as the first. Then you do the same again and again. Now do you understand?'

'Yes. And overstitch?'

'Why do you suddenly want to know these things?'

'It is odd, I agree, but that's how I am. As soon as I feel the

312

urge to know something, then I have to find out.'

'I didn't know you were subject to such caprices.'

'Aren't you?'

'No, not at all.'

'I don't believe you. It's impossible. The female imagination, which is far more sensitive than the male one, cannot possibly be immune to such minor caprices. In my view, the caprice is evidence of moral superiority. Anyway, let's go on with my lesson.'

'What do you want to know now?'

'Show me how you do overstitch.'

Cecília patiently explained, just as she had with backstitch. And Carlos was finally satisfied, although the discussion of such matters continued for a while longer.

Carlos remained serious throughout, whereas Cecília kept laughing as she conducted this strange lesson, which she had never expected to give to a student of the opposite sex.

During almost all the evenings spent at Manuel Quintino's house, the conversations between Carlos and Cecília focused on equally significant subjects and were held in the same grave tone.

The reader will think that nothing could be more inoffensive or inconsequential, but there you would be wrong. Remember the poet's words about love, written *ex professo*:

Parva leves capiunt animos.

Small things captivate small minds. Indeed, in the state of mind in which we find Carlos and Cecília, nothing has more influence on the heart than such frivolous, insignificant talk.

The more trifling and trivial the subject matter, the closer the hearts of those engaged in the dialogue become.

The amorous dialogues we have grown accustomed to hearing between romantic leads on stage or in novels, full of heartfelt words and subtle theories about the nature of desire, are the exception in real life, and when they do occur, the participants emerge from them freer, more inclined to forget and less inclined to dream; they serve as a way of giving vent to accumulated feelings, feelings that often vanish altogether. But the awkward silences from which the imagination vainly tries to liberate itself and, above all, those enforced debates about a thousand banal, futile things, they are far more perilous, because, while that reciprocal exchange of banalities is going on, the heart is sending out other secret, invisible emissaries who do much to advance any pending negotiations and manage to achieve the surrender of the garrison without any apparent struggle.

Ask any of the numerous enraptured couples for whom the hours fly by and the world about them disappears while they are immersed in one of those interminable dialogues, and which are often mocked by the envious people who can't enjoy them; ask those same couples if, when their affections were at their most intense, their minds and emotions were absorbed in transcendent, metaphysical speculations about love; ask them if, when they tried to recall their impressions at the end of one of those happy days, they could think of anything other than those somewhat dull dialogues or banal exchanges about uninteresting topics, under whose guise their hearts had found a way of speaking more fulsomely and eloquently than any poet, even Petrarch in his three hundred and eighteen sonnets.

This was certainly the case with Carlos Whitestone. After that seemingly inconsequential chat about sewing, he returned home filled with the deep, indefinable joy of someone experiencing the kindling of a passion. And so it went on. The overly prudent doctor charged with treating Manuel Quintino had deemed that he must stay in bed for yet another week.

Carlos felt nervous about that deadline. Could he, without it seeming odd, continue those visits which had become so necessary to him? Up until then, his excuse had been that he needed to report to Manuel Quintino on the events of the day, but afterwards?

Carlos continued to work diligently at the office, and Mr Richard had still not come to terms with this change in his son.

As for Manuel Quintino, he was probably the only one who did not suspect an ulterior motive for Carlos' assiduousness, which had long been a topic of discussion for Antónia and for José Fortunato.

And Cecília? I will leave that for the reader to decide.

One night, Senhor José Fortunato was about to go home, and was already at the front door, when he and Antónia had the following conversation.

'So, Senhora Antónia, what do think about this Englishman who seems to have taken up permanent residence here?'

'What amazes me is that Senhor Manuel Quintino hasn't even noticed.'

'Well, tell him.'

'Me? Certainly not. You're the one who should…'

'Me? No, I'm not getting involved, but you almost have a duty to…'

'No, I won't say a word, not until I've learned the truth. I need to find out more about this Englishman, and then…'

'But who will you ask?'

'Immediately opposite his house lives the sister-in-law of the husband of the niece of a great friend of mine. Tomorrow, if I have time, I'll go and see her. Because I reckon that lad is a rapscallion of the first order.'

'Oh, anyone can see that!'

'Of course.'

And with that they said goodnight, José Fortunato in order to brood over his private griefs, Antónia in order to go to bed and ponder how to obtain from the sister-in-law of the husband of the niece of that friend of hers the information she needed in her search for the truth.

XXIV

In which Senhora Antónia goes in search of the Truth

As Senhora Antónia had explained, the sister-in-law of the husband of the niece of her friend lived right opposite Mr Richard Whitestone. It was a small one-storey house, and its tenant spent most of her time at her front door, observing or passing on to others the results of her observations.

If, etymologically, the word 'philosopher' means a lover of knowledge, it would be hard to find anyone more deserving of that disputed title than Senhora Josefinha da Água-Benta, as she was known throughout the neighbourhood.

It was more than a mere love of knowledge, it was a yearning, a fever, a delirium!

At nine o'clock on the morning after José Fortunato and Antónia had, as we have seen, begun their conspiracy, Manuel Quintino's diligent servant, afire with domestic ardour, was standing at her friend's door with the laudable intention of gathering information about Carlos Whitestone.

'Senhora Josefinha!' Senhora Antónia called out in what one might describe as a grating falsetto.

'Coming!' responded a rather similar voice from within.

'How are you?'

'Who's asking?'

And the figure of a middle-aged woman, the perfect image of the town gossip, gradually emerged out of the gloom and

317

appeared at last at the door.

'Oh, it's you, Senhora Antónia. Come in.'

'No, I won't if you don't mind, I can't stop.'

'Why the hurry?'

'Well, it's nine o'clock already and I have the main meal of the day to prepare.'

'That still leaves you plenty of time,' said Senhora Josefinha, leaning in the doorway. 'Anyway, what brings you to these parts?'

'I had an errand to run for my master, and thought I'd drop in and see how you are.'

'How very kind of you. And everything's all right at home, is it?'

'Oh, getting by, and, given the general state of things, it could be worse.'

'Oh, you're right there. I imagine the pay isn't all that it could be, but...'

'Some might be better paid, but others are far worse off,' said Senhora Antónia, who preferred not to give too much away about her private life, and, besides, that wasn't why she had come.

'And I suppose he can't afford to be over-generous,' Senhora Josefinha went on, 'with him being just a book-keeper I mean...'

'Oh, some bosses are much harder pressed than he is.'

'You're telling me. Look at my Luísa, for example. You know the one I mean, don't you? Our António's daughter. She spent six months working for Comendador Colaço and had to leave because the conditions were just appalling. The servants had almost nothing to eat. Sometimes all they had for supper was stale bread and salted sardines. But when you saw him out and about in the street, you'd think he was as wealthy as a bishop.'

'Goodness! I assume the servants at least got paid on time.'

'No, there was one maid who worked there for three years, and they still owe her a whole year's wages. They obviously have no conscience these people.'

'What do you expect? Living the high life is very expensive.'

'You're right there. You know that ne'er-do-well, he's something or other in government, a good-looking man, always has his dog with him...'

'Oh, I know the one. He's the brother-in-law of that military man, the one people say is...'

'The very man. Well, I don't know if you've noticed how his wife and daughters dress, but you should see the way they're got up. They passed by here a few days ago, and I could hardly believe my eyes! Not even a queen gets all tarted up like that! And yet, the father claims he only earns three hundred *mil réis* a year. Since there's no such thing as miracles and money doesn't grow on trees...'

'Where does he get it from, then?'

'Exactly. Well, I found out who pays for all those luxuries. His wife stooped so low as to borrow money from a young girl, the daughter of a friend of mine, who served there for many years. The poor girl slaves away, because she does all the starching and ironing, you see, and she was too embarrassed to say No, and so that was that.'

'Well, she was clearly a fool, but that's no excuse for taking advantage of her.'

'That's what I mean. So you've nothing to complain about really.'

'No, thank God, I haven't.'

'And the food's good, is it?'

'Oh yes, no doubt about that.'

'You're very cooped up, though, aren't you, because they

319

don't seem to go out much, apart from on Sundays to go to church.'

'Well, the boss is hardly ever at home, and she's on her own...'

'Surely she's got a young man... she must have.'

'Not that I know of.'

'Oh, she must have. Especially nowadays. Just look at Senhora Antoninha, that girl from Rua do Cosme Vilas-Boas, not much more than a child really, well, the trouble she's got into because of the scrivener's boy!'

'Why, what happened?'

'It hardly bears thinking about. It was so shocking! The other day, her father caught him talking to his daughter and he went for the lad with a knife. The lad ran off, and then his mother turned up and really laid into the old man. The language!'

'There are some very rum people in the world...'

'Apparently her father wanted her to marry that rich fellow back from Brazil who's having all those houses built up in Santa Catarina.'

'She'd be well set up there!'

'I know, but the silly girl went back to the scrivener's son.'

'Little fool!'

'And he's certainly not much of a looker! Do you know him?'

'No, I don't.'

'He's an ugly little chap and none too bright either.'

'There's no accounting for tastes, I suppose.'

'No, you're right. Anyway, what about your young mistress?'

'Oh, well, she's rather like your neighbour really.'

'Which neighbour?'

'The daughter of the Englishman, my master's boss.'

'Oh her. She's a very good girl, and kind to the poor to boot. She's a bit odd, as all English people are, but otherwise, I haven't heard a bad word about her since we've been neighbours. She's never to be seen at the window, and when she walks past, she always greets me very politely.'

'She's great friends with my mistress.'

'She is. I've often seen her visiting.'

'They're a good family.'

'Oh, no one could deny that.'

'The father seems a pretty capable fellow.'

'He's a bit eccentric, but not a bad sort. He has his peculiarities, like all Englishmen, but…'

'And the son?'

'Senhor Carlos? Oh, don't get me started on him.'

Senhora Antónia had finally reached the matter that had brought her there.

'Why's that?'

'Oh, he's a real piece of work.'

'Meaning?'

'He's a wastrel, that's what he is. He comes home in the early hours and sleeps until midday. You can imagine the kind of life he leads.'

'You mean he gambles?'

'Gambles, smokes, spends his time in bars and theatres, drinks and keeps bad company.'

'Goodness!'

'Oh, you've no idea. The whole house is in uproar because of him. He doesn't speak to his father, and he makes his sister's life a hell. Susana, my cousin, worked there for a week, and she said he's completely shameless. He sometimes turns on his sister and goes on and on at her, until she, poor thing, cries enough to break your heart. That's all she does some days.'

'The Judas!'

'And yet everything always goes his way. Do you know what I mean? A real lady's man. Luís worked for him for a long time, and, according to him, his master received so many letters from so many women…'

'The rascal. What he needs is…'

'They say he spent his father's money on an actress. His father threatened to send him to England.'

'Good riddance say I!'

'Oh, he's a devil all right. And they say he drinks too!'

'Of course.'

'But then he's English, isn't he? Sometimes, he comes home when the sun's already up, and he has to be helped into bed, because he can barely stand.'

'Shameful! And he's from a good family too.'

'Not long ago, I went to my door when it was already getting light, and I saw him just arriving home. He was all pale and dishevelled, and I could just imagine the state he was in.'

'Well, *he*'s not going to last long.'

'He might be better off dead.'

'He's probably still sleeping now.'

'No, he just opened his windows. He's up early today.'

'So is that his room?'

'Yes, right above the front door. His father and his sister left the house first thing. Apparently, they've gone to visit a very rich Englishman who's just arrived in Oporto with his daughter. According to Doroteia, the pantry maid, the old man wants his son to marry the daughter.'

'And what does the son think about that?'

'Presumably not very much, since he didn't even go and visit them.'

322

They had just reached this point in the conversation when a hired carriage drawn by two sturdy horses drew up outside Mr Richard Whitestone's house.

The coachman immediately jumped down to take orders from his passenger, who was completely hidden from view by the blinds on the carriage windows.

He then went to ring the bell, and, a moment later, Carlos' personal servant appeared; after a few brief words, he went back inside and returned shortly afterwards with a reply.

The coachman then opened the carriage door and out stepped an elegantly dressed lady, all in black, her face covered by a long veil, impenetrable to the eager eyes of Antónia and her friend.

This lady went in through the garden gate accompanied by Carlos' servant.

Senhora Antónia and Senhora Josefinha exchanged meaningful looks.

'But...' murmured Antónia.

'What? Speak.'

'Didn't you say his father and sister had gone out?'

'More than an hour ago.'

'So...'

'So...'

Their eyes filled in the gaps in this dialogue. Then Senhora Antónia said: 'That's scandalous!'

'Didn't I tell you?'

'Did you recognise her?'

'No.'

'But it's so brazen.'

'Absolutely.'

'Well, I'm not leaving here until I find out who she is or at least...'

'You see what I mean about lowering the tone of the neighbourhood.'

And they continued in this same disapproving vein. Senhora Josefinha went so far as to question the coachman, who came to ask her for a light. All he could tell her, though, was that the lady was still young and pretty and lived in Santa Catarina.

Antónia meanwhile kept watch in the street.

They continued their conjectures until the object of those conjectures reappeared at the door. She was accompanied now by Carlos who, very gallantly, helped her into her carriage, then got in himself, having first given orders to the coachman.

And the carriage set off again at full speed in the direction it had come from.

The two witnesses to this scene were astonished.

'Did you see that?' said Senhora Josefinha.

'I certainly did.'

'She looked young to me.'

'And pretty.'

'So what do you make of that then?'

'I'm aghast.'

'Have you ever seen such brazen behaviour?'

'No, I certainly haven't.'

Senhora Antónia left, feeling genuinely indignant and determined to say something to her master and unmask the libertine who had wheedled his way into the house on the pretext of providing disinterested help and false friendship.

Antónia had achieved her goal; indeed, she was now so brimming with the truth that it threatened to overflow.

XXV

A Domestic Storm

At four o' clock on that same afternoon, Mr Richard Whitestone was returning slowly home wearing that smug English look we know so well, the look of someone who has concluded the day's serious tasks and has already begun to savour the pleasures of doing nothing. He had spent part of the morning with a compatriot, the father of a pale, fair-haired lady, whom he did indeed hope to see joined in matrimony with his son.

Quite how the discreet Englishman's intentions had managed to reach the pantry maid we do not know, but it's true that, either through logic or some form of occult inspiration, she had been quite right when she informed Senhora Josefinha da Água-Benta of them earlier. Although Mr Richard had been somewhat displeased by his son's failure to accompany him on that morning visit, he consoled himself with the thought that Carlos would perhaps deign to accompany him when he visited again that evening.

This is what he was thinking as he strolled along, preceded by Butterfly, who, impatient with her master's slowness, kept having to run back to his side.

Mr Richard was walking slowly up Rua das Flores humming his favourite song, 'Cheer, boys, cheer', and letting his gaze linger on the displays of gold jewellery in the shops along one side of the street, when he suddenly stopped outside one particular window, as if his eye had been caught by one particular object. He stayed there for a long time.

He had seen something he felt it his duty to investigate, and not being able to do so from out in the street, he went inside.

'May I see a watch that's in the window?' he asked the goldsmith, who, with an amiable smile and delicate manners, immediately did as requested.

Mr Richard examined the watch minutely.

'It's a fine watch,' said the goldsmith. 'And valuable too.'

Mr Richard nodded and continued his silent scrutiny of the object.

'It's English, isn't it?' he said at last.

'It is, sir, and from a very good maker too.'

'So did you have it sent directly from England?'

'No, sir.'

The goldsmith began to study Mr Richard more closely. What he was thinking, I don't know, but a flicker of suspicion appeared to cross his face. A few moments later, he added: 'To be frank, sir, I only bought it a few hours ago.'

'Really? May I ask from whom?'

'I bought it from a young man, who I know by sight, but not by name. I imagine that he, too, is English. He arrived in a carriage with a lady…'

Mr Richard stared at the goldsmith, wide-eyed, then repeated: 'With a lady?'

'Yes, a fairly young lady, all in black, who waited outside for him. He came in, explained that he was about to go abroad and asked if I would like to buy the watch and chain. We reached an agreement…'

'That's of no importance,' said Mr Richard, his lips twitching slightly with repressed rage. 'How much would you sell it for now?'

The goldsmith asserted his right to make a modest profit, to which Mr Richard made no objection, and thus ended up buying, for the second time, the watch and chain he had given to his son.

For he had no doubt, nor should the reader, that this was the exact same watch and chain.

When he left the shop, Mr Richard's face had regained its customary serenity, but if anyone had been able to see beneath the surface, he would have found a rare degree of anger in that otherwise phlegmatic gentleman.

The servant who opened the door when Mr Richard arrived home was the same one who had received that morning's visitor, the one who had so filled Senhora Antónia with indignation.

'What time did Senhor Carlos leave the house today?' Mr Richard asked rather brusquely.

'At… at ten o'clock,' said the servant, feeling rather alarmed.

'Was he alone?'

The servant felt like answering in the affirmative, but Mr Richard fixed him with a look that deprived him of the necessary aplomb required to tell a lie.

'Was he alone?' asked Mr Richard again, more forcefully this time.

'No, sir, he wasn't,' answered the servant.

'Who was he with, then?'

'With… with…'

'Who?' asked Mr Richard, growing ever more imperious.

'With a lady, who… who came asking for him… but… she wasn't a young lady,' added the servant by way of a corrective.

Mr Richard, however, had already turned his back on him and gone into the house. Jenny thought he looked rather

327

strange. She was so skilled at reading his physiognomy that not a single line, however accidental, could go unnoted and not awake in her a desire to decipher it.

Mr Richard responded kindly, but briefly, to Jenny's questions, and asked if Carlos was at home.

On receiving a positive answer, he said that he wanted to go to Carlos' room before supper.

This was such an extraordinary decision that Jenny looked very hard at her father.

She could see that something had happened, something capable of causing one of those violent scenes she did her best to avoid. She tried to fend it off.

'Let's both go,' she said with a smile, preparing to accompany her father.

'No, no,' he said, forcefully, but gently. 'I need to speak to him alone.'

Jenny let go of his arm, discouraged by the barely concealed coldness in those words.

Mr Richard tried to soften this impression, saying: 'It's a business matter. Meanwhile, you can give the order for supper to be served.'

Jenny anxiously watched him leave, trying in vain to guess the reason behind that interview. Meanwhile, Mr Richard entered his son's room without knocking.

Carlos was lying on the sofa, thinking – probably about Cecília – and certainly not expecting a visit from his father.

When he saw his father, who so rarely came to his room, he sprang to his feet with a look of barely disguised alarm on his face.

Mr Richard went over to him and, taking the watch and chain out of his pocket, he said, almost stammering, as always happened when he was in the grip of some violent emotion:

'There you are. When you want... to... to sell gifts... given to you by... by... those who love you... p-please make sure it is for... reasons that do not shame you or... or... besmirch your reputation...'

When Carlos saw the watch, he was so shaken he could not speak. Confused and embarrassed, he blushed deeply and lowered his eyes, as if his conscience were telling him that his father's harsh allegations were perfectly justified.

Mr Richard interpreted this as tacit confirmation of his suspicions, and his anger grew.

'Be as extravagant as... as... you like, but never... never... be base.'

Carlos trembled to hear that word and looked up.

'Father!' he cried, filial respect only just managing to suppress his feelings of outrage.

'Yes, base,' said Mr Richard more loudly this time, as if provoked by that show of rebellion. 'I will not have you make this house the... the venue for your scandalous affairs...'

'But...'

'Remember that here,' his father went on, ignoring his protests, 'that here, under this roof, for which you have failed to show any respect, that it was here your father's hair turned white with grief... where your mother died... and where your sister lives.'

'I don't believe that I have yet given any reason for you...'

'Who came to see you this morning? Who did you share a carriage with? Why did you sell this watch?'

Carlos fell silent, and seemed determined to remain silent as regards those questions; nor was he feeling sufficiently meek to hear those recriminations, made without any proper examination, without also getting angry. His pride rose up.

'I can't explain any of this, but I give you my word...'

Mr Richard interrupted him: 'Nor do I wish to know what you get up to. I've heard many a rumour about your extravagant behaviour, but have always chosen to ignore them. However, I want, demand and, believe me, have the power to enforce this... I want and demand that you respect my name and that of my house. You must understand that...'

'But I've already given you my word that nothing I did this morning could dishonour your name, which is also mine, nor this house, which I respect as...'

'Your word! That's not enough, I'm afraid. I have ample reason to doubt it... and that's why...'

'In that case, since I have no other guarantee to offer, I will say no more. After a response like that, especially coming from my own father, I have no option but to remain silent,' said Carlos, determined now not to continue that conversation, realising, quite rightly, that his natural impetuosity might well lead him to forget who he was speaking to.

Mr Richard fell silent too and began pacing up and down the room. Then, in a voice which, although still stern, was more moderate in tone, he said: 'I assume you would agree with me that I have the right to defend the decorum of my household.'

Carlos did not respond.

'That is the duty of every head of a family. Excessive benevolence can also prove immoral,' his father added.

Again silence from Carlos.

'I hope that your sense of honour has not fallen into such a deep slumber that you cannot understand that duty.'

Still no answer.

Mr Richard, who knew his son, realised that he would wait in vain for some defence or apology from him. He therefore left the room.

When his father had gone, Carlos turned his suppressed fury on a precious Chinese vase, which he hurled to the floor, where it shattered into pieces; then he began striding up and down, and woe betide any object that stood in his way!

Then, at last, the bell for supper rang.

Carlos tried to compose his features into some semblance of serenity, but with little success. Jenny was there to observe him, and she was not taken in by such childish attempts at pretence.

You can imagine how the supper proceeded, having begun so inauspiciously.

The clink of cutlery and glass was the only sound to interrupt the solemn silence. Even the servants came and went on tiptoe, cowed by the oppressive atmosphere in the room.

Jenny tried to smile occasionally, but, poor thing, her smile froze on her lips at the sight of the frowning faces of both father and brother. And she had no idea what had caused this animosity between them! How had that storm blown up so suddenly, without her even having a chance to dispel it?

Supper ended as it had begun, silently and sadly. Carlos was the first to leave the table. Mr Richard would have to enjoy his dessert alone.

He was beginning to undergo a change of heart. He wondered if he had over-reacted to his son's misdemeanour.

He might well have misinterpreted events, and even if he hadn't, it was, after all, merely an act of youthful folly, which did not perhaps deserve such harsh censure.

The tolerant Englishman was now only waiting for the first opportunity to be reconciled – with a certain lofty delicacy on his part, of course. All trace of anger and resentment had vanished.

He was truly mortified, then, when he saw Carlos leave the table, taking with him any hope of that longed-for reconciliation. He glanced at Jenny to see if she might make some attempt to stop her brother leaving.

Jenny, however, was too absorbed in studying Carlos' face to notice her father's glance.

Carlos was already halfway across the room, when Mr Richard spoke for the first time since they had sat down: 'Mr Smithfield arrived from London last night...'

Carlos stopped and stood for a few moments looking at his father, as if waiting to hear something further. Then he continued on to the door.

'Mr Smithfield and his daughter, Alice Smithfield,' added Mr Richard.

Carlos stopped again, then, seeing that his father seemed to have nothing else to add, took a few more steps.

'Our company owes him a great many favours, both commercial... and personal,' said Mr Richard.

These words again stopped Carlos in his tracks, when he had already almost reached the door.

And when Mr Richard again fell silent, Carlos reached out to draw aside the curtain over the door.

'We were there this morning, Jenny and I.'

Carlos said nothing, but waited.

Mr Richard went on: 'And we agreed to go back there tonight. They leave tomorrow for the Minho and... they asked after you.'

It had taken a great effort for Mr Richard to abandon the rather stiff tone in which had addressed his son up until then.

Since it seemed that his father had nothing more to say, Carlos drew the curtain aside, bowed respectfully and left, as if he had failed to understand the meaning behind those words.

Mr Richard watched him leave, and his face clouded over again, and such was the force of his frustration that he managed to crack open a hazelnut with his bare hands.

Jenny watched all this, feeling desperate and unsure what to do. In order to heal this rift, she first had to find out the cause, which she still did not know. She got up and went over to her father.

'What's wrong?' she asked fondly.

'I do everything I can to live in peace with him, but I see now that it's impossible.'

'Why?'

'Didn't you see?'

And he got to his feet and paced restlessly up and down.

'Carlos is twenty years old,' he said, still pacing. 'At that age, we all have certain duties. And if he forgets those duties and forgets that he should and must fulfil them, then I, his father…'

A servant came into the room, interrupting him.

Mr Richard sat down and began reading *The Times*, sunk in a now impenetrable silence. Was it *The Times* that so absorbed him? The fact is that, for the rest of the evening, he did not take his eyes off the first column on the front page.

That column must have been puzzling in the extreme given how long it took him to read!

Jenny went to her brother's room.

XXVI

Jenny's ineffectual Attempt at Mediation

Jenny found her brother apparently absorbed in playing with the ears of his Newfoundland dog, but you didn't need to be an expert on physiognomy to realise that his thoughts were elsewhere.

'What on earth was all that about, Charles?' asked Jenny, her voice still trembling with emotion. 'What *is* going on?'

Carlos looked up and said with a smile: 'Don't be alarmed, Jenny. Father and I were just performing one of the set-pieces from my childhood repertoire. He decided to tell me off as if I were a child, and I did as children usually do, I sulked. When I was ten or twelve years old, such scenes had something of the tragedy about them, now, at twenty, I see them more as out-and-out comedy.'

'But what happened to provoke it?'

'Nothing, or almost nothing. He completely misinterpreted something I did, that's all. I could explain, but I mustn't. I assured him, though, on my word of honour, that the interpretation he placed on it was entirely wrong, and my father, who had just proclaimed himself the keeper of the Whitestone family's good name, was the first to besmirch that name by doubting the word of a fellow member of that family.'

'Oh, good heavens, Charles! Why must you always think so ill of the very person whom you must know could never think ill of you?'

'Well, that's what he said.'

'Poor Pa! Do you imagine he found it easy to tell you off like that? I don't even know what sparked that "set-piece" as you call it, but...'

'It was something completely insignificant. This morning I found myself in need of some money, the need was urgent and the sum of money considerable. And I prefer not to call on someone else when I have my own resources. Besides, I was alone at home. All I could think of was how to get hold of the necessary amount as quickly as possible. I remembered the watch and chain Father gave me when...'

'Oh, Charles, you didn't!' said Jenny, looking disapprovingly at her brother.

'I did remove the little agate seal from the chain, the least valuable part of the present, just as a souvenir. You know that it's never the price of a present I value most. And, yes, I sold the rest. A few hours later, chance was kind enough to lead my father to the very goldsmith's shop where the watch and chain were on display in the window. He recognised them, bought them and re-presented them to me, and the words he spoke then are words I would not have taken from anyone else but him.'

'You must be mad! How could you sell the watch that he, poor thing, took such pleasure in buying for you?'

'Because I needed it for something far more important, far graver, than a father's hurt feelings, however understandable they might be.'

Jenny could not suppress a look of doubt.

'Believe me, Jenny. Please, don't you doubt me too. I swear to you by all that's holy that, if the same problem arose, and despite the consequences, I wouldn't hesitate to sell that same watch and chain again.'

'So what was that grave problem?'

'I can't tell you.'

'You've always told me your secrets before, Charles.'

'This isn't *my* secret.'

Jenny fell silent.

Carlos gazed at his sister for some time, then took her hands in his and said: 'Look at me, Jenny. Do *you* doubt my word as well?'

'No, Charles, I don't.'

'Can you believe that, for all my faults, I could ever do anything that was base?'

'How can you ask me that, Charles?'

'Can you believe that, even for one moment, I could forget the love and respect I owe to you, Jenny? Or the veneration due to the memory of our mother, whom I barely knew?'

'No, Charles. How can you even ask such a thing? I know your heart and your feelings better than anyone. And I always stand up for you,' said Jenny, touched by the evident emotion in Carlos' voice.

'Well, that is what I was accused of just now. And the person accusing me was my own father!'

'And do you think he really meant it, even as he was saying it?'

'If he didn't mean it, then he should have kept silent when he saw how upsetting I found such accusations and the way in which I denied them... but he didn't.'

'Forgive him for that too. Just as I wouldn't do you the injustice of imagining you capable of such evils, I can't believe that my incorrigible brother is being entirely fair either, and might need a little of the forbearance you're refusing to show others. It's over now. You should be like the lakes and meadows, which preserve not a trace of the clouds that cast their shadows over them or obscure the sun. If you had seen my father after you left the table. Poor man. If he did treat you unjustly, then he's paying a high price for that injustice! I'm sure he's more upset than you are. I could already sense in him a desire to ask your forgiveness for something he already regretted. But what do you expect? Such changes can't happen instantly, even with the best will in the world. And you didn't give him time. It would be positively angelic of you, Charles, if you would be so good and generous as to... you could even think of it as a kind of revenge too... if you would be so good and generous as to come back downstairs and accompany your father on this visit to the Smithfields this evening...'

'How can you, who know me so well, suggest such a thing? You know what I'm like. Have you ever noticed in me the slightest talent for dissembling, which is what I would have to do if I did as you ask? I don't bear grudges, it's true, but while they last, I can't disguise my feelings. I may remember nothing of all this tomorrow, but today, now, it would only make matters worse if I were to go to my father so soon.'

Jenny did not insist, because she saw the truth of what he said. Then she added: 'I give this grudge of yours two hours – at most. By tonight, there won't be a trace of it left. Then you can come with us to visit the Smithfields – which would be the best possible present you could give to Pa – and tomorrow we can all enjoy a cloudless day.'

'No, Jenny, I can't go with you tonight.'

'Don't say "No", Charles? Are you really so upset?'

'No, but, I have to be somewhere else tonight.'

'And is that so very urgent that you can't...'

'No, really, I can't not go.'

'Didn't you hear what Pa said, Charles? "Our company

337

owes Mr Smithfield a great many favours…"'

'No, I can't tonight. I'll visit him tomorrow.'

'Tomorrow they leave for the Minho.'

'Too bad. I'll see them on their return.'

'You're going to unleash a real storm by refusing to make such a small sacrifice.'

'Tell the man that I'm a really nasty piece of work, that I'm ungrateful, irascible, coarse and selfish; which is why he shouldn't be surprised by my reluctance to come and wish them *bon voyage*.'

Carlos spoke so heatedly that his sister was quite taken aback.

'You know I could never say such things about you, Charles, nor allow others to say them in my presence.'

Carlos immediately softened when he heard these words.

'Poor Jenny! You're the only person who really knows me.'

'And you're the one who knows himself least,' responded his sister gently, then added: 'Are you coming?'

'I can't.'

'Charles!'

'But I promised… Look, Jenny, if you're my friend, please don't insist. I don't want today to be the dark day when I fall out with the two people I love most.'

This time, Jenny's eyes filled with tears.

'That was precisely what I wanted to avoid, Charles. Forgive me if…'

She was too overcome to say anything more.

Carlos clasped her hands and covered them with kisses.

'My dear Jenny! My generous sister! You're the one who should forgive me, your reckless brother who doesn't even know what he's saying. I should go down on my knees to you, not repay your smiles with tears. You're asking me for forgiveness? Me, Jenny! What, for all the comfort you've always given me? The serenity that gets me through life? The motherly love and care you've shown me? When you're only two years older than this naughty "child" of yours, who does nothing but cause you trouble! Is that what I must forgive you for? Take no notice of my mad ideas. Listen, I would love to do as you wish, but yesterday, Manuel Quintino said he was hoping I would be there to celebrate his last day of enforced confinement after his illness. He'll be allowed out and about tomorrow. It's just a little family party, nothing grand. I couldn't go and see him this morning, as he wanted, and so I was intending to go tonight instead. Do you want me to disappoint the poor man?'

Jenny gazed long and hard at her brother, then looked away with a sigh.

'Answer me, Jenny,' Carlos said, 'and if you think that, if you were in my shoes, you could do that without a flicker of remorse, then I'll obey you, and I won't go.'

Jenny still said nothing.

'What do you say?'

'What do you want me to say, Charles? I wouldn't hesitate to tell you to go if I was sure you were only responding to that generous urge.'

'So you doubt what I said?'

'No, but I do doubt, and have for a long time, that you really know yourself. You taught me to read you like a book, Charles, in the days when you used to tell me all your thoughts. I acquired that habit then, and I can still read you now, even though you've been so studiously avoiding those long conversations of ours…'

'Avoiding them? Do you imagine…?'

'I don't imagine it, I know. Do you really think I've lost

sight of you despite the safe distance you've been keeping? Well, I haven't.'

'And what have you seen from that safe distance?' asked Carlos, trying to joke.

'Enough to worry me, enough to ask God to give me strength on the day when the clouds above us grow perhaps still darker.'

'A visionary, eh?'

'Ah, if only!'

'Won't you tell me, Jenny, why you're so worried, especially now when it's no mere caprice that has captured your brother's heart?'

'Are you sure of that?'

'Absolutely. This is an entirely new feeling for me. Ah, you see, I'm starting to confide in you just as I used to!'

'This time, Charles, there are two people involved, both of them very dear to me, and that's why I'm so worried. This time, if only one of the parties were sincere – and would that be you? – all the weight of hopeless misfortune would fall on the other, and that makes me tremble too. And if both parties are sincere, won't there still be battles to fight, obstacles to overcome? That's why I'm so worried.'

'Don't be, Jenny. I have more confidence in the future than you do.'

At this point, a servant came in with a message for Jenny from Mr Richard, saying that it was time to get ready for their visit to Mr Smithfield.

'Are you coming, Charles?' she said once more.

'Please, Jenny, don't ask me again. Suffice it to say that nothing could make me break my promise today. All you're doing is destroying my peace of mind for the rest of the night because I didn't do as you wished.'

Jenny bowed her head and left the room.

Carlos ran to stop her at the door in order to say again: 'Forgive me, Jenny.'

All she could say, her voice trembling, was: 'Go.'

A few minutes later, a servant came from Mr Richard asking Carlos if he would go with him to visit his fellow Englishman, Mr Smithfield. Carlos replied that this would not be possible.

When he received this answer from his son, Mr Richard started angrily pulling off the petals of the rose he was holding.

XXVII

The more Compelling Reason

Half an hour later, Carlos heard the sound of the carriage taking Mr Richard and Jenny to the place where Mr Smithfield was staying.

He had imagined he would breathe more easily when, at last, he had the whole evening at his disposal, but he quickly realised he was wrong.

There are situations in life which, however we resolve them, always provoke, to a greater or lesser extent, a sense of regret at having abandoned the others.

Carlos found himself in just such a dilemma.

The previous evening he had made a promise, not to Manuel Quintino, as he had told his sister, but to Cecília – thus lending the promise greater weight – that he would not miss the party, which she had organised as a surprise to celebrate her father's recovery.

It was a kind of innocent conspiracy between the two of them, and the reader, whether male or female, will know with what ardour the heart undertakes such enterprises and embraces such alliances.

Carlos did not have the courage *not* to go, even if that would have quelled the tears he had seen in his sister's eyes. And so, as we saw, he resisted.

However, that resistance left painful traces; the knowledge

that he had wounded Jenny still pained Carlos' heart; he felt a deep, inner ache, which the prospect of pleasure and his imminent encounter with Cecília seemed only to exacerbate.

The human heart is full of such contradictions, and for that same reason, the most doomladen of omens seem to loom largest at moments of greatest happiness, while the vaguest of hopes glow brightest in the darkest of times.

Time, though, was moving on, and Carlos prepared himself for the festive evening ahead.

He took enormous pains over what he would wear, something for which he rarely had the patience. It was as if he were preparing to go to a ball.

'That Mr Smithfield certainly chose a very bad time to visit!' Carlos was thinking, as he stood before the mirror adjusting the knot in his silk cravat. 'It's all his fault that Jenny got so upset. But what is it she's worried about?' And he put on his white waistcoat. 'Knowing Cecília as she does should reassure her. She should even feel glad that my heart has found love so close to home and not in some far distant place. She doesn't trust me, that's all. Understandable, really, since I don't exactly have a good record in that respect. But this time…'

The painful impression left by his sister's words of farewell soon dissipated in the midst of a host of pleasant thoughts, and savouring those thoughts, Carlos completed his careful *toilette* and was about to leave, accompanied by a cortège of hopes so vital and pulsating they even succeeded in blotting out the slight feeling of remorse that had entered his heart alongside them.

He was just about to open the front door, when he was stopped by a sudden hubbub of voices, footsteps and shrill cries, like the screams of someone being tortured.

Troubled, he went to find out what all the noise was about.

'It's Senhora Catarina. She's having one of her attacks,' said the servant he approached.

These attacks were so frequent that, when Carlos learned the source of the noise, he dismissed it as if it were of no importance and again headed for the front door.

However, the screams redoubled in volume and violence and reached such a pitch of terror that Carlos could not stand to hear them and do nothing; obeying that generous impulse, he hurried up the steps and went into the room we once visited with Jenny.

The room was lit by the dimmest of lamps, and all the maids were gathered round the bed, where the poor madwoman was writhing about so violently that the maids could barely keep hold of her.

Gesticulating wildly, uttering shrill screams and random, disconnected words, the poor unfortunate, her clothes and hair all dishevelled, inspired a mixture of compassion and horror. Carlos went over to the bed.

When she saw this young person appear at her side, Old Kate fixed him with an almost savage gaze, then, after a while, she began laughing and clapping, in the childish way common to such states of imbecility.

'Look, it's him, it's him!' she kept repeating, her eyes fixed on Carlos. 'How did he get in here? Lucky he did, though. I'd like to see someone try and hurt me now. Come here, Dick, come here!'

And she beckoned him closer.

Carlos obeyed.

'You see! You see!' said the old woman, stroking Carlos' hair. 'It's the young master I used to know, with no white hairs. I said he'd be back. That other master wasn't the real one. I'm not afraid now of these evil wretches who have kept me locked up here all this time. Just let them try. You won't leave me alone with them again, will you, Dick? They're trying to kill me!'

'Calm down, Kate, calm down,' said Carlos affectionately. 'No one's going to harm you.'

'You don't know what they've done to me. Look, can't you see the chains they placed round my ankles? I can't move my feet now, can't even feel them. And now they've stuck a red-hot iron in my chest. I can feel it inside. It's burning. And have you seen the noose around my neck? See how tight it is. I'm suffocating.'

And breathing with difficulty, she clutched at Carlos' arm.

'Try and rest, Kate,' he said. 'I'll order all those things to be removed.'

'Yes, do, do! For pity's sake, tell them, Dick. Don't let them torture old Kate like this. For the love of your children, Dick! I can't take much more of this pain. I'm very old, Dick, very old. Take pity on me.'

And she burst into such heartfelt sobs that even the maids were moved.

Then she rested her head on Carlos' shoulder, whispering in his ear in a frightened, mysterious voice: 'They were the ones who hurt me, weren't they?'

'No, it's all right, it wasn't them...'

'It was, it was!' she yelled, violently raising her head, her eyes seeming almost to give off sparks, as always happened when she was angry.

'All right, it was, but...'

'Let's not stay here. Let's go back to England, Dick. Why did you ever bring me to this house? Why?'

'Calm down, we will go, but for now you need to be quiet.'

'I am, I am quiet, can't you see that I am? But don't leave

me alone, will you?' she added in a supplicant, almost childish tone.

'You have plenty of people around you. Look.'

'I don't want them. Send them away, all of them, send them all away. I want to be alone with you.'

'But…'

'Send them away, please send them away!'

Carlos did not have the heart to refuse her, and he ordered the maids to go, leaving him alone with her.

'Close that door, close it, so that they won't come back.'

Carlos closed the door.

'And now come and sit down here beside me. I won't be able to sleep if you're not here. And I do want to sleep. I'm so tired.'

And she took Carlos' hands in hers.

Carlos felt her hands growing cold, the kind of icy coldness that provokes in us all an instinctive feeling of revulsion. For the first time, it occurred to him that this might be the poor woman's last night.

This thought made him study her more closely. Even in the dim light, he could see how changed her face was.

The clock struck nine, then ten, and Carlos stayed there beside the old woman who, still clasping his hands, kept shuddering at the slightest movement, as if afraid she might be abandoned again. She was clearly so terrified of being left alone that Carlos felt he could not possibly leave her.

And so the hours, which he had hoped to spend with Cecília, flowed past in the company of that poor, unfortunate octogenarian, who held him there with her incoherent babblings, her mad murmurings and her occasional laughter.

Gradually, her speech began to grow more slurred and unintelligible, her voice fainter, her eyes duller.

'They put these chains on me,' she would mutter occasionally, interrupting her agitated state with other ramblings. 'So they think I'm not Kate, do they? Well, I am Kate, I am! It was the furnaceman's widow I gave that green dress to... The furnaceman died... died at sea. That's because they're not good Christians. It wasn't the cock who crowed, it was the owl... She said they were emeralds... and that's how my sister was lost... The cedar wept bitterly... he was her father, you see...'

Carlos placed one hand on her pulse, which was now so faint as to be almost imperceptible. He tried to leave, to call someone to give her the help she needed, but when she felt him get up, her grip tightened and another shudder ran through her, obliging him to stay where he was.

'And why even try?' he thought. 'No one can save her from death now. At least she can pass away quietly. Best let her die in peace.'

And so there he stayed, the sole spectator of that sad scene, a scene quite unsuited to someone of his age and temperament and to the elegant clothes he had so carefully put on for a very different occasion.

The old woman fell into a profound silence, barely interrupted by a few feeble moans.

The clock was striking midnight when, following a brief period of utter peace, a longer, deeper breath closed the circle of that long life.

Carlos knew that what lay before him now was a corpse. After observing her forlornly for a while, he tenderly, respectfully, closed her eyes.

It was then that Jenny and Mr Richard came looking for him, having been told when they arrived back from their visit that, following another of Kate's violent bouts, Carlos had not

347

left the house.

Mr Richard's anger vanished there and then.

'So he didn't go out?'

'No, sir,' said the servant. 'He was all dressed up to leave, but he's been in Senhora Catarina's room ever since.'

Mr Richard, who was still very fond of his former nanny, was deeply moved when he heard this.

He and Jenny ran to Kate's room.

'She died just this minute,' said Carlos when he saw them come in.

Father and daughter sorrowfully approached the bed.

Jenny could not hold back her tears, for the old woman had been part of her life for as long as she could remember.

Mr Richard also bowed his head before this solemn sight.

Carlos was standing opposite him, beside his sister.

Drying her tears, Jenny turned to him and, as if in response to an irresistible, heartfelt impulse, she embraced him, saying: 'This is the Charles I know. Who could ever now doubt your generous heart?'

Carlos returned his sister's embrace, planting an affectionate kiss on her forehead.

And as he drew away from her, he found Mr Richard's hand reaching out to him.

'You behaved like a good man with a good heart, Charles. It does you honour,' he said in a voice trembling with emotion.

Carlos grasped his father's proffered hand, knelt down and kissed it.

That whole brief domestic storm vanished in the face of that deathbed scene.

And that is how Carlos broke his promise to Cecília, something which, hours earlier, he had thought, and indeed said, nothing could make him do.

He had, it's true, resisted his father's anger and – with far more difficulty – his sister's tears, but he had been unable to resist his feelings of compassion for a poor demented old woman in her dying moments.

He stayed there, in order to close her eyes.

That is what Carlos was like.

XXVIII

The Storm begins to brew Elsewhere

Senhora Antónia had neither wasted her precious time nor failed to take advantage of the knowledge she had acquired during her morning observations.

On her return to the house, she had met Senhor José Fortunato out in the street, and had confided to him, as a loyal ally, the wealth of discoveries she had already added to her treasure trove of information.

José Fortunato was duly shocked by the string of extraordinary facts brought to him by such an authoritative source.

'You can't trust the young men of today,' was his considered judgement, once he had pondered each defamatory article.

'The sly bird never fooled me,' commented Senhora Antónia.

'Yes, I always thought the same.'

'Now what we have to do is open the eyes of those in the household who have chosen not to see.'

'Open them? It would be far better to close certain eyes that have already opened far too wide, if you get my meaning.'

'Oh, I do, I do. Don't you worry.'

And having reassured her protégé and soothed his fears, she went into the house. José Fortunato was left thinking: 'What if I were to warn the father, but in such a way that he wouldn't know the warning came from me...'

Cecília was feeling particularly contented that morning.

Her kind heart was entirely filled with happy thoughts, the kind of playfully agitating thoughts of someone who prefers not to reflect on their origin; thoughts which, when they surface, bask like children in the sunlight, celebrating it with laughter and singing, untainted by any nostalgia for the past, and with no tremulous fears about the future to sour their innocent pleasure.

Poor girl! Little did she know how closely she was being followed by the cloud about to cast a shadow over the glow of her contentment!

Antónia was silently plotting against her. Like a spider lying in treacherous ambush, she was waiting patiently for the wings of the restless butterfly fluttering about her to become caught in her tangled web.

Cecília, however, spent little time with her, or indeed with anyone else. She was like a small caged bird, who, when a day of bright sunshine dawns after a long spell of cloud and rain, flaps her wings, hops from perch to perch, beats against the bars of her cage and once again rehearses the song that has long been left unsung.

Busy with the preparations for what she called her father's party, Cecília did not stop for a moment. She went into the garden to pick some flowers and hide them in her room to make bouquets with which to fill the vases; now and then, she also popped into Manuel Quintino's room, so that he wouldn't wonder where she was and in order to speak a few fond words to him; then she would return to the garden with the light, nimble step appropriate to her lithe, elegant body and excitable nature.

Now and then, she would go over to the window, hoping

that some strange happenstance would satisfy certain secret aspirations, the nature of which the reader can perhaps guess at.

On one such occasion, she and Antónia passed in the corridor, and Antónia announced at pointblank range: 'I saw Senhor Carlos this morning.'

Cecília looked troubled, but, affecting indifference, asked: 'Where?'

'He was coming out of his house. He got into a carriage with a young lady.'

'It must have been Jenny, his sister…'

'No, it wasn't her. She'd left earlier with her father, or so Senhora Josefinha told me. This other woman arrived later. She looked to me like one of those actresses he goes around with.'

'Actresses?' said Cecília, making no attempt now to conceal her disquiet.

After this prelude, Senhora Antónia did not hold back. She told Cecília everything she had heard and seen, and – thanks to her vigorous, logical, deductive skills, which were one of that lady's major gifts – everything she had thought and concluded from what she had heard and seen.

Although Cecília considered her maid's opinions rather extreme, she could feel her heart growing gloomier as she listened, and the laughing, singing mood in which she had begun the day was becoming transformed into an irresistible urge to weep.

In summer, in Portugal, the day sometimes dawns very clear and bright; the sky is blue, the sun's rays resplendent; the wind stirring the leaves is warm and perfumed; then, little by little, the sun seems to fade; the blue of the sky dims; the hot air grows oppressive; blue-black clouds gather on the horizon, then spread across the whole firmament; a storm is brewing.

That morning, Cecília was very like one of those summer days.

When Antónia had finished her grave reflections on Carlos' life and character, and proved beyond doubt that he was possessed of all the world's very worst qualities, Cecília abruptly left her side and shut herself up in her room.

She appeared at the lunch table with pale cheeks and red eyes. Her attempt at a smile was so at odds with those vestiges of sadness that she succeeded only in looking still sadder.

Manuel Quintino's heart turned over when he saw her; she had been so happy that morning and now this! He kept looking at his daughter, but dared not question her.

Cecília did her best to appear cheerful; she chatted away throughout supper, but her vivacity was so false that no one would have been taken in, least of all her father!

For the rest of the day, there reigned between father and daughter a kind of mutual wariness, as always happens when there is a secret hanging between two people, a secret kept by one and suspected by the other, and which both avoid mentioning.

It was growing dark.

José Fortunato arrived punctually.

Cecília was becoming increasingly agitated; the hope mingled with fear that Carlos would arrive at the promised hour vied in her heart with a feeling telling her that he would not come that night.

The irritation this provoked in her revealed itself in the smallest things. The darker it got, the more marked became the state of nervous excitement into which she had been thrown by the events of the day.

She was even rather cruel to José Fortunato.

Sometimes, there was even a bitter edge to her responses to her father, which she immediately regretted, and her overly fervent apologies only increased his anxiety.

As before, he continued to attribute this to illness, and only to illness, and sometimes he would call his daughter over, kiss her cheek, and then insist on taking her pulse.

Manuel Quintino, who understood nothing about the nervous system, thought he could see in Cecília's pulse rate evidence of fever and, if he'd had his way, he would have surrounded her with the kind of medical fuss which, on the pretext of combatting a supposed illness, often turns what is a slight upset into something far more serious.

The clock struck seven, eight, nine, and still Carlos did not come.

Senhora Antónia looked triumphant. José Fortunato and she exchanged knowing glances.

'I'm surprised Carlos isn't here yet!' said Manuel Quintino. 'Perhaps he's decided not to come.'

'We'd better bring the tea in,' said Antónia.

'It would be better to wait until someone asks for it to be brought in,' said Cecília coldly.

Hearing the tone of that riposte, Manuel Quintino fixed his gaze sadly on his daughter. This wasn't like her at all.

'It would seem that Senhor Carlos has found other things to do today,' remarked José Fortunato.

'It does indeed,' said Antónia.

'What's got into you all?' asked Manuel Quintino.

'It's just that…' Antónia began, but Cecília interrupted her.

'Go on then, Antónia, have the tea brought in. Quickly now.'

And she said this in a brusque tone that brooked no delay.

Antónia obeyed. Cecília also left the room for a moment.

Senhor José Fortunato took the opportunity to reveal to his friend everything he knew about Carlos.

Much to his surprise and amazement, Manuel Quintino was neither indignant nor aghast; he seemed to find the whole situation most amusing.

'So he's gone off the rails already, has he?' said Manuel Quintino. 'Frankly, I don't know how he stood working in the office for so long! And he worked very hard and very well too. I still can't understand how that young devil picked up so quickly what takes many people years to learn. So the bird has flown the nest, eh? And in a carriage too. Do you think the lady will have escaped with him into the wilderness? Well, in that case, we might as well have our tea, Senhor Fortunato. There was no need to delay things anyway.'

When Cecília returned to the room, Manuel Quintino was still laughing heartily.

'Cecília,' he said, 'let's drink our tea and get back to our old habits. Young birds are sure to fly off if the cage door is left open. The birds who stay, like Senhor José Fortunato, are too old and stiff to escape!'

Senhor José Fortunato was not entirely pleased with this image. Manuel Quintino went on: 'Our friend here just repeated to me the tale Antónia told him about a certain carriage and a certain young man. Very funny!'

José Fortunato laughed too, but he paid a high price for joining in, for Cecília punished him by saying: 'Funny? How unusual. That's not a quality one normally associates with Senhor Fortunato's stories.'

The smile on José Fortunato's face immediately died, and Manuel Quintino gazed at his daughter in amazement.

More such episodes occurred throughout the evening. It was so sad to see the joy that Cecília affected when she brought

355

to her father's room the flowers she had so happily picked and arranged that morning! Melancholy feelings about flowers are normally reserved for when one has to place them on a grave. Her heavy heart made her eyes brim with tears, regardless of the smile on her lips. The evening ended early. Cecília needed to be alone; she wanted to be free of all constraint; she wanted to be able to weep without the risk of being exposed to curious eyes, indiscreet questions, impertinent remarks.

Need I say that she did not sleep that night, and got up the next morning filled with resolve.

'I must have been mad,' she thought, 'it was all a foolish dream, which for some reason I believed, but why? What do I have to complain about? I don't even have the right to feel bitter. I must be patient!' she said to herself with a sigh. Raising one hand to her head, she thought: 'I must find the necessary strength to root out the madness from in here,' and then, after thinking for a while, placed the same hand on her heart and murmured: 'And from here as well?'

That morning, Manuel Quintino went to the office. He had made a complete recovery, but his happiness was less complete, because, when he said goodbye to his daughter, he saw on her face the mournful expression of old.

A few hours later, Carlos, as he usually did, walked past the house, where, ordinarily, Cecília would be watching from the window.

This time, he found the windows closed and the curtains drawn.

He found this odd, and, for a long time, stood staring up at them.

Someone was watching from behind those pitiless curtains, though. Cecília.

You see how hard she was trying to root out what she called

'madness' from her head or, rather, her heart.

But did she really want to root it out?

She watched unseen, following Carlos' every move. She saw him walk past, look eagerly up at the windows, then walk away more slowly only to stop and, as if gripped by a sudden decision, come back, cross the road and go straight over to the front door.

Cecilia recoiled, as if she feared being seen from outside. Then she heard the door bell ring. A shudder ran through her, and she went out into the corridor.

There she found Antónia, who was going down the stairs to see who it was.

'Antónia,' Cecília said, 'if it's for me, tell whoever it is that I can't talk now, that I'm not feeling well. Do you understand?

'I do, Senhora,' replied Antónia, with the smile of one who has understood too much. She was, as a consequence, very brusque with Carlos.

He asked if Manuel Quintino had actually gone to the office that morning, because, seeing all the windows closed, he wondered if perhaps he'd had a relapse.

Antónia answered: 'No, don't worry. He did go to the office. He's completely recovered. And my mistress said to say that she can't talk to anyone now, that she's unwell.'

'Unwell?' said Carlos, so anxiously that Cecília, who was listening, almost regretted the order she had given to Antónia.

'Fortunately, it's nothing serious,' Antónia went on, 'but it's still too early for her to receive *formal* visits. And if you'll excuse me, I have work to do.'

Then came the sound of the door closing.

'Antónia,' said Cecília, as soon as the maid reached the landing, wearing a victorious smile. 'There was no need to be so rude!'

'Oh, don't worry, Miss. Some people deserve it.'

As he walked away, Carlos was thinking: 'Is she annoyed because I didn't come yesterday evening? I hope that's the reason. Later, everything will be explained to my advantage, and then the right to some reward will provide an excellent argument in my defence. Indifference would be much worse.'

Carlos then went to the office, where he congratulated Manuel Quintino on his recovery, adding: 'I'm so sorry I couldn't come yesterday as I intended and celebrate the last day of your convalescence, but I expect you know what happened at home…'

'Yes, I do,' said Manuel Quintino, who seemed somewhat embarrassed.

'I've just been to your house to find out how you were,' Carlos went on, 'and when I saw all the windows closed, I was worried you might be feeling worse. However, I found out that it was your daughter who's unwell.'

'Cecília!?' cried Manuel Quintino in some alarm.

'It's all right,' said Carlos, smiling, because Manuel Quintino's reaction had just confirmed his suspicions. 'Given the way the maid spoke to me, I imagine it's nothing very grave. I didn't even have time to find out more, because she was in such a hurry to shut the door. She seemed to be afraid of me, and she was very sharp with me too.'

Manuel Quintino tried to smile, but it was clear something was worrying him.

After a moment's hesitation, he went over to Carlos, and in the same embarrassed tone, said: 'Senhor Carlos, I believe you to be a decent fellow, and that's why I prefer to speak to you frankly rather than play cat-and-mouse with you, which isn't my style at all, or yours.'

Carlos was surprised to hear these words, which were as

unexpected as they were mysterious.

'What is it, Manuel Quintino? Speak. You seem to have something very serious to tell me,' he said, eyeing him curiously.

'Listen. I know the great favour I owe you and I have absolute faith in your character, and, people can say what they will, but I know you would never be capable of a dishonourable act.'

Carlos was listening in ever greater amazement.

Manuel Quintino's embarrassment seemed to be growing, but nevertheless he went on: 'However, in the world we live in, there is the truth and there are appearances, and while one must give due attention to the former, one must also keep up the latter…'

'What *is* all this about?' asked Carlos.

'It's about, well… a piece of nonsense really, but even though I know it to be nonsense, I have a duty to investigate. This morning, I received an anonymous letter. Would you be so kind as to read it and then tell me what I should do?'

The letter, in a clumsily disguised hand, said this: 'Someone who takes the reputations of his friends very seriously wishes to advise you that the visits Senhor Carlos has been making to your house are giving rise to gossip in the neighbourhood. Given the young man's reputation, he can hardly be deemed a proper visitor to the home of any young woman of eighteen.'

It was signed: 'A disinterested friend.'

Carlos finished reading the letter and handed it back to Manuel Quintino, saying scornfully: 'One should crush such insects underfoot.'

'I'm not in the least taken in by that "disinterested friend" business,' said Manuel Quintino, 'but if it comes from some malevolent creature, he might spread the calumny. I don't care what anyone says about me, but it would break my heart if so much as a single hurtful word should reach Cecilia's ears.'

'You're right,' said Carlos, bowing his head pensively.

'What would you advise me to do? I trust in your judgement as a gentleman, which is why I'm not asking anyone else for their advice.'

'Thank you, Manuel Quintino,' said Carlos, shaking the clerk's hand. 'You must close the doors of your house to me.'

'Carlos, I really don't deserve such irony.'

'I'm not being ironic. I absolutely must stop visiting you. I totally understand your position. It's only right that I should pay for my past frivolous behaviour, which I now recognise was not perhaps appropriate for someone of my temperament, but never mind.'

Manuel Quintino embraced him warmly.

That night, Mr Richard and Carlos and many of their friends attended old Kate's funeral service at the English chapel in Campo Pequeno, where, in keeping with the English custom, Mr Richard sprinkled the first handful of earth over her grave.

Afterwards, Carlos said goodbye to Manuel Quintino, who had come to the funeral.

The good man had grown accustomed to having Carlos' company in the evening, and he could not help saying: 'Come home with me, Carlos, at least tonight. We'll have a good laugh about things. It's not right to go home with one's head full of funereal thoughts. Come home with me. Why deprive ourselves of that pleasure simply because we're afraid of what the world might say?'

'No, Manuel Quintino, it's best if I stop my visits for the moment. Perhaps one day, but... Goodbye.'

And he returned home.

Seeing him so melancholy, Jenny said: 'Charles, there was

a time when you would confide in me about anything that was worrying you. Why don't you do so now?'

The only reply she got was this: 'Give me time, Jenny. It may be that, in a while, I'll have a lot to tell you and will need a lot of advice.'

Carlos was true to his word, and two days passed without the neighbourhood having cause to remark on his frequent appearances in the street and without Senhora Antónia being bothered by his visits.

But if, in that same neighbourhood, anyone happened to be awake after midnight, they might sometimes have seen a man walking past the house and looking up at the closed windows as if hoping they would finally stop being so infuriatingly discreet.

That's how important what Jenny had called a 'fantasy' was to Carlos! For he was that man.

May arrived. It was one of those warm, calm, scented moonlit nights, when some irresistible instinct urges us to seek out the presence of trees and the murmur of fountains. It feels too suffocating to be inside.

Deep in one of those contemplative moods of which only the cold of heart would dare to make fun, Carlos was, as usual, standing beneath Cecília's window when he heard a creaking sound.

Carlos withdrew to the shadowy half of the street and waited. The window opened, and the moonlight, which fell directly onto the house, illuminated Cecília's gentle face.

Carlos did not move.

Cecília was alone, for she was the only person in that household with the necessary imagination to be seduced by the moonlit charms of such a night.

Leaning on the windowsill, she did not move either. There

was such languor in the way she rested her head on her hand, such beauty and poetry in her pale face, made still paler by the fantastical light of the moon, that, even if you lacked Carlos' vivid imagination, it was possible to believe, for a moment, that this was a summer's night apparition like those in popular legends.

What flattering voice whispered to Carlos that she was thinking about him? Who can claim never to have experienced such vanities of the heart, the deceptive illusions of our desires?

Cecília was suddenly woken from that near-dream state – brought on, it seemed, by the bright moon – by the voice of someone beneath the window saying her name.

With a tremor, Cecília recognised that voice. It belonged to Carlos.

'Senhor Carlos!' she cried, startled and instinctively drawing back.

'Listen,' said Carlos, 'listen. I have just a few words I must say to you. I came here with no hope of being able to talk to you. I have made do with far less for several days now. Being able to gaze up at the windows of your house has been enough. But since chance has brought you here, allow me to take this one opportunity to tell you what I wanted…'

'But surely you must see that…'

'Listen. I gave my word to your father that I would not come back to this house. Some interested party wanted to stop my visits and they succeeded, because I myself thought it necessary. Do you imagine this has been easy for me, Cecília?'

Cecília did not respond, because she could not.

'From this day on, there can only be one reason for me to resume my visits to your house, in the broad light of day, and in full public view, but, first, I need to interrogate your heart, Cecília, for your heart alone can give me the authority to act on that reason.'

Cecília finally summoned up the courage to answer.

'Senhor Carlos, my father is no longer ill. Believe me, your generosity during the time of his illness provoked in me feelings of... of gratitude, which I will never forget. I was the one who asked for your help in the first place, and I recognise how great that help was. For our sake you abandoned, and for a long time too, the habits of a life appropriate to your... age and to your... position in society. The last day of my father's convalescence should have been, and was, your first day of freedom. If my father felt that he should demand, or, rather, ask you not to continue to sacrifice your time, I have no right to go against my father's decisions. I see no need, no reason, to renew those visits... and that is why...'

'But Cecília, what if that reason, that strong, irresistible, urgent reason, came from me, from my heart?'

'Senhor Carlos, I hope you will do me the justice of believing...' and here Cecília's voice trembled, 'that I am above such flirtations. If you feel that the circumstances surrounding our first encounter give you licence to address me in those terms, I ask you to remember that Jenny, your sister, still considers me to be her friend even though she knows everything that happened that night.'

'Cecília!'

'Goodbye, Senhor Carlos. I know you harbour the noblest of feelings in your heart, which is why I hope you will understand why this must end. Goodbye.'

And she hurriedly withdrew from the window.

Carlos stood for some time rooted to the spot, unable to find an explanation for her stern words.

A few minutes later, a figure appeared at that same window and said in a mocking tone: 'Good night, sir,' and closed the windows.

It was Senhora Antónia, who had been watching Cecília from a distance, although too far away to overhear her conversation with Carlos, but as soon as her young mistress came back into the house, she ran to see who it was out in the street, and immediately recognised Carlos.

Carlos was startled and left that place feeling deeply troubled.

'Did she know she was being watched, and is that why she spoke like that? Or is she unaware that they're watching her? For her to speak to me like that means that something must have happened, something to my disadvantage. My failure to go the party isn't enough to explain that…'

And he reached his house, still pondering all this.

XXIX

Carlos' Friends

The scene we described in the previous chapter only exacerbated Carlos' mood.

Ever more sunk in himself, he spent hours in his room or wandered up and down the green garden paths. As he grew sadder and sadder, not even Jenny could spark one of those merry moods that had always been so characteristic of him.

Jenny was convinced now that something more than a mere caprice had taken hold of her brother's heart.

And what about Cecília?

Manuel Quintino's daughter had been avoiding her friend's company for some time, and that, too, made Jenny suspicious.

'I need to probe her heart as well, and if I find that she too... then... then...'

She concluded this thought by sitting down at her desk and writing:

Cecília,
Tomorrow is my birthday. Will you reserve for that occasion the pleasant surprise of assuring me that you are still alive? It's been two long months since we saw each other. I will be here waiting for you from dawn onwards.
Your friend,
Jenny

An English Family

The following day really was Jenny's birthday.

Cecília received the letter and could not decide what she should do. She was afraid to go because she feared meeting Carlos; on the other hand, she was reluctant to refuse because she had for so long been avoiding the one person who had always shown herself to be her truest friend! What's more, she could no longer justify her absence with the excuse of her father's illness. And, as well as being Jenny's birthday, it was also a public holiday, which meant that Cecília would be free. She spent the whole night mulling over the problem and said nothing to anyone about the invitation.

The next day dawned and Carlos had woken up full of resolve. He must take a decisive step, for he could not bear living with such uncertainty.

Head in hands and locked in his own inner world, having severed all connection with the outside world, he was trying to discover the best way out of that situation, which, for someone of his character, was unbearable.

I'm not sure I would recommend this as the most efficient of methods. It might be more prudent to think with your eyes open to the world around you, for if you fail to include it as an element in your calculations, you run the risk of making decisions that might, later on, bring a host of nasty shocks and painful conflicts.

Thinking with your eyes closed is only useful when dealing with purely metaphysical matters, but then it's never a wise idea to look for hard-and-fast rules on how to live your life.

The result of Carlos' chosen method of thinking was the following letter, which he wrote in almost febrile haste:

Cecília,

Some days ago, when chance brought me to your side, you refused to listen to what I had to say; please don't allow moral rigour or suspicion to divert your eyes from reading this letter, which I write out of irresistible necessity and because my heart demands it. When I spoke to you with the sincerity that springs from real passion, you took my words as merely flirtatious and refused to hear me out. Was there nothing in my voice that told you I was speaking the truth? How can I hope that this letter will be any more effective, when I cannot include in it the one thing that cannot be put into words, namely, feeling? How can I convince you, Cecília? You have only to imagine the respect and veneration I feel for my sister, to realise that I cannot possibly be lying if I invoke her name when I say that I love you, Cecília. If you believe that I feel for my mother's memory the same love and longing that I saw on your face as you knelt by your mother's grave, then I swear on my mother's memory too. What more do you want? What more do you ask? Don't judge me on my past life; a barrier sprang up between my past and my present existence on the day I began to carry your image in my thoughts, and your name etc. etc...

I will spare the reader the rest of the letter, which continued in the same vein for a few more pages and in a style with which you are doubtless familiar.

Carlos concluded by asking Cecília to reveal her feelings too. 'Whatever your response, it will oblige me to take a decisive step regarding my future.'

He was just signing, sealing and addressing this letter, and was thinking how best to get it to its destination, when he heard the sound of footsteps and voices, which seemed to be growing ever closer, and then many violent blows shook the door of his room, as if intent on breaking it down.

Carlos leapt to his feet, taken aback by this barrage of noise.

'Hello, dear holy hermit,' said a voice through the keyhole, 'will you not open the door to a few poor pilgrims who have come from afar, drawn here by word of your famously pious life?'

'*Monsieur Charles*,' another voice said, '*las des soins d'ici bas, se retira loin du tracas*, like the mouse in the fable who withdrew from the world and took up residence in a block of cheese, may this mouse do likewise…'

'It was because of a woman that Achilles went and sulked in his tent, abandoning his companions. Even the very strongest are prone to such weaknesses.'

'Stop! That is a very grave or, rather, premature insinuation. We must not condemn a man without first hearing his own account of events.'

'Open up, Carlos, we order you to open this door!'

Carlos hesitated for a few moments.

The shouting redoubled; the pounding became more violent.

At last, he decided to open the door.

In they came: the principal companions of his frolicsome past, many of whom we met earlier at that supper in the Golden Eagle. Tired of waiting for him night after night, they had resolved to beard the runaway in his den.

There was a complete change of scene, worthy, in its swiftness, of some English stage play. In a matter of seconds, a gang of youths had invaded the room, occupying chairs, tables, sofa and bed like a swarm of bees. Minutes later, complete disorder reigned.

'So why this mysterious, reclusive life?' asked one, lounging on the sofa in a pose worthy of a sultan.

An English Family

'What lies behind the total eclipse of one of the brightest stars in our own brilliant galaxy? The Venus of the Teatro de São João weeps for you; the genius who presides over the cutlets at the Golden Eagle has lost the will to live; at the Café Guichard the goddess of paradox is mourning the absence of one of her most ardent servants; in short, a whole string of calamities. How do you explain them?'

These words were spoken by another youth, who accidentally spilled half a bottle of perfume over the fine linen sheets.

'You may explain it any way you wish,' said Carlos, sitting down again and making no attempt to conceal his annoyance.

'What is there to explain?' said the man on the sofa. 'When I learned about eclipses at school, I was told that this is usually the result of a planet interposing itself between us and the object being eclipsed. Let us then find the guilty planet...'

'Just assume I was ill,' said Carlos, trying to set the conversation on a different track from the one indicated by his friend.

'Explanation rejected by a majority vote,' bawled a fair-haired lad with a rather effeminate manner – the kind of Apollonian, cake-eating type you see on advertisements for barbers and tailors. He was standing before the mirror, primping the ornate tresses of his monumental hair-do.

'Carried unanimously,' yelled two others.

'I accept his explanation,' said one, busily rummaging through every drawer he could find in search of a light for his cigar. 'Carlos *is* ill, but with an illness that attacks the heart, because what else is love but an illness of the heart?'

The fellow standing at the mirror warbled the lines of an aria from *The Barber of Seville*:

An English Family

Ah che d'amore
la fiamma io sento...

'Your soul is sick, Carlos,' declared a medical student considered to be something of a wit. 'And the pathology of the soul is my speciality.'

'Let science speak, then,' some of the others declared.

The medical student sat down beside Carlos to take his pulse, and, adopting a grave professorial air, said: 'The soul suffers in many different ways. There is the itch of doubt, a chronic ailment among philosophers seeking certainty; then there's the hypertrophy of belief, prevalent among twenty-year-olds; the aneurysm of ambition, very common among young graduates; the jaundice of despair that afflicts fathers of numerous children; the severe character fracture suffered by politicians; the seriously sprained common sense of poets; the paralysis of idleness among civil servants; the dyspepsia of indignation among taxpayers; the *noli me tangere* of susceptibility among indecisive deputies; the convulsive enthusiasm of the godsons of government ministers; the chronic depression of candidates with no one to sponsor them; the cancer of necessity among indispensable diplomats; the epilepsy of jealousy among husbands, and the cataract of love among...'

'Ah, that's what ails Carlos!'

Carlos fidgeted impatiently.

'That is a truly terrible illness!' continued the orator. 'Let's see. Causes: it has been proven beyond doubt that this type of blindness usually starts with the patient being exposed to the blaze and splendour of a fine pair of eyes and to the sweet breath from a woman's lips. To avoid contagion various establishments called monasteries were set up. However, just as happens with genuine epidemics in isolation hospitals and

370

behind cordons sanitaires, the illness was not to be stopped; cases were even found among the famous hermits of Thebaid. While youth is the most favourable state for contracting the disease, it is even more to be feared in old age, where it can have tragic consequences and serious complications.'

Carlos was furiously biting his lip, but, encouraged by the other men's loud guffaws, his friend continued his oration.

'The symptoms are various. Generally speaking, the patient takes on the characteristic physiognomy of a fool; in between attacks, he falls into a kind of beatific state of idiocy, which defies even the application of the most powerful caustic. During such an attack, the patient may tear out his hair, crumple his collar, utter roars that would be the envy of a tiger or coo more sweetly than any dove, much to the despair of the dove. In particularly serious cases, the illness can become malignant, and the patient then turns into a poet. When this happens, the doctor loses all hope and calls for the sacrament of... matrimony.'

'And what treatment would you recommend?' asked some, laughing.

'If a prophylactic has failed to curtail the disease, then hygiene is all, my friends. In Jean-Jacques Rousseau's *Confessions*, he mentioned mathematics as a prophylactic. I disagree. It has been shown that all mathematics does is add a pernicious edge to the illness. The amorous mathematician is the most rebellious patient ever, and often proves incurable. I would prescribe gastronomy, because the functions of stomach and heart stand in opposition to each other. As an antidote to love, I recommend reading Father Theodoro d'Almeida's *The Art of Living Contentedly* and other such sensible works. However, if, despite everything, the illness progresses, then the most heroic and radical remedy is...'

'What?' they all asked in unison.

'Marriage.'

Carlos was the only one not to applaud his friend's speech. He was growing more and more annoyed and had begun pacing up and down the room. Once the storm of laughter had subsided, he said: 'I ask you, please, to leave me in peace.'

'You owe us an explanation,' said the man on the sofa, adopting a still more oriental pose.

'We demand satisfaction,' said another, wielding a fencing foil and placing himself en garde.

Carlos had never disliked his friends more.

'It's simple enough,' he said brusquely. 'As you know, I am, and always have been, a capricious fellow. The agreeable company of you, my friends, was beginning to bore me to death, and so I decided to deprive myself of the enviable pleasure of your company. There you have it. Once the mood has passed, I may – or may not – rejoin you.'

'No, that won't do. The chamber rejects the minister's explanations,' said the man with the fencing foil. 'There are still matters that require clarification. You owe us a full report. What happened with that mysterious, masked woman who, just before you withdrew from the world, you promised to follow to the ends of the Earth? You never said another word about her, and there are some who insist that your sudden conversion began right there and then.'

Carlos was most annoyed by this importunate comment and was tempted to take seriously the aggressive stance of his interlocutor, and give him reason to regret having such a good memory. Instead, he said: 'Don't ask me anything on that subject, because I have nothing to say.'

'Ah, a mystery! It must be love! Yes, love!' cried the man at the mirror, before again launching into song:

An English Family

Dove non ride amore
Giorno non v'ha sereno…

'Leave Carlos alone. Any oath sworn at dead of night, with, as its sole witnesses, the stars and two even brighter eyes, is sacred.'

'I can't tell you anything, because I don't know anything,' said Carlos, annoyed at the interpretation given to his words.

'And you know nothing because you saw nothing, is that it? My friend, your discretion is in very bad taste,' said the man on the sofa, executing a manoeuvre that raised his legs several inches and lowered his head several more.

'Eureka!' cried one friend who had gone over to the desk. 'Here is irrefutable proof of the crime. The evidence! A letter!'

At these words, Carlos shuddered. The man who had made the discovery was triumphantly brandishing the letter Carlos had written only moments before.

'A letter! And what kind of letter is it?' asked the chorus.

'*Papier rose et odeur enivrant,*' said the other man, making a great show of sniffing the letter.

Carlos felt like throwing his friend out of the window when he went on to say: 'And it's addressed to…'

'Who? Who?' they all asked, gathering around him, burning with curiosity.

'Now that is an indiscretion too far!' cried Carlos, going over to try and snatch the letter from him.

The others stopped him.

'Why this sudden maidenly modesty?'

'I forbid you to…' Carlos began, struggling to free himself.

'Don't be so daft,' they responded, laughing and still keeping a firm grip on him. 'Quick, read it, before the lion escapes. He's absolutely furious.'

'Most excellent Senhora,' said the man with the letter, reading very slowly as if to prolong this amusing scene.

'Ah, "Ex-cel-lent Se-nho-ra",' they all repeated, stressing each syllable.

'Cecília...' the man read on.

'Ce-cí-lia! A very musical name!'

'Yes, a most philharmonic invocation!'

'The patron saint of harmony!'

'The inventor of the harp!'

Carlos finally managed to wrench himself free from the group holding him back and, running over to the desk, he snatched the letter from the man's hands.

'There are certain impertinences that I will not tolerate from anyone,' he said, turning pale and shaking with indignation and rage.

Then he tugged violently at the bell, to which his personal servant responded at once.

Carlos handed him the letter, saying: 'Deliver this letter.'

The servant was about to withdraw when Carlos stopped him to issue a further whispered instruction: 'If they ask who it's from, say it's from Miss Jenny.'

The servant clearly understood the order and left.

The others had all now fallen silent and were following Carlos' every move with astonishment.

Once the servant had left, that silence continued for a while, until a voice said: 'An excellent end of act! The servant leaves the stage, Carlos sits down grave-faced, and the other actors regard him, amazed and confused. Imagine the scene!'

The others exchanged glances and, as if they found each other utterly and equally ridiculous, burst out laughing.

Carlos thought it best to smile too, even though, inside, he was still seething.

'Word of honour,' said one, 'I've never seen Carlos like this. He's gone all romantic!'

'Ultra-romantic!'

'And furious too!'

'Like a lion!'

'Like a bull!'

Like a Turk!' said the man with orientalist tendencies.

'Come on, Carlos, where are your manners? Love has turned you into a savage. Come back to civilisation!'

'Tell us about this Cecília.'

'Is she tall or short?'

'Dark or fair?'

'A Greek beauty or more the oriental type?'

'I bet you it's that masked woman.'

'It must be.'

'Come on, man, tell us how it all started.'

'Be careful! A secret passion is a nest of aneurysms,' said the expert on ailments of the soul.

'Cecília! Yes, a most euphonious name!'

'Will you, please, not continue to talk like that about a name which I... respect.'

General laughter greeted this request.

'Oh, you are funny!'

'Hilarious!'

'I've never seen you like this before!'

'Oh Carlos!'

'*Povero amico*!'

Carlos' face flushed with anger.

'I repeat: a name that I *respect*. Surely I'm allowed to be serious occasionally.'

'Of course, but whenever you are, I can't help laughing.'

'*You*, speak seriously?!'

'So you really are in love? Well, tell us about it. That's what friends are for, after all.'

'*Amicus certus…*'

'Sing us your confessional aria, go on, and the chorus will back you up.'

'If you don't, we will search and we will find, and then we will prove implacable, cruel! So watch out!'

'It's that fateful masked woman!'

'Do you really think so?'

'I'm sure of it.'

'Oh, Carlos, take care. You picked a flower from sullied soil, plucked a pearl from some very murky water – a masked ball!'

Carlos again tried to use silence to silence them.

'I refuse to explain anything, so whenever you're ready to cease your pointless importunities, then please do.'

They did not comply, but kept up a noisy, disorderly discussion for more than half an hour, while Carlos pretended to be reading.

At last, they left, and he sighed as if a great weight had been lifted from his chest.

'Goodbye, Carlos, *muchas venturas*!' said one.

'I hope you'll be very happy,' said another.

'Goodbye, Carlos, goodbye.'

One was singing:

Ah, to be once more in Sevilla
Where a sly Spanish lady
In a lace mantilla
Is curling her long black hair.

And thus the cheerful, tumultuous company left the room.

XXX

A Weight that might have its lighter Side

The unfortunate impression his friends' visit had made on him did not immediately disappear with their departure.

I don't know if there is anyone so indifferent and so impervious to other people's opinions that he can hear, without being touched or repelled, the name of some beloved person on another's irreverent lips and spoken of as part of some trivial conversation.

While he was displeased with his friends, Carlos was equally dissatisfied with himself. He had sent off that letter to Cecília without a thought, and only now did he reflect upon his lack of delicacy in doing so, and upon his inappropriate choice of emissary. Something else was worrying him too. When he dispatched his servant with the message, he had forgotten that, since today was a public holiday, Manuel Quintino would probably be at home; and how could Cecília conceal that letter from him, even when told it was from Jenny?

All these considerations were gradually leading Carlos into one of those impatient, agitated states, which, being completely incompatible with bodily repose, demand action and movement.

Since the vague aspirations we feel in such states are far greater than the means we have to satisfy them, we tend to accumulate an excess of energy, which reveals itself in a need

377

for aimless, endless activity, to which we surrender ourselves as if to a physical necessity, which we wisely do not even try to regulate or direct.

This is why Carlos got up and left, as if he found the cramped space of his room suffocating.

He had already gone through the door that opened onto the garden, when the crunch of sand beneath light footsteps alerted him to the presence of someone coming down the street outside.

He nearly gave a cry of delight.

It was Cecília.

This unexpected apparition so completely realised the secret, ill-defined desires troubling him, seemed to chime so mysteriously with his heart's demands, that Carlos almost believed that Cecília's presence there, at that precise moment, was a genuine miracle of love – an illusion comprehensible only to those who have themselves known such feelings. And so convinced was he of this that he did not even attempt to hide his feelings. He saw her and persuaded himself that she had come in answer to his call, that reading his letter had been enough, that, brimming with confidence and trust, she had come to tell him that she accepted the homage of the love he was offering and repaid it with her own.

Gripped by this thought – which will raise a mocking smile only among readers over forty – Carlos held out one tremulous hand to the even more tremulous girl staring at him, and murmured: 'Oh, thank you, Cecília, thank you so much for coming!'

Cecília was gazing at him in amazement, unable to understand the meaning of those words or else fearing that she understood them all too well.

'Listen to me, please, for pity's sake, Cecília, listen. I want to tell you everything that has happened to me since I met you that first time; listen…'

Carlos had, of course, kept hold of Cecília's hand, and she, as if still taken aback by this entirely unexpected encounter, seemed unaware of what was happening and made no attempt to withdraw hers.

Carlos went on: 'The fact that you came, Cecília, means that you believe I was sincere in what I said. Isn't that so? It's true, isn't it, that you will never again think that when I say to you over and over that I love you, it is no mere frivolous flirtation utterly unworthy of someone like you?'

These words almost restored Cecília to her senses. The blood drained from her face only to rush more violently back again; she gave a cry of alarm and tried to withdraw the hand that Carlos was still holding firmly in his.

'Senhor Carlos!' she said, her voice shaking with shock and confusion.

'Don't go, Cecília. Don't be afraid. I love you very much, but I respect you as much as I love you; and…'

He could not go on. The sound of footsteps and voices out in the street, and already close to the garden gate, sent a shudder through him.

Fearing the worst, he instinctively drew Cecília into the room – for that brief scene had taken place just outside – and immediately shut the door.

Cecília was looking at him in great alarm.

She was about to cry out, when Carlos placed one hand over her mouth, saying: 'Please, not a word!'

He was quite right. The garden was once again invaded by that same gang of ne'er-do-wells who, moments earlier, had abandoned the field. They had arrived just in time to see the bedroom door closing and greeted this discovery with loud guffaws.

Moments later, their voices could be heard from inside the room.

'Open the door, open the door! There's no point pretending now, Carlos! We followed her. We had a hunch she would turn up. We saw her come into the garden. It must be her. Don't deny it. Open up!'

When she heard these words, Cecília felt as if she would faint.

'Oh, dear God!' she cried, raising her hands to heaven.

Carlos appeared to be thunderstruck.

'Come on, Carlos. What's wrong with you. You never used to be like this.'

'No, it's not like you at all.'

'We just want a quick peek at her, then we'll go.'

'Yes, we only want to see her and pay our respects.'

'Come on, man.'

For a moment, Carlos was filled with despair. Not really thinking what he was doing, without even considering the consequences, he went over to the door, eyes ablaze and lips trembling with rage.

Cecília stopped him, almost falling to her knees before him.

'Do you want to ruin me, Senhor Carlos?' she said in a voice shaking with emotion. 'Do you want to ruin me?'

Carlos stopped, and trying to help her to her feet, said in no less emotional tones: 'Cecília, I swear by all that's holy that...'

Then, one of the voices said: 'Don't be so mean, Carlos. Don't you want us to see your Cecília?'

Those words sent a shudder through her.

When she heard her name spoken in that leering voice, on the lips of a complete stranger, she sprang back, full of pride and wounded dignity, her face aflame with outrage, she fixed

Carlos with bitter eyes and said: 'What did I do to deserve this, sir?'

'Cecília!' stammered Carlos, turning pale.

Pushing him proudly away from her, she now walked firmly over to the door.

Carlos stood in front of her.

'What are you going to do?' he said.

'Leave me alone! I'm less afraid of meeting those men outside than I am of staying here beneath your "generous" protection.'

That word 'generous' was spoken with infinite scorn.

'Cecília, you can't possibly think…'

'They might prove cruel and immune to my tears, but rather that than your infamous behaviour… which has cut me to the quick.'

And the tone in which she said this revealed that the initial energetic impulse that had inspired her response was already beginning to fade.

With that word 'infamous' all Carlos' lack of resolution dissolved, and again taking Cecília's hands in his and looking her in the eye, he said in a voice imbued with the eloquence of sincerity: 'Cecília, I don't have time now to explain, but I swear on the memory of my mother, on the life of my father, and on the happiness of my sister, that I do not deserve your suspicions.'

A hypocrite could have sworn that same oath, but not in that truthful, persuasive voice.

No one can lie like that.

Cecília believed him, and all the suspicions that had, for a moment, clouded her mind, vanished.

Once her sense of outrage had departed along with the fictitious strength it had brought with it, she regained the gentleness proper to her sex and reverted to a woman's most irresistible weapon. Her eyes filled with tears, and sobbing, she clasped Carlos' hand and murmured: 'Save me, then Senhor Carlos, or else I'm ruined!'

The hubbub of voices which had continued throughout this brief scene – which happened far more quickly than it has taken to describe it – now increased in volume.

Carlos could think of only one way out of the situation. He ran to the library and opened the door. Cecília entered and, almost instinctively, locked the door behind her.

This was still a risky manoeuvre, because the servants might have noticed Cecília suddenly appearing from that part of house, which would have been equally compromising. But no other idea occurred to Carlos at the time.

Having taken a few moments to try and calm himself after that alarming scene, he finally opened the door to his importunate friends.

'Have you chosen me to be the butt of all your jokes today, gentlemen?'

'Oh, stop playing the stage villain, it doesn't suit you. We've come to find out where she's gone?'

'Who?'

'What do you mean "who"? The girl!'

'So the joke continues…'

'Look, don't try and deny it, man. We saw her on the corner. And one of us, I can't remember who, suddenly had a hunch it was her and so we followed her at a distance. She hesitated briefly when she reached your house. An infallible sign! Then she went in and we ran after her. We even saw the door closing… and then there was this rather unkind delay on your part. Some of us even thought we heard voices inside. Come on. Confess.'

'Yes, don't go all soppy on us. Why so sentimental?'

'You were always the first to demand explanations from others, and always defended the rights of camaraderie above all else!'

'Yes, do you remember that time in Carriça?'

'Or in Leça with me? Your curiosity then almost drove me to distraction.'

'Do you want us to go and look for her?'

'Do you want me to be uncivil and order you to leave?'

'You're the one who's being uncivil.'

'And you're the one who's making a drama out of it, Carlos. I hardly recognise you.'

'That's it, then,' said the rather effeminate fair-haired young man. 'He won't budge. The remedy is easy. We'll go looking for her. He'll hardly have given her into the safe keeping of his family. She must be hiding somewhere.'

'Into the bushes, lads, and we'll drive out our gazelle.'

And they immediately launched into a disorderly search of the whole room. Not a piece of furniture, not a hiding place, was left unexamined.

'What about the library?' said a voice at last.

'Yes, the library!' cried the others.

And off they went.

Carlos trembled for Cecília.

'I forbid you to open that door!' he exclaimed, his voice shaking.

'Aha! So we were right! Did you hear his voice?'

'Oh, damn, it's locked from the inside.'

Carlos gave a sigh of relief.

'I've never known it to be locked before. How mysterious! I wonder if we can see through the keyhole...'

'Carlos, open this door or else order it to be opened.'

'There's the sound of voices inside.'

'Let me listen.'

'It's her.'

The man peering through the keyhole went on: 'I think I just caught a glimpse of a woman's dress.'

'Ah!'

'She's gone in there to read *Paul et Virginie*. You know how Carlos loves romantic novels.'

They all roared with laughter.

'Shh. Be quiet!'

Carlos was becoming desperate.

'This is too much. I demand that you leave this instant.'

'And I demand silence. Someone's coming over to the door. It's her! *Incessu patuit dea…* She's far more reasonable than you. About time too.'

Carlos remembered Cecília's earlier decision to confront his friends and feared she might be about to do just that.

He could do nothing now to stop her. He lost all hope, all courage.

The key turned in the lock.

'Hats off, gentlemen! Here she is!' said one of the gang.

Carlos closed his eyes, as if in the presence of imminent danger. His hand closed into a fist on the pistol case lying next to him.

However, instead of the expected tumult – which might have led to who knows what excesses on his part – there ensued a profound silence, that made him look up in surprise.

All those hitherto rowdy young men had doffed their hats and were retreating in respectful silence, as if trying to hide behind each other.

At the open door stood the pure, serene figure of Jenny, with her arm about Cecília's waist, while Cecília, wearing a slightly melancholy smile, rested her head on Jenny's shoulder.

Jenny remained there for a few moments, looking at them all with a composed, enquiring expression, which seemed to subjugate them.

It made for an impressive scene.

Jenny's angelic features exuded sweetness and nobility, while Cecília's face betrayed such melancholy and such confidence in the friend supporting her, that the more frivolous of the gang bowed their heads respectfully before those two women.

Only Carlos, who had long been a student of his sister's face, noticed a slight tremor on her lips, indicating that her apparent calm did not correspond to an equally complete serenity of heart.

And yet she spoke to Carlos' friends in a firm, friendly voice.

'I'm so sorry to have kept you waiting. We thought my brother had already gone out and we came here looking for a book.'

Then, indicating Cecília, she added: 'This is my friend, well, more than a friend, almost my sister.' And she added with a smile. 'Because you soon will be, won't you?'

Cecília trembled and gazed at Jenny in astonishment. She seemed about to speak.

Jenny stopped her with a squeeze of her hand, then, smiling, went on: 'Forgive me, Cecília, if I'm being indiscreet, although perhaps I'm not, given that these gentlemen are… my brother Carlos' friends.'

And Jenny uttered these words with just a hint of irony in her voice, which only increased the embarrassment of those 'friends'.

Bowing slightly to them, Jenny left the library with Cecília.

Carlos did not even dare to look at his sister.

When he saw her leave, he turned to his former companions, who were beginning to mouth excuses, and said to them with provocative coldness: 'I hope your curiosity is satisfied. Was there anything else you wanted?'

'I'm sorry, Carlos, we thought…'

'We had no idea…'

'You must believe…'

'I really thought it was that woman from the masked ball.'

'So did I.'

'I hope you're not too offended.'

'It was just a joke.'

'Goodbye, Carlos, and don't be so elusive.'

'Sincere apologies and… and congratulations.'

And they left the room.

Out in the street, they were saying: 'Goodness!'

'Carlos! Getting married!'

'*Requiescat in pace!*'

'Amen.'

The door closed on the last of them, and Carlos ran back to find his sister, where he knelt at her feet.

'Jenny! Jenny! The love I bore you is as nothing to the love I owe you now. Who could not adore you, sister?'

Jenny drew him to his feet, with an expression that was at once sad and tender. She said: 'Leave such excessive love for someone who, from now on, has more right to demand it than I do.'

And she indicated Cecília, who was weeping, her face pressed to her friend's bosom.

Deeply moved, Carlos spoke to her: 'Cecília, Cecília, can you ever forgive me?'

Cecília did not respond or look up, but held out her hand to him.

Carlos bent to kiss it.

Raising tearful eyes to heaven, Jenny murmured, perhaps addressing her mother's image, which was there in her imagination.

'Thank you! Thank you!'

What was Jenny thanking her for? Doubtless for the inspiration she had sent her.

XXXI

What went on in Manuel Quintino's House

Let's go back to the morning of that same day and observe what happened in Manuel Quintino's house, since this is essential to an understanding of subsequent events.

When she woke that morning, Cecília was still undecided as to whether or not to accept Jenny's invitation.

It was, as we said, a holiday, and so Manuel Quintino did not have to leave early to go to the office. Having spent more care than usual on his toilette, he donned his favourite wide-collared cape – an item of clothing rich in memories – and went for a stroll in the garden until it was time for mass. Walking along the tree-lined paths – the leaves already lush and green – Manuel Quintino was enjoying the cloudless Spring sun, but barely noticed the burgeoning flower beds or the birds singing in the trees above, celebrating the morning.

His thoughts were far away.

The sombre cortège of sad ideas aroused in him recently by Cecília's melancholy mood returned to haunt him with renewed persistence.

'I suppose her life here is very dull, with so few distractions. And she's only eighteen after all! She needs to get out more. Instead of idling about here, I should be taking her out and about.'

And with this idea in mind, he walked back to the house.

'Cecília,' he said when he found her, 'it's such a lovely morning, why don't we go out somewhere?'

'Where?'

'Oh, somewhere. We could go for a stroll before mass. What are we doing shut up indoors like this?'

Cecília agreed, thinking that this would please her father.

Half an hour later, they set off, with Cecília still hesitating over whether she should go to Jenny's birthday party or not.

Father and daughter spoke little during their walk. They ended up in Cedofeita, where they attended mass.

After their usual visit to the cemetery, Cecília seemed, for the first time, to emerge from the hesitant state she had been in ever since the previous day and, stopping at the end of the street that was the shortest route to Mr Richard Whitestone's house, she said: 'I'm not sure what to do, Pa. Jenny invited me to spend the day with her.'

'Today?'

'Yes, she wrote me a note, asking me…'

'Well, you do as you wish, my dear, although, of course, today is a holiday and I…'

Manuel Quintino was about to say how sad he would be not to enjoy his daughter's company, but held back, afraid he might make her feel guilty. Cecília, however, understood.

'I know, Pa. I know you don't like being left alone when you have a day at home – which isn't very often – but some companions only succeed in making us feel even sadder than if we were alone, and I really wouldn't make for very cheerful company today.'

'What do you mean, Cecília? How can you say that?'

'No, I mean it.'

'But why?'

'Because I feel sad, and however hard I tried I just wouldn't be able to pretend otherwise.'

Manuel Quintino was so moved that his eyes filled with tears.

'I'd noticed you were sad, Cecília, so that's nothing new to me. I've been worrying about it for a while, but now that you yourself have spoken of it, please tell me the reason. What is it that's troubling you, what's wrong? Are you ill?'

'No, Pa, don't ask, because I can't… because I really don't know the answer.'

Manuel Quintino stood for a while looking at his daughter, who averted her eyes, unable to speak. Finally, he said: 'Go and see Jenny, go on. She's such a kind girl, and she'll do a better job than I will of cheering you up. I wouldn't want to be the one to keep you from visiting that young angel.'

Cecília kissed her father's hand, and, as they parted, he noticed she had tears in her eyes.

He waited at the top of the road until she had disappeared from view.

'Why those tears?' he murmured, annoyed that he could find no explanation. 'Seeing her like that makes me want to cry too. It's obviously something very serious.'

And he walked back home, head bowed. Indeed, he was so distracted that, most unusually for him, he didn't even greet the neighbours, and very nearly walked straight past his own house.

Surprised to see him return home alone, Antónia asked: 'Where's the young mistress?'

'She won't be lunching with us today.'

'Well, she might have told me earlier.'

'She didn't know until just now.'

'Honestly! So where is she having lunch?'

'With Jenny.'

'Who?'

'Jenny, Mr Whitestone's daughter…'

'Do you mean…'

'Yes, at Mr Richard Whitestone's house.'

'Well, that's a fine thing, that is.'

'What's wrong?'

'Oh, nothing. So, it's only you for lunch, then?'

'Yes.'

Manuel Quintino ate little, for, as far as he was concerned, any lunch without Cecília's presence was not a proper lunch.

'Aren't you eating?' Antónia kept asking.

'No, I'm not hungry.'

'Suit yourself.'

Manuel Quintino left the table and went and sat by the window.

After shaking the crumbs off the table cloth, Antónia cleared her throat as if she had something important to say.

Manuel Quintino failed to notice, and so Antónia decided to take the initiative.

'Now that you've had your lunch, sir, there's something I'd like to tell you.'

'What's that?'

'Although, to be honest, I probably shouldn't…'

'Then don't tell me.'

'On the other hand, I do feel it's my duty…'

'Then tell me.'

Antónia could see that her master was not in the most receptive of moods, so she decided to try a more direct approach.

'Are you blind, sir?'

'I don't believe so, no.'

'Well, you could have fooled me. Haven't you noticed a

change in the young mistress lately?'

This question had an immediate effect on Manuel Quintino, who spun round to face Antónia: 'I have, yes. Have you?'

'Of course! She's not her usual self at all.'

'No, she's not, Antónia, she certainly isn't.'

'Not in the least.'

'And do you know what's wrong? Has she complained to you of feeling unwell, of some illness?'

'Not that I know of, besides there are so many types of illnesses!'

'I know that.'

'Yes, but there are some you might not have thought of... an illness of the heart, for example.'

'The heart!' exclaimed Manuel Quintino, turning pale. 'Has Cecília complained about her heart? What are you talking about, woman?'

'No, you don't understand. I mean... look... to speak plainly. She's eighteen years old...'

'Well, that's hardly news! I know that, but what is it she complains of?'

'If you really can't think of some other malady of the heart, Senhor Manuel Quintino, then I give up.'

An idea entered Manuel Quintino's head, one that had, admittedly, taken its time.

'Is that possible?' he said, and turning again to Antónia, he added gravely: 'Antónia, tell me what you know. I'll need to look into this. Speak, woman.'

'Well, in that case, sir,' she said, as if she had needed his permission in order to be persuaded to speak, 'I wouldn't want it weighing on my conscience, but I would say that, for your own good, you need to keep an eye on this business.'

'What "business" must I keep an eye on? I don't understand.'

'Have you really not noticed what's going on?'

'No, and as you well know, I pay no heed to gossip...'

'What about all those visits from the Englishman's son...'

'Oh, is that all it is?' retorted Manuel Quintino with a shrug. 'Not you as well. Poor lad. Just because he's got up to mischief in the past, he can't even enter someone's house without tongues wagging... Honestly, what a world!'

'So you don't believe me, then? Fine, believe what you like.'

'Did you really think...? But you know why the poor boy came here that first time, don't you?'

'No, sir, and I've given the matter a lot of thought...'

'Don't you remember that evening when I was so late coming home, and Cecília...'

'But that wasn't the first time.'

'Yes, it was.'

'No, sir, it wasn't.'

'Really, woman! What's wrong with your memory? Do you really not remember?'

'I remember that, long before that evening, the same gentleman came to this house and asked to speak to the young mistress. I showed him into the parlour, and she came downstairs to greet him. When she saw him, though, she turned as red as a pomegranate, and told me to leave the room. They talked for nearly half an hour.'

'Are you mad, woman?'

'No, sir, I'm not.'

'When was this?'

'Just after Carnival. It was a few days after you'd let the young mistress go off with the Matos girls, something that, I, in your place, would never have done, but...'

'Cecília never told me about that.'

'I know.'

'What do you mean you know?'

'The mistress told me not to tell you, because they were preparing a surprise for you, not that she would tell me what the surprise was.'

Manuel Quintino was beginning to feel worried. Nevertheless, he had such confidence in Cecília that, despite all he knew of Carlos' flighty nature, he still hesitated to feel concerned about what he was hearing now for the first time.

'And did he come back again?'

'No, not until the day you fell ill, but he did sometimes appear beneath her window at certain hours of the morning and at dusk.'

'Yes, I do remember that sometimes…'

'It was the tobacconist's wife who pointed that out to me.'

'Yes, but…'

'I know there's nothing wrong with that, but the mistress was almost always at the window at the same time…'

'Cecília?!'

'It's true. And that's when I noticed the change in her.'

Manuel Quintino ran his hand over his head as if to brush away a troublesome thought.

'Afterwards,' Antónia went on, 'he came here because of your illness and to help you out with office business, and of course there he was, firmly installed in the house. Do you really think he would have the patience to go to all that trouble unless…'

'Be quiet, woman!' cried Manuel Quintino angrily. 'Carlos is a very generous young man. He would never hesitate for a moment to help a friend, whatever sacrifices that might involve.'

'Maybe, but I'm not the only one who had my suspicions.'

'You would have to be an utterly despicable human being to abuse the trust of an old man, an honest old man and ill to boot. No, neither Carlos nor Cecília would ever enter into such a vile compact!'

'I'm not saying they were both involved, no, but, as I say, I wasn't the only one who thought that…'

'I know. I even received an anonymous letter. I showed it to Carlos, and he himself resolved not to come here any more.'

'Oh, really? I didn't know that. Now, though, I see the kind of man he is. Shall I tell you something else? One night, after he stopped coming here, I heard the bolt being drawn on the garden gate. It was a moonlit night, and I was still up, so I looked out of the window. I saw the mistress going down the stairs into the hallway.'

Manuel Quintino was staring at Antónia now with a look of horror on his face and almost holding his breath.

'And then?'

'I can tell you, my heart was really thumping, but I tiptoed down the stairs after her into the hallway. She was standing at the barred window and talking to someone out in the street. Afraid I might be seen, I couldn't get close enough to hear what they were saying, so I went round behind the lemon trees where I could hear better, but by the time I got there, she'd gone. I went over to the same barred window and saw him standing there…'

'You're lying, woman! You're a shameless liar!'

'Really, Senhor Manuel Quintino! As God is my witness, would I say something like that if it wasn't true?'

Manuel Quintino sprang to his feet and started pacing anxiously up and down.

'Is it possible that a man's heart can contain such evil? Carlos, who I've loved like my own son, who I've always defended when anyone accused him of being a wastrel! Carlos, who claimed to be my friend! Who seemed incapable of any kind of vile action!'

'And yet at the same time, he was riding around in a carriage with actresses...'

'If this is true, that means Cecília was also pretending... that she was deceiving me.'

And the poor old man could not speak for crying.

'I'm very sorry to upset you like this, sir, but what else could I do?' Antónia said. 'When you told me she'd gone to have lunch at the Englishman's house... knowing what I know... you can imagine my feelings.'

'The invitation came from Jenny, and so I have no reason to fear for Cecília. I could doubt anyone else – and who knows what I may yet find out – but never Jenny!'

'But was it really Jenny who invited her?'

Manuel Quintino shot her a look ablaze with indignation.

'Are you determined to worry me? Why? Why ask such a question, you viper? Don't you see that such poisoned words could be the death of me, you devil?'

'May God forgive me, sir, I'm not doing it out of malice. You know how devoted I am to the family, and I would hate any misfortune to befall...'

'Silence, woman! I know your intentions are good, but Cecília told me that Jenny had invited her.'

'I'm not denying that. I know the mistress did receive a letter from Senhora Jenny yesterday, but she didn't tell me what it said, and I didn't ask. This morning, though, just after you'd both gone out, a servant came from her with another letter; it wasn't the same servant, but one I saw the day I watched Senhor Carlos ride off in a carriage with an actress, and it seemed, by his manner, that he's Senhor Carlos' personal servant. "Who's this letter from?" I asked him. "It comes," the rascal said with a wicked smile, "it comes from Miss Jenny." But I'm not so sure… it doesn't look anything like the ones that…'

'Where is this letter?' Manuel Quintino demanded furiously.

'It's upstairs.'

'And did Cecília…?'

'She hasn't read it yet, because it arrived after you'd both left.'

'Go and fetch it.'

'But it might be from the Englishman's daughter, I…'

'Fetch it,' boomed Manuel Quintino.

António obediently hurried off.

Manuel Quintino was pacing up and down, clasping his head in his hands, his eyes closed, his breathing irregular, as if he were in the grip of madness.

Antónia brought him the letter. Manuel Quintino glanced at the envelope and shuddered.

He had recognised Carlos' handwriting!

In despair, he sank down onto the nearest chair.

'Oh my God! Why is this happening to me?' he murmured, tears streaming down his face.

Then he was about to rip open the letter he still held in his hands, but a lingering sense of propriety stopped him.

'No, I won't open it! No act of villainy justifies another.'

Antónia, dying of curiosity, gave a sigh of disappointment: 'So you're not going to read it?'

'No,' said Manuel Quintino brusquely, and resumed his pacing. Then, with sudden resolve, he stopped, looked up and said: 'Antónia, bring me my hat and my coat.'

Antónia opened her eyes wide with alarm.

'Goodness! What are you going to do, sir?'

'Bring me my hat and my coat!'

'But where are you going, sir? You're not yourself!'

'Did you not hear me, woman? Bring me my hat and my coat!'

His voice had taken on a strange quality, so entirely new to Antónia that she couldn't tell what it might portend, and so she prudently decided to say nothing and do as she was told.

She promptly returned with the requested items, saying fearfully: 'But where are you going, sir?'

'To find out the truth,' answered Manuel Quintino, and without any further explanation, he raced off down the stairs.

Antónia seemed paralysed with shock.

'Heavens!' she said. 'The man's mad. I just hope to God he doesn't do anything rash. May Our Lady keep us safe from the temptations of the Devil and the evil enemies of the soul.'

For Senhora Antónia professed an entirely sincere hatred of those particular enemies.

XXXII

Mr Richard's Guests

On the same morning as the events described in the previous two chapters, after having laboured away in the garden and the greenhouse, transplanting, pruning, propagating, sowing and watering the various plants in his collection – thereby inflicting no little harm on many of them – Mr Whitestone finally withdrew to his study, and, out of curiosity, opened his copy of *The Life and Opinions of Tristram Shandy*, which remained an inexhaustible source of pleasure and instruction for that kindly English gentleman. Every time he read it – and it was rare for twenty-four hours to pass without him doing so – he would discover new things, some serious, comic or philosophical, others of deep speculative value and practical utility, in short, everything. Mr Richard was utterly convinced of the rightness of Sterne's own opinion regarding that singular and unclassifiable work: 'True *Shandeism*,' he says somewhere, 'opens the heart and lungs, and like all those affections which partake of its nature, it forces the blood and other vital fluids of the body to run freely through its channels, and makes the wheel of life run long and cheerfully round.'

Indeed, half an hour spent reading one of Sterne's humorous pages was, for Mr Richard, an efficacious remedy against life's sadnesses and difficulties.

Mr Richard had opened the book at random and was now

reading the page that describes how Tristram's father, on learning of the death of one of his children, found consolation in the fact that this provided him with a pretext for some philosophical thoughts about death. Tristram says: 'A blessing which tied up my father's tongue, and a misfortune which set it loose with a good grace, were pretty equal: sometimes, indeed, the misfortune was the better of the two.'

These words gave Mr Richard much food for thought; he was like those connoisseurs of wine who savour each mouthful and regard with indignation those coarse drinkers who gulp down a glass of that precious beverage in one.

'It's true,' he thought, setting the book aside to savour the words he had just read. 'It's the same for more or less everyone. If it were possible to change the world so that it fulfilled all the wishes of those who constantly rage against it, leaving them with nothing to complain about, they would be most put out.'

These thoughts were interrupted by a servant, who came in to announce: 'Mr Morlays.'

'Verbi gratia,' thought Mr Richard, having given orders for the guest to be shown in.

The Englishman who had just arrived was one of those pessimists for whom the entire universe is painted in the dingiest of colours; he was a victim, at once to be pitied and loathed, of the ill humour that the learned Baron von Feuchtersleben calls the vulgar prose of life, brother of tedium and idleness and a poison that eventually brings about death.

Mr Whitestone, a hard-working man contented with the world, was in constant opposition to his friend and compatriot, who was the sort of Englishman who had given the London fog an undeserved reputation as a fomentor of spleen, a reputation that thinking men are quite rightly beginning to dispute, having discovered that the real cause of that suicidal malaise lies in the idleness of certain fabulously wealthy aristocrats.

Ancient medicine would have seen in Mr Morlays' appearance a clear case of that mysterious humour designated black bile. He was one of those rather swarthy Englishmen, and his dark complexion was reflected in his moods.

The study in which the two men were sitting was a compendium of everything that could possibly smooth life's path; it positively oozed comfort; everything favoured the sweet repose enjoyed nowhere more sweetly than by those of Her Majesty's subjects resident in our southern climes.

Chairs of various forms and fashions, in which the inventive genius had outdone itself in multiplying and modulating springs, distributing joints, and shaping angles and excrescences to accommodate, as far as possible, all postures, however capricious and eccentric; rugs, into which the feet sank as if into a field of grass; curtains that lessened the intensity of the light; and, finally, the fire crackling and licking the grate with its red-hot tongue, an inseparable companion for those from northerly nations – even in that almost-summer month. Mr Whitestone agreed with St Francis de Sales, who, it was said, believed that one should keep a fire burning in the hearth for twelve months of the year.

Mr Morlays found many bileful reasons to disapprove.

'A very bad habit, Mr Richard, very bad! It is just such enervating habits as these that have brought about the degeneration of the human race. Scrofula for example…'

'Mercy, Mr Morlays! What an ugly word to use just before lunch!' exclaimed Mr Richard, laughing.

'There are two evils of civilisation, and after sugar, the worst enemy of good health is the open fire.'

'So you're against sugar too?'

'I am indeed! In my opinion, that insidious substance is

the most pernicious of mankind's discoveries, treacherously poisoning our whole body and mingling with our blood...'

'Come now! I was under the impression that Mr Morlays had a very sweet tooth!'

'And what does that prove? That's human nature for you. Once you acquire a bad habit, even the pain it causes becomes indispensable.'

Mr Richard said nothing for a moment, as if meditating on his friend's theory of the law of habits.

Then he asked: 'Is there not even half an hour when you view this world with kindly eyes?'

'The defect is not in my eyes, you know, but in what is constantly being shown to them. Believe me, this is the worst of all possible worlds.'

'Tristram Shandy,' said Mr Richard with a smile, 'also regrets not having been born on the moon or on any of the planets, except Jupiter and Saturn, because they are too cold, his reasoning being that he could not have fared worse on any of them than he has on this one, which he judged to have been made up of the shreds and clippings of the rest. You, I see, wouldn't hesitate to say the same, eh?'

'Why would I?'

The servant came in again, this time announcing the arrival of Mr Brains.

'Ah,' cried Mr Richard, 'the antidote to your pessimistic influence.'

'Oh, he sees everything through rose-tinted glasses!' commented Mr Morlays with a pitying smile.

Out in the corridor, they heard a cheery voice singing:

God save Victoria!
Long live Victoria!
God save the Queen!

And Mr Brains, an Englishman who stubbornly rebelled against the usual commonsensical English etiquette, bounded into the room bowing to left and right as if crowds of people were gathered there to greet him.

'My lords, ladies and gentlemen, please don't get up!' he cried; then, going over to Mr Richard, he declared: 'Good afternoon, Lord Whitestone, delighted to see you looking so well. Oh, and our loyal subject, Lord Morlays! And how is that black devil who accompanies you everywhere?'

'Not in quite such a good mood as Mr Brains' rose-tinted one.'

'Oh, he let me down badly today, by scoffing all the oysters in the market and leaving me not a single one. I even started to think that perhaps Mr Morlays was right. The world does have its thorny moments!'

'Laugh if you want. I confess that I find it hard to imagine a worse world.'

'To do that one would need only to banish all the oysters, thereby losing fifty per cent of the world's value. A light meal, easy on the stomach, indeed, it prepares one for a more substantial repast.'

We will not accompany any further the long, substantial conversation, with its many ups and downs, that took place among those three Englishmen.

They covered absolutely everything that morning: all the grave questions troubling minds and clogging up the embassies of Europe with paperwork; the fate of nations, the future of mankind; these things were categorically dealt with and decided, safe in the knowledge that the decisions reached were infallible, something only possible among English subjects, whose privileges, from that point of view, know no bounds. Monarchs, generals, ministers, diplomats, lawyers passed in a long procession before the eyes of that triumvirate, who judged and sentenced them with a boldness and precision proper to the British spirit.

They gave their own account of the Crimean War: exalting the role of England and bitterly criticising France, whose army was known only for the occasional show of bravado, which, sometimes, by sheer chance, met with some success.

Needless to say, this whole discussion was peppered with lugubrious reflections from Mr Morlays and jovial asides from Mr Brains. The former, with the intention of doing down France, invented examples of cruelty, even cannibalism, committed by the French troops; the latter, with the same patriotic aim, told comical anecdotes as proof of the quixotic nature of old England's allies. Mr Whitestone happily accepted both arguments.

The conclusion Mr Morlays drew from his was almost always the same: 'This world's a nest of perfidious vipers!'

Mr Brains usually came up with something like: 'No, all the world's a stage.'

Gradually, the discussion shifted onto more sublime matters. The matter of politics opened up the still vaster question of society, in which the two Englishmen brought their very individual views to bear, both in the service of their shared homeland.

Mr Brains the optimist warmly embraced utopias. As he looked towards future centuries, he could see, far off, the longed-for coming together of different peoples in one nation, with one legislature, one common language, and the suppression of the word 'war' from the universal vocabulary, because there would be no need for it; with matter subjugated to the intellect and obliged to work, leaving the mind free from having to attend to the impertinent demands of physical life and more able to enter into speculations of a superior, metaphysical kind.

'Then man's ultimate goal on earth will have been achieved! If only I could live to see that day, Mr Whitestone, to welcome in that great day! To be able to say "Good morning" to the rising sun in the universal language of the time!'

With the smile of someone who has little faith in such a golden future, Mr Richard asked: 'And what language will that be, Mr Brains? One that exists already and that will become generalised, or a new one yet to be formulated?'

'Who can say, Mr Richard? That is a secret known only to the future. But there are clearly many plausible arguments in favour of English.'

'Oh really?'

'Definitely. First of all, England is the foremost colonial nation, and English is a familiar tongue in every corner of the world. Young America – at least in its most vigorous elements, which are sure to overcome all others – is also English in origin. And then, my dear Mr Richard, France carries within it the destructive germ that will end up killing it, namely, Popery, which is tantamount to a death sentence. Not to mention the philosophical nature of the English language…'

We will not follow him any further in his philological dissertation, which concluded that, with the passing centuries, all humanity would speak English, something which, if it happened, would perhaps untune the celebrated harmony of the spheres, at least as regards humanity.

Mr Morlays took the floor then, in order to do battle with his compatriot.

Predictably enough, Mr Morlays' vision of society's fate was rather less flattering. Humanity, especially non-English humanity, he thought, would have no reason to applaud the future he foresaw.

Whenever Mr Morlays thought about these things, he saw catastrophes not utopias, which is why he said in gloomy tones: 'I really don't believe, Mr Brains, that such a universal nationality is possible as humanity progresses. According to what I've read, the world we live in has always been subject to convulsions; it contains a fiery nucleus which is constantly rising to the surface. Humanity has already witnessed great cataclysms, and who knows how many more it will see? According to what I've read, the continents we inhabit were once partially covered by water, which leads naturalists to believe that any nations living before us now lie buried at the bottom of the sea. If such geological revolutions should occur in the future, as seems perfectly plausible, the continental part of the globe will be submerged, and out of the waters will emerge new unpopulated areas. One possibility is that, due to England's geography and its island nature, it will escape the same fate as the large continents, and might survive ruin and submersion and even add to its territory any new lands raised up from the depths by the cataclysm. Then, and only then, will the future that Mr Brains imagines come into being, with the English as the sole lords of the globe.'

Then, as if concerned that such an extravagant, not to say patriotic, geological theory might be misunderstood, he added: 'Take this hat, for example,' and he picked up the floppy hat Mr Richard wore when labouring in the garden. 'Imagine the crown to be the world, with the various lumps and bumps representing the continents, and any dips and creases the seas, well, that small bump in the middle, cut off from the others, is England. If you press down on the other bumps, the cavities rise up and increase the size of the central bump. Do you see?'

And so as not to give in to this potentially hopeful possibility, he concluded:

'Although it might be best if all the bumps went under together.'

As you see, dear reader, these two compatriots of Robert Peel were both eagerly awaiting the same phenomenon in the history of the future, namely England's sovereignty over the whole world – albeit by very different routes.

This, in fact, is what every true Englishman believes, with, as with the two great examples here, a few variations on how this might happen.

Mr Richard smiled at his friend's historico-geographical theory.

'To be on the safe side, we had better move back to the island, Mr Morlays. Living on the bottom of the sea would not be a good idea, and even Her Majesty's consul wouldn't have the power to exempt us from being swallowed up like mere Portuguese citizens.'

Mr Brains heartily applauded his friend Mr Richard's remark.

As the morning progressed and the odoriferous smells from the kitchen advanced through the rooms and reached the guests' Englishly alert nostrils, the conversation began to descend from the clouds, where it had been hovering, to deal with more earthly, more comestible matters.

At three o'clock, feeling instinct drive them to the lunch table, the three Englishmen left Mr Richard's study and moved into the parlor, where Jenny and Cecília were sitting close together, deep in conversation.

XXXIII

In Jenny's Honour

'Oh, how good that you could come, Cecília,' said Mr Richard, walking towards her, hand outstretched, 'you'll add to the gaiety of the occasion.'

'Add to the gaiety!' said Cecília, giving Jenny an ironic, melancholy look.

'Yes,' responded Jenny, squeezing her hands affectionately. 'Your presence alone adds gaiety enough.'

Cecília sighed.

'Are you not feeling well, Cecília?' asked Mr Richard, noticing the weary look on Cecília's face.

'A slight indisposition, from which she has promised to recover in honour of my birthday, isn't that right?' said Jenny, laughing and answering on Cecília's behalf.

Mr Morlays the Glum chose this moment to go over to Jenny.

'Miss Jenny,' he said, 'I usually joyfully celebrate the birthdays of people I care about as one more step towards their liberation from life.'

'Oh, Mr Morlays,' cried Jenny with a smile, 'does the tyranny of life weigh so heavily on you that you long for it to end?'

'Ignore him, Miss Jenny,' said Mr Brains, 'his ill humour can be explained by the presence of a few silver threads among the gold and by the appearance of two sinister crow's feet around his eyes.'

Mr Morlays pulled a face and shrugged, but said nothing.

'We, however,' added Mr Brains, 'we ugly, but sturdy members of humanity, ha ha, we have good reason to regret the approach of our sunset hours, but those who serve as our stars in life, they always shine brightly, because even as the sun is setting, we still delight in the stars. Therefore, Miss Jenny, do not fear time's passing.'

Mr Morlays disapproved of this very British piece of gallantry.

'The comparison is most inexact,' he said sagely. 'How can one compare the stars to a man's life? The fall and extinction of the stars is pure fiction. They hide from us, but they do not burn out. It would be more accurate to compare life to a sky rocket.'

'A sky rocket?' cried Mr Brains, laughing. 'Now there's a strange comparison!'

'Yes, explain yourself,' said Mr Richard Whitestone, sitting down.

Mr Morlays began pacing the room, preparing to develop this image.

'Like the sky rocket, man is brought to life by an igniting spark, then rises blazing and blaring into the sky, where he pauses for a moment before exploding, and, once extinguished, falls swiftly and silently to Earth, leaving only his now inanimate skeleton.'

Mr Richard smiled at his friend and guest's original image.

'Mr Morlays is right.'

'And when will we explode?' asked Mr Brains, beaming and revealing a row of orderly teeth, before adding: 'I agree with Mr Morlays, but I would just point out that while there are sky rockets that fall to Earth silent and dead, the pyrotechnical arts have also invented some whose descent is lit by brightly coloured tears, which accompany the rocket earthwards. For my part, I will imitate one of those rockets.'

The conversation continued in this vein until Carlos arrived.

When she saw him, Cecília immediately went over to the window, where Jenny soon joined her.

Mr Brains greeted Carlos, singing: *I'm afloat! I'm afloat! on the fierce rolling tide/The ocean's my home, and my bark is my bride!* – these being the opening lines of a popular English song.

Carlos responded to his greeting with a smile.

Mr Morlays' response was equally characteristic.

'Another year on, Mr Charles, and here we are again. Who knows where we will have to go to seek each other out next year?'

Mr Brains was quick to answer: 'Certainly not to the cemetery, Mr Morlays, because, when you do decide to go there, you won't be in any mood to do any business deals.'

Mr Morlays did not share in the laughter that followed, but instead grew even more sombre.

Once his son had arrived, Mr Whitestone went over to the piano and began running his fingers over the keys with a jarring rapidity tolerable only to his English ear. This rather eccentric pastime was one in which he often indulged.

Fortunately for the two guests, they were as tone-deaf as Mr Richard, otherwise who knows what damage that barbarous entertainment might have caused.

Cecília, Jenny and Carlos were too absorbed in their own thoughts to be bothered by the wild musical exploits of Mr Whitestone, beneath whose fingers the magnificent Erhard piano – the victim of those unmusical *capriccios* – groaned as if under torture.

While this was going on, Cecília was saying to Jenny: 'Please, Jenny, I beg you, let me stay in here. I don't know if I can resist the sadness in my heart for much longer. I'm afraid I might cry.'

'Don't be such a child,' answered Jenny. 'I'm here by your side. Don't be so weak. Has that heart of yours started inventing impossible misfortunes?'

'Impossible?'

'Yes, impossible. Look, Cecília, initially, I was the one who could only imagine a bleak future. You were still laughing then, and I was the serious one. That brother of mine has often made me feel like that, and especially this time…'

'Oh, Jenny!'

'Yes, because I knew that, this time, he had met with a true and loyal heart, and I feared that he, madcap that he is, might not notice, and might break that heart. I told him so.'

'Oh, Jenny!'

'Yes, I did, Cecília, because all sacrifices are painful. Sacrificing pride, vanity, even mere whims, is painful, but sacrificing a heart, now that…'

'Can kill,' concluded Cecília almost unconsciously.

'Exactly. I knew that, or, rather,' she corrected herself with a smile, 'I presumed that this was so. And that's why I asked Carlos to forget about you, yes, because much less harm would have been done had the matter stopped there and then.'

Cecília did not respond, but the deep sigh she gave responded for her.

'And who knows,' Jenny went on, looking at Cecília, 'perhaps I was wrong to think that. Anyway, my brother clearly did not obey me.'

'Really?' asked Cecília doubtfully.

'No, far from forgetting, he simply couldn't shake off those first impressions and, within a few days, they had put down such deep roots that I began to feel afraid.'

Cecília was still shaking her head as if in disbelief.

'Don't look at me like that, Cecília. Who taught you to be so distrustful? Where did you learn to smile so cynically at your young age?'

Cecília silently bowed her head.

'Anyway, convinced that something unusual was taking place in my brother's heart...'

'So you were convinced?'

'I was. This clearly wasn't one of those passing fancies with which I was so familiar. It wasn't one of those fantasies that fitted so well with his habitual way of life and certainly never obliged him to change those habits.'

'It wasn't?'

'No. To my astonishment, I saw him change, and he did this voluntarily too, which he never had when I'd pleaded with him before, even though I think he would always like to have done as I asked. When I saw this, when I saw how different he was, I changed my way of thinking too. My sole concern, Cecília, was Carlos' happiness and yours. As long as I judged that there was still time to stop the whole affair, I did my best to speed matters up, but as soon as I realised it was too late to stop and that stopping would bring no one any happiness, I changed direction.'

The supper bell rang.

The two Englishmen, so oblivious to the musical outrages being perpetrated by Mr Richard, trembled at the sound of that instrument being played upon so freely by the butler.

'Dinner is served!' cried Mr Richard, finally leaving the piano in peace. 'And there's no need to wait for anyone else.'

Kate's death was still so recent that invitations had only been extended to those two close friends of the household, Mr Morlays and Mr Brains.

The two Englishmen and Carlos walked towards the two ladies.

Seeing them approach, Cecília grabbed Jenny's hand and said: 'Jenny, if you truly are my friend, then please don't make me go into supper!'

'What are you saying, Cecília?'

'I just can't go in there, I just can't…'

She fell silent, trembling.

Carlos was already by her side, offering her his arm to lead her into the dining room.

Jenny looked very hard at her friend and seemed persuaded that the constraint of being at the supper table really would be too painful for her.

'No, Charles,' she said, still not taking her eyes off her friend, 'Cecília won't be eating with us. She's not well and needs to rest for a while.'

Mr Richard came over then, asking what was wrong.

'Oh, nothing,' said Jenny, 'but it would be cruel to make Cecília join us. It's nothing serious, but she still feels unwell.'

'You should go and rest in Jenny's room.'

Cecília thanked him, but said she would be fine where she was.

Jenny promised to come back soon and keep her company.

Mr Whitestone indicated an armchair where Cecília could rest and then they all went in to supper.

'What does all this mean, Jenny?' asked Carlos when he coincided with his sister in the doorway.

'That the moment has come to bid farewell to youthful folly, Charles. I want to see what wise depths are to be found in my mad brother.'

'But...'

'Look, everyone's waiting for us.'

And going into the dining room, they took their places at the table.

Do not expect me, dear reader, to give a detailed account of the variety and abundance of dishes adorning Mr Richard's table. All the typical British dishes were there, from the roast beef to the plum pudding, from the potatoes to the Cheddar cheese.

The three Englishmen duly complimented the skill of the chef. Mr Morlays even smiled, and Mr Brains used every flattering word in the English language to assure them all that one could not dine better even at the Erechtheum Club in St. James' Square. Mr Whitestone, meanwhile, told all his usual stories and set forth his culinary theories.

Jenny and Carlos were the only ones to remain silent and preoccupied. Jenny grew increasingly impatient with the slow progress of the supper and listened only distractedly to her guests' compliments. Carlos trembled as never before at his father's inexhaustible treasury of reminiscences.

Eventually, though, supper reached that critical point in all suppers, especially English ones, when all gravity and etiquette are put aside, when the female contingent ups sticks and flees in terror before the orgiastic flags that are unfurled along with the first toasts, the moment when the male guests, free at last from the one thing holding them back, prepare to reproduce in the dining room scenes that are commonplace in the most vulgar of theatres.

Mr Whitestone's supper had reached that transition point.

Jenny had expressed her gratitude for the toasts addressed to her. Mr Morlays was extraordinarily verbose, and appeared to have modelled his speech on that of some character out of Dickens, as you will see from the following excerpt: 'Since Mr Richard Whitestone is one of those rare creatures, an honest man,' Mr Morlays concluded, 'and since Miss Jenny Whitestone is, in every respect, a worthy daughter to Mr Richard Whitestone, I wish Jenny Whitestone every happiness, thus rewarding Mr Richard Whitestone for his honesty, probity and chivalry, a reward that Mr Richard Whitestone neither can nor should expect from the world. Since Miss Jenny Whitestone is also the beloved sister of that loyal and generous heart, Mr Charles Whitestone, a man who has not an ounce of evil in him, by drinking to *her* health, I am also drinking to the health of Mr Charles Whitestone, because those two souls are connected by fraternal feelings, just as Miss Jenny Whitestone would receive any toast made to Mr Charles Whitestone, her affectionate brother, as if it were a toast to her. And thus, thanks to the warmth that binds this exemplary family together, this individual toast to Miss Jenny Whitestone is transformed into a collective toast to the whole Whitestone family. To Miss Jenny Whitestone!'

And with that he drank.

'Hear, hear!' cried Mr Brains, rapping his knuckles on the table, as he had done repeatedly throughout that speech, more out of force of habit than out of any real need to attract the attention of such a small and attentive group of people.

Jenny modestly thanked Mr Morlays for his eloquent speech.

Mr Richard toasted his guests equally briefly.

And Carlos also did his duty in a few short words.

And so the toasts went on and on, and the level of the wine went down and down in the cut-glass carafes.

Jenny stood up. It was time to leave the guests alone. The

hour of freedom was about to chime.

Carlos watched his sister enviously. If only he could leave too, but he stayed.

As soon as the last fold of Jenny's white dress had disappeared through the door curtain, a complete transformation took place around the supper table.

Mr Brains dangled one leg over the arm of his chair and slid down until his head was on a level with the table. Mr Morlays rested his elbows on the table and cupped his head in his hands, so that his face took on the appearance of a very funny caricature; Mr Richard rocked to and fro on the back legs of his chair.

Cigars were lit, the air grew thick with smoke, and glass upon glass was filled and emptied.

The servants discreetly withdrew.

'Give us a song, Mr Brains,' said Mr Richard Whitestone.

'No, let Mr Morlays sing instead,' replied Mr Brains.

'Yes, Mr Morlays could perhaps sing us an aria from a requiem, a *Dies irae, dies illa*,' said Mr Richard, laughing.

Mr Morlays pulled a face intended to be a smile.

'Food usually reconciles Mr Morlays with humanity,' added Mr Brains.

'Yes, the sated beast does tend to be far less fearsome,' said Mr Richard cheerily, clapping his friend Mr Morlays familiarly on the shoulder, and again Mr Morlays smiled, after a fashion.

'Come on, sing!' insisted Mr Richard, once more turning to Mr Brains. 'Give us a song!'

'The presence of friend Morlays makes me fear that we'll have a repeat of what happens in *Lucrezia Borgia*, do you remember? When the wine turns out to be poisoned.'

Once the laughter had died down, Mr Brains began to sing.

We Portuguese, who often describe our British allies as sad

and melancholy, are perhaps ourselves the gravest and most circumspect of all the European peoples.

I don't believe that even Germany's philosophy and militias, or Russia's sombre politics and liking for flogging, or Spain's firing squads and militarism, or Ireland's political meetings and the Fenian Brotherhood, or France's universal suffrage and Napoleonic fever have managed to make any of those nations more averse to singing than ours. Given our blue skies, our landscape, wines and language and our dislike of worrying our heads about serious matters – for in that respect no one can outdo us – this near-aversion to singing denotes an essentially grave nature, which is most unusual in people from southerly climes.

Who, at some Portuguese supper, would have the courage to do as Mr Brains did, and, granting his host's request, burst into song?

And if someone did, imagine the scandalised looks on the faces of the other guests.

No one is more easily cowed by the fear of appearing ridiculous than the Portuguese, and no one faces it more courageously than the British. Ridicule is rather like the insidious habits of certain dogs, which bite the people who flee from them and are cowed by anyone who stands his ground.

The fact is that Mr Brains – leaning back in his chair, legs outstretched, eyes half-closed, one hand on his chest – began to sing a song made for such occasions and he sang it in a nasal voice that defied classification, in a monotonously English way:

O fill the goblet high, boy
And fearless drain it dry, boy;
For ruby wine makes souls divine

And fits them for the sky, boy!
Shall mortals dare upbraid it,
And say that sins pervade it,
When holy writ
And all admit
That He who saved us made it...

It was inevitable that the vocal gifts and artistic talents of Mr Brains would not be properly appreciated. His comment about the banquet in *Lucrezia Borgia* proved all too true!

In fact, just as he reached that point in the song, a loud noise, growing ever nearer – the sound of running footsteps, a confusion of voices, pleas and threats coming from the room next door – silenced Mr Brains and brought a frown to Mr Whitestone's forehead, for he would not brook interruptions to the solemn supper hour.

Just as he was about to demand to know the cause of this outrage, the door was flung open, and to the astonished eyes of all those present, there appeared the figure of Manuel Quintino, in a state of agitation such as none of them had known before.

At the same moment, Jenny, attracted by the noise, appeared at the other door.

Mr Richard Whitestone gazed in astonishment at his book-keeper.

XXXIV

Manuel Quintino in his Madness

The reader will know – better than any of the characters in this scene – the reasons for Manuel Quintino's sudden arrival in the room and for his troubled state of mind.

Antónia's revelations had, as we saw, caused him to rush to Mr Richard's house. The first person he spoke to when he arrived was Carlos' manservant, who told him that Cecília had entered via the garden, although he thought she had probably already left, since he hadn't seen her inside. The servants who had been serving supper confirmed this conjecture, assuring Manuel Quintino that Cecília had not been present.

It's impossible to say what thoughts raced through Manuel Quintino's mind when he heard all this. A kind of mist clouded his eyes as if he were about to faint. His heart filled with grief and rage; oblivious to any sensible considerations that might hold him back, he pushed his way past the servants surrounding him and, bellowing incoherently, like a true madman, burst into the room, to the utter amazement of Mr Richard and his equally astonished guests.

Manuel Quintino surveyed the room for a moment, wild-eyed, and was alarmed not to find Cecília there.

Full of barely controlled fury, he fixed his gaze on Carlos and then, walking unsteadily over to him, placed one hand on his shoulder and said in a hoarse voice that trembled with the effort of suppressing the increasingly violent wave of emotion rising up inside him: 'Senhor Carlos, I am here to find out what has become of my daughter.'

At these words, Jenny turned pale. The two Englishmen sat open-mouthed. Mr Whitestone kept his penetrating eyes glued on Manuel Quintino and on Carlos.

'Senhor Carlos,' Manuel Quintino repeated in a tone of voice that revealed both his anguish and his anger. 'It's me. A father who has come demanding to know what you have done to his daughter!'

Carlos, apparently paralysed by surprise – well, by surprise and perhaps a few slight twinges of conscience – was staring at Manuel Quintino, his face flushing first bright red, then turning deathly pale, transfixed by the old man's irate, interrogative gaze.

Seeing Carlos so dumbstruck, Manuel Quintino lost all self-control.

'Carlos,' he said, 'you abused the trust of a man who unhesitatingly opened the doors of his house to you; you cruelly mocked the white hairs earned during years of honest service to the family business; you crushed the heart that opened to you like the heart of another father... you, sir, are an utter cad!'

Anyone seeing Carlos' posture and expression would have believed this accusation to be true. He was so taken aback, that he didn't know how to react.

On hearing Manuel Quintino's last words, Mr Whitestone had turned equally pale, a rare and one would have thought impossible phenomenon. Soon, though, the blood rebelled against the shock that had driven it from his cheeks, and flooded back with renewed vigour. His extraordinarily bright eyes did not move from his son, as if waiting to see him protest against such a grave accusation.

Jenny raised her head and with great dignity stepped forward. She, too, had grown red with impatience to see her brother sitting silent before an accusation she knew to be unfair.

With an uncharacteristic fire in both eyes and voice, she spoke to Manuel Quintino: 'Manuel Quintino, you have just made an accusation that does you much dishonour, because it is utterly false.'

The old book-keeper turned to Jenny and, struggling between doubt and hope, asked urgently: 'False you say?'

'Yes, false,' Jenny said firmly, 'as false as it is cruel. I understand your reasons, but if, in the eighteen years of Cecília's life you had learned to know her, if you had placed more faith in your own daughter, you would never accuse her or come here saying things that might ruin her reputation, even though she's innocent…'

Suddenly, the door of the room where Cecília had been waiting also opened, and Cecília appeared, looking pale and alarmed, because she had recognised her father's voice and sensed what might have brought him there.

When Jenny saw her, she rushed over and, putting her arms about her, said to Manuel Quintino: 'The daughter you came looking for was here with me. Do you still fear for her?'

Manuel Quintino ran to Cecília and, in turn, clutched her to him.

However, the suspicions aroused by what Antónia had told him had still not been entirely assuaged.

Seeing his daughter so pale and downcast, and recalling Carlos' earlier confusion, Manuel Quintino gently drew away from her and studied her for a while wordlessly, anxiously, before saying in a sad, fond voice: 'Why so pale, child, why so upset? Whatever has become of your usual cheerful self? Why have you been crying?'

And turning to Carlos, he said, not as vehemently as he had before, but still with a touch of bitterness: 'Who is to blame for those tears, Senhor Carlos? For her tears… and for mine?'

When Cecília heard these words, she again sought refuge in Jenny.

'That's enough, Manuel Quintino,' Jenny said sternly. 'Have some self-respect! This hysteria of yours is unworthy of you. Yes, show some self-respect and ask God's forgiveness for inflicting such pain on your angel of a daughter. Come, Cecília, we should not stay any longer in the presence of someone who ought to be the very first to treat you fairly, and yet who is, instead, the first to offend by doubting you. Come.'

Manuel Quintino held out his hands to Jenny.

'Wait, wait! And if you have the power to remove this crushing weight from my heart, then, please do so! However great the suffering of others, my suffering is still greater!'

There was such genuine pain in the poor man's voice that Jenny stopped to listen.

Manuel Quintino showed her the letter from Carlos, which he had brought with him.

'Who wrote this letter to my daughter?'

Jenny was quite shaken by the sight of the letter; she glanced at Carlos, and the expression on his face told her everything.

Cecília looked up in alarm.

When Manuel Quintino saw the troubled look on Jenny's face, he became still more insistent, and, regardless of his own daughter's reputation, he asked imprudently: 'Who wrote this letter to my daughter, a letter that arrived only a few hours ago? I haven't opened it, as you can see, but you may open it and read it and see if it contains anything to justify my suspicions…'

422

And Manuel Quintino was himself about to open the letter, when Mr Richard's voice stopped him.

'There's no need. I wrote the letter.'

These were the first words he had spoken since the start of this whole scene, a scene he had watched until then in silence. Mr Richard Whitestone was a man who was very quick on the uptake and equally quick at making decisions.

He could grasp what was going on in any situation in a matter of moments and instantly come up with a plan of how to proceed and put that plan into practice. He had already understood everything: Carlos' confusion and his degree of culpability, the basis for Manuel Quintino's accusation, and Jenny's generous and noble intervention. He foresaw his daughter's imminent defeat by that letter, of whose existence he knew nothing; he foresaw the consequences of that scene: the danger to Cecília's reputation; the discredit that would tarnish Carlos' name, his own and Jenny's; and, out of thin air, he created a role for himself in a situation in which he dare not fail.

When Manuel Quintino heard these words spoken by his employer in such a firm, confident tone, he stared at him, nonplussed.

Jenny also stared at her father's impassive face and saw at once what he had done.

That good and generous young woman felt like throwing her arms about his neck to thank him for this prompt and happy solution.

Carlos felt himself blush at his father's magnanimity.

This was the second lesson he had learned from his family that day; the lesson of a great heart, which would save the reputation of a person whom he genuinely loved, but who, by his own thoughtlessness, he had almost ruined for the

423

second time.

'*You* wrote it?' said Manuel Quintino, inadvertently dropping the letter.

Jenny ran to pick it up and handed it to Mr Richard, who gave her a knowing look.

In that moment, they formed a tacit alliance to save the reputation of an innocent, defenceless young woman.

'Yes, I did,' Mr Richard went on, taking the letter and casually opening it. 'I sent it, or, rather, we both did,' he added, pointing to Carlos without actually meeting his eye. 'We wanted to prepare a surprise for Jenny's birthday today by inviting Cecília, who hasn't been to see us for ages. But our plan failed because Jenny, quite rightly, had already invited her. So that's how it came about… the letter was written by Carlos but dictated by me. If you're still in any doubt…' he concluded, making as if to hand the letter to Manuel Quintino.

This was one of those heroic gestures that could have lost or won the battle.

Courageous, confident men resort to such gestures in order not to betray the precariousness of their position, and it is precisely that which almost always guarantees success.

Manuel Quintino did not dare to accept the proof being offered to him. His habitual respect, acquired over long years of service, and which a moment of anger, almost madness, had made him forget, once again took hold of him, restoring to him his natural gentleness and timidity.

'Forgive me,' he said almost humbly, and as if regretting his earlier emotional outburst. 'Forgive me, I thought…'

'That's all right,' said Mr Richard cutting in, as if eager to drop the subject. 'But you should be less easily swayed by certain responses that are purely emotional and, shall we say, inappropriate.'

He hesitated slightly before plumping for that final adjective.

Manuel Quintino was about to open his mouth to apologise, but Mr Richard stopped him.

'Let's speak no more about it, there's no point. Do join us at the table.'

'I'm sorry, Mr Richard, but...'

Mr Richard pretended not to have heard him, and summoned a servant to lay a place for Manuel Quintino, who sat down, almost unaware of what he was doing.

Jenny and Cecília again left the room, and supper continued, although the lively atmosphere had vanished.

What had just happened, plus the awkward, sombre presence of Carlos and Manuel Quintino, foiled all Mr Richard's attempts to reestablish the jolly mood of the evening.

The libations continued, but there were no long speeches.

'To your nephew, Mr Brains!' Mr Richard said, raising his glass.

Mr Brains gave a grateful bow, and the others raised their glasses to their lips.

'To your friend Roxboy, Mr Whitestone!' said Mr Brains.

Mr Whitestone thanked him, and the others repeated the toast.

'Mr Morlays, to your uncle in the Indies!'

Another bow from Mr Morlays, and the others followed suit.

Eventually those laconic toasts ended too, with the atmosphere growing ever more constrained.

Mr Richard made one last attempt to clear the air.

'Give us another song, Mr Brains!' he said, filling his glass.

Mr Brains stared at Mr Richard with startled eyes.

'Me sing? It would perhaps make the change of mood less

abrupt if Mr Morlays were to sing first.'

Mr Morlays gave some incomprehensible, monosyllabic response and drank down the last drop of wine in the glass before him.

'You give us a song then, Mr Morlays,' insisted Mr Richard, with no great hope that his guest would agree.

Contrary to all expectations, the gloomy Englishman stood up and, thrusting his hands into his waistcoat pockets, he pronounced in grim tones the name of the song he intended to sing.

'*The Old Sexton* by Park Benjamin.'

Mr Brains shuddered, but Mr Morlays launched imperturbably into the song, and this is the song which, with exquisite tact, he thought fitting for the occasion:

Nigh to a grave that was newly made,
His work was done, and he paused to wait
The funeral train at the open gate.
A relic of bygone days was he,
And his locks were white as the foamy sea;
And these words came from his lips so thin:
'I gather them in: I gather them in.

'I gather them in! for man and boy,
Year after year of grief and joy,
I've builded the houses that lie around,
In every nook of this burial ground;
Mother and daughter, father and son,
Come to my solitude, one by one:
But come they strangers or come they kin –
I gather them in, I gather them in.

'Many are with me, but still I'm alone,
I'm king of the dead—and I make my throne
On a monument slab of marble cold;
And my sceptre of rule is the spade I hold:
Come they from cottage or come they from hall,
Mankind are my subjects, all, all, all!
Let them loiter in pleasure or toilfully spin –
I gather them in, I gather them in.

'I gather them in, and their final rest
Is here, down here, in the earth's dark breast!'
And the sexton ceased, for the funeral train
Wound mutely o'er that solemn plain!
And I said to my heart, when time is told,
A mightier voice than that sexton's old
Will sound o'er the last trump's dreadful din –
'I gather them in, I gather them in.'

You can imagine the effect on that post-prandial gathering of the singer's voice, not to mention the tune and the words. As sung by Mr Morlays, that repeated refrain, 'I gather them in, I gather them in,' sounded not unlike a death knell.

No stomach could remain untroubled after such a 'dessert'.

With truly satanic malice, the singer observed the effect of the song on his friends' digestive processes.

Mr Brains could barely contain his indignation.

Once he had finished the song, Mr Morlays sat down and drank another glass of wine, and Mr Richard Whitestone offered him only the briefest of monosyllables as thanks.

Mr Morlays' misanthropy, made still sourer by the uproar caused by Manuel Quintino, took delight in its revenge, and everyone there longed to be able to leave the table.

Mr Brains was the first to dare to do so. That English Democritus' jovial nature could not bear the leaden atmosphere he was being forced to breathe. Mr Morlays followed suit. His innate ill humour had grown in keeping with the day's events. The guests' already sensitive digestive systems were at grave risk of being disturbed, and in the eyes of that great hypochondriac, humanity would have to suffer as a consequence.

Carlos also withdrew to his room.

XXXV

The Father passes Sentence

Once alone with his employer, Manuel Quintino felt most uneasy. It was, therefore, with great relief that he received a message from Cecília, asking him to accompany her home.

He said goodbye to Mr Richard, to whom he once again offered his clumsy apologies, which Mr Richard received most affably, albeit with the air of someone who would prefer to hear no more about it.

Manuel Quintino then went to find Cecília, who was with Jenny in the next room.

'Cecília, forgive me for ever doubting you,' he said, his voice breaking. 'And forgive my imprudent behaviour just now, it was pure madness on my part. I see that now. Put it down to the great love your father feels for you...'

Sheer emotion would not allow him to continue.

Cecília threw herself, weeping, into his arms.

'Really, Manuel Quintino,' said Jenny. 'Can't you see you're upsetting her?'

'Miss Jenny,' answered Manuel Quintino, turning to her, 'please forgive me too, for imagining that your saintly protection – yes, saintly, Miss Jenny – that your blessed protection could ever be swayed. And please, always keep watch over my beloved daughter!'

'Cecília is perfectly capable of keeping watch over herself,' responded Jenny. 'She has a brave, strong heart.'

Cecília was still resting her head on her father's chest, and when he heard those last words, he held her still closer and said to Jenny in a soft voice, so that Cecília would not hear: 'Strong? It was... as long as it belonged only to her.'

Jenny looked hard at him.

Those words made her think that he still had some suspicions; that he might well be convinced of his daughter's innocence, that he might well judge Carlos' behaviour less severely and less sceptically, but that he had not yet quite closed his eyes to the evidence, or accepted that there were no shared feelings between those two hearts.

Realising this, she said: 'Her heart will always be brave and strong. Now all that's needed is to make it a happy heart.'

'If anyone can, you can.'

'I'll do my best,' said Jenny, smiling.

'If you can make her heart as serene as yours, then she'll be safe.'

Jenny was embracing Cecília when she heard these words, and, shaking her head, half-glad, half-melancholy, she whispered in her friend's ear: 'Don't worry, that isn't how I intend to make you safe.'

And this was the first time she had addressed Cecília as *tu*.

While this was going on, Carlos – now back in his own room – was plunged deep in thought. His mind was still full of everything that had happened that day, and a hubbub of affections and emotions were making his heart beat faster.

What should he do? How could he get out of the position he now found himself in? What noble resolve, worthy of the feelings stirring his heart, could ever compensate for the invincible timidity he had shown during supper?

This is what Carlos was thinking when his servant entered

the room, saying that Mr Richard Whitestone wished to see him in his study.

Carlos had been expecting such an interview, which, after what had happened, could be deemed inevitable; indeed, he himself might have spontaneously asked to speak to his father, and yet, despite this, he did not feel sufficiently prepared; nor would he, perhaps, have felt any differently given more time. That summons, then, still felt unexpected.

He reluctantly made his way to his father's study, as if he were a prisoner going to court to receive sentence.

When Carlos entered, Mr Richard was standing up, leaning on the marble fireplace. The look on his face was the sternest his English physiognomy could manage, and he was holding Carlos' letter, as if he had just that moment finished reading it.

Carlos stopped in the middle of the room, waiting for his father to speak.

Mr Whitestone brandished the open letter and asked in a clipped, incisive manner: 'How much truth is there in what you say here?'

'It's all true,' answered Carlos, trying to speak with a confidence he did not feel.

Mr Whitestone frowned to hear this answer; he gave a slight shrug and a grimace, then handing the letter to his son, said only: 'There you are. Tear it up, burn it, because that will put paid to any new act of... infamy.'

Carlos blushed furiously

'Father!' he said.

'I repeat: infamy,' Mr Richard went on in still more acrimonious tones. 'I'm not the first to say as much, and given that you remained shamefully silent when confronted by the first accusation, I think you might be expected to hear the second with the same humility.'

431

And having said this, he began pacing up and down, as he usually did when angry. Then he added: 'It's false pride on your part to get upset over a mere word, and yet happily accept the ugly act it describes. That's pure theatre.'

Carlos said: 'I find it strange to hear such an accusation from someone who should know me better, from someone not overwhelmed, as was my first accuser, by an excess of violent, but understandable passion. I find it strange and regrettable that, in the space of only a few days, I've heard my father accuse me of being, first, base, and now infamous.'

Mr Richard, who, while his son was talking, had increased the speed of his pacing, suddenly stopped and fixed Carlos with a fiery gaze.

'Why strange? Do tell me. What other word would serve to describe your actions more accurately? I really can't think of one. You're surely not saying I'm being too severe. I repeat what I said the other day. I have been far too kind to you, I have deliberately closed my eyes to your many misadventures, always attributing them to your youth. However, there are some things one would not forgive even in a child. And whenever a man acts in a manner that is… base…'

Carlos could not help but start forward when he heard that word. Mr Richard saw this and repeated it more loudly, still looking hard at his son: 'Yes, base… and infamous. In both cases, to pardon would be criminal, and no criticism could ever be harsh enough for such a man. There's no point looking at me like that. Your own conscience spoke to you far more sternly earlier on, obliging you to fall silent and bow your head before the allegations of that man whose… whose honour you tried to besmirch.'

'As I said, sir,' Carlos responded with unusual vehemence, 'everything I wrote in that letter is true. It was doubtless imprudent of me to write it, I admit, but my conscience tells me that I am being too harshly judged and that is why...'

'It's a shame your conscience didn't wake up earlier. Then your father and your sister would not have had to hear from an outsider, and in front of witnesses, a very grave accusation and would not have then been obliged to lie in order to save your reputation. Your scruples have arrived rather too late, don't you agree?'

Carlos bowed his head and said nothing.

For a while, Mr Richard also said nothing, then went on: 'You say that everything you wrote in that letter is true, but I would remind you that, only a few days ago, you received a visit in this very house, the house in which your sister lives, a visit from a...'

Carlos would not allow him to continue.

'Please don't bring that up again, sir. I have already given you my word that such an insinuation is entirely unwarranted. I cannot offer you any more convincing proof, but I find it very hard to have that proof rejected. On the day you are alluding to, on the day I first heard my own father describe me as "base", I was already a very different man. Believe me, sir: what I feel for Cecília is not some whim, some youthful passing fancy. She brought about this the most important change in my character without so much as a word, with no deliberate intention, without once betraying her feelings for me. I guessed what her feelings were, but she never once spoke openly to me. Cecília achieved, quite effortlessly, what no amount of scolding from my father, no advice or pleas from Jenny, had ever achieved, which is why I believe in the sincerity of my feelings for her, which is why...'

Mr Richard was listening to his son with manifest impatience; it seemed that he would find it almost as disagreeable to see Carlos succeed in justifying his behaviour in that manner as it would to see him crushed beneath the accusation made against him.

Mr Richard's sense of superiority – because Mr Richard did feel superior in some respects – was none too pleased with Carlos' genuine love for Cecília, the daughter of his book-keeper.

A crowd of prejudices swarmed around that idea, prejudices that Mr Richard's clear, strong reason would normally refuse to accept as legitimate, but which, without him realising, had him in their grip. They were of various types.

They were, to begin with, an Englishman's prejudices, for no son of Great Britain can, with indifference, bear to watch a woman from another country steal the heart of one of his own. There is, deep in the English soul, a profound and more or less overt belief in their own superiority as a race, which prevents them from viewing such an alliance dispassionately.

Then there were the prejudices of the businessman, who, however much he esteemed and respected his book-keeper, could still not quite think of him as his equal, and so he was not exactly thrilled at the thought of his book-keeper's daughter becoming his daughter-in-law.

There were also the prejudices of the capitalist; however much capitalists may philosophise about the vanity of wealth, in practice, they can never quite deny the importance of wealth as key to resolving the problem of happiness. Finally, even certain paternal prejudices obscured the light of his intelligence, because, despite the severity of the allegations levelled at his son, he nevertheless deemed few women in the world to be worthy of his Carlos. For all these reasons, he listened with some reluctance to his son's declaration of love, and indeed interrupted him: 'All right, all right, I really don't need to know the whole history of how your character has changed, and I have to say that your character does seem rather too subject to change. And if that is the sole guarantee of the sincerity of your feelings, you must agree that it is rather weak. However, given what has happened, it hardly seems necessary to tell you what would be the best way forward.'

Carlos looked at his father with a questioning eye.

Mr Richard remained silent for a few moments, then he added: 'In a week's time, a steamship leaves for London…'

'But…'

Mr Richard pretended not to hear that 'but' and went on: 'A face-to-face meeting with Mr Woodfall Hope has long been in the offing, because…'

'I don't know if I will be able to obey you, sir.'

Mr Whitestone spun round to face his son, and, visibly annoyed, said: 'I hope you are not so base as to expect to stay here after what has happened. Please don't make me ashamed to have you as my son.'

Carlos had long since lost the habit of facing down his father, and he felt incapable of confronting his father's stern gaze, so he bowed his head and said nothing.

A few moments later, Mr Richard added in a voice that, while still severe, was less gruff: 'You can go now, and, please, try to behave decently in future. There are some mistakes that leave an indelible mark. You must respect other people's families, because to do otherwise is tantamount to dishonouring your own. How could you forget that you have a sister…'

At this point, someone knocked at the door.

'What is it?' asked Mr Richard impatiently.

It was a servant sent by Jenny to ask if she could talk to Mr Richard.

Mr Richard nodded and, turning again to Carlos, said: 'Off

you go. Your sister needs to speak with me.'

Carlos bowed and left without a word. He was still the prisoner being dismissed by the judge, not the son saying goodbye to his father.

Carlos met his sister in the next room. She held out her hand to him, saying: 'You see the result of your folly?'

'Folly, Jenny? How can you still call it that?'

'I'm beginning, just beginning, to want to call it something else, and that's why I've come.'

'What are you going to do?'

'I'm going to plead the cause of a madcap young man, out of consideration for a poor innocent heart, who is not in the least to blame for joining forces with said hothead.'

'Oh, Jenny!' cried Carlos, clasping his sister's hands in his.

'You'd better let me go. Father's waiting for me.'

And as she left the room, she said, laughing: 'You two have certainly given me a very difficult role to play in this whole story.'

XXXVI

The Sister's Case for the Defence

Jenny slowly opened the door to Mr Richard's study, where, head bowed and hands behind his back, he was still striding up and down.

When he heard the door open, he stopped his pacing and awaited this new arrival.

'Ah Jenny,' he said, when he saw his daughter's face, and he said this in an affable tone in marked contrast to the harsh way he had spoken to Carlos.

Jenny went over to him and, taking his hand, kissed it fondly.

'What's all this, Jenny?' said Mr Richard, trying to withdraw his hand.

'I just want to thank you, sir, for your generous, noble action, an action entirely worthy of you, and which made me feel, more than ever, how proud I am to be your daughter.'

'Oh, really, Jenny, and is that why you came?' asked Mr Richard, smiling, and with no hint of a frown.

'There's something else too,' said Jenny with the respectful familiarity of a daughter who knows her father can refuse her nothing.

'What's that?'

'You know everything, don't you?'

'Unfortunately, yes, I do.'

437

'And what do you intend to do? And forgive my asking, but I feel I can, given how often you have confided in me before…'

'Quite right, Jenny, quite right,' said Mr Richard affectionately. 'I know what a good counsellor you are.'

'So what are you going to do?'

'I've given it some thought and have taken a few decisions. Carlos will leave for London on the next steamship…'

Jenny shook her head disapprovingly.

Seeing this, Mr Whitestone looked at her in silence.

'You don't seem to approve, Jenny.'

Jenny said nothing.

'No, please, tell me frankly what you think of my decision.'

'All right, I will. It isn't at all what I was expecting from you.'

'What were you expecting, then?' asked Mr Richard with just a touch of irritation.

'Your behaviour earlier on made me expect a decision that was more… more… reasonable,' she concluded, after a moment of modest hesitation, tempering the force of her words with the gentleness of her expression.

'What else could I do?'

Instead of answering directly, Jenny went on: 'You want to send Charles away when he will take with him, in his heart, something that will prevent him ever being happy in exile – because you *are* sending him into exile; you want to send him away when to do so would mean condemning someone else to suffer that cruel absence…'

Mr Richard was astonished to hear his daughter speaking like this, but then, in a graver voice than hitherto, he said: 'No, Jenny. I'm sending Charles away in order to bring to a timely end an impulsive relationship that could bring about both his unhappiness and…' he paused, then concluded, 'and hers, the person I assume you are referring to. Can't you see, this is just a two-day wonder for Carlos?'

'No, sir, it isn't. I feel sure of that. I can see that this time he is utterly sincere.'

Mr Whitestone shrugged and smiled: 'You clearly still don't know your brother.'

'I have followed Charles' new love, step by step, right from the beginning. To start with, I felt suspicious too; I feared for Cecília and tried to dissuade Charles from what I thought was no more than a whim. Then I saw I was wrong.'

Mr Richard shook his head doubtfully.

'For how long now have you been convinced of that?'

'Oh, for several days now, ever since…'

Mr Richard smiled.

'And what if I had proof that, even until recently, your brother remained the same wild, thoughtless lad he has always been?'

'Proof?'

'And what if I were to show you that now, just as before, he would not hesitate to satisfy certain mad, indelicate fantasies, to by-pass certain considerations that seem perfectly reasonable to anyone who still has some respect for family feeling, but which he perhaps deems ridiculous?'

'That's most unfair. You're being too hard on Charles.'

'Ask him if that young woman, with whom you imagine he has been in love for some time, was the reason he sold the watch I gave him as a birthday present. That action upset me deeply, not because it was a valuable watch, but because it revealed to me a moral weakness in my son, a lack of dignity, which I had not expected to find.'

'Charles told me he had a really pressing reason for doing that…'

439

'He lied!' said Mr Richard bitterly.

'Sir!' cried Jenny, as if reproaching him for using such a word.

'I know what the reason was...'

'Do you have absolute proof of that?'

Mr Richard hesitated, then said: 'Almost absolute.'

Jenny smiled and said: 'Almost.'

As if provoked by her smile, Mr Richard said: 'Were you, then, the person who came looking for your brother that day and went with him in a carriage to the jeweller's shop where he sold the watch?'

This was the first Jenny had heard of such an encounter, but sustained by the new confidence her brother had inspired in her, she responded at once: 'Are these the only facts on which you base your accusation?'

'Yes, and I think...' Then, with a sudden change of tone, he added: 'Putting that to one side, though, what do *you* think I should do?'

Jenny looked down at a magazine lying on the table and said: 'I don't know what would be so very wrong about giving in to the impulse of those two hearts, seeing that...'

A touch impatiently, Mr Richard brought his hand down hard on the desk where he had finally come to a halt.

'I didn't realise that what you know of the world had been gleaned from novels.'

'No, sir, that isn't where I learned about the world, nor from personal experience. The little I know I learned from you, which is why I'm able to distinguish a good action from a bad, in the light of duty and conscience. Isn't that what you taught me?'

Mr Richard accepted this gentle filial correction with a smile.

'Well, it was in the light of duty and conscience that I made my decision.'

'I thought that, after what had happened, duty would have advised you otherwise.'

'What? Because of some absurd whim, some folly, some mere fantasy? It seems you are a woman after all, Jenny.'

Jenny went over to her father, who had sat down on a chair beside the hearth, and leaning on his shoulder, she said softly and as if half in jest: 'I wish, for just one moment, that I could stop being your daughter.'

'Why?'

'So that I could dare to ask you a question.'

'Permission given, Jenny,' he replied, completely disarmed by his daughter's diplomacy.

'Permission given?'

'Yes, I even command you to ask that question.'

'I am a woman after all, that's what you said, Pa. Maybe, and, as a woman, I do perhaps have a sentimental streak… can be swayed by my heart. Isn't that it? The question I would like to ask, if I were not your daughter, is this: Do you think that, in this case, your strong, upright, enlightened mind is entirely without prejudices?'

'What kind of prejudices?' asked Mr Richard, looking away.

'Who knows? Cecília is the daughter of Manuel Quintino, an honest man, but an employee; faithful, but poor; a generous fellow but educated in the school of obedience; capable of making sacrifices for us, but living off the wages we pay him.'

'Don't be so silly! Will you not at least do me the justice of believing that my reason would be enough to overcome such prejudices… were I to have them?' asked Mr Richard, although in a way that showed Jenny she was right.

'That's exactly what I hoped you would say, that's why…'

'No,' said Mr Richard, interrupting her, 'that isn't what gives me pause. It's because I don't believe Carlos' feelings will last; it's because I know how flighty and fickle he is. That is why I hesitate to make him the head of a family he would not be capable of keeping and on whom he would bring down misfortune.'

'You're being most unfair to your son, sir. He inherited the gifts of your heart. He is loyal and generous. And marriage would be his salvation, and lead him by his heart onto the path of duty.'

'You claim to be Cecília's friend, Jenny, so aren't you worried about endangering her happiness?'

Jenny fixed her father with an almost mischievous gaze. Then she said: 'I have one guarantee on my side, and that is Charles' heart. Only a short time ago, you had someone else in mind as a wife for my brother, an alliance that did not even have that one small advantage. What has happened to the confidence you apparently had then in your son as the future head of a family? Why did you not hesitate then as you do now? Do you not care about the happiness of Alice Smithfield, your friend's daughter? Obviously you do, because you know that if Charles promised to make her happy, he would keep that promise. And now…'

Mr Richard could find no response to his daughter's argument. He stood up and resumed his pacing. Shortly afterwards, he stopped and said to Jenny: 'Besides, what if, after what happened in front of witnesses, I were to follow your advice, would the young woman's reputation not suffer? Would the world not see in that action – which while it might be, indeed, I believe it could well be, only fair, but which is, it must be said, not what people would expect – would they not interpret that action as reparation for some worse offence?'

Encouraged by the new direction in which her father was taking their discussion, Jenny said: 'And would Charles' sudden and unexpected departure, after all that has happened, would that not give rise to gossip that would prove unfavourable to her, to him... and to all of us?'

Mr Whitestone did not answer.

'I know little of the world, it's true,' Jenny went on, 'but it seems to me that, whatever happens, tongues will wag, and it seems to me, too, that what we must do is make our actions look natural and inevitable, so that they excite as little curiosity as possible. Let us conduct ourselves in such a way that people will see only the motives we want them to see, without revealing that this is precisely what we are trying to do, so that no one will suspect our intentions and try to find out the true ones.'

Mr Richard was looking at his daughter and smiling, his mood transformed.

'Bravo! Pure Machiavelli! I had no idea you were such a diplomat. How could we apply that to the matter in hand?'

Jenny was smiling too, but wisely kept her feelings to herself, for she could sense victory.

'It's a question of gradually making the situation seem less strange, and preparing people's minds so that they will accept it as perfectly natural.'

'But how? What should I do?'

'Whatever your heart tells you to do. It's not for me to advise you.'

Mr Whitestone bowed his head in thought.

Jenny began to speak then as if to herself, but in a way that her father was sure to hear.

'That's the way the world works. If you give people the

actual facts, they rarely believe them, but if you come up with a different version, often something less natural and less plausible, they almost always prefer it, especially if the true version is generous and noble, and the false one selfish and mean. If you were to explain Charles' marriage to Manuel Quintino's daughter simply as the union of two loving hearts, it would seem strange and incomprehensible, but if Manuel Quintino were to become a partner in the business rather than a mere book-keeper...'

On hearing these words, Mr Richard looked up at his daughter. She seemed distracted, apparently absorbed in the earnest study of a glass paperweight.

Mr Richard had a thought.

He went over to his desk and, picking up a piece of paper, he wrote a few lines.

Jenny was smiling, as if she could read from afar everything her father was writing.

Then Mr Richard carefully re-read what he had written, folded up the sheet of paper and, handing it to her daughter, said very quickly, as if afraid the decision he had taken might evaporate: 'There you are. Give that to Manuel Quintino. In honour of your twenty-second birthday.'

Jenny had very astutely allowed her father to enjoy all the pleasure and glory of a good idea – one that had originally come from her – and, having immediately sensed what it was he had written, she said gleefully: 'A further example of your generous heart.'

'So you already know what the letter says?'

'I don't need to read it to know. As a mark of respect for Manuel Quintino's long service in the Whitestone family business, my father has, from today, made him a partner in the business. Is that right?'

'Almost word-perfect,' said Mr Richard, tenderly stroking his daughter's cheek.

'Any further orders, Miss Jenny?' he asked jovially.

'One more thing.'

'Which is?'

'Don't send that letter just yet.'

'Why not?'

'This action is intended to prepare public opinion for the other matter... isn't that right?'

'I haven't promised anything yet...'

'This action,' Jenny continued, pretending she hadn't heard, 'would still cause tongues to wag if we didn't first prepare the way.'

'How?'

'I seem to remember that, some time ago, you spoke to me about a business deal in which our company almost got involved, and the decision not to was taken on Manuel Quintino's advice, advice that saved us from possible ruin. Is that right?'

'It is. He showed great commercial acumen!'

'How many people did you tell about what he had done?'

'As far as I can recall, none. It's not always a good idea to discuss such deals, even if, happily, they come to nothing, because it could undermine confidence in the business...'

'If you'll allow me to give you some advice: make an exception to that rule. If I were you, I would make a point this week of telling everyone about that narrow escape. Manuel Quintino's name will be on everyone's lips. Everyone in Rua dos Ingleses will know about his invaluable contribution... and then no one will be surprised when you send that letter to Cecília's father, a letter that contains the happiness of two people.'

'And do you think people find gratitude more natural than a desire for profit? If you remove the element of self-interest from the explanation, it will be incomprehensible.'

'In that case, at the same time, you need to spread a rumour that Manuel Quintino has come into money, and that for our part…'

Mr Richard smiled.

'Yes, public opinion will find that easier to accept, even if… Anyway, thanks to you, I've certainly got my work cut out this week! I'll set to with a will, though, and see what we can do. However, I would hate to see you idle while I'm slaving away. My natural egotism won't allow that.'

'What do you want me to do, then?'

'Justify your brother's behaviour. My agreement to your latest plans, Jenny, is dependent on that one condition. Unless you can convince me that Charles sold that watch for some noble reason, then don't expect me to…'

'But Charles refuses to tell me.'

'If the task were easy, I wouldn't give it to you. This isn't a mere caprice on my part. You must understand how important that justification is to me. Faith isn't enough, I need proof. Your plans are all based on your excessive confidence in your brother; that is a very fragile basis for the happiness of the person whose cause you are defending.'

'I'll do my best.'

'You have a week.'

'All right, a week it is.'

And father and daughter parted on the best of terms.

Mr Richard's prejudices had not been completely banished, but by, so to speak, bringing them out into the open and setting them before her father's eyes, Jenny had succeeded in making him feel sufficiently ashamed to reject them.

Mr Richard might still hope to find some other solution to the present crisis, but under no circumstances would he reveal himself to be subject to his secret prejudices.

XXXVII

How to prepare Public Opinion

The following day, Manuel Quintino left early for the office, having spent all morning pondering the previous evening's events.

The more he reflected upon what had happened then and on other occasions, the more he was convinced that Mr Richard's explanation had not been entirely true. Not that this made him like his employer any the less, indeed, he felt grateful to him. He was alarmed, though, about the state of Cecília's heart. Was there still time to root out the mad affection, which he, so imprudently, had allowed to spring up there?

Manuel Quintino was still ruminating on this when one of the most serious-minded and successful of local businessmen came into the office and, greeting him effusively, praised him for his services to the company, applauding his great good sense in foreseeing the failure of a major London firm and thus saving Whitestone & Son from disaster. Manuel Quintino was taken aback by this unexpected compliment. He had long since forgotten the matter and assumed that Mr Richard – the only other person who knew about it – had forgotten too.

However, he found it all the more pleasing that this praise should come from such a respected businessman. He was even more surprised when another man showered him with similar compliments, as did everyone else who came into the office that morning, heaping him with equally flattering words, with, of course, a few variations.

Mr Whitestone was held in such high regard by the commercial world of Oporto that news of Manuel Quintino's invaluable advice spread rapidly, for the honest Englishman, true to the promise he had made to Jenny, had spoken with unusual energy and emotion – unusual, that is, for a normally phlegmatic Britisher – and his words had thus had even more impact.

As the news spread, Manuel Quintino's reputation grew apace. Public opinion, which had until then ignored him, assuming him to be a complete nonentity, underwent one of those sudden volte-faces with which readers will no doubt be familiar.

That morning, Manuel Quintino was the sole topic of conversation among one particular group of businessmen gathered in Rua dos Ingleses. One man insisted that he had long ago noticed Manuel Quintino's qualities, another proclaimed him the best book-keeper in Oporto, yet another praised his perfect command of the English language, another his impeccable handwriting, still another his energy and his easy way with matters commercial, his long experience, etc. etc. One man, a baron, added: 'Mr Whitestone told me recently that Quintino has a nice little nest-egg squirrelled away too.' For Mr Whitestone had not neglected that part of Jenny's plan either.

'Naturally!' said someone else.

'Do you know what?' commented another man. 'He has the makings of an excellent bank manager.'

'Very true.'

This opinion showed just how far Manuel Quintino's credit had risen in only a matter of hours, for judging him to be capable of becoming a bank manager was the highest of high praise. Jenny's plan was working, and Mr Richard watched with pleasure, his pride as an 'artist' driving out any lingering prejudices. He thought it prudent, however, to take Mr Brains to one side when he saw him in the street and ask him not to mention the scene at supper.

'Because, Mr Brains,' he said, 'the way my fool of a son, Charles, behaved was hardly fitting for an Englishman, and if it came to be known...'

National pride finished that sentence for him, and stopped Mr Brains' tongue; that same comment, combined with Mr Morlays' natural misanthrophic reserve, was enough to stop his tongue too.

Cecília was alone at home that morning and thought she heard a carriage stop outside their front door. Going over to the window, she was pleasantly surprised to see Jenny getting out of an elegant open carriage. Cecília ran to embrace her.

'It's such a lovely day that I just couldn't bear to stay at home, Cecília,' Jenny said, 'so I decided to go for a ride – with you as my companion.'

'Me?'

'Yes, you, and I must say at once that I will accept no excuses. Off you go and get dressed.'

'But Jenny, it's...'

'It's ten o'clock and I can't wait any longer. Must I carry you off by force?'

'But I'm all on my own...'

'Someone's sure to come while you're getting dressed, and if they don't... Anyway, I will brook no objections, however absurd that may seem. How can you possibly refuse?'

Cecília could not help but smile at her friend's capricious insistence, and since Jenny was by nature so uncapricious,

Cecília sensed that there must be something else afoot.

She therefore obediently went off to get dressed.

Jenny was left alone in the parlour, and hadn't been there long when she heard someone coming up the stairs.

It was Antónia, who had no idea Jenny was there. The coachman, to avoid the horse catching a chill, had driven the carriage down to the end of the street, so that when Antónia arrived, she saw no sign of any visitors.

Finding the parlour door open, she assumed Cecília was in there and, while still out in the corridor, she began saying loudly: 'People are quite right when they say time reveals all. I've just found out the address of that woman Senhor Carlos went off with in his carriage that morning. I didn't even have to try. I was just…'

She broke off suddenly, realising that she wasn't speaking to Cecília, but to Jenny.

'Oh, excuse me!' cried Antónia, mortified, but she had already said enough for Jenny not to let her leave.

'Wait, wait! Where exactly does that woman live? Tell me.'

Antónia was visibly embarrassed.

Jenny's very English appearance told her at once that she had unwisely pronounced those words in the presence of Carlos' sister.

Jenny didn't give her time to recover from that first impression and make some excuse.

'No, don't hold back. I'm Carlos' sister, and I know the incident you're referring to. I, too, am keen to know the whereabouts of the person you mention. So, please, finish what you were saying.'

'No, it's not worth it. I didn't mean to…'

Jenny was determined not to let slip this opportunity to solve the mystery she had undertaken to clear up in just one week. She sensed that the result would fully exonerate her brother.

'Go on,' she said in a familiar tone intended to inspire confidence. 'You were saying that you've just found out the woman's address…'

'I didn't…'

'Yes, you did. Listen, I know everything that has gone on between my brother and Cecília.'

'You do?'

Jenny did not, however, know what Senhora Antónia's views were on the subject, and so she proceeded with great caution: 'Yes, and, as you can imagine, as both sister and friend, I must… that is, I need…'

'What do you intend to do?'

'To do my best to save them both from misfortune,' answered Jenny ambiguously.

Antónia put her own interpretation on that response.

'All right, I know you're a decent woman and so I'll tell you, this morning…'

At this point, however, they heard Cecília closing her bedroom door.

'Enough,' said Jenny, 'Cecília's coming. She and I are going out together. Don't tell her anything until you've spoken to me. It's for her own good. Come and see me tomorrow morning. Do you know where I live?'

'Yes, I do, Senhora.'

'Be there, then. I can see you're a sensible person, which is why I want to talk to you. And not a word to Cecília!'

'Don't worry,' said Antónia, completely won over to Jenny's cause by these flattering words.

Cecília came into the room then.

Shortly afterwards, those two undeniably beautiful women,

albeit in their very different ways, had set off in that elegant carriage, laughing and talking with all the blithe carelessness of youth.

Jenny had already devised a route. They took the Foz road, and spent almost the whole morning by the sea. Jenny was like a different person. Her English seriousness had given way to an almost child-like vivacity and contentment. Everything was a reason to be happy, and that happiness gradually infected Cecília too.

There are few things more infectious than the jollity of normally serious people.

The two young women enjoyed a delightful morning, and Cecília had no inkling of how it would end.

At one o'clock, they returned to the carriage, and at two o'clock, to Cecília's great surprise and alarm, they drove down Rua dos Ingleses, which was still full of the hustle and bustle of business.

Their presence caused a sensation. Everyone knew Jenny, while very few, if any, could have said who Cecília was.

An Englishman came to greet Jenny, and she seized the opportunity to introduce him to Cecília. Soon everyone there knew that the lady accompanying Jenny was the daughter of Manuel Quintino.

Mr Whitestone came to welcome Jenny at the door to the office, and when he saw Cecília, he exchanged a knowing glance with Jenny, and very gallantly helped them both out of the carriage.

Manuel Quintino was astonished to see his daughter enter the office.

Jenny laughed out loud at the look of amazement on his face, and Mr Richard did nothing to conceal his amusement either.

Carlos was no less amazed at this encounter, which was the last thing he would have expected.

The same air of invincible constraint persisted between Cecília, Carlos and Manuel Quintino, but, at around three o'clock, the groups of men still standing in the square saw the Whitestone family, along with Cecília and Manuel Quintino, emerge from the office and get into the carriage. Moments later, led by Carlos on his horse, they cut a swathe through those same crowds, leaving behind them a trail of comments.

Manuel Quintino was confused, Cecília pensive and Jenny contented.

XXXVIII

Carlos Vindicated

The following morning, Senhora Antónia was ceremoniously ushered into Jenny's room. So charmed was she by the attentions showered upon her that she was already, body and soul, the servant of the *inglesinha* – 'the wee English girl' – as she called Jenny Whitestone.

Jenny had her sit down beside her and tell her everything she knew about the woman she had mentioned the day before.

With a great many digressions – as was her wont – Antónia explained how, the previous morning, while she was walking down Rua de Santa Catarina, she had spotted Paulo, Mr Richard's junior book-keeper, talking to a woman, who was smiling fondly down at him from a window. Antónia took a closer look and realised that this was the very same woman who had gone to Carlos' house and left with him in a carriage on the morning Antónia had gone in search of Senhora Josefinha da Água-Benta.

'There was no doubt about it, it was her all right. I think she's an actress, because people do say… but forgive me for mentioning such things.'

Jenny pretended not to hear and instead asked: 'And where does she live?'

'In Rua de Santa Catarina.'

And Antónia then gave such a detailed description of the

house that there could be no mistaking it.

Once Jenny had gleaned all she needed to know from António, and had generously rewarded her for her kindness in giving her this information, she added, as if to soothe António's entirely fictitious scruples: 'I'm really grateful to you for telling me all this, and now I have one more favour to ask you.'

'Anything, Senhora, anything.'

'Not a word to a soul that you came here.'

'Of course not!'

'I feel sure I can trust you, but tell me something else, do you really dislike my brother?'

'Me, Senhora?' said António, visibly taken aback by the question.

'You probably do. Almost everyone judges Carlos unfairly, until they know him, that is. Then, when they see how good and generous and kind he is, they always end up adoring him.'

Senhora António immediately began to doubt the critical faculties of the sister-in-law of the husband of the niece of that friend of hers.

'And wouldn't you say,' Jenny went on, ' that your dislike of my brother has no real basis in fact?'

'Well, yes, I mean... to be honest...'

'Good. All I ask is that, for the next few days, you think neither well nor ill of Carlos... until you hear further from me.'

'Really, Senhora, I... I wouldn't...'

'Now off you go, Senhora António, before Cecília gets suspicious. And don't say a word to her about your visit here or about that woman.'

'Don't worry, I won't.'

As soon as António had left, Jenny ordered the carriage to be prepared. And as soon as this was done, she went down to the front door and said to the driver: 'Take me to Rua de Santa Catarina.'

In no time at all, she was there. Having memorised the details Antónia had given her, Jenny instantly recognised the house and asked the driver to stop outside.

Then, for the first time, she hesitated as if she had hitherto been in the grip of an almost violent impulse.

'Whose house am I about to enter?' she thought. 'What kind of woman might she be? Carlos gave me his assurance... but...'

Outside the neighbouring house stood a servant, eyeing Jenny's carriage with great curiosity.

Jenny sent her driver to ask the servant about the woman she was looking for, who, it turned out, was a widow living alone with her son.

Then Jenny hesitated not a moment longer; she jumped out onto the pavement and rang the door bell.

Moments later, she was shown into a modest, but spotlessly clean parlour by a lady who, though not in the first flush of youth, was still rather beautiful.

Jenny came straight to the point.

'Senhora,' she said, 'my name is Jenny Whitestone.'

A tremor of surprise ran through the woman, but Jenny went on with truly English directness: 'I've come on purpose to speak to you, and yet I don't even know to whom I have the honour of speaking. The object of my visit is this. A few days ago, my brother, Carlos Whitestone, left the house in the company of a lady; he then went to a jeweller's shop, where he sold a watch which, shortly before, had been given to him as a present by our father. When our father found out, he was most distressed, and Carlos' action has been unfavourably interpreted and been the cause of a certain amount of domestic strife, which I am trying to mend. My brother assures me that the reason he sacrificed that gift from his father was entirely honourable, but that he cannot tell me what that reason was. I trust Carlos, because I know him, but not everyone shares my confidence. By pure chance I learned that you were the lady who accompanied my brother on that morning. Could you provide me with proof that would justify Carlos' actions?'

While Jenny was speaking, the woman became increasingly agitated, as if battling with various emotions. When she heard Jenny's question, she answered with tears in her eyes: 'I can, Senhora, but once you know that proof, may I ask you not to make use of it?'

'I don't understand,' said Jenny, somewhat confused.

Instead of replying, the woman got up and went over to a desk, which she opened, then returned, holding some papers.

'I am the mother of Paulo, the book-keeper in Mr Whitestone's office.'

'Ah!'

'Please read this letter, Senhora.'

It was a letter from Paulo to his mother.

Jenny read it and, halfway through, her eyes filled with tears, and she understood everything.

In the letter, Paulo confessed to having committed a theft and declared that he was a ruined man. The great love he felt for his mother meant that he could not bear the thought of her suffering the least privation in what had been a very hard life since the death of his father, and now that he was her sole support. This pious sentiment had been his ruin. Since his book-keeper's wages were not enough for him to provide her with the comforts he felt she deserved, he took on various debts; then, to pay these off, he began buying lottery tickets, which only made matters worse; later, during the month that Manuel Quintino was ill, he had stolen a considerable sum from the office safe, closing his eyes to the possible consequences. Carlos was easy to deceive, but on the eve of Manuel Quintino's return to the office, Paulo realised that the suspicious old book-keeper would soon discover everything. This fear was followed by remorse, and remorse by despair. Rather than resort to suicide, he decided to flee the city. In the letter, he advised his mother to seek the protection of Mr Richard and, above all, of Carlos, for the poor boy had absolute faith in the latter's generous nature.

'Good, kind Charles,' said Jenny, when she had finished reading. 'I knew that only some honourable motive would have led you to do such a thing. Now, I understand everything.'

'Your brother is kindness itself, Senhora, and God will reward him bountifully for the tears of gratitude I shed on his account.'

Touched, Jenny squeezed the poor weeping woman's hands.

Paulo's mother described to her in detail what had happened that morning: how, when she woke, she found that her son had gone, leaving her that letter; how she had been plunged into despair, not knowing what she should do or where her son was. Then a clue arrived, a note from an unknown friend of Paulo's arrived, informing Paulo when and where he was to board ship.

She went on to describe her conversation with Carlos – to whom she had turned in desperation – and his immediate willingness to help; how, having sold the watch for the sum Paulo had stolen, Carlos accompanied her to the harbour, to the ship itself, where he restored her son to her, the son she had thought lost for ever.

'Hours later, back at home,' she concluded, 'I received this note from Paulo.'

Jenny read the note. All it said was this: 'My dear mother, all is saved. Senhor Carlos' generosity has saved me from dishonour. All that remains for me now is a duty to reform, which I feel more keenly than ever.'

'Tell me, Senhora, must I accuse my own son? After all, was I not the reason he ruined himself? And can I really repay him like that? I know justice demands that I hand him in, but, forgive me, I simply don't have the courage. Will you forgive a mother's weakness?'

Jenny embraced her tenderly.

'Don't worry, Senhora. I would never ask you to make such a sacrifice. God will show me some way to help everyone. I feel strong enough now to do anything.'

'Poor Paulo! It was his love for me that led him into crime. He's still filled with remorse. He tries to remain cheerful, but I know it weighs on his heart. "If I were alone in the world," he told me a few days ago, "if my misfortune would affect no one else, then I would confess everything. I feel ashamed when I think of my silence." And I would bless the hour when he did spontaneously confess, but I lack the courage to say to him: "Speak!" It seems so ungrateful. It's as if I myself, knowing that he brought dishonour on himself because of me, were to point him out to others as guilty and dishonourable.'

Jenny consoled her as best she could and promised not to reveal to anyone else what she had just told her.

Carlos' generous sister left there with joy in her heart. On the way, she tried to think of the best way to show her father that Carlos was innocent without betraying the trust Paulo's mother had placed in her.

Suddenly, an idea occurred to her that made her smile.

And instead of returning home, as she had intended, she told the driver to go straight to her father's office in Rua dos Ingleses.

Mr Richard was strolling about in the square when he saw his daughter, and he went over to her, smiling: 'You're up early, Jenny.'

'Are you surprised? I've been up and about for hours.'

'Is it market day?'

'No, but today I have to report back on the task you set me.'

'What task?'

'The problem I promised to resolve in a week.'

'Ah, I see.'

'Well, as it turns out, I didn't need a whole week, and I have the solution. Now, though, there remains one small difficulty.'

'Which is?'

'Finding the best way to reveal that solution.'

'Well, that seems easy enough.'

'No, it's not easy at all, because I promised I wouldn't be the one to reveal it.'

'Who can then?'

'That's what I've come here to find out.'

'Here?'

'Upstairs in the office, where, if you don't mind, I will spend some time.'

'Feel free. And may we know if the solution is a satisfactory one?'

'It couldn't be better.'

'Really?'

'You'll see.'

'I will, will I?'

'One word more: do your book-keepers all know English?'

'Manuel Quintino does…'

'Yes, I know, but what about the others?'

'Paulo doesn't speak English, but he understands everything; the other one neither understands nor speaks it.'

'Good, and one other thing: you have to promise me something.'

'What's that?'

'When you find out the solution to the problem and acknowledge that you were too hard on your son, promise me that you will be equally indulgent with the real culprit.'

'Are there culprits, then?'

'Do you promise?'

'But…'

'Do you promise?'

'I promise, but…'

'I'll see you shortly. If I'm not much mistaken, in half an hour, you should know the result.'

'From you?'

'No, not from me. Goodbye for now.'

And with that she vanished up the worm-eaten stairs into the office.

When she went in, Jenny put on one of those grave, pensive airs that so suited her kindly face.

Manuel Quintino, Paulo and the other book-keeper were there, and they all stood up when she entered.

'Please, there's no need to stand up,' she said, taking a seat next to Manuel Quintino. 'I just need to rest for a moment, but you carry on with your work.'

'I certainly wasn't expecting to see you here today, Miss Jenny,' said Manuel Quintino, resuming his work.

'I needed to talk to my father… But you seem sad, Manuel

Quintino. How's Cecília?'

'Thankfully, Cecília's all right.'

'Well, don't be sad then. I'm sad enough for everyone.'

'You sad?'

'Yes, very.'

Manuel Quintino smiled sceptically.

'Why are you smiling? Do you think me incapable of feeling sad?'

'No, but I can't think what could possibly make you sad.'

'Well, listen, and you'll see.'

Jenny suddenly began speaking in English as if she wanted only Manuel Quintino to understand, and she spoke in a confiding voice: 'Charles, as you know, has a very generous heart, but he's not always the most sensible of lads. And that, quite unintentionally on his part, gives rise to all kinds of arguments at home. And one such incident is the cause of my current sadness.'

And Jenny began telling Manuel Quintino about the watch, about Mr Richard's displeasure, about Carlos' insistence on concealing the reason why he had sold the watch, and how he would say nothing about that reason except that it was in no way dishonourable.

'But who would believe him?' Jenny went on. 'Only me and no one else. The generally held view of my brother doesn't really help. Anyway, there's been a coldness, no, a hostility between Charles and my father for some days now. And that really upsets me. The tears I've shed over it, Manuel Quintino!'

Now and then, Jenny would glance furtively across at Paulo, and she saw him change colour, turning first red, then pale, then red again, his hand barely able to hold his pen.

Jenny watched all this with pleasure, assuming that he was

following everything she was saying.

'He's just young!' said Manuel Quintino in Carlos' defence.

'That's as maybe, but it's causing us all a lot of grief.'

Jenny made great play of this, painting the domestic scene in very sombre colours. She was still talking about it when Mr Richard came in. Fearing that any question from him might undo her plan, she ran to greet him and, pretending to embrace him, whispered: 'Not a word about what I told you just now, but stay here in the office.'

Mr Richard nodded and smiled.

Jenny chattered on inconsequentially, always keeping one eye on Paulo, who – Jenny was pleased to see – was clearly wrestling with his conscience.

Finally, she indicated to her father that he should go into his office, which he did.

Paulo was growing increasingly agitated, and Jenny watched every gesture and every change of expression. She saw him put down his pen and stand up, as if filled with some great resolve. Jenny trembled. Then Paulo turned pale again, ran his hand over his brow and sat down again. Jenny lost heart. Finally, he got resolutely to his feet, went over to Mr Richard's office and knocked on the door.

'Enter,' said Mr Richard from within.

Paulo went in, closing the door behind him.

Jenny could barely contain herself and unwittingly blurted out: 'The case is won!'

Manuel Quintino looked at her in surprise, and Jenny burst out laughing: 'You may not know it, Manuel Quintino, but the last small obstacle to your happiness is crumbling even as I speak…'

Manuel Quintino had no idea what she meant, and Jenny said no more.

The interview between Paulo and Mr Richard lasted a long time. From outside only a vague murmur of voices could be heard.

Finally, the door opened again. A shiver of doubt ran through Jenny.

Paulo was the first to emerge, face ablaze and eyes red, but Jenny was reassured to see that, as well as those signs of sadness, there was a certain air of contentment, that of a soul washed clean.

Moments later, Mr Richard emerged too. Behind his apparently cold, impassive exterior, Jenny could see that his heart was rejoicing.

Mr Richard issued a few orders and recommendations, then, turning to his daughter, announced that he was at her disposal, and he left the office at what, for him, was an extraordinarily early hour, with Jenny at his side.

'You performed your task impeccably, Jenny,' said her father, when he was alone with her in the carriage.

'I did, didn't I?'

'And how did you manage that?'

'Not so fast! That is my secret. Anyway, do you think Carlos' actions are now fully justified?'

As a response she received only a smile, a proud, affectionate, contented smile, for her father was experiencing all those emotions at once.

'Carlos has a loyal, generous heart, and I have treated him most unfairly.'

Jenny was thrilled to hear this confession.

'I need hardly ask,' she said, 'if you were appropriately indulgent with the culprit, and forgive me for having demanded that promise from you when I knew you would forgive him anyway.'

'You were wrong. I have punished him.'

Jenny looked at him anxiously.

'Punishment is a moral duty,' he went on. 'It's how people are reformed. Base, weak souls must be punished harshly, and only fear will stop them. But Paulo, although weak, is still honourable, and for such people, the only proper punishment is to reward their crime. On the same day that Manuel Quintino becomes my partner, Paulo will become my chief book-keeper with an increase in salary and the keys to the safe.'

Jenny kissed her father's hands.

'God Himself would not have handed down any other punishment.'

'Don't be so heretical, Jenny.'

They had reached their house.

'Now you can give Manuel Quintino your present,' said Mr Richard.

'And then...'

'And then we will make a slow examination of your other madcap enterprises.'

XXXIX

The Final Act

Manuel Quintino had not yet left home on the following morning when Antónia came to announce that the *inglesinha* had arrived in a carriage and was asking for him.

Cecília and Manuel Quintino ran to meet Jenny.

'Are you surprised to see me here so early? Well, what do you expect? I was so excited about coming here today that I couldn't sleep all night for thinking about it. I wanted to find you still at home, and since I know your morning habits...'

'I still have another half an hour before I have to leave,' said Manuel Quintino, consulting his watch.

'The object of my visit is simply to deliver by hand a message from my father. Would you care to read it?'

And she handed him the letter, whose contents the reader already knows.

While Manuel Quintino was reading the letter, Jenny said to Cecília: 'So how's that heart of yours?'

'My heart?'

'Yes, I want to be the one to make it better, you know.'

'Do you think there's something wrong with it, then?' asked Cecília.

'Do you?' asked Jenny, echoing her question.

Cecília was about to respond when she suddenly glanced across at Manuel Quintino.

'Goodness, whatever's wrong with my father?'

Manuel Quintino, who had just read Mr Richard's letter, was clearly shaken; he had turned pale and was trembling, staring down at the letter, which he was still holding in his hand.

Jenny smiled, and Cecília ran to her father's side.

'What is it? What's wrong?'

Manuel Quintino silently showed her the letter, which Cecília read in an instant. Then she tearfully, gleefully embraced her father.

'Oh, but this is wonderful, Pa!'

He seemed caught between joy at the news and some bitter thought that insisted on dressing that news in mourning.

'I'm sure we owe this good fortune to the influence of that angel over there,' said Cecília, pointing at Jenny.

Manuel Quintino also looked at Jenny, and with a barely disguised tremor in his voice, asked: 'Miss Jenny, to what do I owe such a generous reward?'

'Aren't eighteen years of loyal service enough, Manuel Quintino?' Jenny said. 'Why so suspicious? I can assure you,' she went on in a firm, grave voice, because she could see a glimmer of distrust in Manuel Quintino's eyes, 'I can assure you that I watched my father write this letter and, in gratitude, kissed the hand that wrote it, and I can assure you, too, that you must accept this favour – if favour it is – knowing that you earned it through long years of noble, unstinting service.'

These words completely disarmed Manuel Quintino, and any dark shadows summoned up by the letter vanished.

It had in fact occurred to him that they wanted to reward him for the possibly less than loyal attentions paid to his daughter by Carlos, and that idea revived in his heart feelings of pride and resentment that had still not been fully overcome.

However, the respect he felt for Jenny would not allow him to sustain such scruples, especially when he saw how she herself dismissed them.

Now it was Cecília's turn to become thoughtful.

Once that first rush of happiness had passed – a joy provoked by her father's joy – she, too, was driven to consider Jenny's intentions.

Jenny, who was watching her friend, called her aside: 'Why so serious, Cecília?'

'Miss Jenny, may I ask you a question?'

'No, not if you ask me in that formal way.'

'But…'

'I'll only listen to you if you treat me as your equal. Go on.'

'Miss Jenny…'

At a gesture from Jenny, she corrected herself with a smile: 'Jenny, will you please tell me what all this means?'

'All what?'

'This generous action, which I imagine was your idea.'

'Are you not satisfied with my explanation? Don't you believe that gratitude is enough to…'

'Yes, but given the circumstances… after what happened…'

'What do you mean?'

'Jenny, forgive me, but my conscience obliges me to set aside all reserve and speak to you frankly…'

'Isn't that what you're doing?'

'Answer me. What are your intentions?'

'What intentions?'

'Your intentions as regards me.'

'Oh, only the very best of intentions, namely to make you happy.'

'But Jenny, I can never be happy at the expense of other people's sacrifices.'

'Whose sacrifices?'

'I don't know, but it just occurred to me... I know it's completely mad by the way... but it worries me. Your generosity is capable of anything...'

'Tell me about this mad idea of yours.'

'On the morning of your birthday, when you came to me like an angel of mercy, when I most needed you... do you remember?'

'Yes, but let's forget about the angel of mercy, shall we?'

'At that moment, you said something that frightened me, when you said to your brother to "leave such excessive love for someone who, from now on, has more right to demand it than I do"...meaning me...'

'Well, isn't that true?'

'Listen, Jenny. On that occasion, I was saved by your angelic presence, but if you hadn't been there, if I had been caught *in flagrante* as it were – as could well have happened – if I had been found there alone and subsequently lost my reputation and become the object of shame and scorn, I would have preferred to leave there with a clean conscience rather than feel I had the right to demand someone's affections. Does anyone have a right to demand another person's affections? Wouldn't that be just the appearance of affection rather than the real thing. And what would be the point of that?'

'You're right, Cecília. I agree and yet I still want to make you happy. And I openly admit that what happened today is one step on the path I set out on and which I'm determined to follow to the end.'

'But...'

'Tell me frankly, Cecília, because we don't have time to beat about the bush. Do you or do you not believe in Carlos' love for you?'

'No.'

'That was a very lukewarm No!' retorted Jenny, smiling. 'I'm going to find it very hard to forgive you. You may not know it, but I have taken it upon myself to plead my brother's case. And I've already won several victories. My father admitted yesterday that he had treated him unfairly. Even your maid Antónia is on the road to conversion.'

'Antónia?'

'Yes. I suspected that my brother had found an enemy in her, and I seem to have been proved right. After all, wasn't it Antónia who told you that story about a certain visitor Carlos received?'

Cecília looked away at this reference to the 'crime' Antónia had told her about in such censorious terms.

'I see I was right,' Jenny went on. 'Well, even Antónia will accept defeat in the end. As for that visitor... I will say only that everything has been satisfactorily explained.'

'How?'

'That is a secret only my brother can tell you, when the time comes for there to be no secrets between the two of you...'

'I'll have a long wait, then.'

'Well, until then, you must content yourself with my word, or do you doubt that as well?'

At this point, Manuel Quintino came back into the room, interrupting this dialogue.

Nonetheless, Cecília was left feeling more confident about the future, and during the rest of the morning, she often had a smile on her lips.

News of Manuel Quintino's promotion soon spread throughout the business world. He was showered with congratulatory messages from all sides, and his reputation grew among his fellow men of commerce.

Given the high esteem in which he held the commercial classes, Manuel Quintino could hardly remain indifferent to their new respect for him. He allowed himself to feel a quite legitimate pride which did not, on the other hand, tip over into arrogance.

That same day, Paulo was appointed chief book-keeper with an increase in salary. The poor fellow received the news of his appointment with tears in his eyes. Those tears were Mr Richard's revenge.

Thanks to the sacrifices made by Jenny, the two families were often seen together. One night, Jenny even managed to persuade Cecília to go with her to the theatre.

Carlos' friends recognised her at once, and rumours that Mr Richard's son was about to be married to his new partner's daughter soon began to do the rounds of the city.

The imaginations of some of the rumour-mongers came up with various hidden reasons for this marriage, suggesting that Whitestone and Son owed far more to Manuel Quintino than had previously been thought, and that the old book-keeper's savings had helped stem the damage done by his employer's profligacy. And once a way had been found of introducing self-interest into the plot, everyone happily accepted the situation.

Mr Richard had been right.

A steamship left for London, then another and another, and Mr Richard never once reminded his son of the original sentence he had handed down.

One morning, Mr Richard was in his study, excitedly examining the stuffed golden eagle – or, more accurately, the *Aquila chrysaetos*, a very rare visitor to the London suburbs – which he had received from his friend in Box Hill, where the bird had been caught and killed. His collector's ecstasy was interrupted by the sound of the door opening. Mr Richard turned and saw his daughter's face peering in.

'Come in, Jenny, come in,' he said in the usual affable tone he used when speaking to her.

Jenny entered.

'What brings you here so early in the morning?'

'I wanted to introduce you to someone, if I may.'

'Introduce me? Who to?'

'Someone,' replied Jenny mischievously, 'who wants to know when you're planning to send him off to London. He was supposed to leave days ago.'

Mr Whitestone looked at his daughter and smiled, delighted by her sly words.

'Show your protegé in.'

Jenny opened the door fully and ushered Carlos into the room.

Despite the constraint he always felt in his father's presence, Carlos took courage from knowing that the cause he had come there to present formally had already been won

'Father,' he said, taking a step forward, 'a few days ago, I heard you describe something I had done as infamous; I come to you now to ask that you allow me the only means I have to prove that judgement wrong.'

'Which is?' asked Mr Richard brusquely.

'To go and see Manuel Quintino and ask him to offer my name in marriage – a name my father has honoured by a lifetime of probity – to the young woman whose reputation was nearly ruined by my imprudent behaviour, but never by my intentions. She was saved by my sister's generosity and by yours, sir. Allow me, then, to follow both your noble example as well as the example my heart is telling me I must follow.'

'And have you really thought this through, Carlos,' said Mr Richard, all brusqueness gone. 'Have you thought about what you're doing? Are you not afraid that you might live to regret taking this rash step? Do you not fear once again bringing unhappiness upon that young woman? Are you prepared for the many responsibilities of family life?'

'I know that my past may offer few guarantees in that respect, but I believe that the future will prove me right...'

'You believe?' said Mr Richard, laughing. 'Is belief your only guarantor?'

Jenny placed a hand on her father's shoulder and said gently: 'No, he has me too.'

Mr Richard turned to her: 'You? You will stand guarantor for your brother?'

'I will.'

'That's very bold of you!'

'It's not the first time. And which of us has had cause to repent recently, me of my confidence in Carlos or you of your suspicions?'

'For want of anything better, I accept your guarantee.'

Then turning to his son: 'Off you go, then, Carlos, and remember that once you've taken this step, you will have to be a very different man.'

And Mr Richard held out his hand to his son, who kissed it, then left.

'I don't know if you've done the right thing, Jenny,' said her father, as she was about to leave the study.

'I looked into my mother's eyes and asked her advice. I have absolute faith in the decisions that come to me that way.'

Mr Richard gazed lovingly at his daughter for a while before folding her in his arms and saying: 'May God hear your prayers, as He must, because you deserve Him to.'

'And what about us, Pa, are we just going to stay here?' asked Jenny.

'What more do you want me to do?'

'Obviously Charles should be the first to deal with this matter at Manuel Quintino's house, but is it right that he should go alone?'

Mr Richard rang the bell.

'Have them prepare the carriage straightaway,' he told the servant. Then he asked Jenny: 'Is there anything else you want?'

'Yes, to thank you.'

And having embraced her father, she rushed out of the room.

This scene had the following results in Manuel Quintino's house: he was getting ready to leave for work when he saw Antónia come into the room looking anxious and startled.

'What is it, Antónia? Whatever's wrong?' he said.

'There's someone here asking for you, Senhor Manuel Quintino.'

'Yet another man come to offer me his congratulations, I suppose. When I was just a mere book-keeper, no one came to see me, now though...'

And he went to see who it was.

When Cecília heard Antónia's words, she blushed and withdrew to her room. This was because she had suddenly remembered a note sent by Jenny the previous evening, which said only this: 'I hope and expect you to enjoy a very happy early morning.' And it was signed: 'Your sister, Jenny.'

As soon as Cecília had left, Antónia went over to Manuel Quintino and said in a mysterious voice: 'It's him again!'

'Who?'

'The Englishman's son.'

'Carlos?'

Manuel hurried downstairs to find Carlos waiting below,

and he felt somewhat bemused by Carlos' unusually grave manner and words. The two men were still not fully at ease in each other's company, which is hardly surprising given what had occurred between them. It was Carlos who broke the silence.

'Manuel Quintino, I have come here on a very serious matter, one that is of great importance to us both.'

Then, after a brief pause, he added: 'I have come here to ask for your daughter's hand in marriage.'

Manuel Quintino almost fell off his chair.

'For *what*?'

'For Cecília's hand in marriage,' said Carlos again.

A cloud briefly obscured Manuel Quintino's mind. His barely appeased suspicions resurfaced.

Seeing this, Carlos added: 'I will not conceal from you the fact that I have long felt a great affection for your daughter, which I have tried in vain to ignore. I bowed my head before your accusations, Manuel Quintino, not because I felt myself guilty of any base intentions, but because my imprudent behaviour could so easily have endangered the good reputation of the very person I wanted to protect at all costs. I have not come here to offer any reparation, of which Cecília has no need; I have come here to ask you for my happiness.'

Manuel Quintino was dumbstruck.

'My father has already given his consent, and I have Jenny's approval too. Now I need only…'

'And Cecília?'

'Ask her.'

Barely knowing what he was doing, Manuel Quintino went to the door to call his daughter, who, as you can imagine, was not far away.

When she entered the room, her face told him everything he needed to know, far more eloquently than words.

Casting aside all hesitation and reserve, Manuel Quintino threw his arms about Carlos' neck, embracing him, kissing him, and calling him his beloved son.

'Cecília,' said Carlos, going over to her, 'if, in order to assure myself of your feelings, I were to wait for you to reveal them to me, I would still have my doubts.'

'But you don't?'

'No, because I can guess what you are feeling, at least I think I can.'

'What more do you want then? Alas for those who cannot guess, for they do not truly love. Don't you agree?'

'So you can guess what I am feeling too?'

'I hope so.'

'Yet only a short time ago you were filled with doubt.'

'Or perhaps I wanted to doubt.'

'But you couldn't?'

'No, I believed in you even before I heard your explanation.'

'I promise I will not abuse that trust,' said Carlos, kissing the hand she held out to him.

Senhora Antónia happened to come into the room at this point, and, thrilled to have made this scandalous discovery, ran to tell her master, who was in the next room singing to himself. Imagine her astonishment when he greeted the news of this crime with gales of laughter!

A shaft of light entered that prudent lady's consciousness.

She had sufficient political nous to imitate those deputies who, at the first sign of some ministerial change, move over, lock, stock and barrel, to the opposition, in the hope of waking up the next day on the side with the power.

Senhora Antónia soon had occasion to demonstrate this political tact. The door bell rang, and when Antónia went to open the garden gate, she found herself face to face with

Senhor José Fortunato, who had come to warn her that he had just seen Carlos walking down the street.

'That's hardly surprising, given that he's upstairs!' said Antónia with a shrug.

'Upstairs?' cried Senhor José.

'Things are getting serious, Senhor José.'

'What's getting serious, Senhora Antónia?'

'I believe there may be a marriage in the offing.'

Senhor José Fortunato pulled a face and said: 'A marriage?'

'Yes, well, that's hardly a big surprise, is it? Given that they're made for each other, the same age and…'

She could not go on. Mr Richard's carriage had just stopped outside the door, and Mr Richard had jumped nimbly out before helping Jenny out too.

'Holy Mother of God! Now they're all here!' cried Antónia, running up the stairs to announce the new arrivals.

Senhor José Fortunato's curiosity overcame his wounded pride, and he followed the other guests upstairs to be confronted by a most singular sight.

Jenny had flung her arms about Cecília; Manuel Quintino was gravely embracing Mr Richard; and there was Carlos presenting Cecília to Mr Richard, saying: 'I bring you another daughter, sir.'

And Mr Richard responded by embracing her and saying: 'Thank you, Carlos. You are giving me a real treasure.'

And Cecília fondly kissed his hand. Manuel Quintino was spouting utter nonsense and embracing everyone, while Antónia was offering her congratulations and being roundly ignored.

Senhor José Fortunato saw all this and abruptly turned his back on it. Unnoticed by anyone, he went back down the stairs, where he shook the dust off his shoes and, muttering a few unintelligible words, he left, never to return.

Conclusion

There were a few difficulties to be overcome because the happy couple belonged to different faiths, but once this was done, the two were married. I won't bother giving the conditions of the marriage contract, because they would, I think, be of little interest to the reader.

Manuel Quintino's reputation continued to grow in the eyes of the public, and he went on to become one of those men who, at certain times in Oporto, are judged to be indispensable and whose names figure in every one of that enterprising city's companies, societies and committees. Thus, he became, in turn, the director of a bank, the administrator of the poor house, and a town councillor.

Mr Richard continues with his English habits and his readings of Sterne.

His compatriots, Brains and Morlays, are still the same: one, an Englishman who laughs, the other, an Englishman who weeps.

Need I add that Cecília and Carlos lived happily ever after?

I'm not sure I would have had the courage to write the story of their love if this had not been the case.

And Jenny?

Jenny is still the good angel of the family.

And Mr Richard never had to demand payment from her as Carlos' guarantor, for it was never necessary.

Other Dedalus Books translated from Portuguese

Eça de Queiroz:

Alves & Co.
Cousin Bazílio
The City and the Mountains
The Crime of Father Amaro
The Illustrious House of Ramires
The Maias
The Mandarin and Other Stories
The Mystery of the Sintra Road
The Relic
The Tragedy of the Street of Flowers

Mário de Sá-Carneiro:

Lúcio's Confession
The Great Shadow and Other Stories

Jorge de Sena: *The Prodigious Physician*

Dedalus Africa:

Teolinda Gersão: *The Word Tree*
José Luandino Vieira: *Our Musseque*
Abdulai Sila: *The Ultimate Tragedy*
Dina Salústio: *The Madwoman of Serrano*

Young Dedalus:

Sophia de Mello Breyner Andresen: *The Girl from the Sea and Other Stories*
Afonso Cruz: *The Books that devoured my Father*

Anthologies:

Take Six: Portuguese Women Writers edited by Margaret Jull Costa
The Dedalus Book of Portuguese Fantasy edited by Eugénio Lisboa & Helder Macedo